IN A BUFFALO ROBE

Albert Bennetti

ARCHWAY
PUBLISHING

This is a work of fiction. All of the characters, names, incidents, organizations, and dialogue in this novel are either the products of the author's imagination or are used fictitiously.

Archway Publishing books may be ordered through booksellers or by contacting:

Archway Publishing
1663 Liberty Drive
Bloomington, IN 47403
www.archwaypublishing.com
1 (888) 242-5904

Because of the dynamic nature of the Internet, any web addresses or links contained in this book may have changed since publication and may no longer be valid. The views expressed in this work are solely those of the author and do not necessarily reflect the views of the publisher, and the publisher hereby disclaims any responsibility for them.

Any people depicted in stock imagery provided by Thinkstock are models, and such images are being used for illustrative purposes only.
Certain stock imagery © Thinkstock.

ISBN: 978-1-4808-4815-3 (sc)
ISBN: 978-1-4808-4813-9 (hc)
ISBN: 978-1-4808-4814-6 (e)

Library of Congress Control Number: 2017910219

Print information available on the last page.

Archway Publishing rev. date: 7/28/2017

CONTENTS

1

THE STEPPING OFF POINT

At sixteen years of age, a man should already be making his own way, I thought. There was plenty of business in Saint Joe, with all the wagons waiting to be ferried across the Missouri, and I saw no reason we should be leaving. Besides, there was Jenny. Pa had turned my brother Kurt's and my life over once already when we were younger with his chasing after California gold. Now it was the Rocky Mountain gold rush. Although I knew it was *our* welfare that was on Pa's mind, I saw my happiness right there, as far as we'd gotten, in Saint Joe, there with my Jenny. Still, I couldn't fathom deserting Pa and Kurt. We'd all lost so much when Ma died, and I feared it would break their spirits if I left them too by staying behind. Maybe I was using them as an excuse. Truth of it was, I didn't know if Jenny would even have me as a husband. Ours was more like a childhood relationship, rather than that of a man and woman. Although I had a fear of starting a life with Jenny, I also had fear of the wilderness. Understanding that it was okay for a person to have fears, I was still not going to let fear determine my direction. If Jenny asked me that night if I would stay, I would. And if she didn't, I planned to put the question straight forth to her. If she did want me to stay, I realized, there'd still be Pa to deal with. There was no chance of him seeing what I needed to make my life meaningful. It seemed Pa had only one way of thinking.

"Don't let people tell you money isn't important, boy!" That's what Pa would say. He'd started talking that way right after Ma had come down with the fever and died ten years back. At six years old, I still remember Pa crying at her bedside about how he had let her down. One day, shortly after Ma's death, I told Pa what I had heard at school. "The fever has no more respect for the president than it has for a lowdown Injun."

But Pa had said, "Even though I agree with the fever on that topic, it's through the ghetto that the fever blazes a trail, with only a few sparks on occasion flying up to the big houses." Drawing hard on his cold pipe, he'd continued. "Better to live in a safe place and associate with safe people. The poor have to put themselves in harm's way daily." After a short pause and another hard draw on his pipe, he'd concluded, "The best chance for a long and happy life is through wealth. That's why wealth is worth going after with all your heart!" He'd finished with a burst of tobacco smoke that seemed to be the result of an internal explosion.

There was no use in disputing Pa when he was so strong of opinion, so I didn't mention to him how I had hated having to trade my life in New York City for one of hunting gold in the hills of California. How much fun would it be to hunt for pieces of rock in the hills if we were ever to make it there, anyway? Sure couldn't compare to going down to the seawall with my little brother, Kurt, to hunt for a family of rockfish to fill our pail while Pa landed the big ones.

Although Kurt was a full year younger than me, he still did a good job handling a fishing line. He always seemed to have a lot of luck—like being named Konrad instead of Olof, as I was. Most always, we would fill our pail, and when we sold the fish, Pa would use the dollar we got to pay for a stand at the Fulton Fish Market. Pa always had a pile of blackfish and sea bass. Of course, there was no disputing that his were the largest at the market. Kurt and I derived pleasure from knowing that our catch had paid the dollar for the stand so that Pa could take all the proceeds of his catch home to Ma, and we could watch her eyes open wide "like violets in the morning sun" as Pa would say.

If you're wondering how it could be that Pa was always able to have the largest blackfish at the market—and I'm not joshing about that—I'll tell you how, just the way he told me. The big ones got big because they are the fastest to retreat into the rocks at the first hint of danger. That's exactly what they do when they feel a hook set in. Pulling up on the line wedges it between the rocks, and when the weight pulls up against the rocks, you're totally snagged. Pa created a device to keep the line freed up. As far as I know the Swenson family, that being us, are the only ones to know the means. And I'm not about to put it down on paper, but I will tell you that the answer is as simple as a child's toy and as easily discernible as truth. Like Pa always said, "When you hear the truth, you think it's your own mouth talking. That's because the truth is part of your very being."

It had been ten years since I had carefully bounded across the boulders of the seawall. Being constantly licked by the sea, the rocks sprouted green moss like a line of instant life where the sea touched them, making them slicker than an iced-over pond. The wind off the surf would whip the spray of each slap of a wave across my eyes, numb my ears, and salt my lips. Is every memory held so strongly? I only know that I will not strike out the possibility of one day returning to that life. If I now had to leave Saint Joe and Jenny, it would be even harder to think back on and accept than that memory was. How could I let Pa change my life again?

It was March, just as it had been nine years prior when Pa had settled on a life in Saint Joe for us. Upon our arrival, we'd waited near three months for the grass to be high enough on the plains to feed the team during our crossing. Meanwhile, wagon trains were returning with tales of how it was hard to make a day's wages in a week of panning and how it cost a week's earnings for a day's worth of victuals. There wasn't any reason to doubt their stories either, after taking a look at their scrawny bodies and shambled wares. It was true, the bodies of us Swensons could be considered normally slight, but the ribs on these folks could have been counted as easily as those of a scavenged deer carcass a week after the vultures had lit upon it.

The gold from Pa's new prospecting was going to be found in the pockets of the travelers lining the streets of Saint Joseph and camping on the hillsides about town. Even though the gold rush had ended, many migrants were still seeking opportunities in the West, and an endless number of Mormons were journeying to their newfound promised land as well. Pa felt that the Western expansion had just started and that Saint Joe was going to be crowded with travelers for many years to come. He was right. This was, indeed, the stepping off point to the wilderness. The timing and preparation for their journey, many hundreds of miles across uncivilized, rough, and often-treacherous territory, was critical for each person and wagon. Even if a party did feel capable of embarking straight forth without a holdup in Saint Joe, the Missouri River bade them otherwise. There was not one passer through in that town of disgruntled campers who did not come to realize that there weren't enough ferries in operation to fill the need. Often someone would speculate that the town had set its own interest above that of the travelers. Pa reasoned that this forced stall was a godsend to most emigrants, forcing them to take plenty of time to give proper attention to their preparation for what was known by all to be a life-threatening undertaking.

As these journeying masses mingled beneath the cliffs on the side of town in their closely pitched tents, in wagon camps on the flats of the bluffs to the rear and round yonder, or while sitting in the line through the center of town waiting to be loaded on their scheduled towing rafts, they exchanged stories. The stories, though often exaggerated, were full of enlightenment concerning the perils of the journey ahead. They often prompted a traveler to take on more rations or supplies, to lighten his load of nonessentials, or to improve the condition of his wagon and team. It was not at all unusual to see wagons head back east after a night or two of listening to tales of Injuns, droughts, blizzards, beasts, vermin, rough mountain trails, and dangerous river crossings. This was enough to give any man cause for contemplation. Still, the wide-open territories with land and opportunity enough for every man to take a share of, the magnificence and grandeur of the land, the abundance of game, and the possibility of becoming extremely wealthy through a major gold strike were enough for most men to continue their journey. The Mormons, of course, were steadfast in their pursuit of religious freedom and were almost never discouraged.

Listening to these tales from returning wagons had not convinced Pa that Saint Joe was the end of our westward trail. It was not until it was being said that all the major gold lodes had already been discovered and had been bought out by large mining outfits that Pa had become dissuaded from making the crossing.

Pa had had his heart set on making the California diggings, and had we not spent months waiting for the return of the grasses, his stubbornness would not have been daunted, much less overcome. However, in those months of waiting, he had come to realize that opportunity was plentiful in this town of transients. He had to again call on his "old country" learned skill, just as he had done upon our arrival in New York, in order to find a way to partake of the commerce abounding in Saint Joseph. Back in Helsinki, Pa had learned the skill of fishing from my grandfather, when Pa was just a youth. He arrived in New York a year after marrying Ma, with no means of providing for a family. However, after one look at the Fulton Fish Market, setting on the Hudson Bay at the southeast tip of Manhattan Island, he knew how a living could be made to support Ma and the baby, soon to be arriving—that baby, of course, being me.

The skills Pa was to call upon in Saint Joe had been taught to him by my grandmother. While my grandfather was out to sea, in times of severe weather, which caused Pa to be left behind, he'd help my grandmother with her baking. She'd prepare breads and pies, and sell them right out of her kitchen to the neighbors. Most of these neighbors were also fishermen, but ones lacking a capable wife when they returned home. My grandmother loved the baking, as did Pa. "It's like helping the Lord with creation," was the way Pa put it.

Bob Willets provided the means for Pa to begin to create his culinary wonders in Saint Joe. Willets' Bakery had been in business for a fair spell before we arrived. As Pa jawed with Willets one morn, while the loaves did a bit of cooling, he found out that Willets had a desire to return east. It seemed Willets had a cockamamy idea to open a bread factory, where thousands of loaves would be baked at once, wrapped in paper, and sent round the world. Surely, a paper wrapper wouldn't keep them from turning to rocks in more than a few days. I suspect that there may be some Chinamen living in bread houses about now. Although perhaps a misadventure for Mr. Willets, his resolve on pursuing this foolery came at exactly the right time to give Pa a new field to plow. At first, Willets refused Pa's offer for the bakery, which was the entire stake Pa had been planning to use to buy a wagon, team, and mining supplies. But Pa was able to get some additional backing from Mr. Burcher at the bank, and the deal was made.

What a change this deal made in our lives. We went from living in a tent since we'd arrived in Saint Joe by means of rail and wagon fare to once again living under a roof and sleeping in a bed. Kurt and I had a room above the bakery, and Pa, who was up half the night baking, slept in a room behind the store. The enjoyment of awakening to the oven's warmth wafting up the stairwell, heavy laden with baking aromas, left me with a memory that will never diminish in potency. Perhaps bigger, though, than the physical changes Pa's decision to stay had made on our lives were the psychological ones. No more waking up mornings fearing that Pa had decided the grasses were high enough for feed and our crossing could be scheduled. No more worrying through the night that my courage and strength would be less than what was expected, or needed, in the wilderness country. What a relief! The only challenge confronting me in my new life was far more to my liking.

Pa had crafted two sturdy carts for us. Kurt wanted to paint his name on his, but I sure wasn't going to paint Olof on mine. Pa decided we'd paint them both with Swenson's Baked Goods—same as the store. Every morning, except Sunday of course, we'd set out with our carts. They would be loaded with hot pies, biscuits, and bread. Not once, except for when the weather had flared up through the day, did my cart return with as much as one biscuit unsold. If there were more selling hours left before we were to have chow and set off to the schoolhouse, I'd go around with a second load, and Kurt did the same. The reason we tried so hard with the selling was that Pa would pay us a dollar for every ten dollars of selling we did. Pa held the money for us. But he let us count the dollars at our liking and always assured us that it would be ours to keep forever.

When I had reached the age of ten full years, Kurt and I put Pa's promise to a test. It seemed Pa's idea of "yours to keep" was contrary to our thinking that it was ours to spend. Pa had always been easily persuaded to let us do some spending at the candy counter in Ed's

General Store. We were even allowed to by the toy revolvers Ed had gotten in once, for fifty whole cents apiece. But now we were talking about horses. Pa explained that, "Buying isn't the end of spending when it comes to horses. The cost of keep and feed is more than we can manage. Besides, the cost of saddles and gear is nearly as much as that of the animals."

Pa's words of disapproval, such as these, were always given in finality. It's true that these facts had been in our consideration also. But it seemed Pa's being so dead set against our wanting to spend our earnings was fully contrary to our understanding with him. He had in mind that we should keep most of our savings for the day that we would be starting out on our own—"to help you get started" was the way Pa had put it. His refusal was so enraging to me that I told him straight-out what I believed. "You've just been lying to us to get us to work," I declared. To this day, I don't know how I could have braved those words to Pa, or why they hadn't caused him to raise the roof in response, as so many lesser things had done in the past. He just stared at me for a bit, and then he sent us off to school. Between Kurt and me, one thing remained clear—there'd be no forgiving Pa.

Aware of the unusual hostility in my mood that the row with Pa had caused, Jennifer was prompted to query as to its cause. It was a relief to share with her my resentment over the injustice Pa was subjecting us to—as if by her hearing of and recognizing this injustice, it would be partially avenged. It turned out that Jenny was to be more helpful in this matter than she would have been simply by being a good listener. She told me how her gramps had extra berths in his barn and how she would ask if Kurt and I could use two of them, with suitable compensation for feed and housing of course. "Gramps's charge," she suggested, "would be far more affordable than the rates at Jones' Livery."

New hope! I thought—at least sufficient to delay the need of confronting Pa with our refusal to sell our bakery goods anymore. Perhaps the possibility of cheaper livery at Gramps's place would make our request more acceptable to him.

With this hope, instilled by Jenn's offer as a motivator, I made a detour in town to Jones's Livery. His being a big lover of Swenson's pies, I knew Mr. Jones quite well. He was a tall, loud-spoken man but good in nature. I knew him to be fond of joking. After hearing about the endeavor Kurt and I were pursuing, Mr. Jones proceeded to show me saddles. These were more fanciful than would be appreciated by any normal rider. After hearing the prices of them, and even those of the cheapest of his saddles, I headed for the door with a sinking feeling in the pit of my stomach.

"Of course," I heard Mr. Jones' boisterous voice behind me, "If one were to inquire of pony saddles, it just so happens that Marcus Corbin's colts outgrew a pair a few weeks back." He reached behind the end stall slats and produced a pair of somewhat bruised but wholly intact pony saddles. Then he continued, "Course pony saddles, requiring so much less material in the making, can be sold at but a fraction of the price of regular ones."

"How much, Mr. Jones?" I blurted out with little or no thought.

"Well"—he hesitated for a bit and then continued—"for tiny, little saddle like these, I don't suspect I could ask more than twenty dollars each."

I was thinking hard on the number, but despair was fighting to get its place back in my stomach.

"Yet, if someone were to offer to take both of these saddles and rigs and get them out of my way 'round here, I'd probably let the whole mess go for half that price." He rubbed his whiskered chin and stared at me questioningly out of the corner of his eye. I suspect he saw me take a deep breath and let a smile begin to cross my lips as he added seriously, "Little saddles like them ain't likely going to be of use to anyone around here anyway."

"Twenty dollars for both outfits. I'll take them Mr. Jones," I blurted out—knowing that I couldn't buy them unless I got Pa to agree yet sensing that things going so right must have been fated, like a grant to my wish for a horse.

"God bless, you boy," Mr. Jones replied, in one level lower than his normal roaring voice. "It does my heart good to hear a lad your age already knowing how to work his numbers. For this pleasure, I think, should I see you here with your pa shortly to come and twenty dollars is laid 'cross my palm, then these saddles and rigs will be getting out of my way for some time to come—that is, at least, until they get to be too small for the ponies you and Kurt will be riding."

"Thanks, Mr. Jones. Thanks!" I yelled back as I ran from the livery stable, anxious to tell Pa and Kurt how things had developed.

Pa, shockingly, seemed to disregard my enthusiasm over these developments, coldly responding, "I've still got to hear from Gramps Pley. Could be he'll ask twice the normal price for livery, just to keep you boys from coming around his place."

Mr. Pley had purchased from my wagon on many occasions, and I knew him to be a good-natured, somewhat elderly man, prone to wearing a smile and speaking in pleasantries. I doubted if he would be as inhospitable as Pa was suggesting.

"One thing is for sure," Pa continued, " he's not going to be giving away food for two ponies."

"How much, Pa?" Kurt blurted out.

"What, just for feed?" Pa asked.

"Yes, Pa, how much?" I chimed in. Price seemed to be the determining factor in my plans that could make them feasibility.

"Not so much at first. But, by the end of the year, you'll be lucky to meet the cost of the feed with your entire selling profits," Pa replied discouragingly. "Besides, in six months, you'll be in need of all new gear from Jonesy," he added as a final blow.

Again, the sinking felling had returned to my stomach, and I feared it would not soon be departing.

The feeling of despair remained, as I started out with my wagon the following day. It was Tuesday, my day for climbing the bluff. This one, our hottest in that month of July, was already uncomfortable at dawn. By nine that morning, the sun was scorching, and I was glad to be on the road back. Meeting Kurt at the neck of town, I found that, like me, he was also soaked with sweat. Pa always told us to keep our shirts and hats on when we pulled our wagons. "The name of our bakery is on the sides of your wagons," Pa would say. "We want people to know that we run a sanitary establishment." Kurt and I continued together down the center of town, towing our empty wagons in the blazing sun.

Pa was fixing our lunch boxes on the baking counter when we walked in. He looked us over, hesitated a bit, and then told us to wipe off good with the water pail and sponge before putting on our school clothes. "Get straight home from school. You'll be tending tomorrow's chores tonight—if you intend to go to Martin's corral tomorrow for the auction," he added.

"Are we getting the ponies?" Kurt and I asked simultaneously.

"If they offer any sure of teeth and limb, you will," Pa replied decisively.

"Did you hear back something good from Mr. Pley, then Pa?" I asked, startled once again by an unexpected turn of events and anxious to know to whom it was that I should be grateful.

"No, not yet," Pa responded, disconcertedly.

"But, what if he doesn't help, Pa? We sure can't afford livery." I was desperate for an answer that would confer assurance that a miracle was about to take place. Pa gave it to me.

"I'll pay the livery if need be," Pa's words came back. "You boys ain't the only ones that get to see profit from your selling. Besides, a man's got sons with hearts as big as yours, then he has an obligation to show some heart back. I suspect it will do you both as good as any book learning will to develop horsemanship skills in these parts."

"Thanks, Pa," Kurt shouted, running over to throw his arms around Pa.

My mouth was probably hanging wide open as I stood there for a moment, amazed by the fact that I could actually be victorious in a dispute with Pa. Perhaps I really would be a grown, capable man in times to come, I thought.

"Thanks, Pa. Thanks a lot!" I added sincerely as we walked toward the washtub Pa had prepared in the backroom. Tossing my soggy cap on the rear stoop, I wondered if I would really be able to take care of a horse.

THE TRICK RIDER

My pony turned out to be a black-and-white paint, and Kurt's, a brown pinto. Six years later I could jump that paint, whom I had named Spirit, over a three-foot fence while standing on his haunches. I intended to do exactly that—right after Kurt (as usual) won the Saint Joseph's Town Fair Race, on his pinto, Flash.

John Burns's new white mare jumped out in front before the first turn, but she was sure to tire at the pace she had set.

"Go, Kurt, go!" I yelled, while leaning over the gate and waving him on.

Burns's mare was stretching out her lead as they passed. Damn, Pa should have taken the fifty dollars Jack Thompson had offered him to tell Kurt to lay back some. It looked like Kurt wasn't going to win anyway. As Kurt crossed the finish line, in second place, I started tying my hand rope to Spirit's bridle, while at the same time calming him with words and strokes.

"Looks like you'll be getting it tonight." Kurt spoke from outside the gate, while still seated on Flash.

"Good. What am I getting?" I replied, more sharply than I'd intended.

"Jenn called me over at the starting line. She wanted me to tell you to meet her at Gramps's after dinner. Looks like you finally hit pay dirt with her," was his announcement.

"The only thing I'll get from Jenn is a pair of sore nuts, like always," I answered truthfully.

"It'll be different this time. Girls are glad to give it when they know you won't be around to do any telling," Kurt responded matter-of-factly. Kurt never gave people the slightest credit for individuality, especially women. He sincerely believed that people were like cattle, effortlessly driven in the same direction by their sameness of thought.

"You're double wrong on that one." I spoke with deliberation, trying to contain my anger and attempting to display the same confidence of knowledge that he, though a year younger than I, did so naturally.

"How double?" Kurt smiled in anticipation of my explanation. He was quite aware that his sly remark would force me to reveal my personal motivations. There was no doubt Kurt had the upper hand in such matters—for, to him, we all have the same desires, making us, therefore, totally predictable. With this outlook, he had to be correct the majority of the time. To him, I probably fell into the category of a dreamer, rather than having a personality of my own.

"First, that Ron Mauner and your other buddies at school might think girls are all the same, but they don't know how Jenn is. "And, second"—I was now going to force him to be more cautious with my private concerns by angrily issuing him a warning through a tightened jaw—"I don't even intend to be leaving here tomorrow." I was forced to yell my last declaration so Kurt would be able to hear it over the bullhorn as they announced my ride.

"Ladies and Gentleman, we now have our own local, blond-haired Injun buck, ready to ride. Here comes, St. Joe's own, Fall-Off-Swenson."

"Fall-Off" was a name I'd picked up when kids in town had watched me practicing tricks at Gramp Pley's. Though the widespread adoption of the nickname was probably instigated by Kurt in order to taunt me, I had, in fact, some liking of it. That was probably because it was serving as a replacement for Olof.

Gramps Pley was letting us berth our horses in his barn, in exchange for "a couple of hours of work around the ranch each evening." Turned out, he was more interested in our company than our help. It had been a long time since he'd done any ranching. And it was but on occasion that he would actually be in need of our labor. Instead, he was strong on instructing us on riding and, you might say, "on living." We had heard Gramps's stories a hundred times over, but we also had *gotten to ride*!

Kurt got to liking to take off with some of the other town kids who had a horse for riding. He would head off with them over the hills, but not without first asking Gramps, if, "there would be any need of his help at hand." Most of my evenings were spent trying to improve my riding tricks or trying to learn new ones.

The first riding trick I learned had actually been taught to me by Kurt. We'd already been doing some riding bareback. After our ponies had outgrown their saddles, Gramps had offered us the use of several old ones he had in the barn loft. They'd been used hard in the past, by hands he had working at the ranch, and they'd suffered a bit from wear. Actually, without padding, they seemed a bit harder than the backs of our steeds, the latter at least sporting some flesh and hair between their bones and our bottoms. Consequently, Kurt had learned to ride bareback, same as I had. But he later bought a good saddle and was more comfortable using it.

For the last year, Kurt had stopped going to the schoolhouse. He'd never had a liking for school, and Pa agreed that he could do more work at the bakery instead of going. This was the last year that I had need of going myself, having already mastered the practical skills a man has need of to be properly educated.

The trick shown to me by Kurt had been shown to him by one of the older boys in town. As I held Flash's reins, Kurt ran up from behind him, placed his hands on Flash's haunches, and vaulted up. His effort came up slightly short, and he landed slightly above Flash's tail. Flash bucked a bit, and Kurt slid back off. Being some taller than Kurt, I was confident this trick would be easy for me, and I tried the same thing on Spirit. Vaulting past my arms easily and then thrusting them quickly forward to grab Spirit's mane, I landed in my normal riding position. The impact of my landing was a bit unexpected for Spirit, however, causing him to vault forward. Since Kurt was to Spirit's side, holding the reins, Spirit's head was pulled to that side, and I was thrown off the opposite.

The falling was quite uneventful to me, since I was use to taking more serious falls than that off Spirit during riding and jumping.

One fall resulted in my having a very swollen shoulder, and another ended in a similar condition of the knee. Feeling quite confident at this point that I was somewhat exempt from the breaking of bones, I had little to no fear of a slow-speed fall, unless it was to occur on rocky ground. On occasion, I had even faked falls in front of town kids to lend credence to my nickname of "Fall-Off."

On my second try, I told Kurt to release the reins the second I landed—and he did. Spirit vaulted again, but this time he was free to run, with me seated firmly upon him. Gramps had witnessed our antics and rushed over, excited by the activities. His congratulations seemed to me to be an overreaction to a somewhat simple trick. Gramps later told us stories of the trick riding he had witnessed by Sioux Indians in front of Fort Kearny. He described how they could use their Mustangs as a shield, by sliding down on one side while shooting arrows, and how they could throw their bodies off one side of their Mustangs, bounce off the ground, and spring right back up on their mounts. He described how they would fling their legs over the heads of their mounts and come about, facing a rider chasing them.

As Gramps described their performances, I pictured myself doing the same tricks and knew I could. Seeing how Gramps was so impressed with their performances, I thought there might be value in proving my ability to do the same. The value I sought wasn't monetary, but that of increasing my self-worth. Surely if Gramps was so impressed by the antics of the Indians, others might likewise be impressed if I could perform similar feats.

Several years later, Kurt entered and won Saint Joe's (first) county fair race. The joy and pride this had given Pa made me feel less important to him than Kurt was. If it hadn't been for the betting, I may have entered the following year's race myself. Kurt surely had no concern about the money folks had bet on him, but I would have had. The possibility of erring and causing folks to lose their hard-earned money kept me from entering. So, Kurt raced, and I did my trick riding.

As the bullhorn finished its announcement, Kurt swung the gate open, and I made my appearance standing on Spirit's haunches, using my hand rope to maintain balance as he broke into a gait. The crowd gave a hearted cheer at my appearance. They didn't realize that the hand rope made it nearly impossible for me to lose my balance. Comfortable with Spirit's gait, I bent my knees until I could hang the rope, as a coil, onto a hook I had fashioned on a shoulder strap for Spirit. As I returned to an upright position, the crowd gave an expected second cheer. Little did they realize that the slight bend I retained in my knees absorbed all of the impact of Spirit's bounding, and this was, in fact, a more comfortable ride than was afforded by sitting. After having retrieved my hand rope, a slight forward jerk of my legs gave Spirit the signal to increase his gait. As we vaulted the fence that had been drug to the center of the field, a roar went up from the crowd, undoubtedly producing a smile of pride on Pa's face.

Strange the degree of reward afforded for so simple a task. A simple trick, with little to no danger, produced so much awe from the spectators, simply because they couldn't do the same. If they had witnessed the many falls it had taken to learn to absorb the impact of Spirit's landing, they would know that, by merely pushing off Spirit, and taking a few rolls on the ground to absorb the forward motion, another fall would be no big deal. On a cleared, grassy field, this was completely hazardless to me.

Dismounting and removing Spirit's harness, I patted him several times on the nose, gave him the command to "stay," and let him know that our next trick would be a rear mount. At the mount, Spirit vaulted into a gallop. It truly seemed quite effortless to slide off first one and then the other of Spirit's sides, bouncing off the ground after each and returning to a mounted position.

The ease and pleasure of these maneuvers on their first mastering was so great that it had caused my emoting of whoops of joy. This had pleased Gramps greatly, reminding him, all the more, of the Indian buck performances he had witnessed. Seeing how these whoops were so appreciated by Gramps had been cause to include them in my performance, and doing so gave me an additional pleasure.

Turning toward the gate and pushing back onto Spirit's haunches, I swung my left leg to his right side, and then as I rolled over Spirit's back, I swung my right leg over his head and came up seated in a backward mount. Following this with a whistle told Spirit to come to an abrupt stop.

(Teaching Spirit this trick was easy; I'd simply whistled while, at the same time, using the reins to command him to stop. Successively, I'd been able to reduce the rein use until it could be totally eliminated.)

By placing my hands behind myself, on Spirit's back, I was able to push while kicking out my legs and launching my body off of Spirit. The bullhorn urged on the crowd's cheering as my arms were outstretched in symbolic victory. A smack on Spirit's rump caused him to run back across the field, and then my letting out a whoop told him to turn and run back. As he passed me, I reached under his neck, caught hold and swung myself up onto his back to ride out of the gate mounted.

(This maneuver Kurt had helped me teach him. We had done it many times with Kurt riding him while I gave the commands before Spirit responded to the commands without the prompting of a rider.)

"That was Fall-Off Swenson on his paint, Spirit." The final recognition was given as I exited the field.

I was full of confidence as I road toward town, while inwardly cursing Kurt for his disrespect of Jenny. After dinner, I'd be heading to Gramps's to meet her and find out if she wanted the same thing that I did—a lifetime together in Saint Joseph.

FAREWELLS

Since Pa had sold the bakery to Mr. Burcher at the bank, we were living in the prairie schooner he had bought to haul us to Pike's Peak. Pa had fixed a crate on the back, the rear of which could drop down to serve as a table. We'd been notified that we were scheduled to make the crossing with the other members of our wagon train in the morning, so we had already taken a place in the line that stretched through the center of town. We had taken our position, just before heading down to the fair and returned afterward for dinner. This made for what might seem to be a peculiar setting for dinner. But in Saint Joe, it was normal.

After dinner Kurt told me that Mr. Thompson had come over to Pa after the race and told Pa how he and his boys were losers. Pa told Thompson back that we hadn't lost anything. He told him that we would have been losers if we had taken the fifty dollars, by losing our self-respect. "Besides," Pa had continued, "second ain't losing."

Mr. Thompson had shouted back over his shoulder as he left in a bit of a huff, "Hope you have better luck with the Sioux."

"Mr. Thompson probably lost a bundle betting on Flash, like most of the townsfolk," I commented to Kurt, taking advantage of the opportunity to repay him for his comment about Jenny, although I knew my comment would, likely, not produce much of a response from him.

"If he knew anything about horses, he would have known Flash couldn't beat Burn's mare, even if you had been riding him Olof," Pa stated, to our astonishment. Pa must have known all along that I could still outride Kurt!

Upon hearing this, Kurt's gaze dropped to his plate, and his ears reddened from emotion.

"That's for sure—no way Flash would run as fast for me as he does for Kurt," I replied, trying to undo the damage Pa had done to Kurt's pride. Why was I now going to Kurt's aid? I asked myself, again recalling Kurt's comment about Jenny.

Pa seemed to sense that he had been inconsiderate, by our reactions to his remarks, and joined me in the rescue attempt.

"Su …sure. What I mean is no rider, on any horse in these parts, would have a chance against that mare." Pa stuttered slightly as he quickly formulated a response.

"She looked some short and stocky to me," Kurt remarked, somewhat under his breath, before raising his head, perhaps attempting to show us that he was not upset by Pa's comment.

"That's because she's a Morgan," Pa revealed. "I saw them on show once, back in New York. They're much stronger and faster a breed than our horses. It would take an Injun pony to compete with her."

"You should have bet a pile of money on her then, Pa," I said, even though I knew it would be a completely unacceptable idea to Pa.

He must have anticipated this suggestion, though, for his outlined response came quickly. "Why didn't I bet on him?" Pa posed the question as if addressing himself. "I'm sure you already know one of the three reasons—for I told you boys, not that far back, how I feel about gambling. But in case you've forgotten, I'll tell you again. First, there's no good to be gained from money, less it's earned off the sweat of your brow."

"But, Pa—" I started, anxious to query him on that point.

"Hold on, boy. I said there are three reasons. Doesn't that mean there are two more?"

"Yes, Pa," Kurt answered for me.

"Don't give any strength to your opinion by interrupting. More too, it gives a showing of ignorance before your words of purpose have been uttered. The second reason," Pa continued, as if the interruption had never occurred, "is that just about every cent that we got from selling the bakery went for this wagon; our six oxen; and the grub, tools, and supplies. That doesn't leave a bundle of money to be betting with. And third, what kind of a man would bet against his own son? I hope you don't really think that would be me, Olof."

"No, I know you wouldn't Pa," I said, still anxious to get to where I'd wanted my question to lead originally. "But what good can come, then, of money gained by striking it rich with a gold claim?" I asked.

"Well, boy"—Pa's answer again came too fast to indicate any doubt in his conviction—"you know how hard we all have been working in the bakery. You'll soon be finding that these past days were but a picnic, because the trip we're fixing to take is going to be trying on both our bodies and our spirit. The good Lord finds it proper to bring some into this world with a lifetime of affluence at hand. If we should find riches to be ours at the end of our journey, it will be of His doing and with His approval. That's a fair cry different than winning on a horse race. If the Lord found a reason to impose His will on a horse race, it would more likely be to earth His wrath upon a sinner—which may have been exactly the origin of the lesson Jack Thompson has just begotten."

Pa's argument on this, surely, was not a disputable one. Still, it seemed that staking everything you had on a dangerous exploit to find gold must indeed be a major gamble. Perhaps, the wrong of gambling comes from the causing of someone else to suffer a loss. The answer, I suppose, was, as Pa had always told us, "The greatest proof of God's presence is in our knowing the difference between right and wrong. For even the most unlearned heathen knows this difference in his heart, as surely as he knows to breathe the very air."

I don't know what had made me think there would be any chance of persuading Pa from taking this journey with that lame question anyway. Surely, he had thought plenty long on it, and any ploy would be quite ineffective at this point. Out of a building desperation to force Pa's recognition of the unacceptable implication his plan would impose upon me, there came an impulse to blurt out that I wouldn't be going at all— that I intended to stay right there, with my Jenny. I resisted the impulse, however, knowing that, if it were that she would not have me, I'd have that sorry truth to reveal. Better to wait until my visit to Gramps's had produced the answer that would determine my entire future, I thought. Accordingly, I ate quickly of the stew Pa had ladled into my bowl.

"Why didn't you buy mules?" Kurt queried of Pa between mouthfuls. "Everyone says they bring a better price at the diggings than oxen." Kurt needed an explanation, even from Pa, of anything lacking in conformity.

"Mules aren't as tough as oxen. If we have trouble with the weather or with finding feed and water enough, we could lose one, or maybe even two, of the oxen and still be able to keep the wagon rolling. If this was to come about, I'm sure you wouldn't like the stew that we'd be eating then as much as that the one you're stuffing down right now, if you knew it was meat from the rump of a butchered mule. The thing we want to concern ourselves with is successfully making the crossing. We don't want to be bothering other wagon folk, to their jeopardy, with our needs, should we have trouble befall us, while all the while knowing we had been slack in our preparation."

"We're not prepared for a fight," Kurt announced, a bit audaciously, indicating that this must have been a strong concern of his. "What if we get into an attack from Indians? One rifle for three men isn't good preparing."

"You listen to me, boy," Pa replied with authority. "Nature—that is the danger we'll be confronting. The Injuns are at treaty now. They're not about to attack a lone wagon, let alone a wagon train. Besides, the plague has brought down their numbers to where they'd have no chance against our soldiers. They know that. So, they're not going to do anything that might start another war with the white man. They are fighting for survival now, just as we might be doing if we don't prepare well enough. With all the hunting and trapping we have prompted them to do, for rewards of beads, gum, whiskey and other goods, their food supply is now very low. The game they have left to hunt is often unattainable to them because we have cut them off from their normal hunting areas with our trails, forts, and towns. Often Injun hunting parties have been shot down by emigrants who thought that the Injuns had in mind to threaten them."

"That being so, Pa, shouldn't a man know how to shoot good, if he's heading into the territories?" Kurt responded, trying another angle to gain a concession from Pa.

"There's truth to that, son," Pa conceded, after swallowing down an unusually well-chewed mouthful of stew. "Ed should have the store open some time before we start rolling in the morning. I'll pick up some extra shells so you boys can do some practice shooting when we do a camp down tomorrow."

"Thanks, Pa," Kurt replied, tossing out water from the pan he'd just finished washing. "Get moving, Ol. You'll need time to say your proper farewell to Gramps, *and all,* won't you?" Kurt asked of me, waiting for the angry glance he knew I'd throw at him—and also waiting to be sure I'd seen the knowing grin he was wearing.

"Don't waste any time getting back here with those horses." Pa spoke before I had time to think of a way to let Kurt know that he had a big mouth. "You got to get the oxen tended to when you get back," Pa continued, taking up the water bucket yoke.

He was heading to the well and then back, to start filling the water barrels strapped to the sides of our wagon. Pa had saved this job for last, wanting the water to be as fresh as possible before we started out. Most all of the other wagons only toted one barrel, but Pa wasn't taking any chances, in the case that we would encounter a dry hole en route. Since we had six oxen harnessed to a prairie schooner capable of being drawn by four, the extra weight wouldn't be an overtaxing of the team. Pa had said, "After the folks themselves, the most important things in a wagon train are the water barrels." I suspected that, with nothing else at all, we could make it to Mountain City, rolling along our water barrels.

"I talked to Mr. Pley at the fair and gave him my wholehearted good wishes," Pa continued. "Make sure you do the same. Let him know you realize how indebted you are to him for the years of helping and learning he's so kindly given to you both. And, Olof, if Jenny is there to give you a special send-off, you remember to mind your manners with her. I know you two have been sociable for some time now, but remember, what you leave behind will help you in everything that lies ahead, as long as it's a memory you can proudly call upon."

Damn, he's as presumptuous as Kurt! I thought as I turned to face him.

He stood there beside the wagon, oxen yoke across his shoulders, a water bucket dangling from each end. His dusty white shirt was mostly unbuttoned in the midday heat. He looked so darn superior to me, but I wanted to shout at him that he needn't worry about me leaving Saint Joe with any disrespectful memories, because I had no intention of leaving Jenny at all. But I still didn't know if she would be agreeable to making a life with me. Jenn was still planning on going to school. And I had nothing to offer her—not even a means by which to provide for our life together. Perhaps Jenny would plead with me to stay, I thought reassuringly. She might beg me and promise that, together, we could do anything we wanted. Surely Gramps could be counted on for support.

I thought it all out as I stood there glaring at Pa, but I said nothing.

Kurt's chuckle was something I could retaliate against, however. Turning quickly, I slung my near empty stew pot into his chest. On impact, stew splattered across his face and neck. Kurt dove for my waist and tumbled me to the ground, laughing in delight at my anger. A picture of his stew-splattered face remained in my mind as the impact of the ground against my shoulder forced a roaring laugh from my chest. How could I laugh with such pressing problems at hand, I wondered? But, I didn't care; it felt good to laugh.

"Don't forget, we have a long, hard day before us in the morn," Pa called back as he headed down the road, past the line of lead wagons, toward the well—while, Kurt and I continued to tussle.

Working my way out from under Kurt's grasp, as our struggle grew in intensity, I tried to roll on top of him. But he stiff-armed me as we rolled, sending me headlong into the wagon wheel. From the pain I felt, I knew that I'd be wearing a welt above my eye and some kind of cut on the bridge of my nose. Great! Now I'd have to stand before the woman I loved, asking her to trust me with the responsibility of her future, looking like I'd just had my tail whipped.

"Are you all right?" Kurt asked, jumping to my aid.

"You're an ass!" I shouted, fuming mad over all that had just transpired.

It seemed both he and Pa were trying to take away what was rightfully mine. To find another girl as kind, pure, and beautiful as Jenny would be impossible, and to lose her would be unbearable.

"I'm going," I told Kurt definitively.

He hastened to catch up but stayed a step or two behind me, following quietly for some spell.

"I wish I could stay here," Kurt said, breaking the silence with this outrageous statement.

"You do?" I asked, actually meaning, *Not as much as I do.*

"A man named Farwell came to me, after the race, and offered me a job."

"Is that so?" I asked, truly interested. Perhaps this would be my answer for finding a means of supporting Jenny.

"All I'd have to do would be to ride hard and fast, delivering messages to San Francisco," Kurt replied.

"That's crazy. You would kill the horse a hundred times over before you got there."

"He said there'd be a station every ten miles or so with a fresh horse. I'd only be riding about six hours a day, a time or two a week, for a hundred dollars a month pay. They intend to call it 'The Pony Express,'" he said.

"What about Injuns? A lone rider wouldn't have a chance in Injun country."

"That's why he wants men who know how to ride hard, shoot, and know the way Injuns like to attack. I think we've heard about every Injun attack story there is, pulling our wagons through the camps. Now if Pa lets me learn how to shoot, I think I might be able to get the job when the service starts," Kurt said, matter-of-factly.

"So, you're planning to hang around Saint Joe for some months, hoping this guy, Farwell, will come back around and give you a job." *If that don't beat all,* I thought. Here I was totally distraught at the thought of leaving him and Pa, and he'd do the same to us, with but the possibility of a job at stake.

"In a second," Kurt replied, "if it weren't for that Brenda Stills."

"What's she got to do with anything?" *Here he goes again with his favorite fantasy*, was my immediate, instinctive thought.

"Remember I told you about the fun we'd been having with her down by the creek, time or two?"

"Sure I do." How could I not? They were fantastic stories about how she'd let the boys do as they pleased with her and pleasured more than the doers by the doing. Certainly, it was a huge exaggeration, if not an outright lie, I had been sure on the hearing of it. Kurt and his buddies seemed to like nothing better than to talk of sexual perversions.

Sure enough, right up through the menfolk of town, when clustered without their women, the talk would more often than not turn toward some disgusting suggestion of an improper sexual account that was hailed by all to be a truism. Once, I even heard as bad from Pa. I'd come into the bakery while Pa was shooting pies to the back of the oven, so he hadn't noticed me passing to the backroom. As I started changing out of my school clothes, I heard Mr. Parker talking to Pa about a new saloon gal that had started working at Rose's. Pa's comments on her looks and his desiring were as crude as the worst hooligans down at Rose's.

What had happened to the belief in the beauty and holiness of love between a man and a woman that I'd learned about in church? Did that only apply to a husband and wife? I wondered. Or could it be that this crude lustfulness was man's normal attitude toward all women. Certainly, I'd never think of Jenny that way. If I were to lie with her, sex would have to come naturally from our love; I was sure.

Yet, am I any different than they are? I wondered. It was true that I had found the same self-satisfaction in fantasizing about Brenda at the creek that I had found so often in fantasies about Jenny. Still, I'd never wanted to go any farther with Jenny during our lovemaking than she let me. Holding her close, squeezing her against me so she could feel my love passing into her was the only true desire Jenny instilled in me—not a desire of the defilement of her body. *How can these two things come together?* I wondered. Perhaps there was a need for impure thoughts to promote sexual response, I thought. Perhaps I would learn to think of Jenny as an object of sexuality if we did marry. I only knew that I wanted to be with her forever.

As we reached Gramps's ranch, and I lifted the hasp from the gatepost, Kurt continued with what I thought to be a fantasy. "Brenda got herself pregnant, and she told me that I was the one that did it."

Surely, Kurt had no reason to invent such a tale. What could be his motivation, I wondered. The truth would own out in short adieu. His tales must not have been fictitious at all! I suddenly realized. This had to be the answer to my dilemma. If birth could be derived from this kind of improper, lustful behavior, it must be a sin that we are enslaved to, a sin the Lord created between every man and woman, which is meant to be the motivator of sexual response. Still, how could I think that way of Jenny? I wondered. And more impossibly, how could she think lustfully of me?

"How can she be sure it was you? The way you told me, it could have been any of you, right?" Now that I knew these were not fabricated stories about Brenda, I was interested in more details. Perhaps, I should have gone with Kurt and his buddies as he had requested on several occasions. Perhaps then I would now be able to offer Jenny a man as a husband, instead of a child. Did this then, make Kurt more of a man than me? I didn't, however, believe there could be any truth in the proposition.

"She says a woman just knows. But, she always had a liking of me. Now she wants to use the pregnancy to trap me into marrying her—is what I think. That's why I'm heading out of here with Pa tomorrow," he explained.

That is, indeed, the thinking of a true man, I thought. Kurt had no concern for Brenda, nor me or Pa. One hundred percent self-interest was his only motivation—a true child of God, sinful through and through. "You'd better talk to Pa about this when we get back," I said, offering Kurt the option I always fell back on when things were beyond my control.

We completed the walk to Gramps's in pensive silence. Noticing immediately that Jenn's horse wasn't in its stall, I knew she'd be waiting for me at the rock near the pond, where we had met many times since sharing our first kiss there, three years earlier. "Don't go in to see Gramps yet," I ordered Kurt. "Do Flash's grooming first, so I have some time with Jenny before Gramps asks about my whereabouts."

"Sure," Kurt replied, eager to help me down what he thought to be the same road that had led him into his current predicament with Brenda. "Reap the harvest while it's ripe," he added knowingly.

Being expectant of some such comment from Kurt, I found it easy to hide my irritation, and I coldly responded, "Jenn's not as stupid as some girls. Nor am I as some boys. I'll be back before your grooming's done," I said, as I led Spirit across the grass.

We jumped the fence to the road and then stopped, turned, and looked back at the house. There was no sign of Gramps. Kurt was brushing Flash and singing, "I seek for one as fair and gay, but find none to remind me. / How sweet the hours I passed away, with the girl I left behind me."

Jenny had spread her saddle blanket on the far side of the rock and was tossing kernels of corn, one at a time, to the expectant goldfish. After tying Spirit to a spruce next to Sunbeam, Jenn's golden mare, I joined her on the blanket.

"Jenn, I really don't want to leave," I began, but Jenn put her fingers against my lips, hushing me.

"What in the world have you done to yourself?" she asked as she leaned forward and kissed the bruises that hitting the wagon wheel had left on my forehead and nose, as if they were actually of some consequence. Then, without waiting for a response, she brought her kiss to my mouth, kissing me more passionately than she had in our many previous rendezvous. *She must be as desperate as I am*, I thought as we devoured each other.

Lowering her down onto the blanket, I let my hands begin their familiar exploration of her body. As often as I had tried, I could never remember the feel of her as I thought of her at night. Perhaps, after today it would not be necessary. Perhaps, from now on, I would have her with me at night, I thought.

As Jenn began to react to my touches, I let my hand slide under the frill of her bodice and over the softness of her voluptuous breast, trying desperately to picture what my fingers were touching, while knowing that at any second Jenn would end this ecstasy before it got out of her control. When she didn't, I knew she indeed wanted to be mine! Having been granted this victory, I started toward yet another conquest. Moving my hand to her knee, I slid it upward toward the softness between her thighs. On the occasions that she had allowed me there before, it was but for a second, so I knew she would be pulling away and jumping up before I went any further—but she didn't.

Instead, she gave me free access to explore everything I had dreamed of a thousand times over. She actually wanted to give herself to me—to be mine forever. There was no mistaking it; my dream was actually coming true. She wanted me to do it to her, right then and there! But how could I?

The realization came instantly and turned my ecstasy to shame. I had long since realized that, in our lovemaking, I had no longer been obtaining an erection. While at the same time, I had continued longing so desperately to make Jenny mine. I had attributed this to my realization that gratification would be kept from me—that no gratification would come, until I gave it to myself, alone and in hiding. My hope had been that, when I did know Jenny wanted to be mine, my body would react instinctively. But I knew at that second that I had been deceiving myself. Pa's words of warning had come true.

Returning home one day previously, after making out with Jenny, I'd headed straight to the outhouse, anxious to release my desires while the feel and smell of her were still fresh in my mind. In my haste, I had neglected to engage the catch on the door, and Pa had thrown it wide open as I'd stood there with my erect member in my hand.

"Sorry," he said, quickly closing the door. Then he added, "You know, if you get to liking that too much, you won't have a liking for the real thing when it comes your way."

These words had haunted me, as did shame, every time I resorted to this self-abasement. Yet I felt compelled to do so, while, in my heart, I feared that I was sacrificing the ability to have a normal relationship with a woman by my sinfulness. I often contemplated the prophecy that states, "He who spills his seed on the ground shall go without child." Had I brought this affliction upon myself? I wondered. I believed what Pa had often said that "the only true happiness in life comes from doing for your wife and children." Where would my life be, then, if I had stripped myself of the ability to father?

"Don't stop. I want you to," she said, with an uncharacteristic, impish smile.

"I can't do that to you Jenn," I replied. "I'm leaving tomorrow. I won't take that from you and then leave you cold. It wouldn't be right." I couldn't tell her why I really couldn't. And I was longing to hear her say that she wanted me to stay. Surely, I would find a way to work out my problem if we had a lifetime together, awaiting us.

"But I want you to have something to remember me by, Ollie. What if you are killed in an Indian attack, or something? Wouldn't you want to know that you had slept with a woman at least once in your lifetime?"

Damn! Kurt was right. She only wants to do it now because she thinks that she won't be seeing me again, I thought. *She's only trying to collect a memory.* "It wouldn't be right, Jenn. I couldn't do that to you," I said, wishing at that point that I could.

"Then why have you been trying to all these years?" she shot back at me, her welting anger obvious in her response.

The blood burning in my ears would undoubtedly be a dead giveaway to her that I, too, was upset by this turn of events, I realized. How could I explain to her? There was but one choice—resort to the truth. "Jenn, all I really want is you. But not just for this moment. I love you. I want to spend my whole life with you," I admitted as I knelt down on the blanket and reached for her

"But that can't happen now that you are leaving," she replied bluntly, quickly rising to her feet and brushing the wrinkles out of her dress.

"Then I'll stay, and we'll marry!" I proclaimed, happy to have found myself at a point where I could make the suggestion.

"That's stupid!" she declared definitively. "I'm still going to school, and you don't have any means of supporting us. How could we marry?"

Pleasure shot through my body on hearing this utterance. Only her schooling and my lack of work kept her from agreeing to marry me. She hadn't said that she didn't want me! "I'll come back to you when things are right, Jenn," I said, including to myself the resolution of the true problem that was keeping us apart at that very moment.

"Sure, come back rich and we can be happy ever after," she replied sarcastically but also charitably, as she tried to inject an air of sincerity in her statement. She had rolled up the blanket and was heading back to Sunshine.

Moving quickly to her side, I took the blanket, and strapped it to her saddle. Then I turned and took her in my arms, anxious for the pleasure I expected from her—the pleasure I derived from holding her close and feeling the ecstatic relief and tranquility that loving her had always brought to me.

However, this time, Jenn kept her elbows forward, holding me at bay. "This is not our time, then," she explained, pushing me aside as she mounted her mare.

"Don't give up on me, Jenn. The day will come. You will see. I swear it," I said, finding myself at a point of desperation.

"You just take care of yourself, Olof Swenson," she said, keeping all of her options open as she gave Sunshine a nudge with her calf.

Mounting Spirit quickly and following her, I felt quite foolish, having the realization that Jenn had attempted a commitment to me, and that she was probably riding toward the next man in her life. But if I had lost her, it seemed, then, more bearable, since Kurt had been right about her being the same as all the other girls. How much of a loss would she be? She surely wasn't the special, perfect being that I had adored so.

One thing was for sure: I had been doing too much fantasizing about everything in Saint Joe. Suddenly, I felt a need to head into the wilderness, into a world that would force me into reality and force the reaction of a man to emerge from the body of a boy. Suddenly, it seemed I no longer had anything to lose by going. *Good thing I held my lip tight with Pa*, I thought. Perhaps I had expected this outcome all along. As for Jenny, time would tell.

By the time we had reached Gramps's, Jenny had returned to the sweet, understanding creature that had led me to love her so.

Gramps had a seriously concerned look on his face when we entered, but it seemed to ebb after Jenn's normal salutation indicated that she was not unusually happy or overly talkative. Now that we were all back to our normal comfortable personalities, it was easy to say our adieus. But Gramps had surprises waiting for Kurt and me before he'd allow us to leave.

He presented me with a necklace he had received from an Injun scout. He had rescued the scout from the Arkansas River after the scout's pony had been spooked by a rattler. The Injun had told him that the necklace would always return him home safely to his family. It was made from a piece of tanned hide, outlined by red and yellow beads that surrounded a large claw. The claw was too long and thin to be that of a bear. I suspected it was from some kind of a large cat. On either side of the claw, there hung two black feathers. "Perhaps it will do the same for you," Gramps said with a knowing smile. As if my personal longing was an obvious item.

I put the necklace on, proud to be the recipient of this notably significant article and, after having done so, felt a slight reassurance from its perpetuated power.

"That's sharp enough for shaving," Gramps said, handing Kurt a buckskin belt and sheathe. "That's the single most valuable item, outside of water, that a man can carry, in order to keep himself alive in the wilderness. It did so many a time for me. You get yourself one, some the same too, Ollie. It'll make the job a whole lot easier for that there necklace."

There was no doubting the fact that Kurt and I were very important to Gramps, yet he said his farewell as quite a matter of course. I suspected that the early pioneers, like Gramps, had come to accept the hand of providence as natural, rather than punishing—just as a wounded animal immediately adapts to its handicap, without self-pity. Of course, it's quite normal for youths to lack appropriate appreciation toward the caring and giving elder that mold their adulthood.

Kurt and I, being true to form, accepted our departure gifts, with a quick, "Thanks, Gramps." If the thought had crossed our minds that this might be the last we would be seeing old Gramps, we certainly did not dwell upon it—and, of course, Gramps would have it no other way.

Heading out the door, Jenn kissed us both on the cheek, and I could do no more. But as we exited, I managed a last direct look into her eyes. Though somewhat teary, her smile seemed to be one of true pleasure. Perhaps, I thought, any heartfelt memory was enough for her.

"I'll be back, Jenn," I yelled to her as we road toward the gate, believing it with all my heart.

"How was it?" Kurt asked, smiling broadly as we rode off.

"Better than you can imagine," I answered.

"What makes you think she's so great?" Kurt asked, arrogantly.

"It's something that you wouldn't understand," I replied. "It's an entirely more enjoyable experience when it's with someone that you're in love with."

This had to be good advice, though it didn't apply to my situation. In any case, I didn't want Kurt to think that he was farther along to manhood than I was. This remark seemed to put me back in the position of a knowledgeable, older brother and possibly did. I got the impression that Kurt was reflecting a great deal on my statement, since he was quiet all the way back to our wagon.

Pa was standing on the stool, pouring water into one of the barrels when we arrived. "The farewells all said?" he asked as we tied our horses to the wagon rail and joined him.

"Yeah Pa," Kurt alone responded.

I was not about to start volunteering the information I knew he would be searching for.

"Did you say your proper farewells to the lassie, then, Olof," Pa asked imposingly. I knew he would continue to dig out what he wanted to know with words like *proper*. What's proper, anyway? I thought.

"I'm not the one you need to be counseling about 'proper,' Pa," I answered out of anger but also to put Kurt on the spot and force him to reveal his problem to Pa.

"You got something to tell me about, boy?" Pa asked, changing his interrogation from me to Kurt.

Kurt reluctantly explained his predicament to Pa, quietly, containing his shame to our campsite.

"I have a mind to give you a damned good whipping," Pa said after hearing the telling, the redness on his face visible beyond the glow of his recently started campfire. "I would, too, if I thought it would make you use your head more in these matters. Things like this can lead to someone getting killed. There's nothing more cherished than a woman's virtue to them that love her," Pa stated in his most serious tone.

Or no more sought after by those that want to love her, I thought while watching Kurt's fear of Pa wane, since the conversation had progressed past the danger point.

"The way Brenda tells it, no one in her family ever had concern over her virtue," Kurt spoke out, his courage having returned.

"Well, that would be a sad thing be it true, and one that wouldn't surprise me knowing Mr. Stimpson the way I do," Pa said. "Nevertheless, you need to keep in mind that men and women need to be married before taking a chance on bringing a life into this world. They need to make a commitment to love and protect that life. What's to become of this child? That's the sin!" Pa shouted, leaning menacingly towards Kurt. After a moment of contemplation Pa continued, "So you're telling me all four of you boys had your way with her?"

"Yes, Pa," Kurt replied without hesitation.

"Are you sure of that?" Pa asked sternly, suggesting that this held great importance.

"Yes, I am Pa," Kurt replied with confidence.

"Do you think she has also been with other boys?" Pa asked, continuing his query.

"I suspect so Pa. Anybody could be with her for merely the asking— except, maybe, for Wilber Barns," Kurt replied, seemingly amused by this detail.

"That's Mr. Barns the undertaker's boy? And why do you say not he?" Pa asked.

"He's strange—never talks to a soul, and those thick spectacles and all make him look weird. All he ever does is schoolwork—never gets into a game with us," Kurt replied.

"Nobody's friends with Wilber," I explained, "not even Brenda."

"Sure, there's no sense in extending a little friendship to someone who would appreciate it. You kids are a cruel bunch," Pa said, obviously irritated by our comments.

"Aw, Pa, Wilber really wants to be in his own world. At least that's how he shows it," Kurt replied, defensively.

"That's not likely. Many young folk have problems to work through, and a little help from a neighbor can do a lot for them. Once Wilber has worked through his problems, he's going to have the advantage of the extra book learning he's getting now and likely will become someone of importance in days to come—while you 'normal' youth will have spent all your time pursuing fun—with the result of poor education and unwanted fatherhood!

"It's a bad way to be leaving town, having blame put on you, and not being here to set it straight. But we got to concentrate on the journey ahead of us, and I'll be expecting you boys to be mindful of your actions. There'll be three men with our wagon—not a dad and his boys. I'm going to have to be able to depend on you both to keep your wits about you, and right now, that means tending them animals. I have a couple more trips to the well to make, and then we turn in. We have a big day ahead of us tomorrow, with making the river crossing, assembling the wagon train, and all," Pa concluded, as he walked off with the water pails.

That was all there was to it! Kurt had possibly fathered a child, and Pa dismissed it that simply. Surely, fornication must then be a normal activity of life, I thought, which made it more ridiculous to have been attributing it to extreme sinfulness. Certainly, I would never have been able to respond to Brenda the way Kurt apparently had. The idea of having sex in the accompaniment of others would, in itself, be totally humiliating to me. But to take advantage of Brenda like that would be an act totally disgusting to me.

Yet, if I continued to analyze sexual activity so, would I ever be able to perform normally? I wondered. Sex, obviously, required instinctive, animal response, not analysis and certainly not love. Parents, preachers, and teachers were all total hypocrites on the subject of sex, I thought—for, surely, no moral person could respond with the animal lust it required.

I knew that, to make this conclusion, would be disastrous to my future love life. It would mean that my problem would be self-perpetuating, for surely I could not turn off my mind when needed. Yet, Pa had said, "Many youths have problems to work through." Surely, I didn't have as many problems as Wilber Barns. There must be an easy solution to my problem, for the obvious hypocrisies of sex must be apparent to any thinking person, I reasoned. So, just like Pa I would head West, hoping to make a discovery—hoping that, perhaps, the demands of wilderness life would turn me into a less pensive individual.

"I can't believe Pa let you off that easily," I said to Kurt as we wrestled a bale of hay off the back of the wagon from atop the bushels of oats we were bringing for Spirit and Flash. All the animals would do their own foraging for food when we unhitched them at night from here out, but we had oats and corn, should the grazing turn bad.

As the bale thudded to the ground, Kurt replied, "He knows what it's all about."

"Yea, it's being irresponsible and selfish," I blurted out the words I had expected Pa to impart, not trying to conceal my anger.

"She had just as much fun as we did. Besides, you could be leaving Jenny in just the same fix. What makes you any better?" Kurt retorted as we jumped off the wagon beside the bale of hay.

"If Jenn was in that condition, I'd not be leaving," I stated, with the certainty I wished to actually exist. "If it turns out she is," I continued, perpetuating the hoax that this could actually be a possibility, "she'll send word with one of the wagon trains. And when I get it, I'll be back here faster than a jackrabbit chasing a hare."

While saying this, I saw a smile cross Kurt's face, which was alit with the glow of the setting sun as he heisted the other end of the bale. This made me wonder if he had seen through my fantasy, but his mind was doing its own imagining I found, as he replied joyously, "Maybe I'll be delivering you the news via the Pony Express. Wouldn't that be the cat's tail?" Kurt joked.

"I thought you said it was just to go between Saint Joe and San Francisco?" I queried, happy to know that Kurt had given no more thought to my end of our conversation.

"Yeah, I know," Kurt replied, losing the smile as he used the sabre Gramps had given him to cut open the bale.

He probably just liked rekindling the possibility of getting this prestigious job, doing his favorite of all things—speed riding across the countryside. It would be just his luck too that it would come about, and I'd be stuck alone with Pa in the hills, hunting for his precious gold nuggets.

Why had I been making such a big deal out of leaving them? Surely, it was natural for a man to be making his own way at my age. Still, somehow, it seemed hard to picture Pa and Kurt going on without me, as if I were a strong link needed to connect them. I don't know why I thought myself to have such importance. It probably was unjustified. Yet, so it seemed.

THE CROSSING CHALLENGE

Wagons had started loading onto the river rafts at first light. With only a dozen parties ahead of us, we'd be loading before noon, so we hitched our team of oxen and made ready to start moving up. While tightening the straps on the oxen, I saw a terrifying but not entirely unexpected figure riding hard up the line of wagons to our rear. It was Mr. Stimpson. "Pa," I shouted, "Stimpson's coming with a shotgun!"

Pa was on the other side of the wagon draping a cover over our supplies to protect them from the sun. Kurt was behind the wagon setting down pails of water for our horses.

"Kurt, jump in the wagon and get low," Pa shouted.

"Should I get your rifle, Pa?" I asked, surprised that he wasn't already moving toward it.

Pa didn't answer. He leaned against the wagon with his arms folded and one foot raised behind him against the wagon wheel as he watched Mister Stimpson ride up.

Stimpson looked as mean as ever. A heavy, burly, unshaven and unkempt man, his appearance was typical of a fur trader. Kurt and I had sometimes sold him bread or muffins, when he was in town with his furs. As was the way of the traders, he'd go off for many months to trade at the Injun camps, later returning with beaver and buffalo pelts. He smelled a good bit worse than the buffalo hides and could gobble down an entire loaf of bread faster than Spirit could consume a cup of oats.

"Hold up now, Jake," Pa shouted as Stimpson road up.

"Where's your youngin'?" Stimpson barked. "He's got some marrying to do."

It was somewhat relieving to me, knowing that Stimpson knew I wasn't Kurt.

"Now you just come down off your horse, and we'll talk this out sensible," Pa said, trying to reason with the barbarian as he stepped forward with his hands raised to show Stimpson that he had no weapon.

Doubting that this would deter Stimpson from violence, I glanced at Pa's rifle, resting behind the seat, and tried to determine how long it would take to retrieve it. At the glance, I saw a hand grasp the barrel and pull it into the back of the wagon.

Stimpson trotted toward the front of the wagon shouting, "I know you're in there, boy, and I'm going to blast you out." He held the shotgun in one hand pointed upward and his reins in the other. As he started past me, he quickly turned back, lowering the shotgun barrel toward the front of the wagon (and Kurt). His horse was now right in front of me, his shotgun pointed over my head. Without actually giving any thought to what action I should take, instinctively, I bent down and lunged between the legs of Stimpson's mount. From my show riding practice with Kurt, I knew this was a sure way to get a horse to rear up. It worked! The speed of my action, and perhaps the tenseness of the situation, really frightened his horse. He went straight up and near to fell over backwards. Stimpson's shotgun discharged into the air as he dropped off the back of his upright mount. The discharge caused our team to bolt forward, pulling the wagon along.

Stimpson had dropped the shotgun as he impacted the ground with his back. As his stallion's leg buckled under, it too went down, half seated on Stimpson's thigh. Pa quickly snatched up the shotgun and then grabbed the reins of Stimpson's horse as it quickly arose, causing Stimpson to let out a roar as it rolled across his leg. Pa managed to keep the horse at bay, and I saw our oxen team being pulled up, so I knew Kurt had gotten to their reins. Stimpson was grabbing his thigh, rocking his torso, and groaning with pain as I ran over to Pa and took the reins from his hand. Leading Stimpson's mount to the back of our wagon, I tied it up with our horses. Our wagon had traveled partly around Carter's, which was positioned in front of ours, so Kurt had pulled them up in a fashion that had left the roadway blocked. Fortunately, the entire wagon line was now advancing some, so he was able to get our rig back to its proper position. Some of the wagon folk behind us had come forward to help Pa with Stimpson. Together with Pa, they were carrying him up to our wagon. Kurt grabbed Pa's rifle and put it under the seat, covering it with a blanket.

"It's broken! I know it's broken," Stimpson was moaning, while tears flowed freely from his eyes. They spread some straw on the side of the road, covered it with a blanket, and laid Stimpson's mass upon it.

It seemed strange to see this rugged wilderness man crying openly from his injury. He no longer seemed to be an overwhelmingly threatening force. Doc Heartley had just galloped up and quickly set to examining Stimpson's huge thigh. The doc made him move his leg back and forth as if he were walking and then announced that it was tendon damage and probably a fractured bone. "But it will heal," he declared.

The doc had Pa remove some slats from a crate and tied them on either side of Stimpson's thigh with cloth strips.

"How'd we come to get in this condition, Jake?" The doc asked Stimpson.

"Ugh." Stimpson turned his head and went back to grimacing with pain, without responding.

"It was my fault," Pa answered. "Jake had come to sell me his shotgun there," Pa said, pointing to the gun propped against the wagon wheel, and I dropped it while looking it over. The darn thing went off and spooked the animals. It was lucky that no harm was done by the discharge—just Jake getting thrown from his mount.

"Jake, you don't get yourself cleaned up once in a while and your skin's gonna start rotting off your bones. I'll send a travois back, to drag you back on. Stop by my wagon with five dollars, when you get up and about, and I'll take a look at how it's healing. But you clean up before you do. You hear me?"

"Yeah, sure, Doc," Jake answered," still whining. "Thanks, Doc."

"Look what your boys did to me now," Jake whimpered, after Doc was out of earshot. "How am I going to take care of a pregnant daughter in this condition?" Amazingly, he was actually resorting to an appeal for sympathy.

"That girl of yours can take care of herself, Jake. She always has," Pa replied. "And this condition, you brought upon yourself."

"Swenson, your boy Kurt has to own up to what he's done. I know you teach your boys right from wrong, and you know it's wrong for him to duck out on his responsibility." Now, he was appealing for justice, his pain seemingly gone for the moment. Still, I was glad it was still Kurt he had on his mind—not mentioning me, having been the one who had spooked his horse.

"Now, Jake, I know you've got a problem, but you haven't thought it through. First of all, do you want to see your daughter drug off to a mining camp and married to a man that's contracted to ride for a messenger service called The Pony Express? Why, he'll be gone from home even more than you are. And second, now you listen well to this, Jake, your daughter has been with half the boys in town, and you know it."

Jake groaned loudly again.

"If this is brought to town meeting, her reputation will be destroyed, and it won't do you any good either," Pa continued.

"What do you suppose I do about her problem then, Swenson?" Stimpson asked quietly, from a head hung in remorse.

"I'll tell you what I'd do. Go home and tell that girl that she's lost the privilege of picking out the man that she wants for a husband. She's got to find someone who needs her and snag him quickly," Pa suggested.

"You got someone in mind?" Stimpson asked, turning to look at Pa, obviously interested in Pa's suggestion and anticipating that there was to be more to it.

"Wilber Barns," Pa announced. "Between his appearance, with them glasses and all, plus his standoffishness, it's likely he'd be hard put to get the interest of a young woman. Yet, he's obviously a smart and hardworking young man, whose father has property and a business that the boy will certainly inherit in the future. I'd be willing to bet that old Mr. Barns would be so surprised and happy to see his boy marry that he'd little care if this first child was Wilber's, or not."

"Swenson, you're a genius," Jake pronounced, apparently now cured of pain. "I'm going to have a strong talk with that girl about what's important in a husband as soon as I get back there. You know it won't look right, though, if I'm brought back there with that shotgun in hand, seeing how I was supposed to have brought it up here to sell to you all," Jake added.

"And how much do you suggest I was to have bought the gun for?" Pa asked.

"Fifty dollars would sound a proper amount," Jake had the nerve to suggest, while sporting a telltale smirk.

"That gun ain't worth half—" I started to interject, but was cut off by a harsh glance from Pa as he replied to Stimpson.

"All right, Jake," Pa surprisingly agreed. "But I'll hear no more on this matter—no matter how things go with Barns."

"Put it there, Swenson," Jake said, his arm extended from his now somewhat seated position on the ground. "The fifty I mean," he said with a smile, his arrogance unfretted.

After Jake was drug off, I asked Pa why he'd paid fifty dollars for a gun worth no more than ten.

"If Jake likes how he came out of this affair, we are well rid of him, and it will be fifty dollars well spent. We are, after all, part of the cause of the problems Jake's facing—problems that may not be as easily resolved as I had suggested. Though, I suspect they just might."

"Why is that Pa?" I queried, determined not to lose any information on how Pa had defused this explosive situation so easily.

"The Lord has a hand in such affairs. He brings events together to bring forth a result beneficial to the future. We do His work constantly, while choosing our actions, as long as we keep open hearts and minds."

Though Pa's logic did seem a likely explanation for these extreme events, I had to wonder what events the Lord could possibly bring about to resolve a problem like mine. Could any events or situations be created that would result in the reversal of my dysfunction? Certainly, there were none that I could rationalize.

Holding the tethers of three of our oxen, I stared down through the line of wagons through the center of town. Staring from the bed of the ferry, I was praying that I would see Jenny come prancing down beside them to beg me off this journey. Had it been that I had been able to give her what she had wanted the previous night and done so in the manner of a confident and powerful lover, my prayers might, indeed, have been answered, I suspected. Feeling tears of pity beginning to well up in my eyes, I turned to gaze across the beautiful river we were about to cross. It was brown now from the spring rains. Not showing any movement of its own, it reflected perfectly the scene from beyond, across its expanse. On occasion, a giant stroke would sweep the scene and cause it to sway in soft response. The majesty of this scene was enhanced by the bustle of activity on shore.

Kurt and I had made this crossing often. After we had been settled in Saint Joe for several years, fewer wagons, mostly Mormons, were still heading west through town daily. More go-backers were passing through town than emigrants heading toward the California and Nevada mines. Consequently, long wagon lines had begun to form on the west side of the river, instead of on the east. During these days, Kurt and I would cross with our wagons, usually bartering off fare with coffee and muffins. Though the ferry hands were quite adept at controlling the wagons and animals, there were often accidents on board, usually caused by inept passengers. On one occasion, a traveler backed a horse up into children sitting on the rail, sending them tumbling into the river. On another trip, the trail of a prominent lady's gown became caught up on the wheel of a wagon as it was suddenly rolled from behind her, pulling most of the back of her gown clean off before releasing her from its grasp. The antics occurring here were often enough to draw down a constant audience to the loading dock, as it had become a place of entertainment. Although this was a somewhat inconsiderate pastime, seeing how many serious injuries were a result of the unintentional entertaining, the crossings were still much safer, I had been told, since steam engines had been installed on the ferries.

In days prior to the advent of the steam engine, the ferries would occasionally make landfall on the opposite bank by actually smashing into the loading platform. The cause of this was the ferries' uncontrollable means of propulsion. They utilized the always available river current to propel the raft across it. This was done by connecting the raft to a cable that spanned the river. Two cables were connected from the ferry to this spanning cable by means of pulleys, with a longer cable at the rear of the ferry than at its front. This presented the side of the ferry to the river current flow, angularly, resulting in the ferry acting as a large rudder. The ferry simply, then, rode across the river on the cable, and the cable lengths were reversed for the return trip, allowing the ferry to be poled back across. The problem occurred when the current became too strong, moving the ferry too fast to allow the poling efforts at the shoreline to prevent it from a very abrupt landing. This sent wagons, carts, animals, goods, and passengers plummeting forward. When the engine and water wheel were added to the side of the ferry, it was possible to create a reverse force that slowed the ferry down, allowing for a comfortable landing.

Hearing the blast from the captain's horn, I turned to watch Saint Joe falling away behind us, as I had done so many times in the past, and was startled to see a wee figure running down to the dock. Jenny! Could it be?

No, it was Brenda!

"Kurt, don't forget me!" she called out. "I'll be waiting! I love you!"

What a travesty! More convincing—how could I deny the obvious now? *Only sex is significant*, I thought. She should have been yelling out the truth. "You screwed me! I'm pregnant! I need you," not, "I love you."

Yet it was helpful to me that Brenda had made this desperate plea. Somehow, it made it easier to accept leaving Jenny, anger being easier to bear than sadness.

I spied Kurt on the opposite side of the ferry, shying behind his oxen charge. Pa was glaring at him from the front of the ferry, where he held Spirit and Flash at bay. This was the setting for the start of our journey into the wilderness. The rolling hills, beyond the opposite bank, looked to be an inviting start to our journey. It would be easier to confront the wilderness with its beasts, savages, and natural impediments—entirely easier than to confront love, sex, and morality. There was the spontaneous roar from us passengers when the ferry thumped to a stop. This was the first landing in which I felt the need for a cheer—a cheer that could boost my spirit in preparation for the journey ahead, where in the past it had only served as fun.

When the west bank ferrymen boarded and took charge of the animals, I ran down the ramp to join Pa and Kurt.

"We'll have a drink to celebrate that our feet are on this land," Pa announced to us.

The realization then came to me that Pa had never before made the crossing.

"I want you boys to know how much this means to me," Pa continued. "After I decided to abort our trip west, ten years back, I had to question that decision every time I heard a report of success being obtained by a forty-niner. Sometimes, I'd think that, perhaps, even without financial success, the reward would still have been there, simply in the doing. Even if we find not a dollar's worth of gold, I'm sure much value will be afforded to you both. The value will be in the experiences you will have and the knowledge you will attain. Experience opens a man's mind, and confronting challenges develops his confidence. Though you boys have already shown me that you are quite capable and resourceful, I have no doubt that this journey will add to your growth of character."

Pa had passed the flask to me and, with it, my first challenge in the West. I had gotten myself sick once sneaking sips from whiskey glasses off the sill of an open back window at the saloon house, while the drunken patrons where transfixed by their game of billiards. Since then, when offered a drink of whiskey, I only touched it to my lips and then responded with a pretense of the ague the offering was meant to evoke. This pretense was easily affected by the memory of my previous foolery. However, on this occasion, struck by Pa's acknowledgement of the importance of this moment and determined to best all the challenges by which I was about to be besieged, I bolted down a large gulp of its contents and was rather surprised to find that it produced in me but a passing grimace. It was actually quite soothing to my stomach.

Kurt eyed my actions keenly, and took, perhaps, even a larger gulp from Pa's flask. But rather than going down for him, it came flying back out, spraying Pa's shirt before Kurt was able to turn aside.

Pa jumped back and then looked down at his shirt, holding it out from his chest, and laughed loudly. "Looks like Ollie and I will have a boy to do this traveling with."

"Shoot, I just swallowed wrong's all," Kurt mumbled, still somewhat choked. He started to raise the flask again, but Pa grabbed it back.

"Never mind that. You can try it again once we reach Denver City. I suspect you might be a good bit more aged by then," Pa said, while still chuckling.

"I doubt that Brenda would agree with you about Kurt not being a man yet, Pa," I said, offering this both in Kurt's defense and as an opportunity to get Pa's opinion on the subject of manliness verses sexual ability.

"I just hope he don't use himself up in foolery," Pa replied. "Too much fooling around now, and you won't enjoy it as much when you marry—when it's needed to strengthen your relationship."

Although, I was glad that Pa didn't feel a need to further elaborate on manliness and fathering, he strengthened my fear that too much "foolery" can weaken a man's sex drive. Certainly, I still had plenty of drive, but apparently not when I needed it.

5

EXPERIENCE OF THE WILDERNESS

"Let's help with the grouping," Pa commanded, walking toward our wagon. Pa had Spirit pulling a buckboard, in which he had loaded mining supplies, wagon tools, and other items that didn't require being protected from the elements. The wagon party was now moving to the side of the road for assembly. The party was partly comprised of over a hundred handcarts being pushed and pulled by men on foot, whose meager supplies were being carried in the carts. Some were making the journey with nothing except the clothes on their back, a blanket to keep them warm at night, and canteens full of precious water. These men, having little going for them in life, needed to extend but slight consideration on whether or not to make the journey. The chance for wealth was there for all, but in the case of these men, there was also nothing to lose. Many of them were crude, disreputable fellows. But, as the wagon master had put it, "During this journey, we will be one family, and we will be obliged to support and rely on one another."

There were forty-four prairie schooners, like ours, joining in the crossing. We were to be led by three Sarasota wagons, which belonged to the wagon master, Tom Potts, who was also engaged in goods transportation. The wagon train would also be comprised of over a hundred animal-drawn contraptions. Some were buckboards, like the one Spirit and Flash were to draw. Others were makeshift carts to which wheels had been attached. There were converted stages and some totally contrived conveyances. These were being drawn by mules, horses, or oxen teams of various numbers. Some actually had the entire burden dedicated to a single animal, a few of which already appeared to be suffering from the taxing of their load. Within the groups, each party was assigned a position, which they would maintain throughout the crossing, unless problems caused them to fall out and be left behind. If they managed to catch back up, they would finish that leg at the rear of the train.

Pa had made it clear that we wouldn't be burdening our animals by adding our weight to their load. During the entire crossing, we'd be leading our team on foot or pushing our buckboard to help our horses, since they weren't created to function as pack animals like the oxen. Six hundred miles on foot seemed like an impossible task to Kurt and I, but Pa had said, "We'll only be walking a day's worth of it each day, and that will probably be no more than we'd walk normally, near every day, with our normal activities."

Surely, I thought, looking at the personage of some members of our new family, it would be no trouble to match their stamina. Many of both the old and young had bulging midsections and general flabbiness.

After all of our party had made the river crossing, we spent the remainder of that day and all of the next practicing with our teams. We practiced pulling the wagons up into protective circles for night camp and reassembling and driving them out again in formation. It was obvious that many of the wagon owners had little to no experience with animals. Wagons were going off in all directions at first. Some went backward, and some in no direction at all. But, finally, on our third day west of the Mississippi, after making our formation assemblage, we heard the wagon master's refrain, "Forward ho!" being echoed along the wagon train. Then, each wagon shouted its team into motion. We traveled two wagons abreast and then two handcarts wider still, creating a four-column lineup. Between the columns, at random, walked individuals, pairs, and groups probably making the entire assemblage appear as a solid mass, sliding over the river valley to the scavenger birds circling overhead, waiting to pick through the discards of our meal sites.

Underfoot became another matter. Large ruts and potholes were strewn across the pathway. Spring rains had started on the day of our outset, filling the ruts with mud. They had mostly dried since, but water lay pooled up in places, concealing the depth of the holes. We watched the wagon in front of us, and followed its wheel marks as long as the wagon maintained a steady keel. It wasn't long before all the folk who'd thought they'd be making the crossing in the back of a wagon were walking along beside it. The rocking and bouncing of the wagons was both unbearable and sickening to the riders, after but a short period. We had only moved over the second range of rolling hills when the wagons were drawn up into a circle. The wagon master had ridden ahead and marked off a spot for each wagon, using a tree limb to scratch the ground as he rode. Each end of our wagon circle was left open to allow carts and animals to be led in. The site was selected because the grazing grasses were good, as was the accessibility of the river water.

The day before, several boys had accompanied the wagon master in selecting this spot. They helped him remove brush and flatten the earth in several areas of the river edge, so that animal watering could be done easily. Pa said Kurt and I would have turns in that task in days ahead, but for that night, our tasks were to tend the animals and to set up our cooking spit, after which we were to turn in early. We planned on rising early to allow time to have our bacon and coffee before breaking camp, watering the animals, and hitching them up. The wagon train was to be moving out at first light "with or without us," as the wagon master had made clear to all parties.

As we walked along, we watched for clumps of animal dung, which were usually found caked with weed at the side of the road. We tossed them into the potato sacks Pa had tied to the sides of the wagon. "If it doesn't smell strong, it will burn," Pa had said. We used these as a source of fuel, seeing how the trail had been virtually cleared of anything burnable by the many prior, emigrant wagon trains that had already made the crossing. We brought some fresh vegetables for the first few days and many dried ones for the remainder. Pa was a strong believer that our bodies would take care of themselves if we gave them all the ingredients they required to do so. Most of the wagons brought mainly flour, bacon, sugar, and coffee for the entire trip. Many walkers were limited to bacon, dried beef, and coffee only. As well as all mentioned, we also had brought along, dried and fresh fruits, nuts, rice, hard candy, and even Swenson muffins.

Pa had once commented, "These men are dreadfully afraid of Injuns, while at the same time they are putting their lives at risk with their eating. They'd do better to trade their muskets for a small sack of dried apples and just might end up doing that before reaching Denver City."

We left our wagon hitched up after forming our circle. After chow, we led the team to a watering area and right into the river, until the water reached just below the wheel hubs. Each hour, we moved them up or back a foot or two, so that all the spokes had soaking time. Many other wagons were doing the same through the night. The next day, while on the trail, I found out why that soaking was necessary. After crossing a feeder stream with a sharp rise on its far side, we saw a wagon waylaid on the side of the trail. The team had been removed, as well as the front wheel, which was no longer round.

"That's the result of traveling on dry wheels," Pa remarked as we rode pass them. I was more astonished by the means of repair than by the damage. "Wow, he's strong!" Kurt proclaimed, echoing my astonishment as he did. It was Jimbo. I had seen this huge Negro earlier and knew he worked for the wagon master. "Don't they have a wagon jack, Pa?" I asked, wondering why a man should be subjected to this obviously torturous task.

"Jacks don't always work. Like when you get into mud or soft sand," Pa explained.

"How can you do that?" I asked as we passed, in awe of his strength.

"Ask the Lord," he replied, his grimace only slightly concealing his smile as he responded.

After several days of following the river, I began to think that there was nothing at all to fear of the wilderness. Instead, I had found a place that I swore to myself to someday return to with my Jenny. As far as the eye could see, they were swaying in the breeze. There were yellow, gold, red, blue, and white flowers. They were vibrant close up and then blurred into a soft blanket of colored patchwork in the distance.

"Why hasn't anyone started farming here?" I asked Pa. "The soil sure looks good at growing."

"You can't get everything from the soil, son," Pa replied. "Take you a week to get anything from town. Besides that, you wouldn't want to be out here alone when the winter storms set in, especially not if you had a family's well-being at stake."

So, it would be possible when towns start spreading west from Missouri, I thought. I made it a point to remember this place in the wilderness, while chuckling inwardly. It was closer to paradise than wilderness, I thought. However, I would find that situation to be changing by the weeks end.

The trail had become noticeably more traveled and rutted after it was joined by a trail coming from Nebraska City and even more yet after passing Fort Kearney. There it was again joined, this time by a trail coming from Council Bluff. The combined trail had been traveled by many Mormons during the height of their movement.

It had been raining since our stop at Fort Kearney, and the trail had become a sewer of mud. Our wagon had wide wheels, as a foresight of Pa's, and was making out okay. But, several wagons with thin wheels had to fall out of the wagon train. Their hope was to be able to catch back up to us after the ground had dried some.

The stop at Fort Kearney was my first opportunity to see Indian families in their natural habitat. Some Cheyenne were camped in the front of the fort, as was their custom to avail trading with the soldiers and passing emigrants like ourselves. They seemed serious in their attitude toward whites but quite playful among themselves. There was, in their campground, a squaw in a buckskin dress. She wore beads about her neck and arms and had long, braided hair down her back.

"I don't remember ever seeing a white girl with beauty to compare, except Jenny of course," I commented to Kurt, whom I could see was also struck by the squaw's beauty.

"Better to start leaving her out of it," Kurt replied.

No way, I thought to myself. I needed to keep my Jenny with me, even if she were to remain nothing more than a memory. But I refrained from responding, knowing his to be the more sensible argument in light of our situation.

Before leaving the fort, we got to see a demonstration of the strength and self-control the Indian braves possessed. Several had been drinking whiskey and performing a wild Indian dance in front of a teepee when a pistol in the hand of one of them discharged. The bullet went through the right calf of the brave directly in front of him. Stopping sharply, the brave looked down at the gun in his hand and tossed it away as if it were evil and possibly could strike again. Then, while looking at the injured leg of his companion, he quickly grabbed a knife from the sheath at his side. Raising the knife, he bent forward, while staring at the calf of his own leg. He swung the blade down, intent on plunging it through his own calf in retribution for the wound he had inflicted on his companion. His effort was thwarted, however, by the brave to his rear—who, with a yell, jumped forward and grabbed the knife-wielding arm with both hands. The wounded brave had also drawn his knife as he spun toward his attacker in a slightly hunched stagger. After realizing what had occurred, he straightened up normally and strode the few steps over to his assailant in a perfectly normal gait. He reached out and grabbed the free arm of his assailant above the wrist in a symbol of unity, while speaking a few words in their dialect. As this was occurring, I watched the blood spouting from the hole in his calf.

From between the teepees, a heavyset squaw came running, rambling continuously. On her hands rested a square of hide and, on that, a poultice of what appeared to be mud and thatch. She laid the hide on the ground beside the wounded leg of the brave, scooped up a pile of the poultice in both hands, and pressed a handful to each side of the wound. Another squaw joined in the effort, piling more of the poultice into a cloth, which together they quickly tied around the wounded calf. The wounded brave then picked up the pistol and handed it back to the shooter, making a comment as he did, to which they both laughed. What a contrast this was to Stimpson's carrying on over his leg injury, I thought.

"How can the white man ever prevail over men such as these?" I asked Pa, who was witnessing the events at my side.

"The plight of the Indians has actually become a sad one," Pa replied. "They welcomed and helped the white man, unselfishly, upon his arrival—while, with their superior numbers, they had him totally at their mercy," Pa replied. "The years following the white man's arrival resulted in a mass elimination of the Injun population, mainly due to their contracting European diseases. But this atrocity is now being furthered by the elimination of their necessities. The Injuns that had roamed the plains freely in search of buffalo and other game through the winter months relied on the wooded grooves along the creeks and streams to provide shelter, firewood, and grazing grasses throughout the winter. The best of these oases have been chosen, for the same reasons, as locations for our forts. The constant grazing of our soldier's horses, which are much larger and bigger eaters than those of the Injuns, completely depletes the grasses in these areas now. The wagon trains strip away the grasses and firewood along their paths of travel, and the newly forming towns are consuming everything in their surroundings. The Injuns never had a need to overhunt their game until a desire for the white-man's wares led them to it. Now, a serious lack of game to hunt, along with their other problems, is causing them to die in large numbers," Pa explained.

Indeed, as we left the fort behind, continuing westward along the Platte River, the gruesome reality of the Indian's plight was thrust upon us from the stripped branches of a cottonwood tree. A dead brave was strung across the center limbs of the tree. The carcass had been almost entirely stripped of flesh. The remaining skeleton wore a loincloth and some necklaces. Several crows had lit upon the body and were pecking at its joints for remaining morsels of flesh.

"Don't they have the decency to bury their dead?" I asked Pa, disturbed by this ominous presence as I pushed hard against the wagon Spirit and Flash were pulling.

Pa had told us, on the offset of the journey, that a man has two ways of meeting the challenges set upon him in his lifetime. One is to complain about them and feel sorry for himself. The other is to affix in his mind that he is superior to the challenge and can go beyond its demand. He said that, if we thought the walking was difficult, we should strap a sack of flour on our backs for a spell. This seemed to be a peculiar notion to me. So on the second day out, I decided to put it to a test. Getting behind the wagon our horses were pulling, I began pushing with near to all my strength. I was burdening myself in the manner to which many in our party, without animals had already been. They were pushing and pulling their wares in carts and wheel barrels the entire way. Pa, Kurt, and I were only required to push in this fashion at sharp inclines of the trail or when we were rolling through a muddy area.

"Ollie, don't push the wagon over Flash," Kurt had called out in gest on noticing my endeavor.

Though feeling somewhat dissuaded by Kurt's remark, I continued my effort. By the end of the morning session, I experienced the comforting Pa had alluded to. It was if I had achieved a victory, rather than simply enduring. Merely walking the hundreds of miles to Denver City was no longer enough of a trial. I wanted to make it more of a challenge. After ten miles farther out, I was still pushing with determination and, it seemed, enjoying it. Though my body felt strained, it did not, as I felt it should, pain me at all.

"Maybe they're trying to scare us away," Kurt offered from the front of the oxen team as he helped Pa in leading it.

I was glad to hear Kurt's return to the question I had posed earlier. Perhaps he, like I, found the encounter of the suspended Injun carcass both startling and somewhat horrific.

"No," Pa replied. "They believe that, in this manner of burial, the brave's spirit is free to return to nature. They believe that the spirits of their ancestors are a part of every natural thing on this earth—from the soil to the sun and clouds—and that their spirits are present in future lifetimes."

"Do you think that this belief is the reason they have no fear of dying?" I asked Pa, attempting to confirm what I had overheard in town about their bravery.

"No more than believing we will go to heaven emboldens us Christians," he replied. "But it also makes Injuns more conscious of, and respectful of, the elements of nature. With their religious beliefs and outdoor living, they are at one with their surroundings—while we try to master and control them."

"God should favor the Injun's ways, then," I said, "Why is He allowing them to be killed off, by our coming to their land?"

"The death of a man or a nation is not of concern to the Lord, for life is His to create or destroy at will. But His love of mankind is shown constantly in His providing for our existence. Of one thing you can be sure, man will go down the path most beneficial to mankind, at all times, for that is the one the Lord will unfold, as long as He desires mankind to flourish on this earth. It is our duty to serve Him in this doing," Pa explained.

"I never heard of Him asking anyone for help, Pa," Kurt imparted in denial.

"Your conscience is his bidding. You follow your conscience every day, in all things you do, and you will be serving His will," Pa said, returning to a topic we had heard many times in the past, from both him and our preacher. Pa's words, like the preacher's, seemed to air an unquestionable truth. Yet I didn't know if simply the hearing of them would be enough to make me live by them or if a conscious effort was necessary, as they seemed to indicate.

Nighttime was my time to reflect on problems like these. But, this journey was robbing me of that leisure. On clear nights, I would spread a canvas on the ground and experience the newfound pleasure of gazing into the star-filled heavens while wrapped snugly in my blanket. Wet nights, however, forced me into the tent with Pa and Kurt, where they seemed to instantly go into a very sound sleep, while I lay there, with a mind full of irritation over the annoyance of their snoring, grunting, and groaning. In both instances, however, my exhaustion over the day's efforts resulted in my drifting quickly off to sleep, without the time to reflect on my concerns of the day.

Since leaving Fort Kearney, a new element had been added that was making my nights less peaceful and restful. The constant wailing of coyotes was making it difficult to sleep. Their terrifying cries seemed to be issuing a threat to all—that we were surrounded by the wilderness, which was announcing itself as a constant and invulnerable danger. On the first night of this auditory assault, a gun was fired several times after a few hours of the harassment. This, however, resulted in but a brief cessation of the howling.

This wailing was the first threat to my ability to cope with the wilderness that I found to be of concern. Trouble sleeping was resulting in my feeling weak and tired throughout the day. This was a problem to which there appeared to be no solution—since the coyotes were and would remain an integral part of the plains.

It was so that I sat in helplessness and anger while the others slept one chilly morning as a huge figure approached from outer camp. I'd have taken it for a bear, were it not for the yoke and buckets it had in tote. By size alone, there was no mistaking it to be any but Jimbo. "Why are you not under wraps while you can be so, young man?" he asked, in not much more than a whisper.

"How can anyone stand that confounded howling?" I replied, so anxious to speak these words that they came out much louder than I intended. "It's as though the devil himself were in announcement."

"Ha, ha." Jimbo's deep laugh was unmistakably pleasured. "It's not that way at all, young man. Those coyotes are singing to us in joy. They follow our train because of all the food left behind at our meal sites and the supplies being tossed by them with overloaded wagons. They are letting us know that they are thankful—that they are alive, free, and thankful. We should join them in their song. We're free-ee; we're free-ee. Sing with them." Jimbo echoed the coyotes' refrain in song.

"Were you a slave, Jimbo?" I asked.

"Was and would be, were it not for Mr. Potts. God bless him. Mr. Potts bought me from a market and brought me out here to work the trains."

"Is working the trains so much better than working a plantation?" I asked, exploiting Jimbo for knowledge of, what seemed to be, the heart of the slave question that had come to be such a source of controversy since the Kansas Territory was established.

"Mr. Potts also pays me a good wage that goes right into a bank account with my very own name on it. In a few years, I'm planning to get a home in Philadelphia. That's, the City of Brotherly Love." Jimbo paused and looked me hard in the eyes, to see if I recognized the importance of this designation.

"I'll have my own shop. I'll build wheels that won't need soaking to stay together, and maybe wagons that won't bounce folks to pieces. I'm going to have children, lots of children, running all about the place that I'll raise to be as knowledgeable and capable as those of any other man on this earth. That's what Mr. Potts gave me—plans, plans for a lifetime, a reason to be living. Know you have it. Always know you have it, and sing along with the coyotes."

Jimbo's words didn't require consideration. They were, of themselves, explicitly simply and on the value of freedom that our forefathers so cherished. However, I did reflect on the fact that this reasoning was as thoughtful as any white man's, something many claimed was not possible for the Negros.

"We're free-ee … We're free-ee … We're he-eere … We're happ-eee." I put Jimbo's words to the coyote's cries, and quickly collapsed into sleep.

In the days that followed, I seemed to grow used to their cries, no longer losing much sleep on their account. Perhaps it was Jimbo's insight that had displaced the fright that their howling would invoke in me. Or perhaps the threat the howling had been evoking was overshadowed by a tangible threat—the deteriorating condition of our wagon train. Evidence of failure had begun outlining our very path.

A CHANCE WAGON MEETING

Personal belongings were being strewn on both sides of the trail. Everything from trinkets and clothing to furniture and stoves had been discarded by passerby wagon trains, ours included. Items that would normally be fought over if discarded became valueless as they threatened the life of their owner. With the exception of Mr. Potts, who had a herd of oxen on hand, no one could afford to increase his or her burden or that of their animals—many of which had lost half of the weight with which they had begun the crossing. So the discards remained as such. Even our team, as well as we kept them fed, was noticeably thinner. Some persons threw out their weight in goods—allowing them to ride without further taxing their animals, since they were no longer capable of continuing to walk.

Unfortunately, I had myself fallen into this later group. Pa had always bought us wide-toed, calf leather boots—not the new cutoff ones that only fit on the proper foot, and that one poorly. Pa believed that a man's boots, ultimately, controlled his posture, body alignment, and positioning of his organs. Consequently, he believed they largely contributed to a person's entire well-being and longevity more than any other one thing, except maybe good teeth.

Despite the fact that I had two pair of the best boots money could buy and that Kurt and I were used to walking all day while pulling our bakery carts and that, on this trip, we had been massaging our feet nightly with a bit of vegetable oil, I had still managed to develop large blisters on the soles of both feet. Of course, Kurt had not developed one bit of trouble with his. Pa said it was because I was leaning too much into the buckboard while pushing.

When they first started getting sore, I'd tried walking on the sides and heels of my boots, knowing that, if I told Pa about my problem, he'd be apt to make me start riding. Walking improperly only resulted in swelling in my ankles, and the blistering continued to worsen. Pa noticed my limping and made me confess as to my frailness. He insisted that I keep off my feet till they healed, and sentenced me to riding in the wagon. Since we had two extra oxen in our team, they were all looking healthy, and Pa assured me that they could handle the additional load I would be adding. Afterward, however, I noticed that Pa, who had previously been riding, had suddenly taken to constantly walking. Kurt accused me of putting rocks in my boots. He seemed to be jealous of my having to ride.

Having failed to meet the challenge of the journey, I felt as though I had become a burden to the animals. This was quite devastating to my spirit. On the second day of my riding, there was an instance of redemption of my value toward our effort. The team of a wagon, to the left front of ours, became spooked by a large buzzard that dove quickly in front of them, scoffing up a discarded chicken carcass. As that team turned sharply to the right, ours did the same. The sharp twist of the harness tongue caused the connecting pin to snap at the tree planks. Being seated at the driver's bench, I was able to pull up the team and apply the hand brake, stopping the team and wagon without further damage or any injury occurring. Of course, we had to pull out of the train while we spent time replacing the pin, which we completed just in time to put us in our new position at the rear of the wagon train.

Over the days of travel, several wagons had had problems that were more serious than ours. And they had not been able to join back up with the train at all. They were left to their own devices in the wilderness. Just a day earlier, I had noticed that one of the few wagons in the train with girls aboard had dropped out and was in the process of having a wheel changed. In our passing of them, Pa had commented that their animals were not the best for wear. I was glad to see that they were now directly in front of our wagon, since the fate of those left behind was always questionable. And the broken down wagons and animal carcasses we passed along the way suggested the worst. Besides, knowing that they were still in the train, it was pleasant to again be in the presence of females, though these seemed to be some bedraggled by the journey.

The mother of the girls rode in the wagon, which was being drawn by six waning horses. The horses were being led by her son, who was some older than I and a bit larger in stature. Then there were her two daughters, attractive even in their dirty dresses and pinned-up hair. The similarity of their features suggested that they might be twins. Suspended from their arms was their sister, a child of about two, who skipped along between them with her feet finding the ground but on occasion.

The mother took up the reins of the team, and her son walked to the back of their wagon as ours approached. "Name's Norman Fitzrandolph," he said, introducing himself while displaying a friendly smile.

"Olof Swenson," I replied, smiling too broadly as I knew was my nature.

"You heading to the diggings?" he queried.

"Of course," I replied, with true spirit instilled by the anticipation of the company of the young ladies, who were looking back over their shoulders with subtle smiles, while their sister dangled between them, futilely kicking in an attempt to reach the ground.

"We'll be taking the north river. My pa has a lumber business going in Oregon. We had to wait till my sister Lil was old enough to make the crossing. That's her that Liz and Lynn are dragging 'tween them. They're twins, sixteen, and intolerable."

"That's my pa and brother, Kurt, behind the cart." I tried to respond without showing my disappointment at hearing of their heading north. "Hope them horses of yours don't give out on you," I said, prompting him for insight on the seriousness of their situation.

"I know they won't," he said emphatically. "We're planning on making a deal for new ones at the next fort."

"I hope they'll get you there," I replied, letting him know I thought their situation to be precarious.

"I know they're about spent. The fellow who sold them to me in Saint Joseph said they were of excellent stock, but they aren't proving to be."

"Was that Harlan?" I asked.

"Sure was. You know him, do you?" Norman asked.

"Know he buys worn animals from parties heading east, gives them time to reconstitute, and then sells them at a high profit. I suspect that, with the demand for animals being so great, he skimped on the recovery time for these."

"We talked to Mr. Potts about a deal on an oxen team, but his prices are four times what they were asking in Saint Joe, and he won't give us much for these horses. The bottom line is we'd be pulling the wagon with two oxen, all the way to Oregon, and with no funds to improve the situation. If we can't afford a new team at the fort, we'll get word to my pa to send us help. And we'll be waiting there until it arrives."

I was wondering if he was hoping I would suggest that we might sell them a pair of our animals. He wouldn't be the first one in the wagon train who'd had that idea. But I knew Pa wasn't giving up any oxen, and Kurt and I surely weren't giving up our horses. "This is a trying journey," I stated, implying that all of us were at risk.

"Hopefully, we'll all make it to our destinations in good health," Norman replied, not indicating any offense to my uncharitable response as he quickened his pace to catch up with his team.

"I'm sure we will," I called out to him, with forced optimism, before he was out of earshot.

As he walked away, my eyes shifted back to the girls. It was an immediate lift to my spirit, once again being in the presence of females. Too bad they wouldn't be heading all the way to Denver City with us, I thought. Several days earlier, I had heard someone say that it would be a week before we reached the fork in the Platte. That meant that I would only be enjoying their company for the next couple of days. What had he said their names were? I should have made it a point to pay more attention, I thought, as I watched them walking beside their wagon. Their features did appear to be identical from that distance. It appeared that they had either chestnut or blond hair, depending on how much dust they were wearing upon their heads. At that point, we were all wearing a thick coat of dust, as was everything else in the wagon train.

When the wagon train pulled up for a bit, as it often did for one problem or another along the line, the girls climbed up into the back of their wagon.

"Hi, girls," I heard myself call out instinctively.

Only the baby responded, displaying a full and lasting smile. The acknowledgement by the twins was but a quick glance. Then, they turned to each other, and the one on the left said something to her sister, apparent only by the movement of her lips. She appeared to be somewhat heavier or more filled out than her sister. Her comment, I assumed had been a mocking one of me, for they both dropped their heads in an effort to hold in the chuckles it invoked in them. Although this was the response I would have expected from them, had I premeditated my calling out, I still found it to be some discouraging. So this was the last time I tried to initiate a conversation with them till mealtime.

Pa had invited them to eat with us. Mrs. Fitzrandolph was not at all reluctant, but she was insistent that they would bring their own food. Pa persisted and won out, upholding that we were oversupplied for the remainder of the journey. Pa couldn't have been sincere in this. For, with over a third of the journey still remaining, no margin of safety would satisfy Pa—unless he felt our animals were not up to pulling the load, but to this he had already commented to the contrary. We were not in the situation confronted by some folks, who had been forced to give away sacks of flour and rice in order to lighten their load.

Mrs. Fitz and Pa were doing all the talking during our meal. I had to wonder if Pa was turned on by her, like Kurt and I were by the twins. The resemblance between her and her daughters was obvious, and she probably was also very attractive in her youth, I thought. But with the wrinkled, sagging skin she now had, I imagined that she could only be loved as a mother is. To want to have sex with a woman of her age seemed unimaginable to me. Still, it was obviously being done by men all over the world, all the time, and that was certainly as nature intended. I wanted to think that someday, it would be the same for me. But at that point doing so seemed quite impossible to me.

Having hashed over my disastrous lovemaking with Jenny many times, I realized that I had a total lack of confidence in my ability to perform, and I knew this would surely override a normal response in even the most arousing sexual situation. Yet it seemed that this was a predicament many men should be affected by. Since I had never heard tell of even one such situation, I thought there must be an explanation I was missing. I prayed that it was so.

Pa had started the conversation by introducing us, and Mrs. Fitz had then done the same of hers. This time, I made a point of remembering the girls' names and that Liz was the better built of the two. Pa then went through the history of our lives, starting with his arrival in America with Ma. Continuing, he seemed to go from one to another of what he considered to be Kurt's and my accomplishments—from our fishing skills to our joint effort in operating the bakery. He described how we cajoled him into buying our horses when we were, as he put it, just children and how Kurt had won the town fair race.

"Every year since it started, on that horse right there, Flash," Kurt interjected, pointing at Flash, while wearing a broad smile as he looked from one twin to the other. His statement prompted a comment from Liz.

"Don't you ever win?" she asked me directly.

"He's a trick rider," Pa said, coming to my rescue as I sat widemouthed, "And a damned good one," he continued. "Maybe he'll give you a little show after dinner," Pa added quickly, smiling as broadly as he ever smiled. For a moment, I felt exhilarated. This would certainly be an opportunity to win the attention of the twins from Kurt. After all, what could he do, ride around in circles? I thought. Then, the reality of our situation returned to me.

"No, I won't do that to Spirit, Pa," I said, glancing questioningly at him.

"Of course not, son," Pa responded apologetically. "I forgot about our current situation for the second." His explanation introduced a hint of embarrassment through its intonation.

"Near to did myself," I responded directly to Pa, making sure he saw my sneer and knowing he would realize that I was thanking him for being on my team.

"Woe art I—ere to go through life ne'er having seen the great 'Fall-Off Swenson,'" Kurt orated melodramatically.

"I've heard of you! " Norman announced excitedly. "Least I think I did," he said, correcting his announcement and excitement in retrospect. "I heard a fellow in Philadelphia mention a 'Fall-Off Something.' He said the guy could do something unbelievable, like jumping over a fence while standing on a bare back pony."

"You got the right guy. He could do it as many times as he likes," Pa confirmed, smiling broadly.

"Sure would like to see that," Norman stated sincerely. "I'd like to be able to tell my dad I'd seen it, when we get to Oregon."

Wow! Who needed women? Who needed children? I could have a meaningful life as a trick rider. People would be talking about me from Philadelphia to Oregon—across the entire country! I thought in astonishment. But I said, "I'm truly sorry I can't oblige you," in honestly and sincere disappointment.

"Shucks, we all know he can do it. Lie a little and tell your dad you seen it," Kurt said jokingly. "My brother craves the notoriety."

"Notability," I barked at him, trying to discredit his statement by correcting it—then, realizing that I had, in fact, validated his insinuation by my response.

"Big deal," the very impudent Liz uttered.

"Not to you, but it is to me," I told her sincerely.

"You're mean, Liz," Lynn declared.

"Come on, girls. Show a little politeness. Men take pride in their horsemanship," Mrs. Fitz interjected.

Horsemanship! Is that all she thinks it to be. Now, I thought, I can see where Liz gets her ignorance.

"Yea, he's a real horseman," Kurt said, snickering joyously while fanning the campfire.

What would they think if I strangled him? I contemplated.

Mrs. Fitz sent the girls to their tent to put Lil to bed and ready themselves for the same. Pa sent Kurt and I to water the animals. Mrs. Fitz and he continued with adult talk till we finished our chores.

The girls went from their tent to their wagon while we were breaking camp the next morn. They were wrapped in blankets, but their flowered pajama bottoms could be seen on their legs below. I suspected that they were planning to go back to sleep as we reformed the train.

About half an hour after sunrise, the draw on the rear of their wagon cover opened, and Liz appeared, giving me what actually appeared to be a smile. She had shed the blanket and was still wearing pajamas. Suddenly I was glad to be stuck in our wagon. In her pajamas, she displayed much more development then she had in her pent-up dress. The girls began playing some sort of game where the twins had climbed up on a crate at the back of the wagon. Little Lil was running in circles in front of them swatting at them and they appeared to be trying to catch her as she passed. There surely was no reason for Liz to open the bonnet ties for this play, except to let me enjoy their activities, I thought. If it was her intention to get me excited as she bounced around on the crate with her backside facing me, her effort was indeed quite successful. Yet, I knew that, if she were to offer herself to me at that very moment, my fear would emerge, and prevent my chance for redemption. Indeed, just having this thought had thwarted my arousal. But not wanting to waste this experience, I renewed my concentration on Liz's exhibition.

On one instance, when Lil reached the crate, she tried to climb up on it, and in the doing, she grabbed Liz's leg at the shin. At that second, the wagon hit a pothole and pitched abruptly to the left side and then swung back to the right upon exiting it. The first pitch caused Lil's grasp to release, and the second sent her crashing into Liz's left leg, causing it to buckle at the knee. To keep from falling, Liz grabbed Lynn's arm, but she was unable to regain her footing, and they fell forward into the wagon together. Liz's leg kicked out as she fell, catching Lil on the shoulder. The child was forced to slide off the crate and over the backboard of the wagon. She let out an ear-piercing scream as she fell off the back of the wagon. Her scream was added to by ones of a slightly lower pitch, emitted by the twins. Lil caught the backboard for a moment as she fell—long enough for her body to straighten out and allowing her to drop to the ground on her feet. She landed, fell forward, and immediately began to crawl on her hands and knees. The moment

Lil rolled over the backboard, I grabbed the break lever and pulled up our team.

"Stay down, Lil," I yelled as I dropped down from the driver's bench to the double tree. There was no reason for me to fear falling between the oxen as I ran down the drop tongue. If the team were to get the wagon back to rolling, they would break their own legs before treading on a person. My only fear was that of a wagon wheel hitting Lil. Reaching Lil behind our front oxen pair, I jumped to the ground and grabbed her up.

"Let me go," she screamed.

Just as ignorant as her sister, I thought as she squealed and squirmed, trying to break free. "Hold them up," I yelled, spotting Kurt climbing up into our wagon. Having heard the screams, he was aware of the situation and had moved to help.

"Let me go!" the brat continued to yell.

"What's he doing to you, little girl?" Kurt taunted from the wagon.

"Come on, Kurt. The oxen are all shook up," I shouted in an attempt to get him to realize the seriousness of the situation.

"I'll take her," Pa, who had been on the other side of the wagon, said as he stepped from between our rear oxen pair. Lil reached for him with outstretched arms. Handing her to Pa, I realized that I was standing in the droppings of a previously passing team. The Fitz's had pulled up their wagon also, and as the twins climbed down from the back of it, they were yelling, "Lilly, Lilly, are you all right?"

"He hurt my side," Lil complained, pointing at me.

"Why he saved you, Lil," Lynn told the child. "If he hadn't grabbed you, the wagon could have rolled clean over you. You should be thanking him with all your heart," she explained.

"Yeah, he's a hero," Liz chimed in. "You are tricky," she said as she walked over and pressed her lips softly to my cheek. "How on earth did you get to her so quickly?" she asked. "Good thing you were looking our way," she continued with an impish smile.

"Get in the wagon," Mrs. Fitz yelled as she stormed towards us. "You're disgracing yourself—half-dressed and in public." "How in the world did she get out of the wagon?" she questioned, in one breath and three long steps.

"We had to open the bonnet to swat out a bee, and then we weren't sure it was gone, so we left it that way. Lil fell out when we were playing London Bridge," Liz offered in explanation.

"And Olof saved her," Lynn chimed in, while staring at me with a big smile.

"You have my eternal gratitude," Mrs. Fitz said sincerely as she walked to my Pa and took Lil in her arms.

"He hurt me here, Mommy," Lil whimpered, pointing at her side and breaking out in tears again.

"She's only scared," Mrs. Fitz explained. "I better get her into the wagon. "Thank you again, Olof. We'll not be forgetting this."

"Yes, sure was a good thing you were looking our way," Liz said, again impishly, repeating her accusation within a comment.

"I generally do watch the wagon in front of me when I'm driving the team," I replied a bit harshly, to imply that I had no other motive in looking in their direction.

"Don't be modest, Olof," Pa said, joining in the conversation. "You acted very quickly. You can be proud of your fast thinking."

"I didn't think, Pa. I just saw her tumble back, and next thing I knew, I was jumping down to get her—like it wasn't me that was controlling my body."

"Perhaps that's because it wasn't," Pa offered in explanation. "But it was you that chose to do it. That's the important thing. His will has been done. Now, let's move the wagons quickly, and catch back up to the train," he ordered, while walking back toward the buckboard.

"Your Pa's a religious man?" Liz questioned as she started turning toward her wagon.

"Sort of," I replied, knowing he wasn't really a "churchgoing" Christian.

"I'll see you later, Olof," Liz called out, waving back at me with a smile as she returned to her wagon.

Allowing myself a glimpse of her as she pranced back to her wagon, I knew she was after my attention, and she definitely had it. There was no denying that I would have liked to get closer to her. She could never replace Jenny, but she was nice, and she was there. Perhaps she could help me get over my problem, so I could return to Jenny a whole man, I thought. It was relieving to think that a woman would again be a part of my life, even if it were only for a few days.

As our wagons began rolling again, Liz reappeared at the back of theirs, hesitated for a moment, and then drew the bonnet tight.

"Must be nice to be able to ride and get to be considered a hero at the same time," Kurt taunted from beside the wagon. He was the only one to recognize that my action required no courage at all. "Messed up the show though, didn't it?"

It was no surprise that he knew I had been watching the twins—nor was I embarrassed to have been. He'd have done the same in my place. My shame came from not being able to carry my own weight, on my own feet.

"Take a turn topside?" I asked Kurt, with very little thought. Not having felt the blisters at all during these recent activities, I felt it was time to take a try at walking again.

Kurt offered no protest, perhaps himself happy to be in a position to, possibly, be able to interact with the twins.

On seeing this, Pa protested. But I insisted, and so I walked.

When we made our noontime stop, Pa set out our cooking pots while I watered the animals, and Kurt gave them a ration of oats. After we set them grazing, I had some time to spare before the stew would be ready. I grabbed my laundry sack and headed down to the river. Having seen the twins heading that way earlier, I thought it might be possible to run into them without contending with Kurt's badgering. He was busy throwing his knife, and I knew, once he started throwing, he'd keep at it till something pulled him away. This was a perfect opportunity to speak to the girls in private.

The afternoon was growing quite warm, and the river was somewhat shallow along the bank, offering tantalizingly cool rapids at the shoreline. After removing my boots, I sat in the water, between the rocks, at the edge of the riverbed. Reaching back, I opened my laundry sack, withdrew two pair of trousers, and let them trail along beside me in the rapids. The current dragging through them did their washing, as well as that of the pair I was wearing. After wringing most of the water out of them, I returned them to my sack, and completed the remainder of my laundering in this same pleasurable manner.

As I started walking back to our wagon, somewhat chilled in my wet clothing, I heard Liz call, "Ollie, come see." She called me Ollie.

There were several boulders off to the side of the trail. The twins were standing to the side of the large one on the end. Walking over, I found that Liz had removed a charred stick from an old campfire site, and was holding it in her hand. Lynn stood alongside of her wearing a timid smile between her flushed cheeks. With a twist of her head, Liz gestured for me to look at the rock. On it she had scribed, "Liz + Lynn +?"

"Are you good in math?" she asked me.

Somewhat shocked by her boldness and not very clever with words, I was at a loss for a response that would indicate my desire to be added in. Yet, I wondered if I was being set up for a joke, since she certainly wasn't expecting me to have a relationship with Lynn, as well as herself. My response was, as usual, cautious. "I don't know. I've never seen a problem like that one before," I replied.

"Well it's not that hard—is it?" Liz questioned, smiling devilishly, obviously enjoying her control over my emotions. "How about solving an easier problem? Do you know how you can tell me from Liz?" she asked.

"But *you* are Liz," I quickly responded, happy to be able to show her that I was not completely gullible.

"Well, how'd you know that?" she asked with a false air of sincerity. "It certainly isn't by our faces," she said, putting her face next to her twin's, which was starting to look a little distraught.

The wind seemed to have kicked up, and I was trying to keep from shivering. Liz grabbed Lynn's hand and pulled her a couple of steps to the side so they were behind the large rock. They were both wearing shirts and jeans. Liz was unbuttoning her shirt and offered to show me the difference between her and Lynn if I would do the same. There was no way I was about to show them my miserably shriveled-up member so that they could humiliate me with laughter. I suspected that, had it been Kurt they had selected for this adventure, he would have been eager and able to give them whatever it was that they were after. And since we would be parting trails shortly, I suspected that would have been quite a lot.

"What, here" I asked, "where someone's apt to show up at any second to do their business? Why, I saw a fellow relieve himself right there where you are standing just a short while back."

"Ugh, that's disgusting!" she squealed. She grabbed Lynn by the arm and started pulling her back toward the camp.

Perhaps if she knew how much I would have liked not having had to disappoint her, she wouldn't have become so angered. My fear had, once again, overpowered my natural desire and left me destitute. Liz called me Olof again after that encounter, but Lynn had actually become a little friendlier.

We were all sad when it came time to part ways. Pa went quite out of character and surprised us all by selling Mrs. Fitz the two oxen at the rear of our team. Our strongest pair was harnessed at the head of the team, and the weakest pair was at the center. These were our second healthiest pair. Pa said that they would likely be able to pull the Fitz wagon on their own for a good distance, if need be, assuming they were kept properly fed and watered. Mrs. Fitz got tearful and tried to refuse, but Pa insisted.

"My boy didn't rescue Lil so she could be stuck out here in the middle of the wilderness," Pa explained jestingly but, I knew, with sincerity.

"If you're ever in Oregon, you will look us up and give us a chance to repay this kindness," Mrs. Fitz demanded.

"Yes, Ollie," Liz added, once again befriending me by name and by smile.

Her mom gave her a curious look and then laughed. "Any of you," she said, rising to her feet and giving each of us a kiss on the cheek.

That might be the last I'd ever see of the twins, I thought, but it certainly would not be the last I'd think of them.

7

JIMBO'S AMAZING ABILITY

Having had the extra oxen on our team for the first two-thirds of our journey resulted in the four we were relying on now still having most of their body weight. Our horses, too, were quite healthy in appearance. So Pa decided we could take the shorter South Platte Trail, while many wagons in the train were forced to follow the North Platte to Fort Laramie for rest and supplies.

The sand on the South Platte trail was as thick and loose as that on the beaches of the North Atlantic coast that I had loved so in my childhood. It was foreseeing this hazard that had inspired Pa to invest in wide wagon wheels, which made pulling our wagon through it much easier on our team than on the oxen pulling the narrow-wheeled wagons. The trail to Fort Laramie, though quite pitted, was worn hard by the years of California emigrants and Mormons who had traveled it. Wagons with thin wheels, weak animals, low supplies, or in need of repair were forced to head to the fort.

After the splitting of our wagon train at the parting of the Platte Rivers, our party was now down to fourteen wagons. One wagon had turned back on our first day out of Saint Joe. Many wagons had broken down or had their teams go lame along the way. There were some wagon parties that had developed plans for homesteading and had simply remained behind to start doing so. The last wagon to depart remained in Julesburg, the owner intent on opening a commissary there. Julesburg had recently been established by the Pike's Peak Express Company, as had other depots along the trail. They were spaced every twenty miles or so, in order to supply the stage coaches with fresh teams. Some, like Julesburg, had towns growing up around them, increasing the availability of supplies. Their prices seemed outrageous, but Pa said they were "quite appropriate."

Pa had had our oxen shod in Julesburg for forty dollars. When I told him that I thought that price was robbery, he asked me, "How would you like to spend a year or two here, making a fortune shoeing emigrant cattle?" Looking around at that dust bowl of a town, having only the depot, a warehouse, stable, supply store, and saloon, in its entirety, I realized why Pa had not protested the blacksmith's price. We were, in actuality, in his debt for providing his services at the desolate outpost.

Although we had been warned that the sand of the South Platte would put an additional strain on our animals, some, perhaps in their anxiety to rush to the diggings, had not heeded the advice. The second day out, a team was unable to continue. The wagon had to be drug off the trail, and the four horses of the team were put down by simultaneous shots to the head. The wagon's slogan, "To God's Country" seemed to take on a second significance as I gazed back on the ominous setting. "Have the vultures already lit upon their carcasses?" I asked Pa, not really expecting an answer. Pa and Kurt were forward of the wagon at the time, while I was walking behind the buckboard, so I suspected they were actually out of earshot.

"Would be a strange vulture, what wore but a single feather," I heard from the voice of Jimbo. Looking more closely, I saw that he was right. There were several Indians crouching behind the bodies of the horses, and one quickly sprung up into the wagon bed.

"Injuns?" I asked, somewhat startled as I turned to see the huge, dark figure of a man standing beside me, his arms outstretched and his hands planted on the wagon beside ours.

"They've taken to following the trains in these parts, knowing that we will leave a trail of discards behind. Your father prepared well, but it was foolish of him giving up them two oxen," Jimbo said.

"Pa don't let folks he likes go unaided," I retorted, somewhat taken aback by Jimbo's criticism of him.

"I know he's a good man, boy. That's why I just threw one of Parker's bags in your wagon with the others."

The Parkers were the owners of the wagon that was just abandoned. The four members of their family were now occupants of three adopting wagons. The three wagons in which they now rode as guests were allowed to confiscate any of the Parkers' food and grain supply that they wanted. But, increasing the passenger weight of their own wagon, farther limited their team's reliability. Noting the fate of the Parker team, they cautiously took little. The remainder of the Parker's stores were now being distributed among the remaining wagons, as had been those of several wagons previously left behind. What would have happen if all had refused them passage, I wondered? But, aware of the God-fearing belief shared by the members of our party, I thought on this only briefly.

Pa knows our team is strong enough to finish the journey," I said to Jimbo in Pa's defense.

"That might be so. And that extra feed can help to keep them that way. It's only the animals that keep us folks alive out here."

"I suspect them redskins would take all our animals and supplies if they could," I said, trying to get an opinion from Jimbo as to the degree of threat that the Indians presented.

"There's no doubt that they could," Jimbo replied. "But believe me, they'd rather be bringing down their own game than taking anything we have. Problem is, we're using up the wildlife. And someday, there'll be nothing left for them but that of our bringing. These will become untraveled trails when that day arrives," Jimbo predicted.

"Can't we help them?" I asked.

"It would take the hand of God to pull them from the despair they are facing. They are the best of hunters and horseman on earth, but they rely on the Spirits to provide them with their game. It is a foolish man what leaves his fate to providence."

"Jimbo," an unfamiliar voice called out, as two mounted riders approached. They were dressed like traders in their dirt-caked buckskins. "Fill a jug or two with water from the barrel there," the trader continued.

"That's Mr. Swenson, right there," Jimbo said, pointing at Pa. "You can ask him, do he have that notion, and if so, I'll gladly do the fetching," Jimbo replied.

"Worthless nigger." The trader's voice trailed off as he turned toward Pa. The men rode at Pa's side for a few moments. Then I saw Pa walk to the water barrel with a jug that one of the horsemen had handed him. Pa filled the jug as the stranger hollered out that he was only going as far as Valley Depot, where he had heard there were some Cheyenne trading beaver pelts and buffalo robes. "Jules has become too independent, with all the emigrant business at hand," he professed. "He's trying to get twice the normal price for his furs. He claims the Injuns want the extra, but I know it's just he's a growing greedy. These parts are gettin' just too citified," the trapper added as they started off down the trail toward the forward wagon.

"Right polite pair of fellows, those two are," Pa shouted back to us sarcastically.

"Too long without family turns a man's heart cold," Jimbo spoke to Pa while stepping out from behind the buckboard and walking toward him. "Had they two fine lads by them, as you have here, Mr. Swenson, I suspect they'd have a much more pleasant disposition toward others."

"I suspect you are right, Jimbo. But what keeps you heading on the proper course?" Pa asked in reply.

"Just that, Mr. Swenson—exactly that," Jimbo said, looking back at Pa in passing with a broad smile on his face.

When we stopped for our noontime camping, I asked Pa what Jimbo had meant by "Exactly that." Pa told me that it was a man's family that gave him a reason for living, and so too, it was for Jimbo. Having heard this belief from Pa in the past was what had made me worry so about not being able to create a family of my own.

As I fell into my old depressed state, I heard Kurt shout, "Let's see what's up! Cavalry's a coming!"

Joining Kurt, we ran to the head of the wagon train just as a company of soldiers was arriving. Their captain directed his conversation to the captain of our wagon train, Mr. Wiley, with whom he obviously had a former acquaintance. Captain Wiley was Wagon Master Pott's controlling force. He rode beside the wagons, attending to any difficulties that were hampering our advance. "Hi, Will," the Calvary Captain called out.

"John," was the reply.

"Had any Injun trouble lately?" the Calvary Captain inquired from his mount.

"Not a bit," was the response.

"You'll need to keep a sharp eye. A party of Sioux ambushed a lone wagon a bit back. I sent a company to deal with them; just passed. Surprised you didn't see them. A couple of trappers ahead of you said they'd seen it happen—about six miles east, just off the trail. The wagon was marked 'To God's Country.' Sadly appropriate I'm afraid."

Running toward our wagon on hearing this, I yelled back, "We got to stop them!" If it could be done, I was confident Spirit's speed would be the fastest means of intercepting the soldiers before they encountered the Indians.

"Where's he going?" the cavalry captain inquired of Mr. Wiley on noticing my antics.

"He knows that wagon was abandoned by our train and the team put down for lameness," Mr. Wiley replied.

"The Injuns were just taking the animals for need of food," Kurt input. "My brother knows that. And he wants to stop your men."

"Stop that boy," the captain called out on hearing this. "He's got no chance of overtaking them on a traveled mount—wouldn't have one on a fresh one. They'd near to be there by now," the captain proclaimed.

I explained the situation to Pa while untying Spirit from the cart. As I turned to mount, Pa took hold of his reins.

"You'll succeed in nothing but killing Spirit in his condition and overtaxing Flash with the extra pulling. Forget it, boy!" Pa exclaimed, protesting my efforts.

At that moment, Kurt came running toward us repeating the cavalry captain's statements.

Once these warnings had sunk in, I realized how foolishly I was acting. "You're right, Pa," I said. "I don't know what I was thinking." I was embarrassed by my thoughtlessness and the lack of responsibility it indicated.

"You weren't *thinking*, boy. You were acting—acting out of concern. There's nothing wrong with that," Pa said, reassuringly. He didn't seem to feel the concern that I did over my foolishness. But I made a promise to myself that I would maintain my sense in the future, when startled by events.

We heard later that the Indians were loading the horse meat on their dregs when, upon seeing the soldiers ride up, they quickly mounted in an attempt to flee. The three were immediately shot dead.

"How could those trappers do something so downright evil?" I asked Pa, on our hearing of this news. "They had to know the Injuns were just scavenging."

"There are men without souls," Pa responded. "They have no purpose but to serve God's will," he replied.

"To serve God's will? Was it God's will that those Injuns be killed for no reason?" I asked.

"Nothing is done that is not the work of the Lord. Perhaps those Injuns would have created a great evil in days to come. Or perhaps the significance of their death may serve in some fashion. We cannot see as He does."

What of our Ma? I felt like asking Pa. Was it that she was fixing to do such a wrong that the Lord needed to take her from us? Must it then also be that the Lord is responsible for removing my ability to father? Perhaps it is His will that my offspring do not walk the earth, in the fear and confusion that I would impart to them. It seemed logical that an all-knowing God would have His will imposed in matters of life and death, at the least, I thought. "But the Injuns are the innocents. Would it be wrong for them to retaliate for the losses they suffer, since the losses are through His will? There has to be an injustice in that. Can any good come from this evil?"

"Perhaps this event will prevent some greater wrong," Pa responded. "Perhaps it will influence the cavalry not to make future attacks on the Injuns, which would result in many being killed. Perhaps a new treaty will result from this wrong that will ensure their tribe's survival. The Lord creates our future, my son. There is no need to question His means."

Why then should I fret over the inevitable? I allowed myself the pleasure of thinking this, while realizing that any deeper thought on this subject would lead to obligation and responsibility. It seemed that my questioning was useful to me only when cursorily considered. The sacrifice required for a lifetime of piousness was beyond that which I was inspired to through my partial devotion to religion.

"There they are!" These words were being yelled back from the forward wagon as we emerged from the thicket of Beaver Creek. To the right of the forward wagon could distinctively be seen the peaks of a mountain with a range of ridges trailing off to both sides of the horizon.

"That's Pike's Peak?" I asked Pa, almost reflexively.

''Suspect so," Pa called back.

"Not that one—beg your pardon for correcting, Mr. Swenson. That one's known as Long's Peak." The words came from the unmistakable gruff voice of Jimbo, who was passing us on foot, toting empty seed pails. We had seen him seated on a rail, straddling those pails as we passed a short while back. He had apparently delivered them, full, from Mr. Wiley to a wagon in the rear, and now was returning to the front of the train. He strode alongside our wagon so that Pa, along with Kurt and I, could hear his booming announcement. "Well named that it is too, I'd say, for it will be a long week we'll be seeing it before we get to a hard day's ride of its shadow. You'd go well to keep from looking at it as much as you can. It can become downright discouraging when, during each day of walking, that mountain peak doesn't appear to get one bit closer. No sense in being discouraged the whole day through, now be there?"

"Well thanks for the advice, Jimbo. It certainly will be heeded by me, and I would suggest to my boys to do the same," Pa replied.

"Hopefully, these last days will pass as quickly and favorably as those we left back along the trail," Jimbo continued in friendly chat.

Pa concluded with an agreement of sincerity, and Jimbo quickened his pace, making his way back toward the lead wagon.

"Those don't sound like the words you'd expect to hear from an idiot, do they, Pa?" Kurt questioned from the other side of the wagon team, as Pa and I walked behind our cart, pushing.

I had found Pa's advice on hardship to be quite useful. By attacking toil with more than the required effort, I felt satisfaction, rather than helplessness. My exertion seemed to give me confidence in my ability to master and control the situation, and I was doing so now, with calluses that had replaced the blisters on my feet. Spirit and Flash were conditioned to staying slightly ahead of the lead oxen. That way, Pa, Kurt, and I were able to stay abreast of each other and converse as we felt the need, while either pushing the cart or leading the oxen. I was listening intently to their conversation. Having heard similar comments to Kurt's on occasion in Saint Joe, I had been somewhat astonished by the blasphemousness of them. Yet I had not the knowledge to explore their failings.

"No, not at all," Pa shot back, obviously displeased. "And what makes you think Jimbo to be an idiot?"

"Cowboys talking at camp said it. They said the niggers are better off being slaved 'cause they are but idiots and, so being, can't do for themselves, as we whites can," Kurt explained.

"If those folks were as superior in knowledge as the think themselves to be, they might not be so anxious to sit in judgment. When I arrived in this country, with no knowledge of the language or most of the ways of its inhabitants, I surely gave the appearance of ignorance—as did most other foreigners," Pa said, somewhat in a huff, as if he were surprised that Kurt could not make this deduction on his own.

Since Kurt had had acquaintance with Negroes in Saint Joe, both slave and free, as we peddled our bakery goods, I doubted that he gave any credence to such statements. It was likely that, like me, Kurt was interested in pulling out Pa's insight on this issue, since it seemed to be used by the slavers as a justification for their inhumanity.

"But, Pa, isn't it true that they lived like savages in the jungles, never developing tools to build houses with or cities and all the other stuff of our civilization?" Kurt continued, drawing again from the conversations we had heard on occasion at the camps.

"There are many different types of civilizations, son. It depends upon the needs and desires of the inhabitants to determine how their energy should be invested. The answer to your question is all around us. You've heard the natives of this land also referred to as savages. That's because they haven't developed the same civilization that Europeans have. But it is obvious that they have never had the same need or desire to do so. When people are blessed with a land that can amply supply its populous with their requirements, they have no need to develop means of survival required by persons who are forced to forage for food and shelter in barren and inhospitable lands. Rather than developing a mechanized society, they have had the time and energy to interact and develop a spiritual bond with nature, as well as a respect for their surroundings.

"None of the emigrants," Pa continued, after a moment of thought, "that experienced Injun confrontations, would feel advantaged by intelligence in a trade of wits with them. In fact, most fear such engagements to their preclusion. I'd so suspect that the same would be true of white man's confrontation with natives anywhere in the world, if they were forced into a confrontation with equal armaments and numbers in the environs of the natives. You can be sure an African wouldn't give up his life in the wilderness in exchange for one in the city. Nor would an Injun be willing to give up his. And why should they? Who is to say that our cities are a better place to live than the very world with which God has blessed us? Sometimes I wonder why He has allowed the white population the dominance of this world. I suspect that it might be the ability of our mechanization to support huge populations. Perhaps it is pleasurable to our Lord to have as many persons alive on this planet as possible. Perhaps when there is a person standing on every square foot, of every landmass on this earth, the Lord will come down for dinner."

"Ah, Pa," Kurt said as we both broke out in laughter.

"Don't laugh. You know the Lord is to be feared," Pa said, his smile showing.

"I think I'd rather be an Injun," I avowed defiantly.

"Me too," Kurt added, somewhat out of obligation to the implication of my statement.

"Me too," Pa added softly, after a moment's thought, and probably with more sincerity than Kurt or I had had.

"The abolitionists are right, then, Pa? We should force the Southerners to free their slaves?" I asked.

"There are two kinds of freedom fighters among the abolitionists," Pa responded quickly, suggesting that he had already given sufficient thought to this subject to establish an opinion. "The first kind is religious. He believes in treating his fellow man as he wishes to be treated in kind—with love and respect. The second fights slavery because it runs contrary to the expansion of industrialization. Plantations are not public enterprise and don't trade on the stock exchange. The consequence of the Western territories passing a vote allowing slavery was a disastrous blow to the industrialists. This second type of abolitionist seeks to abolish slavery so that the industry of the North can expand through the Western territories and have the Western ports to add to their goods trading ability—thereby adding to their profits and power. God-fearing, neighbor-loving citizens do not rely on force as a means of correcting the ungodliness of their neighbors. It is this second type of freedom fighter— who places power and wealth above kindness and compassion—that uses freedom fighting as a justification for killing.

"Enslaving and exploiting our fellow man was not discovered by the Southerners," Pa continued in explanation. "It has been common throughout history in all civilizations, including those of the Injuns and blacks. If the abolitionists have their way and slavery is outlawed throughout our nation, the South will most certainly succeed from the Union. If they do so, the North and South will go into competition in world markets, and the Lord will bring success and greatness to that nation which supports the world he desires. I would predict failure and despair to the South, since it would be founded on principles contrary to His will. The will of the Lord is worked by the Lord, not by taking up arms against our neighbors. In any case, I don't believe there can be any support for a war against our fellow Americans. And I certainly would forbid you boys from taking part in it, were it to be so."

It was good to hear that Pa's moral reasoning had led him to this conclusion. For I truly had no desire to go to war, even if morality did dictate the cause to be just. There was one more factor that I felt needed consideration before agreeing to going to any war for a cause: Would it be worth dying for? No one seemed to bring that question up in such discussions, as if it were insignificant. Perhaps it is assumed by all that young men have no concern in matters of their own life or death. Possibly an expression of such a concern would contain an implication of cowardice. *Is it cowardly to want to stay alive?* I wondered.

Yet, if my country were to have ordered me to serve in a war, I would have certainly complied, for I knew it to be the responsibility of every family to pay its dues for the privileges the family enjoyed in our country. Just as the early settlers had done, in driving out the Brits, I believed we must all be willing to risk death in order to maintain our freedoms. Though my personal motivations would lie stronger in survival than in the attainment of victory, I would surely do what was required of me to satisfy my family's obligation to this land. I concluded this thought warily.

PA'S PROSPECTING PLAN

Upon arrival at our original destination—the two cities straddling Cherry Creek, Aurora and Denver—we found they had become near too ghost towns. All that could be seen in the streets were shopkeepers and a few women and children. We discovered that most of the prior residents were off to Gregory's Diggings. There had been two dozen strong claims filed there in recent weeks, and the word was that panning any stream in the Clear Creek area was producing a week to a month's wages, daily!

Most of our wagons had decided to put up a spell in Denver before heading to the new diggings—more out of necessity than desire. Pa explained to us that, if we put up, every day that passed would make it harder to start out again. Although I didn't doubt his reasoning, I had trouble trying to regain an attitude of determination after such a disappointment.

Gregory's Gulch was another three to four days of uphill traveling. Afternoons had become blisteringly hot while nights made us appreciative of Pa's having traded for buffalo robes back at the fort. Temperatures after sundown were often dropping below freezing. Some days, the wind blew so hard we had to take the covering off our wagon to keep the canvas from tearing apart. With both feet planted on the earth, a man might be blown clean to the ground. At times we were so caked with dust that it was hard to recognize one another. The dust had filled our wagons and invaded our food supply.

"Summer's not on us yet," Pa said. "Days are only going to get hotter while we wait."

"Let's go then," I blurted out at him.

"Yeah, let's get it over with," Kurt added.

"We can't be overanxious, though," Pa cautioned. "This will be the hardest leg of the journey. The animals are tired, and we are too, more than we realize. This is the time when keeping a clear head can become our toughest battle. Keep faith in each other, and we will have the strength we need," Pa concluded as we trudged back toward the wagon.

Once the wheels were rolling, and I was again leaning into the wagon, I felt my strength return, perhaps even invulnerability.

Gregory's Gulch reminded me of the hills around Saint Joseph. Every nook and cranny was stretched across by canvas or jammed by wagons, shanties, or lean-tos. In addition, among these there were interlaced brush structures, designed to be basic shelters. This multitude of contrivances surrounded the few legitimate structures along the street—several cabins, a livery supply store, and a saloon. "What a place this'd be for a bakery," Pa declared as we mounted a rise overlooking the town. Kurt and I looked at each other with mouths agape. Was this what we had put so much effort into attaining—another bakery!

"That is, if those hills weren't waiting there, laden with gold and waiting for the harvesting," Pa added, smiling broader than he was known to.

"Sure looks like there's no lack of harvesters on hand either," Kurt said, rebutting Pa's trickery.

"That won't bother us none, son. Long as these streams are seeded with nuggets of gold, they'll not stray far from their banks. Somewhere back in the history of the world, those nuggets were knocked loose from their mother and washed down to these basin creeks. It's up there where it will be found," Pa said, pointing to the hills beyond the valley basin. "The source of untold wealth lies up in them hills."

"Those ain't hills, Pa," Kurt stated. "They've got to be the highest mountains on earth. Are you planning on taking us climbing over them?"

"No I'm not," Pa replied. And after a pause he continued. "First, let's deal with the problems at hand. We've got to establish some lodging and then trade off this wagon and team for the supplies we will need. After that, we'll figure on a plan for prospecting."

Obviously, Pa already had a plan figured out but for some reason wasn't ready to let us in on it. I gave little consideration to this conversation, intent on enjoying the realization that we had actually reached our destination.

We traded off our wagon and team at the base of the ravine, below Gregory's claim, at what was commonly being called Mountain City. Pa got some coffee and dried fruit in the deal, as well as a pack mule. The cost of these items was nearly ten times what they'd have cost in Saint Joe.

"You boys will need to learn to harvest the fruit from this land, to offset the price of bought goods," Pa proclaimed as we loaded our purchases into the buckboard. "These hills are said to be teaming with wildlife. We can also deal with the Injuns for food." A large group of them was encamped at the base of the mountain, and individual tepees were scattered about town. "They market corn, fish, meat, berries, and such, if you lack the time to harvest your own food. That being the case if gold harvesting proves to be a more valuable investment of your time."

"Sounds like you're planning yourself out of our future, Pa," I said.

"It's not that I've been trying to be secretive on you, Ollie. Just I wanted to see exactly what was here before I made a decision. I wanted to be sure there was enough civilization and resources established here so that I won't have to worry about the two of you," Pa explained. "They say there are over three hundred working claims in this digging now. So I doubt there will be many new, major leads to be discovered. But it is also said that, in a day of sincere panning, a good day's pay is fairly assured, with occasional large bonuses. Also, many of the smaller claims offer work at a percentage of their take, and the larger ones pay good straight wages. I'm sure you'll find it easy to make a much better day's wages here then you did peddling our baked goods. I intend to head to the high peaks to the southwest, where I believe there is a good possibility of surface leads still waiting to be discovered. If I can find a stream with pay color, I'll pan my way up to the mother lode, just as Gregory did here."

"Why didn't you leave us back in Saint Joe? Seeing how you're breaking up the family anyway!" I shouted at Pa, angered by his lack of concern over the alliance I'd felt to be so necessary to protect in my decision to leave Saint Joe with him. I had been surprised to see how little our family meant to Kurt, but now Pa too? Had I been inflating this value as an excuse for not confronting the challenges of a life, with the responsibilities that surviving alone would bring, I wondered.

"We'll definitely be back together by October, Olof. The mountains are unworkable and unlivable through the winter. And, I'll be back on occasion for supplies and to check on your welfare. Then, too, if I should find myself in dire straits, I'll have you boys to fall back on for support," Pa said, with apparent sincerity. "Hopefully, I'll have success in making a strike, and the claim will be ours to work together. I know I've been asking a lot, in expecting you boys to accept my reasoning in this endeavor. But it's not selfishness that drives me," Pa continued. "If I were not blessed with the wonderful sons that I have been, I would not have had the motivation to make this journey. It is the real possibility of a short stay in these hills resulting in a major improvement in the quality of life you and the families you will one day have that proves this to be a worthwhile pursuit. I would also propose to you that the worldliness and knowledge that you are adding to your persons will benefit both of you throughout your lifetimes."

"We'll go with you into the mountains, Pa. We've already done the long stretch. Surely a couple of mountains wouldn't be insurmountable for us." I was taking liberty in speaking for both of us and noticed Kurt's head snap quickly toward me, as if prepared to offer a rebuttal. But instead, he waited to hear Pa's response.

"I've asked too much of you boys already in making this journey. There's no life for youths in the wilderness. These are the days of your lives when associations will develop your virtues and character. Besides, going over the same territory as I do would add little to the possibility of a discovery, and the imposition of hauling triple supplies would restrict the speed and extent of my efforts."

"I don't believe you'd leave us behind for anything, Pa, except our own safety. You know it's too dangerous out there with savages surrounding you. If it's too dangerous for us, we don't want you out there either. Let's work the gulch together and we'll be ready to move, first in, on the next find that comes up, hereabout," I argued.

"If your safety was my concern, you'd be correct, but Injuns take no pleasure in attacking lone persons in the wilderness. They feel all men share in the ownership of the earth. I would have concern if it were Mormon country on which we were encroaching. Also, Injuns feel there is no glory in defeating a nonthreatening party. You boys have proven yourselves to be men. Now, some time with independence from a father's care will strengthen your confidence in yourself. Also, I'll be depending on your being earners, as I likely will not be one for some time."

Building of confidence? Did Pa actually know that I needed to build my confidence? There was enough direct connection to my situation to convince me of Pa's wisdom, and I dropped my challenge entirely. "Dried beef and bacon will be set aside for you, anytime you come over the hill, Pa," I said, to let him know that I was behind his decision.

"I hope we can find our fortune this year. Next one I'll be off riding mail," Kurt added, with his normal disconcerted attitude.

We spent that night camped below Mountain City with the other new arrivals. The entire following day was spent making the journey up to the top of Bald Mountain and the town of Nevada. Over the length of the gulch, the mining activities were bustling. Slough boxes and cradles, as I was later to learn they were called, were strewn along the creek among the prospectors panning or shoveling the banks and the creek bottom. Wheelbarrows, gravel, and buckets of water were being conveyed in every direction as pickaxes clanked into the rock of the mountainside. For a two-mile stretch, which included Gregory's claims, a huge slough box was being constructed to facilitate hydromining of the slope by the Russell Mining Company, which had purchased all the working claims over this stretch of the creek.

The miners were a vast combination of characters and attitudes. Since pulling up stakes and making an immediate sojourn is natural to hobos, vagabonds, gamblers, and thieves, many vulgar and unsavory characters embodied the populous. There was, however, often laboring directly beside one of these personages, an obviously sophisticated professional, who, for his own personal reasons, had found a calling to these diggings. As diverse as the miners were in character, their diverseness was just as evident in their attitude toward their endeavor. Some could be observed cursing or throwing down their tools in discuss at times, while others could be seen smiling or even singing while performing their toil. Some would greet us pleasantly, with words of encouragement, while others would suggest that no space was available for newcomers or that all workable soil had been worked clean of pay dirt. The greatest discouragement, however, came from the large number of go-backers we passed on the roadway. Those among this group had come to the conclusion that the reward was not worth the effort this lifestyle demanded. Unfortunately, one characteristic was common to near every individual I had seen at this digging—they were all male!

Great, I fretted, the confidence I was hoping to develop in my manhood was surely not going to develop in this single-sex community. So this was to be the conclusive assurance that my life would be spent as one of a celibate. In this surrounding, Pa's plan of building my confidence would be totally destructive to the confidence I longed to develop so badly.

Perhaps it was time to accept the inevitability of my situation. The constant concern, guilt, and regret my sex life had brought me, to this point, was certainly blighting to my character. Perhaps I could revise my opinion of a life without a family from being one that has no chance of being meaningful or fulfilling. Perhaps this was the perfect place for me to accept a life in which women played no part—since here, it appeared they would not . But, not ready to make this concession, I rejected the thought. Still, I had to wonder how everyone else seemed to be able to avoid a pitfall that seemed so unavoidable. Lack of confidence would surely result in failure in sex, which would, in turn, result in an inflated lack of confidence. This prophecy had to be self-fulfilling, I concluded. Yet, since mankind had managed to flourish on this planet, there must be a way out of the loop, I thought in retrospection—a way that I had not, to that point, discovered. Perhaps the girls would appear on Sunday displaying their finery at the church house, I theorized optimistically.

The Nevada General Supply and Hardware Store had all we needed to prepare our shelter. Pa had hoped that we'd be able to construct a dugout at the base of a rise in the mountainside, by digging and prying out old, fallen rock. This effort, for the most part, had already been completed for us by prospectors, who had turned every movable stone and had engaged in removing the irremovable, in pursuit of a glimpse of a golden color. They had now taken to working the higher levels by spiking their way up the rock and then tying on. Their efforts had resulted in a scarring of the solid rock foundation of the newly founded city of Nevada. Pa had wanted to use the mountain walls as the best protection from storms, as well as for their ability to hold warmth. Since, this was not safe, with miners picking overhead, he selected a lot centermost in the city, expecting that other structures would be arising around ours that would serve as a wind barrier. Some actually had, before we had completed the construction of our shanty.

A consequence of the instant arising of this mining community was quite visible and had, in fact, given Bald Mountain its telltale name. There was not a stitch of available timber in the entire area of Gregory's gulch that wouldn't require extensive effort to secure. This made the building of a cabin quite impractical.

The supply store was, however, a convenient source of framing and sheathing lumber. We were able to construct a sturdy adobe shanty in less than four days with these materials. In addition, it was pleasantly surprising to find that we were able to purchase a wood-burning stove that would serve as both a heating source and cooking plate. The high cost of these items, at the Nevada City rate, had stripped Pa of near to all of his savings, but he still was able to open a fifty-dollar account for Kurt and me at the Nevada City Bank. It was painful to realize that we could have made the same purchases much more cheaply if we had done so the previous day in Mountain City or at half the price less than a week earlier in Amaria; in fact, we had passed several stoves on the trail that were free to the hauler. With the situation we were in (that of a rush), time had become our major concern—aside from the safety of ourselves and our animals. Time saved in not having had to haul an item added to the item's value at each location.

We spent the warmest night since leaving Denver, in our new adobe shack. The smell of the lumber seemed to give the warmth of the coals an embodiment. As usual, Kurt and Pa went out instantly, and I momentarily thought that I might not be able to sleep in that noisy confinement. Then the realization that this would be the last night that I would have to contend with Pa's noisy snoring, possibly forever, came to me. My noise sensitivity, which I attributed to a weakness of character, dissolved with that thought, and on that night, I experienced no further annoyance from my companions.

After breakfast, Pa showed us how to hang our buffalo robes, which had kept us warm through the night, against the wall and door to block wind drafts. Then he made us a map on which he marked the route and areas he intended to prospect in. "I feel that I'm leaving two strong and capable men as my rear backup. I have no doubt that you will make a stand here that will be honorable and rewarding. Still, I feel I need to caution you on the one character trait that I feel to be a danger to you both. Folks in Saint Joe were tolerant to the honest outspokenness of youths. Here, your words will be judged as those of men and will be taken exception to on occasion. Judge your company and weigh your words against the tolerance of your audience. In particular, there are many Southerners here. They are known to be extremely prideful and base their lives on codes of honor. Avoid competing with them, for losing is often unacceptable to them. Many men are killed over another's pride, as a result of a mismanaged conversation."

"I'm not about to coward over a man's pride. I'd rather fight him," Kurt responded angrily.

'I've watched you boys grow. I know you better than you know yourselves. And I know there's not a streak of cowardice in either of you. I'm not suggesting that you develop one now. I'm asking that you use your intelligence to negotiate your way through situations in a manner that won't require you to put your life on the line over an argument, or challenge, that could have been avoided by an equally brave man who had a notion to stay alive despite his bravery."

"I'm not walking through life on cat's feet, Pa." Kurt's anger could still be detected in his voice, which seemed to be forced from his bowed and frowning countenance. I was sure Kurt had no desire to disagree with Pa, but a concession on this topic was more than he could stomach.

"How about if those cat feet actually belong to a lion?" I said, hoping to help them out of this conversation.

"You boys take care of each other," Pa said to me, pausing until we had a full eye contact. Then, turning to Kurt, "And use some discretion in your conversing, please." He summarized his position with the directness he knew Kurt to be most affected by—though I hadn't heard him resort to "please" since Kurt had acquired the ability to talk back.

It was Kurt's position on this issue that impressed me. It was as if he demanded to be allowed to prance through life free of tether, like a wild stallion on the plains. He would sacrifice a lifetime of domesticated living for another moment of the freedom. He refused to surrender. I envied him for having this rash attitude, which I believed to be an indicator of confidence and manliness, or so it seemed.

BEGINNER'S LUCK

We watched Pa disappear over a ridge and then reappear as he continued up the neighboring mountainside. "There, you see—Pa has reappeared," I said to Kurt," with an inference to Pa's eventual returning. We continued to watch as he again disappeared over the summit. "Next time we see him may be in the fall," I suggested.

"Yeah, if I can stay alive that long," Kurt responded, obviously still angry over his conversation with Pa.

"What say we see what we can learn about this panning?" I asked Kurt, looking for a change of venues.

"I'm game," Kurt replied in a tone of normality. We grabbed our shovels, pans, and a bucket and then started down to the head of the creek. Following the bends of the creek, we passed many parties operating cradles and then a crew installing a water diverter for a Long Tom being constructed at the side of the creek on an active claim site. Below this, where the creek flow was below the rock bed, sat a large, sparsely haired prospector. He was an older fellow, clad somewhat like a businessman but as unkempt as any of the trail dusters. He was pouring the ounce or so of soil he had in the bottom of his pan into a sack, which he had drawn from his inside jacket pocket.

"Excuse us, sir." I spoke pointedly. "Would it be improper for us to observe your panning technique? Seeing as this is a new occupation for us, and we are too undertrained to possibly succeed at it."

There was no indication from the mass of humanity spread across the ledge below us that my words had been acknowledged.

I simplified my salutation to, "Excuse me, sir," in a somewhat strengthened voice, to eliminate the possibility that my words were being directed to partially deaf ears.

Still no response as he finished shaking the last grain of black soil into the sack, tied it off, and returned it to his jacket pocket.

"Forget it," Kurt called out, giving my arm a tug and turning to step back up the creek bank.

Agreeing with him that we obviously were being ignored, I joined him in the ascent. Just then, we heard from below, "Hold on. You've already had your initial lesson in panning. Don't let any interruption distract you until the precious black dirt is secured—less you return it to the creek in its former elusive condition, and with an increase in discouragement having need to be overcome as well."

"Thank you, sir," I replied to the businesslike orator responding from below.

"First, let's set forth the conditions of this verbal contract in which we are, on this date and at this time, about to engage. Do you agree?"

"So speak then," I declared in as serious a voice as I could muster, indicating that I would be willing to play along in the fashion in which he was proposing.

"I, Ralph Pastore, will show the young lads in my presence ... State your names."

"Olof Swenson," I stated.

"Kurt Swenson," Kurt said, with a slight negative shake of his head as he glanced in my direction.

"Ollie Swenson," he repeated my name in his more melodious version, "and Kurt Swenson are the principal parties. These said parties hereby propose to be instructed by one Ralph Pastore in the most professional and optimally effective method of extracting—through the placer method of mining, commonly referred to as panning—the precious metals thus-wise extractable from one panful of soil each. They forth wise agree to relinquish these precious metals, in the form of black dirt, flake, and/or dust, to Ralph Pastore in partial payment for the service rendered in the previously mentioned instructions. The remainder of the payment for the said instructions shall consist of a visit to the establishment of Ralph's Men's Wear, if ever the said principals should find themselves in the City of Brotherly Love, commonly referred to as Philadelphia. The principals also acknowledge that, in relinquishing the said first panful of slough, they may be relinquishing the result of what is commonly referred to as 'beginner's luck. Do I have the agreement of the principals?" Ralph asked, concluding his legal dissertation.

"I take it you're a lawyer?" I asked, initializing my own inquiry before making a commitment to this stranger.

"No—have been there, but now have advanced to the even more materialistic profession of businessman."

"Do your stated instructions include the process of quicksilver extraction?" Kurt queried bluntly, somewhat shocking the stranger and myself.

"It does now. After that learned negotiation. Can we call it a deal then?" Ralph asked.

"You're the proprietor of a men's clothing store in Philadelphia?" I was hesitant to become involved in even a nonconsequential agreement with someone without engaging in as much as a brief conversation.

"Not currently, but directly. I must now insist on an answer, since time is of the essence. For I will now engage in the sifting of my next panful of slough, whether it becomes one contractual or uncommitted."

"I'd be glad to commit to the terms of your offer," I pronounced, realizing that I had nothing to lose but a pan of properly sifted slough that Ralph could more easily process on his own and that I would, otherwise, have no ability to process at all. Of course, the prospect of relinquishing beginner's luck could not be construed as a tangible and, therefore, didn't require serious consideration.

Ralph had me use my shovel to push aside the loose gravel at the base of the three-inch waterfall on the far side of the creek and then go as deep as possible with the shovel, trying to remove the subearth. Two such efforts and my pan became virtually full. He then instructed me to stand facing him and joined me in holding the pan. Together we submerged it in the pool in front of Ralph and then proceeded to shake it with a slight jarring motion, causing some of the slough to wash over the edge of the pan. When the slough had been reduced to a quantity that, basically, covered only the bottom of the pan, he changed his technique to one whereby he would fill the pan with water and then lift it out of the creek and proceed to swirl it in a circular direction, causing the slough to rise to the brim of the pan with a small portion being expelled. The remaining slough was much darker in color. Lastly, ralph lowered the pan to below water level, and began swaying and abruptly stopping it, so that something of a cloud would be formed in the water above it. The cloud would then be partially washed away by the current flow. Subsequently, the cloud was reduced in density until it was barely visible. At this point there was a small amount of a dark black, granular substance intermixed with some, hardly detectable, gold flakes. Ralph flicked some of the dirt to the side of the pan repeatedly and, in the process, revealed two small and one even smaller flakes of gold color. These he removed and dropped into a small, glass jar that he had produced from the other side of his massive jacket. This jar was about half-full of small flakes of gold.

"Do you have a serum bottle?" he asked, holding one toward me. "I'll throw this one into the deal," he said, after seeing my head shake in a negative response.

"Were those flakes you removed actually worth something?" I asked.

"Perhaps fifty cents," Ralph estimated. Not bad for a panful. Some full days of panning sometimes produce less. Yet this is definitely not a beginner's luck quantity. I seriously believe you were holding the pan too loosely to transfer the luckiness—which could be construed as cheating and, therefore, a breach of contract. Yet, since we have no clause covering this condition, I can only proceed with the offer of a second lesson, if you would like to improve your grip on the pan—that is, your grip of panning."

"I really think I have the basics down. Besides, my fingers are painfully numb from this cold water. How about we give my brother a try and see who is the luckiest?"

"I would gladly so proceed," Ralph pronounced, continuing with his legal phraseology, "but, I'm afraid that I have not yet acquired agreement from the stated second principal, one Kurt Swenson."

"Kurt Swenson will require one stated 20 percent discount from the said clothing store for himself, as well as for principal number one, his stated brother—who wasn't said to be smart enough to improve on his own deal," Kurt said jestingly.

"So, the Philadelphia lawyer has met his match in this young Pike's Peaker," Ralph replied. "The concession has been made. Grab your shovel and fill your pan."

Kurt half-heartedly pushed aside some of the pebbles on the top of the creek bed in the center of the creek and then took a shovelful of whatever was easily scooped. There was a definite indication that his heart wasn't going to be in this work. Before the first shake of Kurt's pan, Ralph quickly reached into it and removed a gold-colored pebble from the edge. He unceremoniously deposited this in the front pocket of his jacket, which sagged slightly from the weight accountable to this newly acquired content.

"Was that a nugget?" Kurt queried loudly, after a brief, wide-eyed stare at the bulging suit pocket.

"We'll discuss that after the lesson," Ralph countered.

"I want to see it." Kurt demanded.

"That matter will be brought to the floor at the conclusion of the, as stated, agreement," Ralph responded placidly.

They proceeded to swing the pan below the water surface, but Kurt's eyes returned to Ralph's pocket with a reddened face and grinding teeth.

"Okay. I'm afraid that, if we don't resolve the nugget issue now, the entire value of the lesson will be nullified by the distraction. So let's address this complication." With this statement, Ralph removed the object from his pocket and held it out between his thumb and forefinger, allowing us to observe it fully. "This object, produced by the process of panning of two pans of slough, is commonly referred to as a gold nugget. Unfortunately, no provision was set forth in the contract pertaining to the discovery of such an object, due to the rareness of occurrence of such a condition. We do, however, have a reference to the disposition of the rewards of beginner's luck. And common knowledge withstanding, I have been working my pan at this very spot for over a week. In that time not one comparable nugget or even half-comparable nugget has been produced. Surely, the principal of beginner's luck has manifested on this occasion—therefore, indicating that the nugget should properly be construed as the stated payment for said instruction."

At this point Kurt's face was strained with anger.

"At least Kurt should get part," I heard myself demand.

"Please, this matter has not been concluded," Ralph replied, resuming his oration. "Since this nugget," he continued, "similar in size to a large robin's egg, would have a weight of two ounces or so, its value would be in the neighborhood of forty dollars. Since, this would obviously be realized as an overpayment for so short a period of instruction by any reasonable thinking person, the nugget shall be declared to remain solely in the possession of principal number two, one Kurt Swenson, for now and forever. Looks like I'm still underestimating the power of beginner's luck," Ralph said, in a newly developed, serious tone, while handing the nugget to Kurt.

When they resumed panning, they located two more nuggets, a little less than half the size of the first. Ralph refused to take even one of these as payment, referring again to overpayment as being unacceptable. It seemed he found greater pleasure in seeing the elation these discoveries brought to Kurt and me than he would have had the discoveries been his own.

After Ralph demonstrated the process of passing the quicksilver through a cloth sack and squeezing out the mud to leave a gold- and silver-rich, black deposit in the sack, we shook Ralph's hand, thanking him sincerely, before departing in haste toward the assayer's office to sell the nuggets. After doing so, we proceeded to the bank, arriving just before closing, and deposited most of the cash we had received, in our savings account. This increased its value from the $50 Pa had deposited for us to $166. This was done on our first day of panning! The banker again reminded us of the beginner's luck principle. Yet I felt I knew a principle that he was unaware of—the "Kurt's luck principle," which I had had a lifetime of experience with.

After a somewhat colder night, Kurt suggested that we should get some of the money back out of the bank and buy more buffalo robes to hang on our walls, as well as some materials to construct sleeping cots in our shanty. I didn't feel that I was in any position to caution him on this spending. Nor did I have a desire to. It was shocking how picking up a few stones from a creek bed could so improve our lives. There it was—the inescapable lore of *gold*.

Perhaps Pa was right. Perhaps we would be leaving here wealthy and into a new, improved lifestyle. My portion of beginner's luck didn't materialize at the Sunday church gathering as I had hoped, either. Only two females were in attendance. Both were in the accompaniment of their husbands. One of them was an Injun squaw, and the other a crusty-faced frontier woman.

Certainly, it would be easy to maintain loyalty to my Jenny in this community, for what that was worth. However, this was one place where I wasn't in any worse shape than near to ever other man in town when it came to not having a female relationship. Did any, or perhaps all of them, harbor the fear of losing their virility as had been haunting me? I wondered. If so, you would never guess it, considering their constant reference to sex acts in normal conversation, just as had been the case with the menfolk of Saint Joe. The hopelessness of the situation here made it seem sensible to respond by dispelling any concern over sex for the length of our stay. This would certainly bring me a welcome relief from the mental stress to which I had been subjecting myself. It would not, however, bring about any change in my desire for Jenny. On that thought, I wrote her my first letter from the diggings, wanting to share with her my optimism over our initial efforts and to express to her that I might indeed be returning to Saint Joe shortly, in the personification of a man of means. This premature optimism, and enthusiasm, was analogous to the entire gold rush fiasco.

10

CONFRONTATION WITH
TEXANS AND BROTHELS

When we arrived in Mountain City, there were perhaps three thousand people between it, Nevada, and the Gulch (Gregory's), including those scattered between the towns on either side of the contributing branch of Clear Creek, which meandered from one town to the other. This same confluence, three weeks later, boasted a population of over twenty thousand, many of whom had already become discouraged with prospecting. They believed that they had been deceived by news articles that had been generated by speculators who were invested in the development of the new city. Another such city had materialized halfway down the gulch toward Mountain City; it had become known as the City of Central.

The nuggets Kurt had discovered on our first day of panning were all that were to be obtained from what we had come to refer to as Ralph's puddle. Indeed, Ralph himself was no longer locatable. We were told by a prospector at the spot where we had met Ralph that, on hearing of the opening of the overland stage, Ralph had quickly arranged passage back east, joining the daily procession of go-backers.

Their decision to return was completely understandable after but a brief encounter with the process of prospecting. The misconception we all shared was that prospecting would require very little effort and that the excitement created by the constant possibility of a discovery would be an inspiring motivator. In actuality, the process was quite labor intensive and was often made painful by constant contact with the icy creek water in the presence of a blustering wind. Bending, squatting, digging and hauling became quite difficult, particularly when, time after time, your efforts proved to be fruitless.

Yet, on two separate occasions, Kurt and I came into soil quite rich in color, resulting in a one-day earning of more than ten dollars each. While separating the multitude of flakes from the soil we had become elated and began prophesizing on a future life of prosperity. But on both occasions the color was completely panned out before we had expanded our normal, daily effort at panning. On most days, our efforts resulted in one to two dollars of earning for each of us, while some days proved to be totally profitless. Overall, our earnings were superior to what a normal job would have afforded us, but they required a determined effort in the obtaining. In addition, a good bit of what we were earning was absorbed by the cost of our purchases of food, coal, and other necessities from Nevada's outrageous merchants. Only by thrifty management were we able to continue to increase our savings at the bank.

Still, overall, I was excited over the prospect of returning to Jenny with the seed money we could use to start a life together. The proof would be there—I could be a successful provider. But the thought of my other inadequacy still plagued me.

Basically, these earnings were all that were expected of Kurt and me by Pa. He felt that he had the ability to make a major strike while we were doing this earning. Although the general opinion of wandering prospectors was that they were somewhat crazed, we knew Pa to be totally rational and realistic. Day by day, we anticipated his return—a triumphant one.

Anxious to see the progress being made down below, in the City of Central—which was only slightly visible from Nevada—we loaded our camping gear into the buckboard one sunny August morning and headed down the valley. Half the hillside beside the city seemed to have been removed. Digging and probing of the earth was ongoing in every nook and cranny. Determined to have a sample of the color, from this section of the creek, we bucketed some soil from an unyielding, pick-resistant surface mound. This proving to be a hopeless effort, we found an abandoned claim marker and wadded into the stream.

"Hey you," I heard someone shout.

Looking downstream, I saw two men working a cradle. They looked about our age and were dressed like cowpokes. Kurt was standing 'tween them and I, catching their gaze.

"Howdy," Kurt responded.

"You're an asshole!" was the outrageous reply from the one nearest us.

Kurt stood, staring openmouthed, as if in shock.

"What's your problem?" I asked, almost instinctively.

"You suck!" was the immediate reply.

"Why are you looking for …trouble?" I replied, myself shocked by this unprovoked insulting.

"Not very friendly, are you?" the same guy replied.

"Not when we're talked to like that." My words came out unreserved.

"How about stepping up atop the bank?" he answered as if his statement had been preplanned. This guy actually wanted to provoke a fight with me for no reason whatsoever. If it were an acquaintance so challenging me, I believe I would have sought an explanation and sought to dispel whatever the provocation. Such an insult from a total stranger seemed inexcusable. When I reached the top of the bank, I was charged by a raging bull! He had both hands flaying wildly when he reached me but abruptly stopped the charge when my fist slammed into the center of his face. Both arms continued swinging in my direction, leaving me no choice but to continue pushing my fist into his face.

After two failed attempts to flatten my nuts with his boot toe, he lunged into me, attempting to knock me to the ground. He was somewhat shorter, though a good bit heavier, than I. This wrestling situation was more familiar to me than boxing, as Kurt and I engaged in it near to daily, up to recent days. It was instinctive for me to immediately turn my forearm into his shoulder and force this fellow to lose his balance. Catching himself from a staggered fall, he landed on all fours in front of me. Quickly straddling his back, I pumped my fist into the back of his head until he collapsed below me. Then, grabbing a handful of hair,

I pulled his head back and smashed my fist into his temple. It was my intention to assure that he would not get back up and resume his attack.

I pulled his head up a second time, but wondering if I should continue this brutality, I looked up at Kurt who was standing beside me holding back the other cowpoke. Kurt nodded his head yes, and I again smashed the head with my right fist.

Then as a voice shouted out, "Get off him!" I felt a body knock into me from the side. Feeling a second impact, I knew Kurt had joined into our scuffle.

At that time, the voice of one of the bystanders who had gathered for the pleasure of watching us fight sounded loudly, "That's enough, boys!" This was yelled several times as hands began pulling us apart.

When I rose to my feet, I spied a badge-wearing lawman approaching us.

"What's happened here?" the marshal asked me directly.

"We had a misunderstanding," I replied, surprised to notice a trembling in my voice. I'd had no fear of being harmed during this confrontation, but I suddenly felt endangered.

The bystanders had rolled the flattened cowpoke onto his back and were splashing water onto his face.

The marshal looked toward the other cowpoke, who was standing beside me and said "Earl, if you and Simon cause but one more disruption in this town, I'll see you both clean out of this Colorado Territory— so help me!" Colorado Territory had just been formed by the federal government as a result of the rapid growth in the area.

"Okay, Marshal," Earl replied.

Simon was slowly rising to his feet, while staring at me with distain. Hearing the sheriff's rebuff, I felt somewhat relieved.

"Simon, I want you to apologize to these men, for being such a jackass."

"But, Marshal, these Yanks are squeezing in on what's ours. We got to keep them in their place," Simon replied.

"You feel someone's encroaching on your claim, you come see me. You know that! There'll be no more talking about it. If you hadn't already been disciplined by this fellow here, I'd have a notion to give you a whopping myself."

Simon hung his head. His anger was still apparent on his swollen and reddened face.

"Now, the four of you, shake hands and talk out your problem, civil like. You hear me, Simon?"

Simon gave the marshal half a nod while approaching me. "You're lucky these wet boots had my feet slipping out from under me. Or I'd a really given you a whacking."

"For what?" I yelled at him, in an attempt to convey my incomprehension.

Glaring at me, as though justification were on his side, he replied, "We'll not be tread over by Yankee vermin."

"We have no intention of encroaching on anyone's claim. Show us your marker, and we'll be sure to stay well upstream of it. We pan up in Nevada regular," I offered, hoping sensible conversation might result in a sensible reply.

"You kicked my ass, but you'd never outfight me on a battlefield," Simon replied, slowly and distinctly, so as to be sure I got the message.

"What are you talking about?" I asked, speaking quite loudly out of frustration from this cowpoke's nonsensical taunting.

"You can't outshoot us. You can't outride us. You can't outrope us. You can't outhunt us, and you damned sure won't whoop us in a war."

"We can outride you," I responded to Simon matter-of-factly, along with giving him an intentionally hard, eye-to-eye stare.

"How about having a friendly, four-man street race?" Kurt asked, joining in my ploy. "No entry fee. Winner takes all."

"Our horses still need recovering," Earl said in response. "You'll have to wait a spell for that whooping."

Contemplating on how Kurt was setting up these Southerners, I found myself remembering Pa's warning of how they were unable to accept defeat. "I'll give you a quick demonstration of what you'll be up against," I told the cowpunchers as I headed over to the buckboard to unhitch Spirit. He had regained near to all of his weight, and I had been exercising him regular.

"That pony able to hold you?" I heard Earl ask, mockingly.

As I turned, leading Spirit out, I noticed Kurt's frown of displeasure. I knew he'd disapprove of a demonstration of my ability, since it would likely scare these fellows out of the race he had arranged. But, heeding Pa's advice, I would do it anyway. I stood Spirit in the street, did a running mount and then took him, full-out, down the center of the street to town, leaning and swaying in and out 'tween the wagons and carts along the roadway. As I pulled him up and turned him at the start of town, I noticed the marshal under the first porch overhang, his hands on his hips and a glare in his eye. I did some side-to-side touchdowns on my way back and then came in standing upright on Spirit's haunches, dropped back down again, straddled, and slid off his back, pulling him up abruptly, directly in front of my audience.

"You'd make a damned good cowhand," Simon said, wearing the slightest hint of a smile, while I paid my appreciation to Spirit with an offering of oats from the buckboard. "Where you all from?" he asked, as a normal human being might.

"Saint Joe," I responded.

"Missourians, no wonder. Hell, that's a slave state too. You all are with the South yourselves. Why didn't you say so?" Simon asked, in his new, friendly persona.

"That's because you're on your own planet!" I responded, frustrated once more by the invulnerability of his self-centered mind frame.

Kurt burst out in laughter at my comment, and I expected we might get back into fisticuffs shortly.

But instead, Simon went into a somewhat sensible explanation of his depravity. "It was just told us, 'fore we spied you all—word is the Yank businessmen aim to destroy our plantations and ruin our way of life. They started that settlement in Lawrence, Kansas and then armed the town with repeaters, so they could run out or murder the slave-state folk. This Colorado should proper be a slave territory now. And we'd have some niggers up here a feeding this cradle for us. Folks back home are saying we should secede from the North and start over with our own country. If we do, we'll take these Western territories with us. The Northern city slickers got no rights to these lands that are part of the

Southern settlings. The ones pouring into these parts now are going to have to be dealt with sooner or later, and I'd as soon do it now, before they squeeze us out of these diggings."

"It wouldn't do anything for your health or character, watching some darkies doing the work for you. In a short spell you'd be wider than the creek bed, like this Philadelphia lawyer we were panning with a few days back," I said.

"Not that we'd have them doing all of the work, but these rockers are better worked by four than two, its known," Simon explained.

"We wouldn't mind giving it a try. If you'd be willing to share the take," Kurt offered, surprising me with his lack of hostility toward these boisterous egotists.

"It's our claim and our rocker. If we're splitting even, you all will have to do the digging and the hauling," Earl contributed.

"If that's what suits you, you've got a deal," I said, adding my consent to the arrangement. I'd been wondering how well a cradle would produce, and as far as handling the labor end went, it would have been my preference anyway.

"We just did a washout, so let's jump on down, and we'll start a new run together," Earl imparted, also adding his consent to the arrangement.

"Simon and Earl Dalton," Simon said as we made our way down to the creek bed.

"Ollie and Kurt Swenson," I responded, somewhat embarrassed by the swelling on Simon's face that had now become visible.

"Really did a job on my head," Simon said as he patted his swollen cheek with a soaked bandana.

"You didn't give me much choice," I responded defensively. That was the last we spoke of the fight.

The cradle proved to be a much more efficient processing method. In the first day, for a half-day's effort, we measured out over two dollars each worth of flakes and powder. This was about the same take we had for each of the three days following.

After a week of working side by side with the Dalton brothers, we had become quite friendly. We had been sharing tales of our hometowns and travels while prospecting with the cradle. Their upbringing in El

Paso, amid conflicts with both the Mexicans and Indians, made Kurt's and my experiences seem rather lame. During the conversing, I managed to convince the Daltons to load their cradle and gear into our buckboard and ride up to Nevada with us for a try at the pay dirt there.

We did even better there, at our old hole. So the Daltons rode down to Central a few days later and managed to sell their claim for five hundred dollars at the Russell site. Since they had moved their tents with them, they now had become new Nevada citizens. On many occasions, we went on hunting expeditions with them. Each trip was both a rewarding as well as a learning experience for Kurt and me. We always had game to sell afterward, since we killed more than we could consume. In addition, we split the take for the furs and hides of our kills. I felt a debt of gratitude toward our Texan companions for this valuable and pleasurable training. How superiorly rewarding their lives had been compared to ours as bakery vendors, I thought.

On these hunting excursions, as well as buffalo, we landed some elk, bears, antelope, dear rabbits, beaver, several types of fowl, and buckets of pike and bass. How had Pa disregarded this lifestyle? I wondered. I would have preferred it to any a man of wealth could buy.

On one occasion, we found ourselves directly in the middle of a huge herd of passing antelope and dropped them as quickly as we could reload. One night, as we sat before a spit of venison simmering above our campfire, I remarked to Kurt, "Wouldn't you think that anyone could find satisfaction simply by hunting for a living?"

"They'd have to be here to do it this well," Simon replied. "There's no other place like this in the world. Then, too, he'd have to deal with the Injuns at some point, I suspect," Simon added prophetically.

No one disputed that notion.

Kurt and I offered a little of our method of enjoying a day of pleasure as well. We had the Daltons join us in a bit of rock climbing. They were not very proficient in this endeavor. I suspected that their pointed boots were a bit of a handicap. We also took them to a waterfall pond we knew of, for swimming and diving. It had a rock slide that dumped you into another pool at its terminus. The Daltons seemed to be uncomfortable with this type of activity, as if embarrassed by it. I suspected they were not use to engaging in any type of playful behavior.

One night, after a successful day of rocking the cradle, Simon suggested that we should travel down to Madame Kate's brothel in the morning. The Daltons had been there on its day of opening, and they had bragged about it almost daily since we had made their acquaintance. I had feared the inevitable rising of this proposition ever since.

"Sounds great!" Kurt's enthusiastic and expected response boomed out.

"Are you thinking?" I queried of Kurt. "These girls go through one guy after another, night after night. It's a sure thing you'll come back with crabs, maybe worse."

"'Taint no big deal," Simon replied on Kurt's behalf.

"You intend to go through life without it?" Kurt asked me, pointedly.

"I have someone I care about waiting for me back home," I responded quickly and, I believed, honestly. "I have no intention of bringing her back that kind of surprise."

"Well I'm in," Kurt said, in display of his indifference to my comment.

"That's your call," I concluded.

Certainly, Kurt had earned the right to make his own decisions. It was a relief to have stated my position on this matter, and I would maintain it if ever I was again reproached for my position on such activity.

Although it was in truth that I expressed my disapproval of their planned venture to the brothel, it was a relief to find that I had been able to justify my refusal to join them without expressing the full extent of my sentiment concerning their proposition, as it was my nature to do in matters about which I had a strong concern. I had restrained from asking, *"How could you desire to lie with a woman that would not find one bit of pleasure from the act, who's only desire is the cash in your wallet?"*

Then there was the question I knew I would never verbalize, but most desired to know the answer to. "How could you get it up under the circumstances?" One thing was sure in my mind; I couldn't. Whether as a result of the disgusting aspects of the proposition or of my self-fulfilling prophecy of failure, failure would certainly be the humiliating result I would be subjected to.

My hope was that, upon seeing Kurt's youthful appearance, the brothel would refuse him entrance. Knowing that they may be encountering unruly characters in this place, I was considering accompanying them, in case they needed help.

The following day, after they had set out for Central, I wrote another letter to my Jenny—this one with more enthusiasm than the previous, since we had of late been saving more of our take. Jenn's replies to my letters were always upbeat and uplifting to my spirit. It was without exception that she would suggest that I should return soon. Knowing that I had something special and wonderful in Jenny, I prayed that I would be able to meet her expectations.

My decision not to join Kurt, even as a protector, was based on the fact that the night would surely include drinking, which would lead to their insistence that I join them in their debauchery and that, in turn, would lead to my blurting out all of my private thoughts and consequently losing the respect of my kid brother.

The following day, when Kurt returned from this pleasure jaunt, he was somewhat disappointed in their outing. "You were right," Kurt acknowledged to me. "Those women were uglier than sin. And, somehow, while we were doing it, this one I had must have slipped the bills out of my wallet—'less there was another under the bed that got into my trousers as they hung on the bedpost. Anyway, Simon tried to make her give back the money, and the proprietor had us thrown out—some over ten dollars blown on a run-down whore."

On hearing the tale, I couldn't refrain from breaking out in laughter.

"It's not funny," Kurt rebutted, before he also subdued to the relief of realizing the hilarity of life and joined me in my merriment.

11

RETURNING TO SAINT JOE WITH RESOLVE

The Daltons had proven to be honest business partners, and in our close working arrangement we had become rather good friends. So it was that Kurt and I were sorry to see them leave when August came to an end. They left their rocker with us so we could continue sifting till Pa got back. We agreed to leave it in our shanty to again use, come spring. Kurt had expectations that he'd be running mail before then, but I expected to be working with the Daltons again next season.

Through September there was a mass exodus from the diggings. It was hard for Kurt and me to put effort into rocking, feeling that we had had enough of it, too, and should be on our way down the mountain. Although we were producing less daily with this attitude and without the help of the Daltons, we found that we were still earning a good bit more than we had previously, with the four-way split. This was no surprise to us, seeing how we had always known we were doing most of the labor.

As December grew to a close, we began to worry as to Pa's well-being. We had had no word from him since he'd headed out in spring. The last day of the month, snow started falling, and Kurt and I decided to bring the rocker in early. We were loading up the buckboard with what we had in supplies, blankets, and such when I saw a lone figure appear over the crest of the mountain. "I think it's Pa!" I hollered out to Kurt, who was just coming out of the shanty with the last of our packs.

"It is!" Kurt replied, excitement clear in his affirmation. We ran to greet him. Pa seemed somewhat bedraggled under the tattered and matted buffalo robe and coonskin cap he was wearing. Yet, his clean-shaven face had better color than we were accustomed to seeing on it, assuring us of his present good health.

"You boys waited?" Pa called out as we approached. "I'd hoped you'd pulled out since several days back. It would have been no problem hunting you down in Denver," he said.

"We were worried about you, Pa. We would have set out hunting for you today if you hadn't shown up."

"That would have been fool-crazy!" Pa replied in anger. Those mountains are no place to be once the winter snows start. How much loading have you got left?"

"This was all, Pa," Kurt responded. "Your timing was perfect."

"Good. We'll start right out then. Jingles here has been cooperating quite well so far—think she knows it's time to go back down," Pa said, referring to his mule.

"You're calling her Jingles, Pa?" Kurt asked.

"I took a couple of spurs and fixed her up that collar. Like that, when she tries to wander off, I can hear the jingling—got her name from that, I suspect. How did you do here? Were your panning efforts profitable?"

"They were, Pa," I said and then went on to tell him of our exploits.

Kurt eagerly jumped in and even went into a description of the brothel escapade he had had. I didn't expect this to go over well. Pa pretty much gave him the same cautions I had about brothel woman but reproached me more severely for not going along.

Pa was right. I was embarrassed by the weakness I had displayed. There was no excuse that I could offer, so I responded guiltily, "You're right, Pa. I should have."

"He'd have probably got to throwing his fists around, and we'd have ended up in the pokey," Kurt said, coming to my defense.

"You boys forgot everything I tried to teach you. Don't get yourselves killed over some meaningless disagreement. You've got long lives to live. At least give me my grandsons first." Pa's temper was obviously ebbing as he spoke.

"God willing," I told Pa honestly, and perhaps with a hint of the true fear I was harboring—that being that this matter was, in fact, out of my hands.

"I've been writing to Jenny, Pa. She wants me to spend the winter in Saint Joe. That's why I've been hoping you'd be giving up on prospecting. She said her family would put me up. And with my share of our savings, I'd be able to stake a place for us." As I spoke to Pa, Kurt and I had begun to hitch Spirit and Flash to the buckboard, readying them for the forthcoming downhill journey.

"Hold on, boys," Pa said sharply. "I have something to show you." He opened the sack that was tied on Jingles's rump, removed a cloth-wrapped object, and placed it on the buckboard seat for us to inspect. "Have you heard of a flowstone?"

"Is that what it is, Pa?" Kurt asked.

"One probably containing near to two pounds of gold. But it's worth a fortune more in information." The rock was smooth white quartz under an exterior crust. Pa had obviously broken it into two halves. A dull, porous gold center radiated gold arms like the tentacles of an octopus. "I found it at the base of a creek. It had to come from somewhere in the surrounding hillside. Somewhere in that hillside there is a quartz outgrowth. That outgrowth is the exposed body of the mother lode. Keep in mind that this is not speculation but a certainty. I found the stone my second week out, and have been trying to uncover the outgrowth since. I've done extensive picking over half of the valley's surrounding hillside. It's sure I will turn it up soon. It couldn't take more than another season to uncover it. I made this drawing, showing the canyon and creek." Pa lifted the stones from the cloth so that we could see the drawing below. It showed Gregory's Gulch and the surrounding mountain ranges and creeks, with an X where the stone was found. "We have to keep this a total secret till I've found the source and filed a claim. I'll be putting this in a bank safety box in Denver, inside of a locked case. We can't breathe a word about it to anyone."

It now appeared that Pa had been right about everything. Kurt and I had done well, and he was on the verge of a bonanza. A flowstone was known to be a definite indicator of the presence of a quartz lead, which in those mountains always promised tremendous quantities of both gold and silver.

"Could we help you find it quicker?" I asked.

"No. We can't change our routine. We don't want to draw any attention to our efforts. If just one other prospector becomes attracted to that valley, we might end up being robbed of what looks to be ours. Of course I have an advantage in finding it, knowing a good bit about where it's not."

"When can you start back?" I asked, realizing the eminent possibility of discovery Pa had been afforded.

"March would be the soonest. It depends on the snows," he relied.

"No wonder you were so late getting back," I offered. You must have kept thinking that the next strike of the pick could reveal the vein. It must have been devastating to have to quit after all that searching," I said.

"You'll find it, Pa," Kurt added sympathetically. "Next summer, they'll be swarming into Swenson's Valley, after you've staked your claim."

"That'll probably be true, if in truth I do find it," Pa replied.

We were all silent for a while, contemplating the possibilities forthcoming as we started down to Denver.

There were only a handful of prospectors left at the diggings, and they were in the process of readying for departure as we passed. The following week, snow fell frequently, and the streets of Denver were difficult to transverse due to snow and the mud and ice it generated.

"Pack your things, Olof," Pa commanded as he entered our room above the livery, in downtown Denver. "You're getting out of here while the stage is still running," he continued, dropping a ticket on the table next to the discarded cards pile Kurt and I had created in our game of rummy.

Picking up the ticket, I immediately saw "Saint Joseph Missouri" printed boldly across its face. "I can't. I can't leave you two. That wouldn't be fair," I blurted out impulsively.

"It was Kurt's idea," Pa said. "He'll be running mail soon as the weather breaks, and you know how much you will be seeing of me, as soon as I can get back up into the hills. This goes with you too," he continued as he handed me an envelope. "There's six hundred dollars in there. Kurt's giving you his share of savings too. I'll return it to him when I sell off the flowstone. If you decide to come back in spring, leave any cash you have left in Saint Joe, where it can be waiting for you when you go back to stay. You have to put your face back in front of that Jenny's pretty eyes, or she'll be finding a replacement for it soon."

"What about the ticket cost?" I asked.

"That'll be a wedding present from me—if there is one. I had another savings account in Nevada that I didn't tell you boys about, because I wanted you to make a sincere effort at prospecting. The banker had directions from me to transfer the money into your savings account if your balance ever went below ten dollars. I used some of the money from that account for your ticket."

"That was pretty slick, Pa," I said laughingly, while realizing how great my family was. "Thanks," I said as sincerely as I could. "And you too, Kurt, thanks," I added, turning to look him in the eye.

This was as sentimental as we allowed ourselves to get. Perhaps the death of Ma had taught us the necessity of maintaining a strong countenance as a defense against our vulnerability. "I have to write to Jenn and tell her I'm coming."

"Why do that? You'll be there as soon as the letter will," Kurt said.

"That's right," I said, laughing out of embarrassment that my excitement had so affected my thinking. "I better start packing." *And getting my mind to concentrate on the actuality of the situation*, I thought.

Gathering my belongings in my knapsack, I realized I was elated. Since we'd left Nevada City, I had been focusing on Pa's discovery of the flowstone. The excitement the possibilities of this discovery presented were subdued by a nagging feeling that something was seriously wrong. It was a feeling that I had not wanted to directly address. This discovery meant that we would be staying—staying long enough to destroy any serious hope I had left of establishing a life together with Jenny. This was the same feeling of despair that I had been dealing with whenever I realized the hopelessness of expecting a normal, childbearing relationship with her. Perhaps this was a foolish trip to be taking, but I had to try.

I had to give myself a chance at happiness, as hopeless as obtaining it might seem. Regardless of the outcome of my efforts, there remained the joy of knowing that, soon, I would again be back with my Jenny.

Nothing had ever impressed on me the value of money as much as Pa's purchasing the Overland Stage ticket for travel from Denver to Leavenworth at a cost of $120. To be back in Missouri in a little over seven days, rather than spending the months of torturous travel the multitude of us had endured en route to the diggings was a profound monetary indulgence. There were twenty-five depots along the trail to Leavenworth, each about twenty-five miles apart. Fresh drivers and horses were exchanged for old at the depots, allowing the stage to continue rolling and complete the crossing in this incredible time. I expected to be buying a return trip ticket in spring. In addition to this, I would be paying for round-trip passage from Leavenworth to Saint Joe on the riverboat and my living expenses during my stay in Saint Joe with the money Pa had given me. My intention was to earn enough while in Saint Joe to offset the expenses.

The guilt I felt over spending so much of our savings on this trip was increased by my partaking of the lavishness of the riverboat ride to Saint Joe. The earth-laden river displayed a reflection of beauty and harmony from the life flourishing along its banks that was softened rhythmically by gentle ripples and swirls. This tranquility was overwhelming; it demanded recognition and sharing. I wished Kurt and Pa could experience it with me and that this peacefulness could continue with us forever.

The journey's end came at Saint Joe's landing, which seemed at first unrecognizable to me. This caused me to fear that changes may have disassociated me with my adoptive home. Shortly, I realized that the change was simply caused by the vantage point of the upstream view presented—this being one not afforded to me by my memory.

The surroundings were quite familiar to me once I disembarked and ventured onto the roadway. Wagons were lined clear to the setting sun on the western horizon, waiting to be ferried back across the river. These had begun their return long before summer's end, suggesting that they were partied by disillusioned go-backers, returning in disappointment. This was a situation that I had anticipated. The surprise was that there were several long wagon trains waiting for ferrying westward. These folks were venturing on what could be a disastrous journey, in light of the onset of winter storms in the western territories. Their impudence was manifested by their determination to be in the forefront of the upcoming season of prospecting. This was a clear indication that the influx of emigrants and development in the diggings would not be waning in the coming spring. Saint Joe was inundated with transients, intent on waiting out the winter. It was still the last bastion before the wilderness. This presented a situation that was essential to the town's prosperity. It was basically the same as we had left it. However, one change was obvious to me. The sign in front of our old bakery had been changed to read "Robbins Bakery." It was somewhat thrilling and exciting to walk through those streets again, where every sight instilled the sensation of a memory.

It was twilight by the time that I reached Gramps Pley's homestead. I was glad to see that there was still a light on in the window, suggesting that he had not yet retired for the day. Hearing his hound barking, Gramps appeared in his doorway wearing a robe and slippers, a pipe hanging from his lips.

"Who's that?" he called out as I approached. "Ollie, my boy—you've come back. How wonderful!" Before I had time to respond he grabbed my arm and pulled me into a hug. "Over the gold fever and back with the living, I hope. Where's your brother? You still riding that magnificent Spirit, are you?"

"I came alone, by stage, Gramps. Kurt and Pa are still in Denver. I left Spirit with them."

"Then you've come by yourself?" Gramps questioned. "Oh, of course, you've come for Jenny," he added, revealing his understanding of my intentions.

"I've come to see her, Gramps," I explained, not really confident that I could expect more than that at this point. "I was afraid that, if I stayed away any longer, she would forget about me," I stated honestly.

"You can rest assured you are always on her mind, son, but it's wise you are to realize what you have at stake. How much time are you expecting to stay with us then?" Gramps asked, somewhat sullenly.

"'Unless things work out differently, I expect to be leaving early April," I replied, revealing a bit of my true aspirations.

"Well, that's time enough for me to get some repairs done around here," Gramps said, with the intent of assuring me of my welcome and a smile apparently reflecting appreciation of his own cleverness. "We'll put a cot right there by the fireplace for you. You're welcome to stay as long as you have a notion. God knows I could use a hand around here with the animals and garden, and all—if you find you have some time on your hands, that is."

"I'd be glad to do what I can, Gramps. I'm hoping to find some paying work too, though—to repay my Pa for the traveling money."

"You might try Jim Burke at the Rig and Fitting Depot. He always has work revamping the come-back wagons and selling them to the new group of adventurers. So, tell me son—did you have any luck in finding those precious gold nuggets?"

"We did manage a good return for our work, but only by doing extra to survive off the local game. Had we store-bought all of our needs, at the outrageous mountain prices, we'd have about spent all we earned. We had enough success, though, to bring up hope for a big find in one more season of effort. I know that sounds a little optimistic, but we do have some reason for being hopeful … How's Jenn, Gramps?" I couldn't wait any longer to initiate conversation on my all-consuming desire.

"Just as lovely as when you left. Tomorrow's Saturday. She'll be here soon after the sun's high, as she always is, to tend and ride her Sunshine. It'll be one super surprise for her to find you're back in our company. You know, this place will be Jenn's one day soon. If you two were to get together now, it'd be fine for you to make it your own, right off. And, I'd gladly become a burden on you for the days I've got left—grateful for the blessing of companionship and perhaps for some great-grand offspring."

"Well, Gramps, that sounds like a wonderful and generous offering. But I don't know if we'd be ready to start a family yet," I said, really unsure if I could then or ever have that blessing.

"Know that the offer stands, Ollie. Mention it to Jenny if you like. It may influence her positively, knowing that you have a start awaiting you here."

"Thanks, Gramps," I said with as much sincerity as possible. I hoped he'd realize how important and valuable this offer was to me.

It was necessary to reevaluate my entire situation from this new vantage point. Did I really have any need of establishing a savings to give us a start in a life together, or was Gramps providing us with the entire means, just as he had done when he allowed Kurt and me to bring horses into our lives many years earlier? It certainly appeared as if fate were taking a hand in bringing me and Jenny together. Yet I had to contend with the unresolved problem of my inability to become a normal, sexually functioning individual. Perhaps I was fooling not only Gramps, but also Pa, Kurt, and myself with my unachievable expectations. Was I also about to bring Jenny into this selfish farce of an undertaking? I loved Jenny too much to hurt her that way. Yet faith in God's control of our lives led me to believe that he was bringing us together and that I should trust Him to work things out in His given time. *Certainly, a family is a blessing He regularly bestows on humans as His plan for mankind is perpetuated*, I thought.

It seemed the responsible thing to do would be to explain my dilemma to Jenn and let her decide if this was a problem she would be willing to confront with me. But how could I seriously expect her to want a husband who had disabled himself sexually by selfishly indulging in the sinful and unnatural act of self-gratification. Surely, this would make it impossible for her to love and admire me for a lifetime as her husband. If I were able to overcome my lack of confidence and perform naturally for her, wouldn't this shortcoming be better left undisclosed—for her well-being and contentment, as well as my own? Though honesty is a necessity between a husband and wife, isn't it best for some things to go unsaid? I wondered. Certainly, premarital affairs were not a necessary disclosure between a husband and wife. The depth of my love for her might overcome my dysfunction, or it might not. My concern could not be alleviated by reasoning, and that would, in itself, be destructive. It would not allow the natural resolution I would so welcome, of a coming together in spontaneous lovemaking. I prayed to the Lord for his forgiveness and blessing.

12

AN ENCOUNTERING WITH JENNY

It was with hopeful expectation that I awaited Jenn at Sunshine's stall that following morning. God's hand, my love and time would eventually resolve the situation, I had decided. Although, I wanted to surprise Jenny, I was afraid of startling her, since she would not be expecting to see anyone in the stable. I watched as she approached through a space between the doors until I saw her approaching. The sight of her was startling. Her beauty was even greater than my memory had attributed to her. She was voluptuously shaped in her tight riding pants. Her shirt was tucked in at her tiny waist, and then it flared to almost impossible breath over her sumptuous breasts. She was shocking to behold. Flowing curls of auburn surrounded her flawless beauty. Tumbling down over her shoulders, they framed an oval face with catlike, hazel eyes set above high cheekbones; a tiny, unimposing nose; and a succulent lower lip. She would surely infuse desire in any man setting eyes upon her, and so she did in me. Yet, my desire was only to have her love—not to force myself on her sexually as nature was supposed to demand.

In an attempt to present a manly, yet nonthreatening figure to Jenny when she entered, I sat myself upon a saddle that was draped over the wall of Sunshine's stall.

"Ollie," Jenny yelled upon seeing me. She ran over and pulled me down toward her, forcing me to use my grip on the stall to keep from falling heavily upon her. Still, I couldn't keep from tumbling into the hay on the ground with her. We kissed for a long while, but I didn't try to do more, out of respect for her, fear, or both. It was exultation having a woman of extraordinary beauty desiring or perhaps even loving me.

"What are you doing here, Ollie?" Jenny finally said, through heavy breathing, after breaking our embrace.

"I was afraid to stay away any longer, Jenn. I didn't want you to forget me."

"But isn't it more important to become rich first? I thought you wanted to become stinking rich, so that every woman would be letting you into her pants," she said with a smile.

"That's not at all true. I only wanted enough to allow us to make a start. As far as needing to make a bonanza strike goes, that's more Pa's ambition than my own."

"Well, it's an admirable one," she said, much to my surprise. "Wanting to improve your life and to be willing to endure extreme hardships and even risk death to do so is nothing less than heroic to me."

Once again, Jenn had surprised me with her perception and intelligence, just as she'd seemed to do in every conversation we'd had in the past. "But I might have wasted time that we could have been using to build a life of our own. I was talking to Gramps, and it seems that he—"

"What would we do?" she said, cutting me off, as if she knew where my conversation was going and felt that topic to be worthless. Apparently, Gramps had already presented her with his plan of our taking over his homestead. "Should we scrape a life of poverty out of the soil, as Gramps has done?"

"I thought maybe we'd raise thoroughbreds. We could enlarge the stable in time and make our ranch famous across the country."

"And how many thoroughbreds of any quality do you think you could afford from pie selling? We'd never see that dream come true. That was the downfall of our parents and near to all of the emigrants of this country. The problem is the daily chore of staying alive doesn't leave any time for the building of dreams. You have to do something about building your income before being bogged down with chores and child rearing. Be realistic. Ollie. You know that as well as I do."

There she was, right again, and making me feel foolish for my ignorance. "What are you suggesting? Should I go back come spring and give Pa's dream more of a try?"

"Sure," she replied immediately and with enthusiasm. "In the meantime, I'll be doing something to improve my own stature."

"What's that?" I questioned, somewhat taken back by this announcement.

"My teacher, Mr. Jenkins, says I have the potential to continue academic studies at a university after this year's graduation. He's sending a letter to the Simpson College in Des Moines to see if I would be accepted to attend there next winter."

"You are talking about *years* of being apart!"

"Not if you come to me in the summer as you have now," she said with a smile. "Ollie, I want to become a teacher. I want to feel like I'm doing something important and useful with my life—not just spending it in a farmhouse."

"What about raising your own children, Jenn? Could anything be more important than that?"

"That won't change. Schoolteachers have children too. My mom would help if I had children. Anyway, who knows if that would ever happen?"

"It won't for us if you have your way," I said, too distraught by her pronouncement to withhold my disapproval.

"Are you saying you won't be able to stay in love with me over the years if we're not together every minute?"

"No, I'm trying to say that I don't know if I'll be able to love you like a husband is meant to love his wife. God, I don't even know if I can do that now," I said, the words seeming to come from my mouth on their own. My frustration had grown to the point of desperation. Feeling the tears welling up in my eyes, I had to pause and collect myself before addressing the astonished look I saw in her eyes. Honesty seemed to be the only recourse at this point and the disgrace and embarrassment it entailed would be unavoidable, since the alternative would be to accept her plan of more years of estrangement. That would certainly be a situation disastrous to my hope of becoming a normal sexual partner for her.

"I see. You lost your desire for me while you were away. You don't want me anymore. Is that it?" she asked.

"No, that's not true. I want you. I have always wanted you too much. That's the problem. All these years, I've given in to my lust for you. I've disgraced myself, Jenn. I've spilled the seed that was meant for you, over and over again. I'm sorry, Jenny. I don't believe I'm capable of being a real man anymore. I'm afraid that the only way I can have sex now is by doing it alone." Tears had actually escaped from my eyes at this admission. But what did it matter? She now knew the truth of my weakness and uselessness.

"I want to see you do it," she said. There was no sign of disappointment in her words or on her face. She actually looked somewhat pleased.

The thought of what she was proposing put me into something of a state of shock. I started to respond to her demand unquestioningly. I unbuttoned my trousers and started performing right in front of her. There was no fear of failure due to a lack of confidence to deal with in doing this for her. If it pleased her, I would surely enjoy obliging. Yet the possibility that she wanted to see me in self-abuse so that she could leave me with a picture in her mind of my unworthiness was a real one. If she were to do so, I would have no remorse. Nor would I hold any blame against her. I was finally being honest about myself to both of us.

"No, take them down. I want to see everything," she said, her fixed stare and hurried words indicating an excitement.

Could it be that she had no repulsion at all over my failing? She seemed merely sexually interested in the workings of my body. I did as she asked and provided her with the show that she requested, surprising myself with my lack of humility in doing so. But, for once, I didn't have to imagine her beauty. She was right there in front of me, seated in the hay. "You see how it comes to life when I touch it. It's like magic," I said as she watched intently.

"I'll do it for you," she said and did for a short while. "No you. You know how to do it better than I do," she said, seemingly more content on watching me.

So, now she knew, and she accepted everything!

"I'm sick of bathtubs and mirrors," she said, touching herself as she watched. "Let's do it together," she added—and to my amazement, she unbuttoned and pulled down her riding pants. "Come over here," she said, seeing how excited I had become as I knelt in front of her, watching her in total fascination and excitement. "Rub it here," she said. And, in a trance, I did as she asked. Then it happened! As I entered her, I was surprised at how excited she had become. "Put it all the way in, but pull it out before you climax," she said magically.

I was actually inside of her—my Jenny. That was all. In but an instant, I had to do as she requested, and my seed was still not where nature had intended. But this time, for the first time, I felt no shame. To the contrary, I felt elation and had to laugh at the incredible change in my situation. Just like that, the fears I had developed over the past years had been dissolved. I had to laugh at myself for being so concerned over something so easily resolvable. Was it Jenny's doing? Did she know exactly how to resolve my problem, or had this just occurred spontaneously?

"Get off me," she said through her laughter, while giving me a slight shove. "Get covered up. Gramps might come out. You were my first, you know," she continued. "Sorry, I broke the skin myself one day, when I got carried away with a bar of soap. There, you told me your shame, and I told you mine. I always intended to tell you it happened while horseback riding. From now on, we can be honest with each other about everything," she said, as I used the side of my boot to push the wet straw down into the pile.

Then I turned and took Jenny into my arms, kissed her, and squeezed her to me. This was still the best part. I wanted to hold her against me forever. "We'll ride the river together," I told her.

13

THE INJUN THREAT

After that day in the stable, Jenny and I made up for lost time. We spent the winter finding different ways to please each other, while taking care to prevent a pregnancy from resulting. She got her acceptance to Simpson College midwinter and became ecstatic over it. I was somewhat taken aback that she felt so little regret over leaving me, now that we had truly become lovers in the full sense of the word—that is, sex sharers. In honesty, I have to admit that I had come to agree with her as to her outlook on the future. Jenny realized, just as Pa did, the importance of wealth to the quality of our lives. I wanted to get back to the diggings, and had become somewhat anxious about it and about trying to make our dreams a reality.

It seemed that I was not the only one who had that anxiety. Saint Joe had become more crowded over the winter than it had been the previous year. The crowd was almost entirely made up of would be "Pike's Peakers." Many started making their way westward during the March thaw in the Rockies. This was a definite indication of their determination to be among the earliest group of new arrivals to the diggings, since their journey across the plains would certainly be a treacherous and punishing one when experienced before the onset of spring.

Having booked passage on the Overland Express in early April, I was assured of arriving in Denver prior to the earliest of these wagon trains. I was looking forward to the downstream riverboat ride but not to weeks of sitting all day as the staged bounced over the rutted plains trail. This had proven to be a torturous, as well as boring, experience on my trip east.

The stage ride back proved itself not to be as boring as I had anticipated. Every night was noticeably colder than the previous as we made our way westward. It snowed the most of one night and quite heavily the following one. Yet the heat of the afternoon sun reduced the fluffy, white mounds to a thin covering of slush atop the muddy earth, which was already saturated by the winter thaw.

At one point, to facilitate the fording of a ravine, we passengers had to abandon the stage. We were in the process of aiding the team by pushing the stage to keep it moving through the boot-deep mire when the team suddenly came to a stop. Looking up at the driver, who was staring wide-eyed toward the front of the team, I followed his stare to a group of five mounted Sioux braves standing several feet in front of the team. Each was holding a bow with an arrow set for flight.

Without real thought, I jumped toward the stage door intent on quickly getting my hands on the rifle I had seen leaning against the stage seat. The futility of my effort became immediately apparent on my first step, as my boot sank and lodged in the mud, where it stayed when I pulled my leg up. After I bent forward to recover the boot, my head was yanked back up by yet another brave on horseback, who had grabbed a handful of my hair. Twisting my head to the side, as best I could, I saw him sneering down at me. He held my hair with his left hand and was bringing his right, which was holding a tomahawk, toward the back of my head!

I raised my arm in what I knew would be a futile attempt to bring it behind me in time to fend off the inevitable. Simultaneously trying to twist around, my effort was thwarted by the uncooperative surface below me. Strangely, I felt something of a relief, realizing that, in a second, my scalp or possibly my entire head would be lopped off. It was a relief, I realized, since it would bring to an end the need of meeting the challenges and suffering that lay before me. *So it will end now*, I thought.

The second did, but I felt no change in my cranium. My hair had been released, allowing me to turn toward the Indian. I saw him holding the Cherokee necklace Gramps had given me before my first westward crossing. He had sliced the necklace off and was speaking to his companions while examining it. Then he dropped it down to my hand, and shoving me to the side with a moccasin-clad foot, he stepped his pony to the stage door, opened it, and swung in.

"Let them take what they want, and they'll probably let us live," there came Swainton, our stage driver's raspy voice.

On hearing his instructions, the foolishness of my action became apparent to me. At this range, the five braves with bows would surely be able to kill the five of us, unprotected in front of them, before we could so much as draw a single weapon on them. Our weapons were the first things they collected. Then, as they went through our bags, a razor, a looking mirror, a brush, shoe polish, jewelry, and some garments were bagged and slung over a pony. While glaring at us, they made some remarks in their language that terminated in a chorus of threatening chuckles. Then, they galloped off, yelping triumphantly as they did.

Swainton explained to us how hijackings had been occurring regularly upon wagon trains of late, but this was the first he had heard of one against a stage.

"Why doesn't the army go after them?" I asked, thinking that they were acting quite belligerently in face of the fact that our numerous forts in the area had a far superior manpower to pit against them.

"I suspect they recognize that the Injuns have had some justification in their actions. When the Injuns returned to the mountains for winter shelter this year, they found that their normal refuges had been raped by our settlers through the summer. Their normal oases, at the stream mouths, were bare of firewood. And most of the game that they were used to finding abounding in them had been killed or run off. The result was that this has been a disastrous year for the Injuns. Starvation and pneumonia has devastated their numbers, just as the plague did years earlier. In most of their raids, they have only taken horses and food, wagons full at times, but they have been making a point of not harming anyone."

"In other words, they've been taking back some of what we've taken from them?" I asked.

"That's true. But it's not going to end there, I suspect," Mr. Swainton added sullenly. "We have a situation that can only get worse. The more the emigrants move out here, the worse things will get for the Injuns, and the more they'll be set on retribution. I see major confrontations brewing, and I fear they'll be unavoidable." Mr. Swainton's prediction seemed to be the likely outcome. It was one that painted a fearful picture in my mind—that of Pa going back into the mountains alone, save for his mule, Jingles.

"Kurt's out riding for the Pony Express," Pa informed me upon my arrival in Denver. "He'll be making fifty dollars a week for riding but only one weekday. He makes a run of about a hundred miles, changing horses every ten or fifteen. As the speed delivery service grows, he'll be making more runs and more money. For every extra run he makes, he earns another fifty. He thinks he could end up earning a good bit more than he has been at the diggings, and you know how Kurt loves riding. He could eventually earn several hundred dollars a week. That would be comparable to the best week of panning, and it could be done on a consistent basis. A remarkable income for doing something in itself pleasurable, don't you think?"

It was hard to picture Kurt spending his days at depot stations or wilderness forts for long. I hoped that he'd tire of it soon, and I told Pa why. "Things are changing with the Injuns," I responded. "They hijacked our stage on the way here and made off with our weapons and anything else they had a notion to. It's plum crazy for riders to be crossing this territory alone. The Injuns may start picking them off just for target practice."

"What sensible reason do you suppose they'd have for doing that?" Pa queried of me, the calmness in his voice indicating that he was not sharing my concern.

"They might start killing white men out of hatred, if we keep making it harder for them to survive. Don't you think so, Pa?"

"No, that's not like the Injuns. They believe that all their worldly needs are provided to them by Spirits. And, if they are not provided, it's their own responsibility for having failed to please those Spirits."

"That may be so, Pa, but I'm sure they know who has cut down their trees," I replied somewhat angrily, feeling that Pa was being unrealistic about a matter on which Kurt's welfare depended.

"They do, but they also believe it to be the will of the Spirits that the white men have come, or else they would not have. And there is merit to that concept. Besides, think about what is actually happening. The riders are being provided with fresh horses every ten miles or so. Would the Injuns want to run down their ponies trying to catch fresh ones in order to capture a mochila of mail, in which they have absolutely no interest? It doesn't seem a likely possibility to me," Pa concluded. He was attempting to reassure me of Kurt's safety. Yet I sensed that he felt some apprehension about Kurt's venture himself. We both seemed at a loss for words at that point. The silence, in itself, exposed the depth of our concern.

"Wagons were lined up deep on both sides of the crossing," I began, recanting my days in Saint Joe to Pa.

After I had told all that I thought was of interest, he asked, out of the heart of a concerned father, "And where's the bride?"

"She didn't want that yet. She wants to go to college and study what's needed to become a teacher. I decided that it wasn't what I wanted either. When I go back, I want to have something to offer her."

"Well, that's the first I've heard you converse about that girl that I didn't feel you had yourself in a state of torturous confusion. For the peace of mind it seems to have brought you, I'd declare the trip a successful one."

Pa was right. I'd feared that he wouldn't understand why I needed to go back to Jenny, even though nothing seemed to have been accomplished by my doing so. It was relieving to see that he understood.

Then Pa had his turn at storytelling. As he described the magnificence of the storms that had blown through the town and the digging out of the streets by tunneling afterward, his pleasure was apparent. Listening to him, I gathered that having experienced the power of the event was, in itself, satisfying. As he described the necessity of blazing a trail to the stable, while being lashed by winds strong enough to force a smile on his face by stretching back the skin of his cheeks, it was obvious that he'd found exaltation in the experience.

"How's the weather been since Kurt started riding?" I asked.

"We've had some storming, but that comes much less where he's been riding, I'm told. His home station is back in Julesburg. I had hoped you would run into him on your way back here."

"No. We changed teams there, at night, and I used the break to get some shut-eye. So, I didn't see much of anything."

"You wouldn't miss the riders if they had their topcoats off," Pa said. "They've got them all uniformed in blue trousers and red shirts so they will stand out to all onlookers. They even gave them two revolvers, shouldered at their sides, as well as a saber, bandana, and boots. Kurt left his old rifle and saber with me, since they insist that all the riders use only company uniforms, gear, and clothing. They sit upon a Mexican mochila that is both a saddle and carrying bags. That way, both can be transferred to a new mount quickly at the depots. Quite a sight they must present to onlookers as they race across the countryside," Pa added. His pride in Kurt's actions was detectable during this telling.

The impression I wondered about was the one they would have on the Injuns. But, I didn't see any purpose in pursuing my fears any further with Pa. "When are we heading back to Nevada?" I asked him.

"First light—I'm hoping," he replied.

"I'm going to help you search out that quartz outgrowth, Pa."

"No, you're not. I need you back at the diggings, same as last year," Pa replied, "where you can be earning something for your efforts," he added in explanation.

"No you're not, Pa. You're not pulling that one on me again. You know there's plenty enough game out there for us to get by on. And I know plenty about hunting now. With my help, you'll have more time to do what you need to be doing. Prospectors will be spreading more into the mountains this year, and we got to make that find fast."

"I'm not going to argue about this. I don't want you out there with me!" Pa barked back angrily.

"You can't order me anymore, Pa. I'm a grown man now. I'm supposed to be able to take a wife and raise a family. I came back out here to get the means to make that possible. I don't want to have to come back again next year to do it, either. Listen, Pa, I know it's because you think it's not safe out there with the Injuns. If it's not safe for me, then I don't want you out there either."

"It's not the Injuns that scare me," Pa replied sullenly but went on to say, "Okay. You're right, son. It'll be nice to have someone besides Jingles to talk to," he added, while allowing a smile to momentarily cross his face. "Let's get our supplies and load the buckboard. We'll stop at the stable and settle, so we can take the animals and set out at first light."

"We'll be passing through Nevada City? Or is there a faster route?" I asked.

"There may be a faster route. But, if so, I don't know it."

"Good. I'd like to see if the Dalton brothers are up there again. I was thinking that we might want to ask them if they'd be interested in buying the cabin. I don't see us needing it anymore. Do you, Pa?"

"Probably not. That would be a right smart thing to do. We'll search out those friends of yours when we get up there."

With the early start we got in the morning, and pushing a little hard, we got to Central City late in the afternoon three days later. On our arrival, I saw the marshal outside the stage depot, so we pulled up and waited for him to conduct his business with another party. Apparently, that business was about Injun trouble.

"Sounds like the same trouble I had coming out to Denver," I told the marshal after he finished talking to the other driver.

"It's getting to be a serious problem," he replied, nodding in consent. I don't know how we're going to keep running the stages—unless we get the army to give us an armed escort to make the trip with them. Any lone wagons or stages are gambling when making a crossing these days. Luckily, the Injuns haven't killed anyone yet. But I see things getting worse, with the number of emigrants we're expecting."

"Has anyone tried to fight them off, instead of giving into them?" I asked. This was a question that I was glad to have the opportunity to ask. The answer might help me settle some misgivings I'd had about my reaction to the robbing of our stage.

"No, not that had the least bit of success. And I suspect that's why there hasn't been any killing here yet. It'd be damn foolish for a few men using single-shot rifles to go up against a group of braves. They'd never have a chance to get off a second shot. And even if they were close enough to use revolvers, they'd be lucky to get more than an Injun or two, unless they had a real fast gun hand with them. I'm just hoping the army does something to help get things under control. Are you planning on spending another season working the creek, Olof?" the marshal asked.

"No, actually I'm not. I'm going with my pa into the mountains."

"Marshal Jackson," the marshal said in introduction as he turned toward Pa. "Which way you planning on heading?"

"Olof senior. I'm glad to meet you, Marshal. There's a large valley, about a day and a half to the southeast. You come to it after passing through a walled canyon," Pa replied.

"Much color in the streams?" the Marshall queried.

"It does have promising terrain though," Pa responded with a slight shake of his head to the negative and the deliberate omission of a mention of the flowstone. Mentioning this detail would, of course, be an unnecessary gambling of our privileged information.

"You know there are Injuns out there, everywhere. If they come to you, I'd not offer any resistance to their demands. The other choice is to be killed," the marshal stated emphatically.

"That's advice we'll be sure to follow. It's not our plan to die trying to improve our living," Pa replied, assuring the marshal of his understanding. "Thanks for the warning, Marshal. And we'll be sure to come and visit you when we come back down to stake our claim," Pa concluded, before we turned back to the uphill side of the road.

"Do you really agree with what the marshal had to say?" I asked Pa.

"You don't know me to say what I mean?" Pa responded gruffly.

I hadn't told Pa how the brave had sliced my necklace off during the robbery, as I had been embarrassed by my inaction at the occurrence. Relating the event to him, I also explained how I realized that I would have to stay more alert in the presence of Injuns or even white men that appeared dangerous in the future, if I was going to survive in this part of the country.

"Surely, that Injun could have slit my throat, just as quickly and easily as the necklace. If I'd been alert, I could have grabbed his arm soon as he reached down at me."

"So, the brave sliced your necklace. He even gave it back to you. What would you have done after grabbing his arm—pulled him off his pony? Would you be willing to give up your life trying to stop him from taking it? If you realized he wanted the necklace, you should have offered it to him. That would have been the best alternative. The Injuns have come under some very trying times. Their numbers have been reduced from a multitude to a few. They are facing desperation at this point, as well as great humiliation. For them, it might be worth dying to strike out against the whites. But you have to ask yourself if it is worth dying to engage them on the account. Most often, it is pride that motivates men to die over some relatively insignificant matter. I suggest that you always ask yourself if the cause is worth dying for, before gambling your life for it."

Though I understood Pa's point, I still believed it would be a good idea to remain defensively alert in the future.

14

CRATER VALLEY

We approached the cabin just as the sun started setting and were surprised to see smoke coming from the chimney. Simon and Earl had arrived at dawn, after spending the night in Mountain City. They had spent the day stacking firewood and bringing in game. There were two rabbits on a spit over the fire, creating an appetizingly delicious aroma.

"Glad you boys had no trouble making yourself at home," Pa said, in a pleasant and humorous tone.

"We wanted to have these hares on a plate waiting when you arrived, but we're running a bit late. Got you a good supply of firewood though," Earl proclaimed in jest.

"Yeah and run all the vermin off the place for you too," Simon added. "Get yourselves comfortable at the table, and we'll divide up these critters," he added.

"No need to do that," Pa replied. "We have a buckboard full of goods out there to fill our gullets with."

"No way, Pa," I retorted. "I want to sink my teeth into one of them cottontails."

"We've got several more hanging out back. We can throw those on while eating these," Simon offered.

"All right!" I responded, noticing that Pa offered no further protest.

"We need to set a place out for Kurt too, I suspect," Earl stated, believing that Kurt would be following us in.

"No, he's not with us. He took that job riding for the Pony Express," I explained.

"Damn, they're supposed to recruit orphans for that job. It's too damn dangerous for persons with family," Simon said. "If I didn't know what a fast rider Kurt is, I'd be worried about him, he added, perhaps trying to dampen his spontaneous statement somewhat.

"And they get a fresh mount every ten miles, so they're always at full gallop," I added, watching Earl drop a portion of rabbit on Pa's plate.

"How safe is anybody in these parts?" Pa asked. "He'll probably be safer than us prospectors up in them hills who aren't even setting a mount," he said, pulling off a slice of meat and audibly savoring its aroma. "You're softening me up with this morsel, just as I'm about to start some serious business negotiations," Pa said between chews. "Ollie's going up into the hills with me this season. So we won't be using this here cabin at all. If you fellows expect to have a need of it, we'd be glad to let you have it, as it stands, for, say, two hundred dollars? That being a little less than we spent on it in total."

"I'd say that's a mighty fine offer," Simon said.

"That it is," Earl agreed. "But you're dealing with fellows just back from a winter of serious hell-raising in San Antonio. We'll be living off our earnings right off," Earl added.

"We can settle up on that when we get back down. Or if you pull out before we're back, you can sell it and leave the money with the banker for us," Pa offered.

"Looks like we have a roof over our heads this year," Simon said, turning toward Earl.

"Yes, but who's going to help load the cradle?" Earl asked.

"We've worked it alone before. At least when we hit pay dirt, we won't have a four-way split anymore," Simon answered.

"That's a good point" Earl agreed with a chuckle.

"Have you got something to go on or just striking out cold?" Simon asked.

"We figure these streams are about played out as far as something big is concerned. So, we're shooting for all or nothing," I replied. "Pa liked the looks of the terrain of a valley about fifteen miles to the southwest.

The marshal says it's called Crater Valley. We're expecting to give it a hard going over. In case anyone has a reason to know our location, that's where they'll find us. Perhaps Kurt may come by and want to search us out."

"Are there any creeks with color there?" Simon asked.

"Not much," Pa replied. "But, that doesn't always tell the whole story. Even a little had to come from somewhere."

"Guess you're right about that," Simon replied, with no discernible excitement in his voice. "We'll be hoping you find the source and it turns out to be a mother lode. After you stake a claim on it, Earl and I can get rich helping you work it."

"That sounds good to me," Pa responded.

"Yes, it does," I added in agreement.

"Let's have a drink on it then," Simon suggested, producing a bottle of whiskey from within the pantry.

"Only one thing," Pa announced, delaying the celebration. "The deal on the cabin doesn't go through till we leave in the morning. That means that Ollie and I get to sleep on the bunks tonight."

The drink that sealed the deal, of course, turned out to be just the opener. Simon and Earl got to recanting tales of their winter exploits, allowing the drinking to go on into the night. And they were some amazing tales they had to tell. My adventure with the Indian ambush on our stage was all I had to offer. And my part in that was more of an embarrassment than an experience worth bragging on. Even more embarrassing was answering Earl's question, "And what of that little lassie you've been doting on, over in Saint Joseph?"

"She's tending to go to college and get the learning needed to be able to teach children," I answered, trying to sound positive about Jenny's plans.

"That's the last you'll see of her," Simon stated, quite authoritatively.

"Maybe so," I replied flatly.

Simon's sharp, almost instantaneous response caused me to realize, for the first time, that this was actually the likelihood. Jenny would probably find a more attractive, intelligent, and wealthier companion than me at college and forget I ever existed. What was I doing here then?

This was the road she had chosen for us. But would it really end up being for us? Perhaps, I should have been more forceful with her. If I had given her an ultimatum, she may have chosen me over college. And I would still be there with her. Simon's remark had set me to doubt. But, perhaps I should give Jenny more credit than he was giving her, I thought. After all, she had remained faithful to me so far. Of course, college would certainly offer her much more temptation.

"We'd better get sacked out, if we're going to get an early start," I told Pa, at that point realizing that my best course of action was to get done what we had come out there to do and get back to Jenny as soon as possible.

Pa agreed with sacking out, and we did.

Yet it was somewhat late in the morning before we got our start. We packed our tools and supplies on Spirit, Flash, and Jingles and left the buckboard with Earl and Simon. Two days later, we passed through the walled canyon, which opened into the surprisingly immense Crater Valley. The view was similar to looking up at Nevada from the bottom of the diggings at Mountain City. It was somewhat upsetting to see a prospector working a pan in the creek, about a mile to our front. "Looks like someone's got the jump on us," I said to Pa, wondering how much of a concern this should be to us.

"You'll see lots of prospectors passing through and giving these hills a try. I hope that's all it amounts to. One thing you can be sure of—after finding the stone, I thought the source would be visible in some manner, so I tried every outgrowth and surface disturbance from here clean round this valley and back. Wherever it is, it's not jumping out at anybody. Course that's not saying it isn't possible for someone to stick a pick into the right spot before we do. We can only hope that the Lord will find us deserving and let our efforts be the fruitful ones."

Pa pointed off to the side of the creek at a pile of stones that had obviously served as a cooking pit at one time. "That's where I set up my first campsite in the valley. I was getting stones from right here, at this bend of the creek," he said, bending down beside the creek bed in an area that showed signs of a good amount of digging and turning of the earth. "The stone was lying right here," he said, picking up a stone and laying it in the exact location the flowstone had occupied. "I pried it out of the bank and carried it, with another, up to that campsite. It wasn't till I stacked it on the pile that I saw the broken end was exposing a quartz composition. This is the reality; that quartz flowstone, shot through with gold as it was, was lying right here. It had to come out of those hills from somewhere," he said. His eyes scanned the top of the mountain range from one side to the other. "That's why I keep looking," he concluded, while staring up at the hillside.

"We'll find it too," I said, letting Pa know that I understood his determination, as we continued into the valley following the creek.

After a short greeting and small-talk of panning expectations, with a man named Pfeiffer, the prospector we had seen panning the creek, we made our way through the sage and up the rise of the valley wall to a large crevice at the base of a cliff face. From the ash on the ground and soot covering the walls, it was obvious that this had served many times as a campsite. Pa took a canvas tarp with ropes tied to each corner from Jingles's pack. He had me climb on his shoulders and hook the rope on spikes he had driven on each side of the crevice opening. "How'd you manage this on your own?" I asked.

"I had to use Jingles to imitate your trick riding. It took me near to a day to get her to cooperate long enough to drive the spikes and another to recover from the falls," Pa replied.

"Maybe you and Jingles can join my act next show," I jested.

"Find that outgrowth for me, and I'll consider it," Pa replied with a laugh.

The canvas covered most of the opening, save for a narrow space at the top. Pa tied the lower corners round boulders to the sides of the crevice, one side tight to the wall and the other creating a shoulder width's opening that would serve as an entrance.

"If we keep a good fire going in there through the day, the bricks will hold the heat till morning," Pa said. "We'll throw a good pile of brush under our bedrolls, and you'll find the nights quite comfortable. The main thing is, keep your bedding dry and you'll keep warm. Of course, you know that; I know," he said. "Well, that's it. Home sweet home—unless you want to take the time to build a cabin?"

"Home it is then," I replied, starting to untie Spirit's packs. "That Pfeiffer seemed like a nice enough fellow," I continued, while unloading the packs.

"You'll find most of the honest prospectors to be so. We're all in the same boat, so to speak," Pa said.

"What do you mean by honest prospectors?" I asked.

"You've got a lot of swindlers roaming about in these hills," he explained. They try to find a way to infringe on a man's claim or buy him out for a fraction of a claim's worth and then sell it to a mining company for big money. There are also outright thieves that travel about, who will try to find the location of a prospector's stash and then relieve him of it at nightfall. We keep our wits about us when dealing with strangers—right, son?"

"Right, Pa," I replied, now having more appreciation for Mr. Pfeiffer, considering him to be an ally, rather than a competitor.

"This time, when I return to you, it will be for good. I'll never let us be apart again. Love always, Ollie." After finishing my letter to Jenny I placed it in my knapsack.

Later, I would give it to one of the prospectors who were heading back to town as I had done with the three I had previously written her— one each month since we arrived in the valley. There were always other prospectors working the valley while we were. Most would continue on, farther out from the diggings. Some were just passing through the valley on their way back—although, day by day, more were heading back, disappointed.

It was also common to see Indians about the valley. Most often it was a group of braves hunting with dogs. Sometimes, a group of braves and squaws would pass through, using dogs or horses to pull dregs that were laden with trading goods or supplies. Pa said the Injuns about those parts, at that time of year, were resigned to accepting a lifestyle that relied on relations with white men. The independent tribes were off hunting the migrating herds of bison that were making their north-to-south migration. These stationary tribes were not likely to be hostile, since they had accepted the white man's contribution to their livelihood. Still, although relieved by Pa's assurances, I could not help but feel threatened when I was within their view.

With the sun setting and Pa already curled up in his bedding for the night, I scanned the valley from the point we had started working it. Pa had seriously worked about a third of it the previous year, alone. And we'd picked up from the point where he had stopped. We had matched his effort already, but a third of the valley still remained untouched. After completing that, the slow process of picking at the cliff faces, while dangling on a rope sling, would be confronting us. This would surely be a slow process.

"Pa, are you sleeping?" I asked in but a whisper, in case he had already gone off to sleep.

"No. What is it Ollie?" he responded, not surprised that I would address him at this time, as I often had a desire for discussion when our day had been completed.

"I don't think we're going to have enough time to complete the whole valley before winter sets in, unless we cover more ground daily."

"Well, I'm hoping we come upon the quartz before we have to cover every square inch of the valley," Pa replied.

"But what if we don't? We probably won't even get to the cliff face this year. It may be up there that it came from."

"I'm not going to start leaving unturned earth that might let us skip right over the vein," Pa said. "If we do that and end up not finding it, we'll have to redo the entire area. We have to continue working up and down the hillside in controlled steps, so we can be sure that what we cover has been completely covered. Ollie, you know—we've been over this before. We have to do it right the first time," Pa explained.

"But, Pa, I don't want to have to come back again next year, if we don't make the find."

"You won't have to, Ollie. In fact, you can head out tomorrow if you like. You know I'll find it for us, sooner or later, if it takes the rest of my life to do it."

This didn't surprise me. But it was a little shocking to hear him put into words just how determined he actually was.

"I'll see this year out, but I don't want to make another season of it."

"I understand that, Ollie. Maybe tomorrow you ought to go out and hunt us down some fresh meat. It's been near a week since we've had any. And you know how hunting always lifts your spirit."

"You're right. A successful hunt always makes me feel like I've done something useful with my time," I replied, not mentioning how contrary this seemed compared to our time spent prospecting.

"You have to admit that it also brings you pleasure to be roaming through the hills, surrounded by nature's creatures," he added.

"Yeah, I guess it does at that," I confessed

Pa was right about my enjoying being among the creatures, but I could have added, "Only the four-legged ones." I always felt a little intimidated to be in the woods alone, knowing that Indians were also roaming about. I still hadn't resolved the issue of the correctness of my passive response to the Indians who'd robbed our stage. On one hand, I wished that I had grabbed the brave's arm and held his hand at bay. But on the other, a physical confrontation with him might have had disastrous consequences for my companions and me. Yet, since the same consequences could have been endured after a passive response to his aggression, wouldn't it make sense to choose the action that would, at least, leave me with my self-respect? I vowed to myself that I would maintain a state of awareness if I again found myself in the presence of Indian braves.

I had brought along Jingles for the hunt. My plan was to land an elk or deer and bring back the carcass slung across her back. If it were too big to lift, I would quarter it on site, finishing the butchering back at our camp. The weather was great to be riding in. Although the early-morning air was crisp, there was minimal wind. And the bright sun and clear sky made the morning quite enjoyable. I rode to an area to the northwest of Crater Valley, where the hills were heavily forested and attracted a large amount of wildlife. There was an open field, in the thick of the forest, where the high grasses made a great grazing spot for would-be prey. On two prior trips I had had success in this field, killing pheasants. But on this trip, I intended to wait out a larger prey, the tracks of which I had found to be plentiful in the area on those previous trips.

15

AN INSTANCE OF KILLING

Once I located the field, I let Jingles and Spirit graze until I saw that their hunger was waning. Then I led them back several hundred meters and tied them securely, out of sight, behind a thicket of thatch. Returning to the opening, I took up a position near the center of the circular field, knowing the high grasses would conceal me. My hope was that a large grazer would eventually step into the clearing, tempted by the grasses in the area, and opposite the downwind travel of my scent. With my musket fully loaded, I sat cross-legged, listening to the sound of the critters about me—sounds that increased in intensity as my presence ceased to affect the activities normal and eternal to these forests.

Several hours had passed as I sat waiting for the intensity and rhythm of the din about me to vary, indicating the presence of a visitor. While contemplating settling for anything capable of providing a meal or two for Pa and me, my attention was caught by activity at the face of some long reeds to the right of my musket barrel. A spider had spun an intricate web between the reeds, and a small, white moth had found himself caught up in its adhesive latticework. It was frantically fluttering its one free wing. My instinct was to break open the web with my musket barrel, setting free the desperate creature. But remembering that I was to be a nonintrusive visitor to this area's environ, I decided not to intervene on the normal course of this natural encounter. Quickly, a thin, somewhat long-legged spider moved halfway out from its position of hiding, paused, and apparently waited for the fluttering to repeat.

Then he again ran forward till his head pressed against the body of the moth, which fluttered only once more.

Upon hearing a loud cracking sound in the woods to my immediate front, the sense of remorse I had been experiencing by not going to the aid of the forlorn creature was overpowered by excitement. A series of lesser cracks of twigs in the underbrush followed, indicating the rapid approach of a large animal. The brush waved momentarily and then flattened fully, revealing a huge, fully racked venison buck. My musket was up at the ready when he appeared. I set my bead directly between his muscular shoulders, but before I could get off a steady barreled round, the buck lunged forward as his left leg collapsed beneath him, and his body dropped to the side, following his head in a downward plunge.

The disappearance of the buck from my sight was immediately replaced by another appearance, to his rear. This one, however, had shoulder-length hair; wore a loincloth; and carried a shiny bladed dagger in his right hand. My mind flashed back to the Indian at the stage who had cut off my necklace. As I tried to determine if they were one and the same, I heard my musket fire. It wasn't till after I'd seen the bullet splatter against his chest, with the slap of heavy impact that I realized I had fired it. Jumping up from my kneeling position, I rushed toward the brave. He had stopped sharply, dropped to his knees, and then fallen face-first into the brush. Blind to the huge deer right in front of me, I tripped over his legs with both of my feet and was sent sprawling, facedown on the ground, immediately in front of the brave. The hope that he was, somehow not seriously hurt by my shot was shattered by the sight of a pool of blood filling the gaping hole between his shoulder blades, where the musket ball had exited.

My fright climaxed at the realization that no blood was surging from the wound. Hunting experience had taught me that, if an animal's heart was still pumping, blood would surge from any deep wound received by an animal. I was sure the Indian brave was dead. I had killed him! What would the consequences be? Should I take the brave back to Pa or to town? Or should I just leave him here?

Perhaps I should go far from this area and hunt as if nothing had happened. He might have friends showing up at any minute. Since he was not carrying a bow, he had apparently run the deer down. His friends would be tracking him quickly on horseback to help with the carcass. If they found me with him, they would surely kill me. I had to get away from him. That was for sure. What of the deer? I could load him on Jingles, but I would have to halve the carcass, at the least, to be able to lift it. This was out of the question. I determined that I had to leave immediately.

My legs were feeling weak as I ran back to Jingles, and I had a terrible need to relieve my bowels. But I couldn't take the time. Before reaching her, it came to me that the Indians would have no trouble tracking me, especially with two animals. Even riding over the rocky hilltops would not be of use as a means of shaking them from my trail. It was about four hours back to our camp. If I were to head to town, it would be a day-and-a-half trip. I would surely be overtaken by the braves before I reached town.

Yet I didn't want to lead the Indians to Pa. It would be better to accept the responsibility for my deed on my own than to endanger him also. I had to resolve myself to my fate. I would act correctly, I decided. I would do as a man is expected and accept my fate as it befell me. After deciding to retie the animals and answer nature's call to relieve myself, I set off, somewhat calmer. Though surprising myself by having the ability to shake off the panic of fear, I was sickened by the thought of the dead brave and wondered as to the strength of my resolve, if his friends were to overtake me and string me up for a skinning.

Starting toward town, I gave more thought to the aspect of confronting the wrath of the dead brave's companions. If there were but a couple, I would stand it off with them—the slight chance being that I might prevail in the conflict. Three or more, and I would accept my fate and use my musket to take myself out of this world. How had this day turned into such a tragedy? I wondered. Reflecting on the fact that the brave was not carrying a bow, as would be normal for a brave to do—in fact, with nothing on his person but a knife, a loincloth, and moccasins, it was obvious that he had run down the buck, as Indians were known to often do. He had run it down to the point of collapse, which had occurred directly in front of me. How coincidental that the brave had chased it to the exact spot where I had taken my stand. Then to have the animal collapse, directly prior to my pulling my musket trigger—these were impossible coincidences. This was a depiction of the kind of bad luck that could only be attributed to fate taking a hand—an uncontroversial explanation for a man's demise. It felt like I was in a suspension between life and death that was certain to be of short duration.

Even at the slow trot Jingles was forcing us to maintain, Spirit would tire before covering the distance remaining before us. It had been close to an hour since we'd set out, and my instincts were telling me that I was going to be overtaken at any second. The brave surely couldn't have been planning to haul that carcass over any distance on his own. He had to have companions following up his trail with pack animals. And if they'd set right out after me, I was lucky to have gotten this far. Staying on the high ground past Crater Valley, I intended that Pa would not chance upon and join me en route. The normal path was running down below me, and as I rounded a turn in the ridge, I could see the trail from the southwest pass joining up with it. A group of horses were coming down the trail toward the valley below me. Staring through the dust their mounts were creating around them, I was able to make out cavalry uniforms. The bank below me was clearly too steep to descend to the valley trail. And it would be miles farther before I could reach a spot with a more gently sloped hillside. The quickest way to reach the soldiers would be to backtrack, toward what would likely be revenge-hungry Indian braves.

We did this in something close to a gallop, with Jingles slowing us down and nearly pulling Spirit over on several occasions.

Breaking from the trail and descending the hillside, it appeared that my route would bring me down right behind the troops, who were then almost directly below me. At that instant, I felt a sharp stabbing in the ribs, on the left side of my back, below my shoulder blade. Though not serious enough to slow my descent, it caused in me the reflexive action of turning to look over my shoulder and, in so doing, espy a brave sitting a mount at the top of the slope. He was not coming down but sat motionless, holding a bow in his left hand while staring down at me. It must have been an arrow, lacking the force to do serious damage over the distance it had traveled, that had struck me in the back, I realized. I suspected that I would find a significant cut where it had struck, for a stinging was still noticeable at the wound.

"Hello!" I shouted at the group of about twenty soldiers that I was approaching from their left rear.

"Whoa!" I heard resound from several of the soldiers, loud enough to put the entire party on notice to pull up. The lead soldier, whose uniform decoration indicated a position of importance, turned his mount to the side of the group and rode toward me.

"Excuse me, sir," I said as he approached, "but I have come into something of a desperate circumstance and need to impose myself on a person of authority to intervene at this point."

"That would be me. I'm in command of this company—name's Captain West. Perhaps, there may be a small way in which I could offer some assistance. For instance, would you be in gratitude were I to pull that arrow out of your back?" The formality of the captain's response, and the chuckles of those in earshot indicated to me that the soldiers must have been aware that I was unaware of the seriousness of my own distress.

Embarrassed by the ridiculousness of my behavior, I reached for the spot where I had been struck while responding, "Oh. I didn't think it stuck." Not being able to get my hand up far enough to reach the arrow, I felt its shaft touch against the top of my hand, just behind the thumb, creating an increase in the stabbing feeling in my back, which had become more painful since I'd become aware of the arrow's presence.

The captain had his troops pull up for a smoke break and called a medic over to help with my injury. The medic knelt behind me as I sat beside the captain. Immediately, I felt a sharp pain in the wound and saw the arrow land on the ground between the captain and me. The tip of the arrow was colored by my blood.

"It was wedged between his ribs," the medic said. "It didn't hit hard enough to break through. Take your shirt off, son," he continued. "This is going to sting a bit—hold fast," he warned, while unscrewing the cap of a medicine bottle.

My leg did an uncontrollable kick, and I had to let out a groan, as the pain was quite substantial for an instant as he poured the liquid over my wound.

"Tell me, son," the captain said. "How'd you come to be in your current predicament?"

"I killed an Injun brave." I recalled the event while speaking the words. It was a harsh realization that I had allowed this horrible deed of mine to slip from my concern as I became engulfed in my own welfare.

"I might say the same myself," the captain replied, and I thought I heard the medic chuckle a bit as he wrapped a bandage around my torso. "Tell me the exact circumstances that prompted you to perform this noble deed. And I will prepare a report for the Indian Council."

There was a definite chuckle from the medic at this remark.

The captain produced writing implements from his saddle pouch and then nodded to me. "Go ahead," he said.

"My Pa and I are prospecting Crater Valley," I replied, turning to point up toward the valley. As I did, a cutting pain from my back caused me to wince a bit.

"I know the valley," the captain said, frowning at my antics. "Go on."

"I went up yonder to the thick forest to hunt down some game. I took up a position in a clearing and waited for a grazer to wander into the opening. When an eight-point buck ran out, I jumped up and took aim on him. But he lunged forward and dropped just as I did so. As he fell, a redskin replaced him in my sight. I thought for a moment that it might be the same Injun that had held up our stage when I came out here several months ago. But before I completed the thought, I heard my musket fire. The ball went clean through his chest, and he fell dead— right there," I explained.

"Did you do anything before you left?" the captain asked. "Did you check his pulse—do anything with the deer or anything else?"

"I could see he was dead by the small amount of blood that had come from the wound. And I didn't think taking his pulse would be any use—seeing how I don't know how to do it right anyway."

"You just put your fingers here," the captain explained, placing his fingertips on his wrist.

"How do you know that it's not the pulse in your fingers that you are feeling?" I asked.

"You can't feel the pulse in your fingers," he answered, appearing to have become somewhat irritated by my ignorance. "So, you just looked at his body and left?"

"Well, no. First, I had to relieve my bowels, in the bushes, back where I had my animals hitched," I related.

"That brave you killed must have been kin or companion to the one that followed you, to have caused him to set off after you like that. He could see you didn't kill for the game, since you left it where it dropped. And the defecation that you took the time to leave behind, when you could have been using that time to put distance between him and yourself let him know that you didn't have the stomach of a killer. What all this means is, it's not a good thing for you that he took out after you. If he's seeking revenge, he may not stop until he gets it."

"What should I do?" I asked.

"First, let me get this report written."

I had noticed that the captain had, so far, not done any writing on the pad. "Tell me your name," he requested.

I did. And, he wrote it down.

"How old are you?"

"Eighteen years," I responded.

"And your father's name?"

"Same as mine," I said.

"How long have you been in these parts?" he asked.

"We came out here June of fifty-nine, with my brother Kurt. He's riding with the Pony Express now," I said, realizing that Kurt's position seemed to make me feel somewhat more important. "Last winter I spent back in Saint Joe."

"Go back to see your old lassie?" the captain asked, smiling.

"How'd you know that?" I asked, somewhat amazed by his insight.

"I deal with young men daily. I know what drives you," he answered matter-of-factly.

"So, your family's from Saint Joseph?"

"Yes," I replied.

"Now, listen to me carefully. I'll fill in the incident report for you. If you are ever requested to tell it back, use these same words—so as not to be misunderstood: A deer came out of the woods. I fired at it and missed. The deer feel, shocked by my weapon's report and apparently suffering from exhaustion. Then I saw an Injun brave fall out of the brush.

"You didn't set out to hurt that Injun, did you, son?"

"Not on purpose. No, sir, I didn't."

"Then stop feeling you had anything to do with the *accident*," he said.

Again I was amazed, and perhaps somewhat angered, by this officer's insight. "Thank you sir," I replied.

"Now, I'll tell you what we can do to try and keep you alive. You tell me where and exactly how to find your father. We'll send a man ahead to explain the situation to him. If there are any braves following us, we don't want them to make a connection between him and you. You'll come into Denver with us and get some doctoring. You might contemplate another trip back to Saint Joe to see that little lassie of yours and let some grass grow under your feet. It may be that that brave will be satisfied knowing he left that sticker in you," he said, lifting the arrow from the ground as he did. "But who knows? This is Arapaho," he announced, while examining the arrow. It's probably from a local tribe. He may keep you in mind for a long time. Even if he didn't get a good sighting of you, that Paint of yours is a good means for him to find you by. I don't think you should ride him in these parts again. Do you feel up to riding?" he asked.

"Yes, I'm fine," I replied, believing it to be true.

"We'll give my trooper time to get ahead some. Then we'll be going," he said, rising and moving back to the circle his men had formed around a coffeepot.

"Don't go waving to him now," the captain said to me as we rode past and below, my Pa, who was standing beside our campsite looking down at me.

I gave him but a slight nod and thought I saw him respond in kind.

"He told my trooper that he'd be looking for you in Nevada if you were not back in three weeks. Leave a note for him in the depot if you move on," the captain instructed. "I think you might want to leave your animals there for him also and move on down to the city of Golden with us. I'll get off a message to Washington from there and have you reassigned to my company. We'll fix you up with a new mount, outfit you, and have you added to the payroll. A fellow who takes an arrow in the back as lightly as you do is sure to make a fine Indian fighter."

"Tell you the truth, sir, every time I think of that Indian I killed, I get to feeling quite sick in my stomach."

"That's only because you haven't seen the cruelty they're capable of inflicting on whites or even on their own kind for that matter."

"I'm proud to have had the asking, sir, but I really have only one thing in mind right now."

"I know," the officer interjected. "That lassie we were discussing. Keep one thing in mind, Mr. Swenson. You're planning on settling down at a young age. Every man is cut from his own mold. Some don't have a need to be part of the making of the world. They're happy to put down roots and make that their place for life. But your being out here tells me that you have an adventurous heart."

"Actually, it was mostly my Pa's doing—my being here. And frankly, I think today has just about given me my fill of adventure," I replied.

"So be it then, Mr. Swenson. We'll be leaving you in the good hands of Dr. Hardin when we part company in Nevada."

"Thank you, sir," I replied quite sincerely.

With that, the captain rode up to the head of the column. I contemplated the decision our discussion had led me to. The truth was that I really had had enough of this wilderness.

16

A CHANGE IN MOTIVATION

When we reached Nevada, the captain walked me to the door of the doctor and asked him to tend to my wounds. Then, after wishing me well, he departed. "I'll be able to pay you just as soon as I get over to the bank," I informed the doctor.

"That'd be just fine, son," he replied. "Now, let's just see what you've got there."

After unbinding my wound, he declared that I was lucky, seeing how it was clean. Applying a poultice of moss and sulfur, he told me that I'd have to come in daily for a week or so to let him look at it.

So, I'll have to stick around for a while, I thought. "I'll do that, Doc," I replied.

With my bandage reapplied, I headed to town center, planning to draw out some cash from my savings. Then I headed to the depot to see if there was any mail there from Jenny or Kurt and to send the letters in my saddlebag off to them. From there, I'd head over to our shack. Night should be falling by then, and Simon and Earl would likely be about, I thought.

It was disappointing to find that only two letters had arrived from Jenny and not surprising that there was but one from Kurt. I had a letter for him also, but I had decided to add another page to it, telling him about the accident I had had, which would surely be of interest to him. Being shot and escaping the Indian who had hunted me actually made me feel proud as I wrote it. I hoped that I wasn't so small a person that

I could actually feel proud of accidentally killing an innocent man. It was important to be sure to word the letter correctly so that Kurt would understand how remorseful and distraught I was over my actions, I determined.

Simon and Earl were already sacked out when I arrived at the cabin. After tying Spirit and Jingles to the hitching post, I curled up in my blanket in some thicket, up the hillside a bit, that smelled of pine bristles. The star-filled sky was so relaxing that I don't believe any thought had time to enter my head before I drifted off into sleep.

The sun had just begun to make an appearance when the smell of bacon on a skillet awakened me. I scurried on down the hillside. After stowing my blanket, I barged in on my old companions—hoping there was some extra grub to be had that would quell the rumbling in my stomach. As I stepped through the doorway, a rope lashed against the side of my head, dropped down over my shoulders, and pulled up tight against my midsection. At the same time, a blanket dropped over my head, blinding me to the surroundings.

"I've got me a polecat!" I heard Simon's voice announce as he tumbled me to the floor.

Immediately, there came another thud on top of him and Earl's voice. "Let's finish him off."

"Get off me you, guys. I've been shot!" I said, trying to convey the message in a serious tone—knowing that they would likely believe I was just trying to bluff my way back to freedom.

"And it's fitting that you should be," Simon said as he rose off me, lifting Earl and the blanket with him as he did. "Where ya hit then?" Simon asked, while looking me over.

"Get this off, and I'll show you," I said, straining at the rope that was still confining my arms to my body.

When he undid the noose, I pulled my shirt up some, and replied, "Dr. Hardin bandaged me clean round. I had an arrow stuck in my back." While phrasing these words, I reminded myself not to look for glory from the terrible death I had inflicted upon, as far as I knew, what had been an innocent person.

"Damn you really was shot," Earl said, surprised to find that I had not been bluffing.

"Yeah, sort of," I replied. "It was just one Indian—after me … for killing another one." I had a little trouble getting out that sentence.

"You killed an Injun?" Simon asked, his tone suddenly serious.

"It was an accident," I responded remorsefully.

"How'd you do it?" Earl snapped out, predictably.

I remembered the way Captain West had directed me to answer this question. But I wanted to hear myself express it the way it had really happened and hear the response I would get. Surely, there was no danger in telling these two, my friends, the truth. And so, I did.

After hearing my story, Simon said, "Sounds like you got even for the stage attack to me."

"No, I didn't," I replied, angered by this assumption. "I shot at the deer."

"That deer couldn't have dropped faster than a bullet flies. Whatever was in your sight when you pulled the trigger was what you shot at," Simon went on, exasperatingly.

"*I didn't mean to shoot him!*" I blurted out, enraged by Simon's analysis.

"Whatever—the good deed is done. That's what counts," Simon replied. His merry dismissal of this travesty was the same as Captain West's had been. Could they really be so coldhearted to another human being's death? Or were they just trying to help me dispel my guilt?

"Perhaps he was a gentle man who never hurt anyone," I suggested, trying not to sound meek.

"He would if he could. They're all savages." Simon's curt response answered my question as to his motivation; he actually believed he was paying me a compliment by crediting me with an Indian killing.

"Well I'm not proud of it," I said, reassured that I was not an Indian hater but not so sure that I had not pulled the trigger out of fearful self-preservation.

"What was the idea of the hostile welcoming I got here, anyway?" I asked.

"I saw your animals when I was heading out to the john," Earl replied. "Then found you sacked out on the hillside. So, we thought we'd surprise you with a welcome fitting to a hustler."

"So, I'm a hustler now too?"

"Don't take much effort to grow notorious in this part of the country, do it?" Earl replied.

"I give up. How'd I get this title?"

"That's right. You rode in at night. You didn't see all the cabins abandoned up here. You can pick one up for a song now. Folks have been pulling out left and right since the beginning of last month. It seems the streams have pretty much played themselves out. And Russell's Mining has been buying up most of the claims," Simon explained.

"We did all right though," Earl broke in, perhaps noticing that I had had my fill of guilt at the moment. "We got eight hundred dollars for our new claim."

"Russell's putting in a two-mile mining slough here. We're hiring on to wash the hillside as soon as another box gets operational. Maybe you'd want to work with us," Simon suggested. Pretty good bucks in it, and it's not as boring as rocking the cradle," he went on.

"I'm not really planning on spending much more time around here," I replied. "The doc says he needs to look after this for a week or so," I said, pointing at my wound. "After that, I intend to head on back to Saint Joe."

"Can't go no longer without getting a hold of that gal of yours, I suspect," Simon commented.

"That—and, just plain not wanting to be part of a country where you can't count on being alive on the following day."

"Well ain't that some rotten apples? If you hadn't come out here, you'd never of had the pleasure of hooking up with two real Texas cowboys," Earl said, hooking his thumbs through his belt loops and posing pompously.

"You know, you're right, Earl," I conceded. "You guys have been the best part of the trip, along with the grand landscape and herding critters. It's just that, now, I feel it's time for getting."

"It's time for getting the bacon out of the pan," Earl announced.

"And for getting it down my gullet," I replied.

"I thought you might be of that notion. There's plenty enough to fill you to the gills." Earl's words came as magic to my ears.

"Afterward, I've got to take some time to put toward my letter writing," I said, anxious to get to my next pleasurable activity. I wanted to tear into Jenny's letters almost as bad as into the slab of bacon Earl had thrown on the plate in front of me.

"You'll have the place to yourself for concentrating, soon as we finish eating," Simon said. "Earl and I have to head down to the claims to help with some wagon unloading."

"Maybe I'll get down there after I see the doc," I said.

"Better ask him what he thinks about you lifting—if you're planning on working," Simon suggested.

"Yes. Guess you're right. Maybe I'll just hang around. We'll see," I said, reflecting the confusion I had as to where my life would be heading from then on. Perhaps Jenny's letters would help, by giving me some confidence in my decision to leave.

When Simon and Earl headed down the valley, I got out my letters and brought out a chair to the roadside where the sun would brighten the pages and let me clearly view each word. Jenny's first letter was dated just two weeks after my leaving Saint Joe. It started:

Hi Ollie,

I'm missing you already. I check every day for a letter from you. I know you're lacking for conveniences and under trying circumstances out there, but do remember that my thoughts revolve around you.

We had a sign-up for Simpson on Tuesday. There are six of us enrolling. It felt good, just knowing that my name was being sent off to them. You know that boy, John English? He was one of those signing up. He wants to be a lawyer, like his father.

Would you believe he actually asked me to go to the prom with him? He had never said a word to me before he found out that I was going to Simpson, too. I guess I'll go with him, seeing how nobody else has asked me. It's not as if I'll actually be going "with" him. He'll just be accompanying me. I'm sure you understand how important it is for me to attend, even if it is not with the man that I love. Please keep me in your heart and do write often.

Love, Jenny

That clinched it. English was a scrawny and quiet sort of fellow that I'd never paid much attention to. He seemed to always have his head in a book, which is probably why he had to wear spectacles. He really didn't seem like a threat. Yet her attending with him would make Jenny seem more available to every other male at the prom, I thought. Although the prom had long since passed on my reading of her letter, having missed the event reinforced my decision that being out west was sheer foolishness on my part.

Jenny's next letter was postmarked July 15. So, it was over a month since she had written again—unless a letter had been lost en route, which was not unlikely with all the stage raids that were going on.

It began:

I got a letter from you a while ago. It was quite crumpled up, but I was still able to read it. I can't believe that your stage was actually attacked by Indians! That's terrible. I really don't think that it's safe, making the crossing with the Indians acting up the way that they've been.

It may not matter though. You may not want to come back after you've heard what I've got to tell you anyway. I'm dating John English now.

I stared at the words in something of a shock. Just like that, she had written them—without any prelude to warn of the impending disheartenment the forthcoming announcement would produce. The letter continued:

I found him to be surprisingly nice. He has his family carriage take us everywhere and always brings me flowers. His father recently built a large hotel on Charles Street. We went to a ball at their mansion house, and I wore a new gown that John had bought for me. He wouldn't let me wear my prom dress because he said, it was "too soon" to be seen in it again. Can you believe that?"

No. I couldn't believe any of this. Was my Jenny actually that shallow? Did she really feel that strongly about material things? The rest of the letter left me no doubt.

It went on:

"Ollie, you wouldn't believe the new world that is opening to me. I'm meeting people that are actually somebody. And I feel that, with going to college and all, I'm going to become somebody, myself. I can't tell you too much about it, but we actually helped some slaves make it to a freedom farm last week. When I get to college, I'm going to join political groups that are working to create a better America.

I know I must sound like a selfish tart to you, but, Ollie, you have to understand how excited I am—after believing all my life that I would be stuck on a farm, doing chores and raising kids.

I sincerely hope that life opens up new opportunities for you, too. Maybe it already has. One thing you can be sure of, I'll always have feelings for you.

Love, Jenny.

So, she's dating a rich bastard, I thought. *She doesn't want me to come back. Yet, she doesn't come right out and say so. She doesn't want to burn her bridges yet*, I determined—*in case things don't work out with him.*

And, what was with this nincompoop? True, Jenny was pretty, but there were other girls who were pretty and who were also rich, like him. I guessed that none of them wanted to get involved with a twerp like him.

He'd probably find one in college that would and throw Jenny over for her. I could go back to Saint Joe, knock his head off, and take her back.

But would I even want her now—knowing how unhappy a simple life with me would make her? She didn't seem to be the Jenny I loved anymore. Not with the values she had recently been revealing. If I hadn't come out here, I thought, I would have been able to keep her love. But would it have lasted throughout her college years and career life? Likely not—seeing now where her values actually lay. Yet, if I took Jenny out of my dreams, where would I be? I needed her love to give my life purpose. What I had to do was to get back there with wealth. And she would be running back to me. I'd return to her in a coach of my own—one of solid gold. Then, I'd decide if I still wanted her.

Starting a new letter to her, I wrote:

Jenny,

I just finished reading your letter. I have several letters here that I haven't had a chance to mail to you. But I have decided to burn them, instead. They really said nothing, except that I miss you and long to get back to you. They seem rather inappropriate now, since I don't expect to be returning to Saint Joe. That is, unless fortune has it that I can do so in the garb of a sophisticated gentleman—as it seems that such is all that is worthy of your acquaintance presently.

Not that it would have changed anything, but I would have gotten the letters off to you long past, were it not that we have been staying in the mountains, far from any civilization. It was just now that I came to be back in Nevada City and that only being for doctoring.

For, you see, I may not be going anywhere, unless the wound in my back decides to heal. It happened while I was hunting alone in the woods. An Injun jumped out in front of me, and I killed him with a ball through the chest. Unfortunately, he must have had a companion that lit out after me. For, shortly thereafter, I was shot in the back with an arrow, while on horseback, by another Injun that had followed me. A cavalry company that I crossed paths with had their medic remove the arrow and gave me some doctoring as we headed back here to Nevada.

Writing this, I hoped my story would be somewhat shocking to her, as repayment for the shocking revelation she had presented me with in her letter.

I continued:

> So it is that I'm laid up here a bit. But, if the wound heals clean, I'll be riding back up into the mountains to find my fortune.
>
> Seeing how circumstances are what they are, I won't be expecting to hear from you, from here on out. Perhaps it's just as well, since we really aren't geared up for letter writing out there, anyway.
>
> If I'm ever passing through them parts, I may stop by and check on you. I guess this is a good-bye. And, I say it with a very heavy heart—as you have been my reason for living and all my dreams to this very day. Farewell my Jenny. I'll always love you.

Ollie.

Kurt's letter was next. I opened it quickly, to get my mind off Jenny. I didn't want to contemplate the loss of her from my life any longer. It seemed unbearable, yet unchangeable. How could I contend with it rationally? All I could do was to divert my thoughts. I hoped that his letter might help do that.

Kurt was making two round-trip mail runs a week now out of Julesburg. So, his salary had increased from fifty to a hundred dollars a week, he explained. He wrote:

> I like making the runs, but the off days are murder. The women in these parts, for pleasing, are squaws that are not much more appealing than old Jingles.
>
> We've been encountering some Injuns on our runs from the start. It seems they like to ride alongside us, whooping, and then

cut across in front of us. Of course, we can't push our animals too hard, or they won't last out the run.

If they ever try passing me when I'm near my end station, I'll let my mount go all-out and see if they're willing to run their ponies to the ground. I heard that one rider had returned with an arrow stuck in each bag of his mochila. But at the range they were shooting from, the Injuns could have just as easily stuck the arrows in him, had they the notion.

Why don't you join up and keep me company down here? We can have some fun with riding contests and such. I've about had it with playing cards. I even got a hold of some books, just past, to pass some time by reading.

I'd take off from this job now, if it wasn't for the bonus they're offering us if we stick it out to the end—$1,000. They say the Express will be debunked as soon as the telegraph reaches San Francisco, a year from now. Between the bonus, and what I'll have accumulated by then, I might come up there and buy a gold mine for you and Pa.

How'd you like to see San Francisco? Maybe we'll get together and raise some hell out there, someday. Anyway, if you see some guys putting up telegraph poles, give them a hand. I wouldn't mind getting some letters to read. So send all you want. Give my love to Pa, for me.

Your kid brother, Kurt

I wrote another page and added it to the letter I had already written Kurt, telling him of my exploits, much more honestly than I had recanted them to Jenny. It was some difficult telling him about Jenny's letter. It shamed me some, to be thrown over by that bumpkin John English.

I concluded:

Why don't you come back and help me and Pa with the prospecting next spring? Crater Valley is some large for two men to try to pick out every few feet of. We'll be dropping down on ropes to do the upper faces, if necessary.

I'm not going to give up on Pa's dream. I'll see it out with him, even if it takes another year. I've really got it in my mind that, like Pa, I'm going to find that gold or die trying. It's come down to a matter of life or death. Wealth has, that is. Hope to see you soon.

Your big brother, Ollie

That *was* what I intended to do. For the first time, I understood Pa's obsession with making a bonanza strike. We do, indeed, need wealth to have a happy life. If I were wealthy, I'd be with Jenny, I thought, instead of her being with that dully English. The flowstone Pa had found came from somewhere in that valley, and I was going to find that source. There was no other consideration at that moment.

Riding back to the valley on Spirit appeared not to be a prudent thing to do, with the likelihood that the Indian who had stalked me would still be in wait. Since we had less than two months of prospecting left in the season, I would put Spirit in livery, I thought, and make the trip back with just Jingles.

If it wasn't for having stiches in my back, I would have started back at that very moment. But I was forced to stay in town for some time, waiting for the doc to finish with me. The weather was pleasant, and I enjoyed working and chatting with the Daltons. Still, my anxiety to return to the valley was reinforced with every thought of Jenny and the need to prove myself to her—I would! I'd find that treasure now, because I had to. From the start I had been chasing Pa's dream, but now I had my own determination and knew it would not be denied.

The determination of most of the prospectors dissolved over the course of the summer. They had arrived in even larger numbers that spring than they had in '59. They had spread out throughout the area surrounding the original diggings. But by the end of the summer, they were heading back in droves, ravaged by discouragement. Our efforts on the cliff faces had required much less time than we had anticipated, because most of the surfaces consisted of an impenetrable rock.

"Think we've done about all we can do," Pa said to me as he raised his rope ladder from the cliff.

"How about we just let our instincts guide us and let into wherever they point," I suggested, while untying my safety rope from a securely driven spike.

"There's only about two weeks left for us up here, anyway. There's no sense in going over ground that's already been picked. It's time to own up to the fact that I've been a fool," Pa said.

"That's not true! You know it's here somewhere," I responded, using my sledgehammer to bang out the spike, with more than the required ferocity.

"Our funds are running low, son. And I don't want to waste another year without earnings. If we go back now, we would still have enough money to set up a small shop," Pa replied, while untying his ladder from its tie down spikes.

"Where would we do that? These towns are dying now. Anyway, I'm not going back to Saint Joseph to face Jenny as a broken man. I'll keep trying on my own if I have to. I can get what I need to live on from the land. I'm not going back till I can be proud of what I am and what I've done."

"Ollie, I'm sorry I led you on this fool chase. I've always felt that, if I were a wealthy man, I wouldn't have lost your mother and that becoming wealthy would somehow bring back my happiness. I know that doesn't make any sense, but I suspect that the same is true for you. It doesn't make any sense to think that wealth will bring Jenny back to you, when she's chosen to be with someone else."

"I don't believe that, Pa," I said, angered by his assumption. And, without collapsing to the truthful element of his statement, I responded, "I'm not trying to get Jenny back. It's just that I've learned the value of having wealth now, just as you have in your life. And, we both know that it has to be right here—waiting for us. How can we give up now, Pa?" I asked, in a voice full of desperation.

"Perhaps, the Lord put that stone in my hand to lead me to dwell in this valley that is so full of His majesty—knowing, that in so doing, I would contemplate how unappreciative I have been of His blessings, of having your mother for the years that He had given her to me and of having the wonderful sons with which she left me."

"That doesn't mean that He wouldn't want us to make our lives better," I responded in rebuttal.

"We'll give it two more weeks then, Ollie," Pa conceded. "But if we don't come upon some promising ore after that, I'm going to start looking for a shop back in Denver. These hill towns might fold up, but the big mines will stay. And they will be in need of Denver as a hub. Besides, there is something clean and refreshing about the air in these mountains that I believe I can't do without now—now that I have the knowledge of it. Don't you agree, Ollie?"

"And sweeter still these mountains would be if we made a strike in them, Pa," I responded, using my youthful impertinence as a means of letting Pa know that I wasn't ready to concede to the dropping of our long-standing dream.

After tying our coiled ropes on Jingles, we began the ride back down to our valley camp. On the way down, I felt much more optimistic than I had in months about the possibility of our making that strike. Finally I could let my instincts lead me and strike out at any point in the valley, instead of following Pa's systematic plan of covering every section.

And so all the stronger was my feeling of desperation and despair as the two weeks passed with our continued lack of success. I even resorted to calling on my mother, in heaven, hoping that her love for me would transcend the void between us and bring me a sign as to the right spot to strike my pick. The realization that Pa might be right about giving up on our quest, made it even more agonizing to leave the valley.

But the agony that was awaiting us in town was even more excruciating.

17

REALITY DEFINED

Mountain City was mostly deserted when we rode in. it was surprising to see Simon and Earl's horses standing at the hitching rail beside the cabin. "I'll bet they hit a big one, Pa," I said, after spotting their mounts. "There's no way they'd still be here, if they hadn't—not with that long haul back to Texas in front of them. They must be pulling out too much to give up the last few days before the snows set in."

The sullen expression on Simon's face on seeing me in the doorway contrasted so harshly with the joyful expression I was wearing that we were momentarily left at a loss for words.

"The marshal said to set them down and get them a drink before saying anything," I heard Earl say from within the cabin, to Simon's rear.

"Simon, Earl, what is it you've got to tell us?" Pa demanded, his voice issuing concern as he stepped into the cabin in front of me.

"We were fixing to leave last week," Simon said. "But we decided to wait till you got back. We thought it'd be better—you hearing it from Kurt's friends, than from the marshal.

"Is he dead?" Pa blurted out, before I had any idea of what was being said.

"It was Injuns." Earl spouted out these words as if he had been choking on them since being assigned the gruesome responsibility of relating them to us.

I saw Pa take a short step forward and then sink slightly on bent knees. He straightened back up, swung around, and lunged out of the cabin door.

As I turned and started to follow, realizing, shockingly, what was being said, Simon grabbed me by the shoulder while shaking his head no, to indicate that I shouldn't follow Pa. Not knowing what to do or say, I had to rely on Simon's advice. Stepping back into the cabin, I dropped into a chair, numb to my own actions. I had lost my brother forever. There'd be no trip to California, no more wrestling with him, no more racing or vying for the correct reaction to life's challenges. I had lost my brother forever. How could this be a reality?

I had never contemplated the possibility of having Kurt totally removed from my life. And what of his planning and dreaming of the reward he would be receiving for the effort he was making? They were gone, as if they had never happened. The finality of a person's life, at death, came to me at that moment—my first realization of life's fragility. Then there came the pain and sorrowing over Kurt's lost future. Knowing that I couldn't deal with this in front of the Daltons, I drove my attention back to Simon, before the tears had a chance of overflowing the swelling in my eyes and asked, "Do you know how it happened?"

"There's a letter here from the Pony Express Agency. About all we know of it is that he was making a run and didn't show up at the next station. They found him a short ways back from it, struck in the head by a tomahawk. They didn't find his horse. I'm sorry, Ollie," Simon said, more sorrowfully than I would have thought him being open to revealing, as he handed me the envelope he'd received from the marshal.

To the kin of Kurt Swenson:

It is with extreme sorrow that we must inform you of the death of Kurt Swenson. He was struck down by an Indian tomahawk while making a delivery in the service of our company.

To maintain the sanctity of his remains, and in the absence of available family members, we took the responsibility of having his body interned at the Julesburg Christian Cemetery, under the auspices of the Honorable Reverend James Townsend.

Please be aware that it is with the obligation gratitude demands that our hearts are concerned over your well-being. Kurt is the only rider we have had killed to date in our service. And it is a situation we have hoped would never arise. Our appreciation for the courage that all our riders display in our service and in that of our expanding nation is impossible to express.

We have, in our humble efforts of concern, arranged for plots to be maintained beside Kurt, for his listed next of kin to avail themselves of upon their passing. Those have been registered in the names of Olof Swenson Senior, father, and Olof Swenson Junior, brother.

Also, we have enclosed a check, payable to Olof Swenson Senior, for the amount of $1,100. This money is pay that is due to your son, as well as a bonus he was to collect at the upcoming dissolving of our company. We know that Kurt intended to continue with us until that end. Therefore, we decided that it would be just to have his kin receive that bonus now.

Also be informed that Kurt has a savings established at the Julesburg National Bank, with the names of Olof Swenson Senior and Junior as beneficiaries. Please contact the bank for information.

Finally, I want to express my personal sorrow and grievance over your loss and to let you know that I will be available to aid you in any way that I can, to help overcome the difficulties your loss may impose.

Very sincerely yours,
Elias Harper
Manager, Pony Express, Western Districts

Simon and Earl had stepped out of the cabin as I read, and Pa was standing beside me as I finished.

"Let me read it, Ollie," he said sullenly, reaching for the letter.

I only glanced at him slightly as I handed him the letter, not wanting to engage him in a meeting of our sorrows, lest we both might be overcome by weakness. He read for a moment and then turned away, gasping silently.

After finishing the letter, he spoke quietly, without looking at me. "I've let down another one. First you mother. Now Kurt. My failure meant their deaths."

"You're not the blame, Pa," I replied in sincere disagreement.

"If I'd been a good provider, I would have been able to keep your mother away from the plague. If I had wealth, Kurt wouldn't have been out there trying to earn a bonus by riding through wilderness territory. No, it's true, Ollie. It's my fault that we've lost them," he said, turning toward me as he finished with reddened eyes, flushed by tears.

"How can you know what fate we would have had if we had wealth, Pa? You always tell me God's will, will be done. And I believe you. If it's God's will that we should be punished, then I'm the one that brought it on us. It was the Injun I killed. I pulled the trigger on him, not the deer! It was my fear of confronting an Injun that caused me to shoot him. I acted out of weakness. The Injun that shot me was probably *his* brother. Now I'm being repaid for the grief that I brought onto him—by God's justice." Expressing these thoughts as they occurred to me, a truth had revealed itself.

"That wasn't fear. That was your natural, instinctive response toward self-preservation," Pa said after a moment of thought. "Men are not responsible for their instinctive reactions. Kurt's death had nothing to do with you, Ollie. If God is punishing someone, it's me—caused by the lack of appreciation I have shown for the wonderful family that he blessed me with."

Recognizing the depth of pain and the confusion Pa was experiencing, I said, "Let's not, either of us blame ourselves then, Pa. Can you agree? I don't know how we can get through this if we continue to."

"You're right, Ollie. We have to accept God's lot and be grateful for each day that we are blessed with His providence."

"Amen," I said, and he echoed it back.

Still, I felt in my heart that the words I had uttered, about my weakness, were sent by Him, to bring me to an awareness of my failing. And, Pa, I was sure, was no more relieved of his failing than I was of mine.

"Yeah!" I called out, recognizing the coded knock on the door that broke the silence as being that of the Daltons.

"Ollie, Mr. Swenson, we're sorry to be intruding, but we got to get a start out, so we can make it down to Blackhawk before nightfall."

"No need to apologize, Simon," Pa said, through a little choking of his voice. "It was real thoughtful of the two of you to wait these extra days for us. That's more than a man could expect from another, knowing how important it is that you should clear the mountains before the snows set in."

"Well, another reason we waited was to let you know that the money we owed you for the cabin was being held for you at the bank," Simon informed us.

"I don't aim to hold you boys to that purchase," Pa replied. "I know these fields are drying up. If you don't return, I would feel I had taken advantage of you."

"No," Earl replied. "We have to come back, to be able to put up the rest of the money for our ranch and herd. We will still be in need of the cabin," he said emphatically.

"Actually, we did quite well up here this season," Simon explained. "Russell's been paying us well. And on our days off, we've been bringing in some good color at the creek, by going deep for it. Instead of blowing our dough, we've been setting it aside—like you do, Ollie. We're planning on getting a nice spread in a year or two and becoming bona fide cattlemen."

"Good for you," Pa exclaimed. "A person needs to have a dream to keep him going in this world."

I wondered if Pa was thinking what I was—that it had actually been over a year since we had saved a red cent.

"We'll just grab our bags then and be on our way," Simon said, grabbing up two duffel bags from the bed and handing one to Earl. "Again, we can't say enough how sorry we are about Kurt. That was about as terrible a message as you can hand to your friends."

"Keep a strong faith," Earl added.

"We'll see you next spring then," I said during our farewell handshake.

Pa turned to me with a cross expression but did not comment as we stepped out of the cabin and watched the Dalton brothers ride off.

"You shouldn't have said that, about seeing them next spring," Pa said when they were out of earshot.

"But Pa—we have money now—between Kurt's earnings and what they paid us for the cabin."

"That's not it," Pa replied harshly. "I'm not taking a chance on losing you too. I've been a damned fool. Not anymore! We're heading out of here at daybreak—for good. We're going to head over to the bank, before they close, and get what we've got coming to us, so we will be ready to let out at first light." His expression left no doubt that discussion of the matter was out of the question.

While Pa headed into the bank, I headed over to the mail office to look for a letter from Jenny. There was none.

The letter I was handed shocked me. I had been trying to convince myself that I'd never be able to talk to Kurt again, and there, right in my hand, were his words.

When Pa came out of the bank, he found me sitting on the road step, staring at the names on the envelope. "It's from Kurt, "I said. "Should we read it back at the cabin?"

"No. Why wait? These will be the last words we'll ever hear from him. I'll take no chance on them losing their way to my ears," Pa said as he sat down on the step beside me.

I was surprised to see "Pa" included in Kurt's salutation. He always addressed his letters to me, expecting I'd receive them and repeat his comments to Pa. It was almost as if Kurt had envisioned the setting this letter would be read in. I read:

Hi, Pa and Ollie,

I'm still sticking out my time at the Julesburg leg of the express. If it wasn't for the bonus offer, I suspect I'd be back with you all in the mountains.

I suspected that these words would add painfully to Pa's feeling of guilt over bringing us out West, but they were Kurt's last to us, and they had to be aired as written. I continued reading:

So, I'm still enjoying making the runs. I especially like trying to dust off the Injun braves when they come a yelping down beside me. I'm planning on bringing a lariat on my next run and showing them a bit of roping. Maybe I can land one of them on the seat of his pants. I'll let you know how it goes.

I've got to apologize to you, Pa. I've, kind of, been hoping that you haven't found that bonanza yet. I want to be the one responsible for the discovery. How would this sound—"Kurt's Gulch"? Not quite melodious, is it? I think I know why.

Pa, didn't you say that that the mountains were formed during a time of violent, explosive eruptions? Why did the stone have to come from the hills above the valley then? Couldn't it have blown up there from down below? Perhaps the pass was formed from a giant bang. "Kurt's Pass"—now that has a good sound.

They're saying it may be as long as a year more before the telegraph reaches California and we get discharged. So I'm sure you'll be back in the hills before I join you. You have my permission to use my insight and let into the pass, if you think I might be onto something. But, the Kurt's Pass thing stays. Find it!

Love, Kurt

So, it wasn't the will of the Lord at work at all. It was the childlike naivety of a spirited youth, bringing down the wrath of one or more prideful Injuns, who, most likely, Kurt had directly humiliated. This letter was a going away present from Kurt, I thought. It released Pa and me from the lifetime of guilt we were prone to enduring—guilt over believing that the Lord had taken him from us as a punishment for our faithlessness.

"What do you think, Ollie?" Pa asked. "It's as though he wrote us this letter as a going away gift," he continued, answering his own question and echoing my own thoughts.

I told Pa of my agreement.

"Indeed, then it must be so. He's telling us where it is. Don't you agree, Ollie?" Pa asked.

Concurring being appropriate considering the context of the letter, I nodded in agreement.

Through the course of the winter, we had no more discussions as to whether we should stay or leave—only on what plan of attack on the pass we should employ. We spent the winter in Denver, after a trip to visit Kurt's grave in Julesburg. We found three stones there of the same appearance, aligned beneath a cottonwood to the side of a church. Pa's and mine, to its right, were marked only with our names. Kurt's, to the right of mine, was the same except for stating a date of birth and death. The headstones made the anomaly quite clear.

The line marked, "Died," should have been filled in from left to right as the stones were arranged—not from right to left. For the first time since hearing of Kurt's death, I was struck by how badly he had been cheated. Up till then, I had only been dealing with how my life would be changed and how I would be deprived of his company. That I could handle. But the thought of Kurt's entire future having been denied him, I found to be unbearable. Kneeling beside his headstone, I collapsed in grief against it and wept uncontrollably.

"It's okay, Ollie," Pa said, placing a hand on my shoulder.

"But, Pa, he's been robbed of everything."

"That's not so," Pa replied in condolence. "He had already experienced near to everything pleasurable that I have in all my years. He's tasted the same foods, had the love of a family and the pleasure of a woman. He also enjoyed the wonders of this country that God has gifted us with. Kurt took life as it came, unquestioningly, and had the pleasure of accepting his place in it. After all, Ollie, in relationship to history, all of us are in this world but for the flicker of an eye. Kurt was, and we will be. Just remember him with love. That's all that any man can ask of the world—to be remembered with love, as we will remember Kurt."

"Excuse me," a voice intervened. It was coming from a man of the cloth, carrying a bag, who was approaching from the direction of the church. "I'm Reverend James Townsend. Might you be the kin of the departed?"

"Yes, we are his family," Pa replied.

"I was given the keeping of his belongings," the reverend declared. "They are in this mail sack."

"Much obliged," Pa responded, taking the sack and examining its contents.

In Kurt's well-worn wallet, there was a photo of the three of us in front of our bakery and a very faded portrait of Ma. Much to my surprise, there was also a photograph of what appeared to be a somewhat pregnant Brenda Stimpson. Besides these items, there were just clothing, camping, eating, and shaving items. We returned the contents to the bag for packing back, thanked the reverend again, and took our leave.

While I had been in Saint Joseph the previous winter, Pa had introduced Kurt to a new pleasure in life, one that I had yet to experience. It was called "snowshoe racing." Kurt had written to me about it with great enthusiasm. I had dismissed it at the time as sounding like a trivial pastime entertainment. Sliding down a hill with boards attached to your feet could certainly not compare to our horse racing. Pa, like most of the Scandinavian emigrants, was familiar with using snowshoes to get around when winter snows defeated all other means of traveling. In the mountains, mail was often delivered by this means. Some mountain men managed to remain hillside clean through the winter using snowshoes to get back and forth to town for supplies. Back in Denver, I found out why Kurt's enthusiasm had been spawned.

For racing, snowshoes were made of half-inch thick boards, four inches wide and a full twelve feet long. We lined up horizontally at the top of a clear section of snow-laden, mountain slope. Using long, thick poles to aid in our descent, we slid down at an incredible speed. To one end of the pole was affixed a basket. These devices were useful in helping us attain speed on start off. They were also used, even more frequently, as props to lean against when up-righting ourselves, after taking one of the plummets we inevitably enjoyed. The briskness of the sport was such that, even on the coldest winter days, I found myself loosening my garments.

By midwinter, large numbers of visitors were arriving to take part in this extraordinary pastime, and to my pleasure, many of them were young females. The women formed their own racing teams and raced both against themselves and against the menfolk. I found myself at liberty to make as many acquaintances with lady folk as I had a liking to—a situation quite new and contenting to my ego. Yet, although I did become intimately involved with several women that winter, my heart remained controlled by the thought of Jenny. Indeed, in every encounter, Jenny was a non-divulged participant. That winter turned out to be one of the most pleasurable periods of my life thanks to this, seemingly trivial, pastime.

My only regret was that Kurt was not there to share my experiences with. It was, however, good to know that he had had the knowledge of the exhilaration of this sport. As pleasurable as the winter had been, I was anxious to return to the mountains again—sure now that Canyon Pass, or Kurt's Pass as I had become determined to rename it, would be the source of reward we would receive for the years of toil and sacrifice that we had expended.

Prospecting the pass was strange after spending so much time in Crater Valley. Travelers passed through at a distance in the valley, but here they were all within clear view and often within earshot. In all the time we had spent in the valley, I had never noticed a single prospector setting an axe to a wall of the pass. Somehow, it didn't seem like a place for prospecting, but more like a hallway, meant only to be traversed as a connection between legitimate prospecting places. So it must have been for all the passersby, as they all seemed to want to address us and inquire as to our activity. Some were a pleasant distraction and quite enjoyable to exchange experiences and aspirations with, while others became quite annoying and impolite in their nosiness.

One such encounter was with a pair of supposed prospectors who were quite insistent on knowing all the details of our prospecting activities, as well as our motivation for working the pass. After they left, Pa pointed out to me that their picks and shovels were still wearing store-bought edges and their canteens had no markings from ever haven been scraped against a hard surface. "They're looking for a way to capitalize off the toils of others," he explained. "They may be looking to buy, steal, or bamboozle the success of anyone foolish enough to negotiate with them. Their kind is best treated with insincerity, since an honest discourse would give them an insight as to your vulnerability." This explained why Pa had been so negative as he'd conversed with the pair when it came to describing his expectations toward the possibility of our achieving any success by working in the pass.

Still, I suspected that Pa's, like my own, initial enthusiasm was somewhat abated after what had been two weeks of working the valley. We had thus far concentrated on the easy, ground level prominences, but that would be changing in a few days. From that point on, we would have to do our picking from rope ladders, as the walls of the pass rose nearly vertical from its floor.

Recalling that, on passing through the diggings, I had found that Simon and Earl had not yet returned. And contemplating on how some friendly companionship might revive my flailing spirit before setting to the hard toil forthcoming, I decided to propose to Pa my taking a trip back to Nevada for a short visit—assuming that they would surely have arrived since our passing. "I could easily make the round trip inside of three days on Spirit and be back before we need to start using ropes again," I suggested.

"Have you forgotten that there still may be an Injun out there looking for a brown and white Paint?" was Pa's reply.

I had been going into neighboring areas again, looking for game, but this would be my first lone, long-distance excursion since our return. At that point, I realized, I had become oblivious to the Indian threat. "I'll stick to the main trail and keep my eyes open," I assured Pa.

"I'd rather you didn't go, but a man makes his own decisions," he replied.

Although I was glad to have Pa's approval, I was somewhat distraught by the realization that Kurt's death seemed to have defined the end of my youth, to both Pa and me.

18

NORTHERN AND SOUTHERN ALLIANCES

A noticeable relief came over me upon reaching the outskirts and safety of Nevada City. Pa's warning had revived my concern over the Indian encounter I had experienced. That concern seemed now to be more over my own safety than over guilt for having pulled the trigger on the brave as it originally had been. Perhaps, if I had not shot him, I may have had a tomahawk embedded in my chest in the second that followed, I rationalized. Who knows how he would have reacted, if he had had time to react. Then, remembering that the brave was only carrying a knife, I revised my recreation of the event. Kurt being murdered had definitely had an effect on my thinking, I thought.

The town looked surprisingly inactive as I approached. Indeed, there had been much more activity on the street when Pa and I had passed through it on our way out. It seemed more what I would have expected had it been the end of the season. There were but a few wagons and carts in the street. But some activity in the center of the street was generating dust in the air and apparently attracting onlookers. I soon discerned it to be a ruckus in front of the saloon—not an uncommon event in Nevada. On closer observance, I saw there were six men involved in the brawl. One man had his arms and legs flaying wildly in an attempt to hold off two attackers. Another was being held behind the head with his arms stretched up behind him by one assailant, while another punched him brutally about the midsection. This turned out to be Earl, and Simon was the flayer on the ground. Galloping to their aid, I slid off Spirit and onto Earl's assailant. My assault didn't seem to daunt his hostility, as he managed to twist around and sock me squarely in the mouth while we tumbled to the ground.

"I'll kill you, rebel," I heard him angrily utter as our shoulders struck the dry, hard roadway. He was turning from me, while trying to rise as I struck him a blow to the side of the head with my left fist. Then I wrapped my right arm around his head, and entrapped his midsection between my legs. My right forearm went across his throat while my upper arm was forcing his head down against it from behind. There was no doubt that continued pressure would result in his strangulation. Relaxing my grip, I again heard him utter his ominous threat.

Simon and Earl were now to my rear. Knowing they were still dealing with three assailants, I couldn't expect any assistance from them. Indeed, one of the other assailants was likely to come to the aid of the one I had temporarily demobilized. Certainly, I couldn't expect to hold him in this fashion until the situation resolved itself. I contemplated snapping his head quickly back and to the side, which I suspected would probably break his neck, removing him from the situation immediately. But I had to wonder if I really wanted to kill a person I didn't even have a quarrel with.

Deciding against that, I released him. But, not wanting to be left in the compromised position of lying flat on my back at his feet, I kicked out at him with both feet as he rose. Unfortunately, he stepped quickly backward, avoiding my feet totally as they kicked blindly into the air—somewhat as Jingles did when her backside was threatened. Then, realizing I was totally vulnerable to being kicked, I tried to rise quickly. But, before I could straighten up, my head was struck several times on both sides by his fists. Hands that came around my throat from behind were pressing my windpipe closed. On occasion, previously, I had wondered if I could use my neck muscles to withstand such a grip—I couldn't!

To make things worse, having my air cut off seemed to weaken my struggling efforts, leaving me quite helpless. At the point where I realized that, unless I was rescued, I would surely be killed, two gunshots sounded beside me, and a voice commanded, "That's enough!"

Looking up from my kneeling position, I saw the marshal. At that instant, the grasp around my neck released.

"There'll be time enough for that a coming," the marshal said as he proceeded down the street, confident that our brawling had concluded or with a lack for concern if it had not.

As we were dusting ourselves off, I heard one of their group mumble, "Rebel bastards."

Simon took a step toward him, but I grabbed him by the shoulder. As he turned to look at me, I saw fire in his eyes and the muscles of his face bulging with strain. As he looked into my face, his countenance changed.

"What happened to you?" he asked, a smile replacing the snarl of a moment earlier.

"That guy beat me up," I responded, pointing to the group walking toward the saloon door. I tasted blood in my mouth and felt a swelling in my cheekbones that I knew from experience would result in blackened eye sockets.

Turning, Simon looked at the group going into the saloon. "I'm not going back in there," he said. "I don't want to get killed unless I do it with the Confederate Army blowing away Yanks," he said, still staring at the saloon doors as if he were visualizing the enemy on the other side.

"What happened?" I asked, realizing that there were some important, underlying agitations responsible for these hostilities.

"One of them Yanks told me that, I'd better stay here, where I'd be safe, while the Yank Army walks through the South and lets the niggers give us back the whippings we've been handing out to them. I let him know that they'd find themselves planting in a tobacco field if they ever set foot over the Virginia line." Simon's anger was obviously returning as he recanted the conversation. "I'm going to see to it that that happens, too!" he barked.

"And I beside you," Earl piped in.

"Hey, don't forget, I've been in the mountains. What's all this talk about war?" I asked.

"The Yanks are trying to blockade all our ports," Earl explained.

"Virginia seceded from the Union last week, becoming the eighth state in the Confederacy. And the rest of the Southern states are expected to do the same shortly," Simon added. "The Yanks started it by sending warships to Fort Sumter," he continued, "instead of abandoning the fort as they should have. We weren't going to let them build up their forces in the middle of Charleston Harbor. So, we took them on—right then and there. There's no doubt that Lincoln will try to stop the succession. And we're ready to give them a whooping. Once the Yanks see that we're not going to let them take control of our properties without a fight to the death, they'll be hightailing it back north for sure."

"You really think the American government would send troops out to kill other Americans?" I asked, rather taken aback by the shocking developments I was currently learning of.

"They were ready to shoot it out with Young and his Mormons just a few years back, when Young tried to employ sovereignty in Utah territory," Simon reminded me. "Earl and I are heading to the bank and then to the general store for supplies," Simon said as we mounted our horses.

"That's the same route I'd be planning too, before going on a hunt for you all," I replied.

"Joining us at the cabin for a bit then, will you be?" Earl asked, in a manner suggestive of anticipated approval.

"That's mainly what brought me to town. I love my Pa, but sometimes I get the urge to see some other faces—ugly as they might be."

"And, maybe an urge to visit Maria over in the Sundown," Simon suggested, referring to a brothel gal down in Central City.

"Yes, maybe that too," I replied, joining the brothers in a short chuckle. That was much easier than trying to explain how I actually felt about prostitutes, an opinion that hadn't changed over the years.

It was hard not revealing the existence of Pa's flowstone to the Daltons as we made our way around town together. As they discussed their prospecting successes, the only explanation I could give for our persistence in working the pass was to attribute it to a hunch of Pa's. This seemed like a lame motivation for our persistence. It also irked me to be put in the position of having to offer a lie to my friends, but I had to uphold the promise of secrecy I had made to Pa.

Our conversation of the war did not return until we had settled in at the cabin.

"You came back at exactly the right time," Simon said, bringing a deck of cards and a bottle of whiskey to the table.

"We're heading south at the end of the week," Earl chimed in. "We'll be signing up for the eleven-dollar-a-month army payroll check, soon as we reach San Antonio."

"I don't believe you're talking about going to war, just like that. Maybe the thing will be talked out before you even get down to Texas," I suggested.

"No way. It's been a long time coming, but now it's come to a head," Simon said. "All the officers pulled out of the Union Army already, heading back to their home states to enlist with the Confederacy."

"And the Union troops were pulled east to add to the invading force," Earl added.

"So you're telling me that half the country is going to shoot it out with the other half? And over what—whether they can own niggers or not in the free territories? That seems a little loco, doesn't it?" I asked.

"Lincoln says the nation can't exist with states having different slavery laws, and he's been trying to abolish it everywhere," Simon stated somewhat angrily, before slugging down a large gulp of whiskey. "You know what's been going on down south. Abolitionists have been coming down and stealing slaves right off the plantation fields."

"And they'll shoot people down to do it, too," Earl stated, more excitedly then was natural to him.

"The problem is, Lincoln gives them sanctuary when they get north," Simon continued to explain. "The courts ruled against that when that Scott nigger was returned, years back, but the law isn't being upheld by the Republicans. Our whole economy depends upon the plantations. And Lincoln wants to destroy them, so the Northern industrialists can have control of the nation," Simon went on. "They're changing the constitution to fit their economy and expect us to remain a part of their Union. They built their cities with indentured servants. That wasn't any different than slavery—sometimes worse," he concluded.

"I don't see why they can't just let the Confederacy secede," I said. "Who's to say that they have to stay with the Union?"

"Lincoln!" Simon answered sharply, his answer seemingly identifying the source of the South's problems.

"Ain't been but a few years that Texas has been a part of the damned Union, and better off we were afore joining it," Earl added heatedly.

"You're shuffling those cards to death," I said to Simon, before I wet my lips with the devil's spirit, as Pa referred to alcohol.

"Five-card draw," Simon stated as he started dealing out our first hand. "You're right. Let's enjoy the game and save our hatred for the Yanks."

The impudence of the Daltons nearly sent me through the roof. They were giving no consideration, at all, to my position on these events. As a Missourian, which I considered myself to be, I was actually a member of the Union. They seemed to assume that I would naturally be in agreement with the South, since Missouri was in support of slavery. But I did not want to open a dispute on the subject.

Yet I didn't want to feel that I was cowering under their resolve. "Doesn't it seem that the nation might be more benefited by staying together?" I asked, reviving my bravado.

"Ain't gonna happen," Simon responded.

"But, Simon, if all it would take was to end slavery to resolve the dispute, perhaps the slavers could be paid a retribution by the government for the money they spent in purchasing their slaves," I suggested. "And perhaps even some assistance in changing the plantations over to become employee operated. There are plenty of Southerners, like you, who don't own slaves. Is it fair to ask all Southerners to defend the practice?"

"Pick up your cards," Simon commanded. "That doesn't mean anything. It isn't the slavery question that's important. The question is, can the Northerners use the government to impose their will on us? Do you think that's right?" he asked.

"Two bits and two cards," I said, using the game as a means to gain some thinking time.

"You must have caught on the deal," Earl replied. "But, I'm in."

"I'll do you one better," Simon said, tossing in an extra two-bit piece.

"Call you," I replied, becoming some worried about the card game by his raise.

"Me too. Give me three," Earl replied.

"And, I'll play these," Simon said, a small grin crossing his face as he did. "You didn't answer my question, Ollie."

"No, I don't think that it's right. But I don't think you should take going to war over it too lightly. The North has a lot more men than the South does." I replied with what I believed—not being able to come up with anything more enlightening.

"Well, you can bet those tenderbellies won't fight like we will," Simon replied in a voice lacking tonally of concern as he dealt out our draw cards.

"Yahoo," Earl exclaimed on picking up his new cards.

"I pass," Simon said, frowning and shaking his head as he stared at Earl's smiling countenance.

"I'll bet a dollar!" Earl shouted.

"I'm out," I responded.

"Who'd you expect to stay in when you act like you just struck a hit on pay dirt?" Simon asked Earl as he also tossed his cards into the discard pile.

"Four kings on the first hand! Can you believe it?" Earl asked, proudly displaying his cards.

"Yeah and I had a pat straight," Simon replied.

"And I came out low, with three jacks up," I added. "You never can tell how the cards will fall."

Simon just grunted. Earl's luck outlasted the booze, and we all found it easy to drop off solidly into sleep.

The next morning, the thing that worried me most about the prior night's conversation was learning of the army's departure from the territories. How safe would we be in the mountains once the Indians had realized that the army had gone? And Pa was out there alone. Instead of sticking it out till the end of the week with the Daltons, as I had planned, I decided to say my adieus, pick up some extra supplies, and then head out. Simon said that we could feel free to use the cabin at our liking—for which I thanked him. If I thought it would have served any purpose to plead with them not to enlist, I would have. But I realized that that would be like asking them to show cowardice. For in their eyes, and, I suspected, in the eyes of all Confederates, they were being bullied by the American government.

"I hope we'll see you guys up here again next spring," was all I decided to say as a farewell.

"You will, if you're here," Simon replied.

"If we don't hit on something big before the weather breaks, I don't suspect we'll be back up here again. But you'll probably find us if you pass through Denver," I replied.

"Just don't go joining up with the Union Army," Earl commented. "I don't want to have to shoot at any person that I'm friends with."

His remark made me chuckle a bit as I responded, "Don't worry. That'd be the last thing I'd be planning on doing. You guys take care of yourselves, you hear," I told them as they turned to ride off.

"Aim to," Simon replied in a confident tone.

"So long, Ollie," Earl called back as they rode off.

I wondered if that would be the last I'd ever see of the Daltons. And I hoped that it wouldn't be.

19

THE FINAL INSULT

Not long after starting back, I saw a group of Indian braves on the hillside. My instinct was to break into a gallop and put some distance between us. But I realized that they'd catch up to me before I could get back to our camp if they wanted to. And I really didn't want to put Pa in danger also. So I resisted the impulse and reacted in a manner more favorable to Spirit's well-being—that being to continue at my present, relaxed trot.

As I approached camp and saw Pa's familiar, pick-wielding form, silhouetted against the canyon wall, I said a short prayer of thanks.

"Back already?" he called out as I approached.

"Don't know if it's safe for us up here now, Pa," I replied. "The army's been pulled east, to prepare for a Union war against the Confederate states. The Injuns might find this to be an opportunity to start more attacks."

"That's not likely, son. Most of the Injuns in this area now rely on trading with the whites for their necessities. They wouldn't be looking to endanger that relationship. When the hunting tribes return for winter shelter, things could get hairy, though. They're not as dependent on us—and not as in acceptance of our presence."

"Maybe we ought to get out a little earlier this fall," I suggested.

"Gladly, if you'd get down here and pull the cover off that vane of gold for me," Pa said in jest.

"I'll tell you what. A cup of java, and you have a deal," I replied, noticing steam rising from the coffeepot in the pit at his side.

"You're in luck," he said as he dropped his pick and started toward the pot. "Now what's this talk of war all about?"

As we used our hardtack to sop up coffee, I filled him in on the events I had learned of from the Daltons.

"This could be the makings of a great tragedy," Pa responded on hearing all of the details. "I'd say it's a good time to be up here, in the splendor of these mountains. Let them folks fight it out to their liking, down below and we'll saunter down from here when the smoke clears."

"Seriously, Pa, could men actually kill each other over what would appear to be a negotiable matter?"

"I don't see any way that it can be avoided at this point. The question is, how long will it take for the South to surrender?"

"You talk like the South doesn't have a chance," I said questioningly.

"Well, the Union has more resources. They've got more available troops. They've got factories that can produce the required arms and foreign business connections that can bring in added support."

"But how hard will they want to fight? Certainly not as hard as men whose homes and way of life are under attack?"

"Soldiers fight on the command of their officers and out of loyalty to their comrades. They don't need any further motivation," Pa explained.

Sipping my coffee, I contemplated Pa's words. He was right. War was coming. Quietly, I said to him, "I know we're not to question the Lord's ways, but how can He be just if He lets war exist at all?" I asked, expressing my frustration.

"Some have also asked how a just Lord can tolerate slavery," Pa responded.

"And, why does He then?" I asked.

"Perhaps He wanted a sampling of all mankind to make up the populous of this vast and diversified continent. Sometimes, I suspect that He may have purposefully created this land to be developed in His name, and to His liking."

"But, Pa, between the Spanish and the British, the wars and the plagues, there's been nothing but killing and death to be found here as far as I can see."

"Apparently, the Lord's love is not as much for man as it is for mankind. Perhaps your mother and brother know the explanation for this dilemma. I don't. All I know is that life is to be treasured by the living."

"Do you think Kurt's dying served a purpose to the Lord?" I asked.

"I'm sure of it. I couldn't venture a guess as to what that purpose might be. But, whenever death occurs, it is with His knowledge and, therefore, through His will—as all things are."

"Kurt said the gold is here, in this pass," I said, remembering his last words to us that he had written in his letter.

"And so it is," Pa acknowledged. Let's get about finding it then," he continued as he finished his coffee and rose to his feet.

"You're on," I responded, taking up my pick and joining him, again anxious to get on with our quest.

In some way, this conversation with Pa left me feeling a little better about death. Since the Lord did, indeed, love all of mankind, which can obviously be seen through the providence of all our necessities on this earth, then his disregard for the individual life served as a conclusive proof of an afterlife. He must know that our individuality on earth is inconsequential, or He'd never permit the injustices life inflicts on so many. This was a reassuring realization. I wondered how long it had taken Pa to make this connection and whether he had had someone to rely on for insight, like I had him.

By the end of August, my anxiety for our quest had become as dry as the canyon floor. We had thoroughly excavated from the valley, down the right side of the canyon to its entrance, and three-fourths of the way back on its left side, without finding more than a few specks of the elusive metal. We had less than a month before the snows would drive us out again, but that would be enough time to allow us to complete the rest of the canyon.

"Too bad we hadn't started on this side of the canyon first," Pa said to me one night as we turned in.

"What's it matter, then we'd be over there right now," I replied, pointing straight across the canyon, aware of the implication of my response.

"So you've given up then," Pa said calmly.

"I have to say, I'm having trouble rallying myself to the task of late, Pa."

"That's quite understandable at this point, son. But don't be of the mind that we cannot still find ourselves to be successful?"

"And, if we're not—after years of trying. How can we deal with that?"

"Dealing with trying and failing is not hard at all, son. What's hard is dealing with not having tried." He stared at me with those words—the way he did when he wanted to be sure that I had embraced his concept. "And no matter how it goes, we'll still have had the pleasure of these mountains. That's a pleasure few ever get to experience."

"I can't wait till snowshoeing starts again," I told Pa, actually anxious to once again be in the company of females. My fantasizing seemed to always go back to Jenny—a fact that made me feel like quite the fool— since I knew that my plan of a life with her was never going to be.

"We're about out of game again," Pa said. "Why don't you take the day tomorrow and see what you can do about that problem?" Pa knew how to bring my spirit back up. Riding in the hills always did it. "And take Flash this time," Pa added. "Give him a little treat too."

"That sounds good, Pa. I'll head out at first light and see what else is up and about."

In the morning, I set out on Spirit. Pa always told me to take Flash, but I never did. He probably feared my old Indian enemy would recognize Spirit and attack me again. Taking Flash did seem the sensible thing to do, but I couldn't get myself to let Spirit see me riding off without him. This doesn't sound like something worth risking your life over, I know. Yet, to do something so against my nature, through fear, would be cowardly on my part, I thought. Indeed, the whole encounter with the Indian brave had left me feeling as if I had been running scared. Kurt would have probably turned back up the hill and confronted the brave's bow, head on. Not wanting to feel like I was in hiding or to further spend my nights in fear of being ambushed, I decided to go back to the field where I had shot down the brave. If I would soon be leaving this place forever, I wanted it to be knowing that I hadn't left any demons behind me.

Arriving at the opening about midmorning, I tied Spirit to the same tree I had on my last visit and crept out into the clearing. About a hundred feet to my right front, a group of turkeys stood, pecking at the wild oats in the grasses. If I had a scattergun, instead of my musket, I could have dropped several with a single shot. But as things were, I took a bead on one in the center of the group, whose entire side was to me and fired.

At the moment I did, the critter, apparently sensing his impending doom, leapt forward as if a feather had been plucked from his tail. Still, fortune was on my side. For unbeknownst to me, another bird, which had had his head down pecking the fallen oats about him, was directly behind the other and received the ball through his breast.

After retrieving and plucking the bird, I hung him by his feet from the branch of a small cottonwood about ten feet behind me. As on my last visit, I seated myself on the pile of rocks, in the center of the clearing and waited for the appearance of a critter through the foliage at the clearings edge to my front. By the end of the day, the bird would be well drained, cured by the sun and a wonderful sight for my Pa's eyes on my return—even if I didn't have any luck with a larger kill.

As the sun began to reach its high point of the day, I kept a keen eye on the brush around me—this being the time of day that critters often made appearances as they set about to the task of getting a good meal before the heat of the afternoon overtook them.

Sure enough, my expectations seemed about to be rewarded as a rustling started in the brush to my front. A chill went through me as I recognized the scene to be exactly as it was on the day on which I had slain the unfortunate brave. For a moment, I expected to see a brave appear in front of me again. Not having contemplated what to do in that instance and not wanting to make the same mistake again, in my dismay, I let my musket lower from the ready as I awaited an appearance. No sooner had I dispelled the chill then the bushes at the edge of the clearing parted, revealing brown fur—huge brown fur, belonging, as it turned out, to the huge, round body of a bounding grizzly. The weight of his body shifted side to side as he ran at me with increasing speed. Before I could get the barrel of my musket back up in line for a shot, he was on me. His head hit me in the chest, knocking me backwards. My body lifted clean off the ground, and I came to rest seated, straight legged, a few feet to his front, my musket off a few feet to my side.

The grizzly stood straight up in front of me and roared. He was as large and wide as a braying stallion before me. And the power of his roar would smother the blast of a locomotive engine's steam whistle. Pulling my saber from its sheave, I expected to make an effort to fend off this mountain of power, while he, most likely, would be ripping me to pieces. However, to my relief, his body turned as he dropped back down, and he sundered off to the cottonwood, where he snatched the turkey from its branch with his jowls. Scurrying to my musket, I was preparing a new cap as he walked past me, toward the same hedge brush from which he had emerged. Perhaps, I could have gotten a ball into his backside, but on contemplating how much harm it would do to him, I though it better to not. Probably, it would only serve to bring him back after me in a state of total fury—a situation I didn't want to contemplate. Better to let him go on his way, and I on mine, even if he was the one with the turkey.

This wouldn't be the first time I'd returned to our camp empty-handed. And the tale I was returning with would surely be ample compensation for Pa. Still, I also knew that telling him of my return to the clearing was apt to fire up his ire. This would demand explaining to him how necessary it was for me to confront the fear that the shooting had left in me—the fear that had caused me to show cowardice by running from the incident. And now, on having returned to the clearing, to have found myself overmatched and again cowering from confrontation would be hard to admit. It was as if the brave I had slain had returned in the form of that huge grizzly to charge me from the bushes, just as he had done on our last encounter. It's said that, on reaching manhood, braves receive a visitation from the spirit of a facet of nature and bond with that spirit. From this bonding, they receive a new name, status, and power. This brave's name, for instance, might have been Charging Bear or Huge, Hungry Standing Grizzly. If his purpose had been to frighten and humiliate me, it had worked. Yet I found that I felt somewhat relieved in having made the return visit.

Crossing the canyon at sunset, I hoped to see a rise of smoke from our campsite, indicating that Pa had started a soup or stew pot, rather than waiting to see if I would return with game for the spit.

On my approach, the first thing I noticed was that vultures were fighting over a sack or carcass in the brush. Fearing that they had broken into our bacon satchel, I kicked Spirit into a gallop. At the edge of the hedge groove, I pulled up sharply, recognizing first a shirt and then shoulders—Pa's!

Jumping from Spirit, I ran to his body—the birds squawking and taking flight to my front. Dropping to my knees at Pa's side, I instantly realized that he was dead. He was lying facedown with his head turned toward me. Most of the flesh had already been plucked from his face and head. His eye socket was gruesomely hollow. His shirt had been pecked open at the collar, and most of the flesh had been eaten off his shoulder and upper arm. Somewhat in shock, I rolled his body into my embracing arms. As he rolled over, an arrow popped up in front of me. It was projecting from his chest. The front of his shirt was soaked with blood, as was the ground where he had been lying. His face was intact on the side that had been down against the ground, but blood and torn flesh covered his skull in place of hair.

"Injuns," I spoke the word aloud, as if Pa could hear it.

My mind seemed to be operating rationally and clearly, but I was not feeling the sadness and terror that this horrid discovery of my Pa's slain body surely should have evoked. Was this what they described as shock? Or was I simply an unfeeling, uncompassionate son, who lacked the human emotion a loving and understanding Pa, such as mine, deserved. Tears filled my eyes at this thought as I stared down at Pa's scalped skull. Ants scurried about in disorientation as I lifted Pa's body and carried him over to our campsite, where I could keep the birds from again feeding off his flesh. The limpness of his body indicated to me that it hadn't been long since he was killed.

If only I had returned home immediately on killing the turkey that morning, I thought—I might have been able to help Pa fight off the Injun, or Injuns. Had it been just the one who'd attacked me after I killed his companion? Or perhaps this was an altogether unrelated attack, by other Injuns.

There was so much disturbance of the loose, sandy soil about our campsite that it was impossible to tell how many unshod hooves had been tramping about. But it did appear as though more than one Injun mount had contributed to the tracks. Thankfully, I had taken Spirit with me and left Flash. If I had left Spirit with Pa, I would have felt that this attack was one meant to be against me. Perhaps it was, even still. Pa's wound, created by the arrow in his chest, was probably the fatal blow. It was inflicted just about in the same location as where my musket ball had fatally wounded the brave. Perhaps his companion wanted to inflict the same loss on me that I had inflicted on him, by killing my companion as I had killed his. If so, he had surpassed his goal. For, in addition to the loss I was suffering, I also had the torment of dealing with the extreme guilt of believing that my weakness and failings had brought this tragedy down on my Pa.

Injuns were so concerned with displaying honor and bravery that they had no concern for truths—or interest in the circumstances that depicted those truths. They probably killed Kurt over what was no more than competitive play to him. Now they had killed my Pa over an involuntary reaction I had had to a charging, armed brave in my gun sight. For nothing more than misplaced pride, they had slaughtered my entire family. Now I had no one left in my life. I felt a need to avenge my loss. And I had nothing to lose in the attempt, since there was nothing left to live for. I wanted to go after them—hunt them down, kill them, and die in the process. If it were not that I had Pa to take care of, I would have set right out after them.

To protect Pa from the vultures, I wrapped his body completely in a blanket and laid him over Flash's back. After packing all our supplies on Jingles, I set out for town. Remembering how pleased Pa had been with the plots the mail express had provided us with at the church in Julesburg, I felt that it would be a small retribution to him for my failings to see that he was buried there, beside Kurt. Still, I swore to myself that I would not relent in my hatred or in my determination—that I would somehow avenge the injustices these savages had inflicted on my family.

Riding back to town, I explained all this to Pa. With pressing situations weighing on my mind, I had always relied on a talk with him for reassurance and enlightenment on the appropriate course of action. And so I talked to him through the entire trip to town—knowing that this would be my last opportunity to do so and realizing how hard it would be to adjust to having lost my ever-present source of knowledge and guidance. On acknowledging this loss, I would have surely cried out, had it not been for Pa's words to me on my having done such at Kurt's burial.

"Analyze your tears," Pa had said to me. "If they are for the things Kurt will be deprived of experiencing, they are manly—for sympathy and pity are honorable traits. But if those tears are being shed over your loss of Kurt's companionship, they are a show of weakness, for it is not manly to cry over our losses. We are expected to appreciate what we have been given and to be grateful for all we have been blessed with. So it's fine for you to cry over what Kurt may have lost, but not over what you are losing. On my death, you will not have the right to shed even a single tear, for, as I stand here, I tell you in honesty that I have experienced all that a man could ask to have experienced and have been blessed with all the things that a man could ask to be blessed with—in having the love of your mother and the delight of our children. So, you see, there will be no pity or sympathy justifiable on my departure."

"What blessings am I carrying forth?" I asked.

Through his unmoving lips, Pa responded, "Memories …love … faith."

I wasn't sure of "faith" anymore. Why had Pa been killed?

The marshal saw me tie up in front of his jailhouse and came out to meet me.

"It's my pa," I told him as he walked toward me. "He's been scalped and stuck in the chest with an arrow," I said matter-of-factly. "I was hoping you could tell me what tribe the arrow would belong to, but I couldn't get myself to dig it out."

"Probably Sioux—but what's going to be the use of that? There's some bad in all the tribes. It won't do you any good to take on a vendetta against one of them. What are you planning on doing with your Pa's body?"

"The church in Julesburg gave us plots next to Kurt's. Pa was pleased by that. So I know it would be to his liking to rest there."

"That's fine, Ollie. But it's a long trip. You should get him down to McCray's and let him prepare the body with fluid so it will last out the journey. If you want, I can write to the church and have them ready the plot for your dad's casket."

"That'd be right nice of you, Marshal. I've been riding all night and am about done in."

"McCray will need a day to get things ready. So I'd suggest you arrange to take the stage the morning after next. I suspect you'll also be in need of a trip to the bank. And I'll be obliged to get a statement from you on the circumstances of your Pa's death, for the Indian Affairs Department. Let's get him down to McCray's, and I'll take a look at him."

At McCray's, we had to lift Pa off Flash in the folded position he had rigor mortised to. The marshal and McCray forced his body straight and removed the blanket.

"They're Comanche feathers," the marshal told me after McCray had wiped off and handed him the arrow he had removed from Pa's chest. "I would have expected Dakota. It's early for Comanche to be coming in for winter. Maybe the hunting has been so bad that they've given up. If that's the case, we may be in for more attacks. Hopefully, they've met up with a herd and filled their travoises.

"Don, have you got a steel point and paper about that we can use?" the marshal asked Mr. McCray as he motioned me toward a desk in the room. "Let me get this statement from you right now, then, Ollie. And we'll both be free to get about with our other business. I want you to write down just what you were doing when your father got killed and everything you know about his death."

"Okay, Marshal," I said, taking the pen and paper from Mr. McCray. I dipped the pen in the well and started writing. "I left our camp before sunrise, setting out to hunt down some game."

"Should I write down that I went back to the spot where I accidently killed that Injun brave last summer, Marshal?" I asked.

"No! I really don't think that would be something we'd want to bring up—unless you are trying to point out to them that you are some short on smarts," the marshal replied sarcastically.

"I know, Marshal," I mumbled, keeping my eyes pointed down at the paper. "I don't suppose they'd want to know about the turkey I shot in the morning or the big grizzly that took it off me in the afternoon either." I realized that these details would be insignificant to Indian Affairs. Yet, their being so significant to me, I felt I had to mention them.

"Good to know that there's still some game about But that's not important either," the marshal replied.

"Did you get a shot at the grizzly?" McCray asked.

"At his back. But I thought better of taking it," I replied.

"That probably would have just brought hardship on one or both of you," the marshal commented. His agreement with my lack of action made me feel better about not having taken that shot.

"When I returned to our camp, at sunset, I found vultures and ants were feeding on my Pa's body," I continued writing.

The marshal had me draw a sketch of our campsite and the location of Pa's body.

"Flash was tied up here—to the big cottonwood?" he asked, pointing at my sketch. "The fire pit was here? And, this is where you found your Pa, in the brush?"

"That's correct," I replied.

"Now, Ollie, I want one more sketch from you, showing me exactly where your campsite was in the canyon."

"That's easy, Marshal," I said, quickly sketching out the entire canyon on another sheet of paper. "This is the large cottonwood—the only really large one on the east side of this end of the canyon," I told him, pointing it out on my sketch as I did.

"Thanks, Ollie," the marshal said. "That should be all I need. But stop in and see me tomorrow."

"And I should be finishing your dad's body by late afternoon. So you can pay me my twenty-dollar fee then. If that suits you," McCray added.

"Sure. That would be fine," I responded.

"Of course you know, there's not much I can do with the left side of his face—if you're expecting viewers."

"No. There'll be no need for a viewing," I replied. "Thank you very much," I said, turning and walking out of his office—followed by the marshal.

"Are you planning on heading to Julesburg with the casket?" the marshal asked. "It's not my place to say, but I really don't think there'll be much more you can do for your Pa. If you're planning on staying in these parts, I can have the reverend in Julesburg say a few words for your Pa and notify us when he has been laid to rest—just for your piece of mind on the matter."

Strangely, I had made the entire trip from the canyon without giving any thought to what I'd be doing with the rest of my life. For sure, I was done trying to find the source of Pa's flowstone. Crater Valley and Canyon Pass would die with Kurt and Pa. There was nothing for me in Saint Joe—not even employment—as far as I knew. There was one thing I knew I didn't want to give up—the snowshoe races, which would be starting up in a month or so.

"I suppose, when your kin are gone, your home is wherever you are. I have no place to go. And I really don't think my Pa would want me sobbing beside his gravesite. So, I think you're right, Marshal. That'd be a needless journey to be taking. I'll say my farewell's to Pa right here."

"That'd be fine, Ollie. I'm sure. I'll make the arrangements with the stage and get a letter off to the reverend today. You get yourself some rest."

After thanking the marshal, I headed back to the outskirts of town, and set up camp for the night under some hemlocks. Though not being one for daylight napping, at this time, I felt it might be good to drop onto my sleeping blanket. Looking up at the sun, peeking through the hemlock branches, I contemplated my situation. The decision I had made to remain for snowshoeing sat well with me. Perhaps, next spring, I'd take up with one of the mining companies. Perhaps, I'd sign up with Simon and Earl at Russell's. No doubt, this war business would be done by then. Pa had said that he saw no way war could be avoided. But I knew in my heart that the first battle fought, if it were one where Americans actually killed other Americans, would also be the last. The news of this, I knew, would certainly bring about an uproar that would force a rational compromise. I felt I had made a good decision in deciding to stay. And there was something else I found pleasing—I had actually made a decision on my own. Perhaps, losing Pa would allow me to finally accept the responsibility of manhood.

Oh God! I mortified myself with the thought that I was so weak as to actually require my father's death to motivate me into manhood. No, that wasn't so, I thought. I wouldn't have wished my Pa to die, even if it was at the stake of my own life. The savages were to blame. They had stolen my family from me, for little more than a moment's satisfaction. If I were truly a man now, I would set my mind back on vengeance. Feeling I could think no more on this, I gave way to repose.

20

AN OMNIBUS RECOURSE

After having the bank switch our savings to my name alone, and drawing out some government currency, I walked out into the street and spotted Captain West at a table in front of the post office. A sign across the front of the table read, "Army Recruitment."

"Afternoon, Captain," I said as I approached him.

"Put your name or mark, on the line, with your date of birth to the right," the captain said without looking up from the papers in his hand.

"It's Ollie Swenson, Captain. We met some days ago in Crater Valley," I said, questioning his memory of me.

"I recall. I see you've made a total recovery from that sticker you were wearing on our last meeting. You're a good, tough lad. You'll make a good contribution to the service."

"Military service," I asked? "I hadn't really considered doing that."

"Well you should. Most of the army has been pulled east, you know. We're relying on volunteers to form up a militia that will keep the savages from preying on people here, in their absence."

"They killed my Pa, just yesterday," I informed the captain.

"That's right—Swenson; you're Olof Swenson," the captain replied, apparently already aware of my father's demise and making the connection between us. "I've already added your father's name to the list of persons who have recently met their death at the hands of the savages."

"I suspect my brother Kurt is on there too."

"Yes, he is. The Pony Express rider out of Julesburg," the captain said, going back a page in the papers he was holding and pointing at Kurt's name toward the top of the list. "These are just 1861," he added. "Don't you think we ought to do something about it?"

I bowed my head in though, without speaking.

"And you—having lost your father and brother—should jump at the chance of possibly bringing justice to their killers."

"But I don't believe I have it in my heart to kill, even in the revenge of my family," I replied to the captain, somewhat surprised with myself for having voiced this admission.

"It wouldn't be like you were executing them or something," the captain explained. "Move aside for a second.

"Sign right here and write your birthdate beside it."

I stepped to the side and watched a boy write, "William Paulson— August 11, 1845."

"That's fine, Bill. Be out here on the street, Friday, 6:00 a.m. sharp. Bring a horse, if you have a good one and a shirt on your back. Uncle Sam will supply the rest."

"Thank you, Captain. I'll be here," the boy exclaimed, as he turned and ran off down the street.

"As I recall, you already killed an Injun. Isn't that right? It wouldn't be any different than that."

"But that was an accident," I quickly responded, somewhat upset by the confusion I was experiencing as a result his comments.

"It was not. You thought he was attacking you. And you shot him," the captain responded, in a somewhat harsh tone.

Now I was confused. I suspected that the captain must have filed an army report on the incident. How had he worded it?

"Listen, if you feel it to be fine to let the savages continue to kill our neighbors, the way they killed your father and brother, you're not a man we'd have any use for anyway.

"Get out of the way of this man," the Captain said, bringing my attention to a somewhat younger lad than the last one walking up behind me.

"I'll need a day to attend to some affairs," I said.

"Friday morning, 6:00 a.m. You can bring that painted stallion, if you still have him."

"I will," I replied, while quickly assigning my, and Spirit's, life to the captain's sheet.

It being too late to do much more that day, I decided to set down for a bit in the saloon—my hope being that some alcohol and conversation might raise my spirit and set me off with a new outlook on the direction my life was taking.

It was somewhat unnervingly pleasant to receive a cheer when I announced my enlistment—on being questioned as to it. Then, as the night drew on, I found there were two available discussions of which to take part in—one being the pending Injun war and the other, the upcoming North-South conflict. Both I found to add to my depression. At length, I decided to retire to the moonlight and write a letter to my old love, Jenny.

Although I had given up on a life with Jenny, I was lost, with no one to turn to. Realizing that her aspirations lay elsewhere, I told her as much. But at this point I needed someone I could confide in, and she was the only such one that I had left. I told her that too—and about my losses, my enlistment, and my despair. Just having written it down seemed to relax me greatly, and I fell quickly and soundly to sleep. The next day, after settling up with the undertaker and the stage company, I said my farewells to Pa, through his wooden casket. Together with the marshal and the stage driver, we loaded the casket onto the top of the stage from the pavilion platform at Town Hall and securely strapped the casket down. The marshal was right about my not needing to go along. I knew Pa was already gone.

The final business I had to conclude added to my distress. Riding Spirit, I walked Flash and Jingles down to the livery. There'd be no way of keeping them at this point, I was sure. To my surprise, the caretaker sent me back to see Captain West about the matter. He informed me that the captain was paying for both mounts and pack animals, as long as they were of good health. At this point, Captain West seemed to be the answer to all of my problems. Not only had he given me a way to address my need to act on behalf of my family against the Injuns, but he also would be taking over the upkeep of my animals as well. He even assured me that he would have them assigned to my company.

It was a relief to have the answer as to what to do with the rest of my life—at least for the next three years. That would be my enlistment period, unless the military requirement was reduced and there was no longer a need of us young recruits. If I was right about the short duration of the war, my enlistment time might indeed be short. But, even so, I could at present totally devoid myself of the need to plan my life any further. For sure, there'd be no more prospecting. I had sold Pa's flowstone to the assayer for sixty-nine dollars and fifty cents, which seemed a trifle of an amount for Pa's years of prospecting.

The Captain had said that our training and home base would be at Camp Weld, outside Denver. So I would certainly have time to partake of the upcoming snowshoeing season. Meanwhile, I'd be provided with room and board from Uncle Sam, as well as a meager but sufficient fourteen dollars a month. There was no doubt that my army uniform would make a big impression on the girls at the slopes. My life at that point seemed to have been put somewhat in order. It being several days before I had to report for our 6:00 a.m. formation, I decided to head up to Pisgah Lake for a couple of days of fishing, sunning, and relaxing at that summer oasis.

There remained only one decision I had not, at that point, made. The necklace Gramps had given me on my departure from Saint Joe still hung around my neck. Gramps had said that it would bring me luck. And previously, I had thought him to be correct. But had it? Losing my family could, certainly, not be considered lucky. Yet, I myself had survived two Injun attacks. Then there was the sentimental esteem Gramps had attached to the necklace, as well as to Kurt's knife. What had become of Kurt's Bowie? I wondered. Through the trauma of dealing with Pa's death, I hadn't given any thought to the knife.

I decided to ask the marshal if he had noticed it about Pa's waist when he removed the blanket in which I had wrapped Pa. Perhaps an Injun had taken the knife off of him. If so, we might be able to identify one of his assailants, by finding it. Or perhaps it was still lying somewhere at our campsite. But I certainly did not intend to return to the canyon to look for it. This was a period of my life that I intended to permanently close the door on. At times, living life in the mountains had been quite enjoyable, but it had become a symbol of loss to me—and one that I had no desire to reflect upon.

"There was nothing on his body but his clothing. I checked that," the marshal said. "But, give me a description of the knife, in case it turns up somewhere."

After doing so, I told the marshal, "I'm going to take a couple days of retreat up at Lake Pisgah before I have to report to Captain West."

"Yes, I heard you made an enlistment," the marshal acknowledged. "You know—we'll have something of the same job now. You'll find, as I have, that it's quite satisfying to know that you are protecting people. The problem is remembering not to get a feeling of superiority and abuse your power. Keep that in mind, and I'm sure you'll find that there's a rewarding career available in the military service."

Though not really relating to his advice, I replied, "Thanks, Marshal. I'll remember that. If there's nothing else, I'll be off to the lake now."

The marshal nodded with a slight smile, which was the most he ever committed to, and I set out.

The first trip I had made to Pisgah was with Kurt, Simon, and Earl. It might be better described as a pond, rather than a lake, not being large or deep. But that made it excellent for soaking in, since the shallow water reached a perfect temperature under the summer sun. After filling a half pail with pan-sized perch, we had ended up wrestling around in the muck at the lake's edge. Fun as it was, the serenity of the place was what had impressed me the most. Nestled in a grotto at the top of Mount Piagel, the small lake was surrounded by spruce and aspens. It served as a haven for birds, animals, and fish alike. There were seldom any visitors there, since Lake Missouri was both larger and more easily accessed. The diggings had been all but cleared out at that time, between the decline in available pay dirt, talk of war starting between the states, and the approach of winter, so I didn't expect to find anyone partaking of the pleasures of the lake. And I was right. It had often occurred to me to return to that peaceful oasis, but this was to be the first time that I would actually be doing so.

With a line in the water, I relaxed while watching the local habitants as they frolicked in their utopian habitat. As well as the rabbits and squirrels running hither thither, pine martens climbed about in the branches above me, and Marmots lumbered about on the lake's banks. Heron lit upon the lake as a hawk circled overhead. The never-summer mountain peaks glistened across the way, while on their slopes and in the valley between them, there could vaguely be seen longhorn and pronghorn sheep, as well as mountain goats grazing at length, or darting in haste.

Of course, there existed the possibility of some intimidating visitors to this oasis. Mountain lions, bears, or an irate Injun brave could appear. Those possibilities may have been a contributing factor in my not sooner having made a return visit. But that concern was beyond affecting me at that point. I seemed to have arrived at a point of fearlessness, reconciling with those entities, as they had become an accepted part of my destiny. So it was that I could relax in total appreciation of this pleasurable environ.

After taking a cutthroat trout and a string of perch from the lake, I decided to walk for a bit in the tepid water. My boots remained on shore, but the rest of my clothing joined me in my soaking, as they were as badly in need of a cleaning as I was. After swimming and thrashing about in the lake until I felt the water had removed as much of the trail dust from my person as it was apt to, I climbed to the rocks above the lake and filled my canteen with the clear, cool spring water that trickled out from between them. Once my canteen was full, I lay down on my stomach and drew a long, refreshing drink off the smooth surface of a rock and then sat back up in splendid awareness of the beauty of life that surrounded me. It was strange, I thought, how, when in this same grotto with Kurt, Simon, and Earl on my last visit, I had given no attention to the bounty of life about me. It seemed that I had been so involved in our conversations and activities that, to do so, would have been a needless expenditure of consciousness. Yet the knowledge of the existence of this bounty was imprinted in my memory, as an indivisible part of the experience.

Indians were said to maintain a continuous consciousness of their surroundings, believing the spirits of their ancestors to be embedded in those surroundings and capable of joining them in experiences. Perhaps, I thought, Kurt's spirit was consciously embedded in the bastion of life surrounding me. He was also aware of its tranquility, but even more so than me. For in the essence of a spirit, he would have become as one with the boundless wonders of creation. As a spiritual presence, he would have the ability to appreciate this beauty and perfection, while simultaneously recognizing all worry and suffering as insignificant, worldly annoyances. Such a state, unimaginable to us in our subordinate form, could possibly be the manifestation of heaven, I thought. Likely, I will never draw on the memories of this day, but my spirit will be strengthened by them, I recall thinking, while preparing my catch for the frying pan.

The morning sun crossed several of the aspen branches that were shading me before arriving at an opening that allowed it direct access to my eyelids, causing me to turn from the brightness. Before me, there lay a unique scene with which to begin my day. The huge head, neck, and rack of antlers belonging to a bull moose were framed motionlessly in the center of the lake. With the water reaching to just below his back, he stood gazing into the valley to our front. There was something surreal about the picture before me. It was as if someone had placed this magnificent head out there as a decoration while I slept. As I watched him looking off into the valley, I wondered if he was searching the hillside for a mate. Perhaps he had come to join me in my loneliness. I was anticipating that his huge head would rise with a boisterous bellow, reverberating from his powerful neck, meant to sound out our beckoning clean down to Center City. Instead, the huge head turned in my direction and then lunged forward, pulling the broad, powerful shoulders up behind it. With several such lunges, aided by the rising and stiffening of his emerging front carcass, this massive creature managed to climb out of the lake. After this quick manifestation of strength, he strode off through the brush and timber. Suspecting that it was my company that had caused him to flee, I felt guilty for having intruded upon his domain—until the unmistakable clatter of the hooves of an approaching horse to my rear became apparent to me.

"Hello there, Ollie," I heard the marshal's voice call out. He pulled his mount up beside me as I sat, half-awake, on my blanket. "Sorry to have to pull you away from this haven, but there's a matter in town that needs to be tended to right now. It's concerning your father. I know you have to report to Captain West with the other volunteers at first light tomorrow, so we've really got to do this now."

"Okay, Marshal, just let me get my stuff together, and we can set out," I said, while rising and starting to roll up my blanket. "What kind of business are you referring to, Marshal?" I asked, my mind jolting back to Pa's casket departing town atop the stage and wondering if complications had arisen concerning his burial.

"I really don't want to get into that right now, Ollie. There's just one question I have for you before we head out. This is the map you made for me showing where your camp was when your father was killed," the marshal said as he climbed down from his horse and removed the folded paper from his shirt pocket. "Could you show me about where he would have been prospecting on that last day?"

"Sure, Marshal, just about exactly," I replied, looking at my drawing as he unfolded it. "We had already picked clean down this side of the canyon and back up here to our campsite—and then another three hundred yards or so down, stopping when we came to a large, flat rock, setting right about here," I said, pointing to the approximate location on the map where we had ended work the day before Pa's death. "Pa would have been starting right at that rock. No doubt about it," I said, wondering why the marshal had asked this. "Did you find the knife there?" I asked him, probing for an insight.

"When we get back," was all he replied as he helped me tie my pack on Spirit.

The marshal set a brisk pace back to town, allowing only for conversation that was directed toward our mounts.

JUSTICE AND INJUSTICE

Entering the marshal's office, I noticed two men in the holding cell. Besides the cell, about all there was in the office was a fireplace sporting a coffeepot; a table; a desk; and a combination gun, coat, and key rack. The men stood facing us, their hands grasping the bars beside their heads.

"That's Brown and Jeffers," I said to the marshal, immediately recognizing the men from their visits to our campsite.

"See. The boy will tell you. We've been prospecting the hills up there for years," Brown said.

"That's right," Jeffers chimed in. "We ain't claim jumpers."

"You—both of you—set down and shut up. Or I swear, I'll come in there and gag you!" the marshal shouted.

"You found Kurt's bowie," I said, pointing to where it lay upon the table.

"You sure that's it?" the marshal asked.

"No doubt about it," I replied. "Look right here in the sheath. Kurt cut his initials in here," I said as I removed the knife and looked at the leather to the inside, rear of the sheath. "Someone's cut them out," I said, seeing that the area where Kurt had cut them had been gutted.

"Let me tell you what has been transpiring these last few days," the marshal said. "Ever since you told me your Pa had Flash at the campsite when he was murdered, I haven't felt right about something. The thing is, Injuns don't leave stallions behind when they raid. They'd be more likely to leave with the stallion and not even hurt your Pa then to kill your Pa and leave the stallion behind. Looking for the knife, I took a ride up to the campsite after you left. And I brought one of Captain West's Navaho scouts, Tuba, with me. Tuba showed me a ridge on the edge of the unshod pony prints. The ridge was from a depression made when shoes are burned into hooves. In other words, those horses had, at one time, worn shoes."

At that point, I had the gist of where all of this was going. "They did it! Didn't they, Marshal?" I shouted, stepping away from the table and toward the holding cell.

The Marshal grabbed me by the shoulder and said sternly, "Now I want you to sit down here and let me finish the telling. You hear me?"

I dropped into the chair but still had my head turned so I could see the faces of the murderers in the cell. Their eyes were open wide at the sight of the revelation unfolding in front of them. "My pa told me they were no good. 'Their picks and shovels always wore store-bought edges,' he said. 'There game is to find a way to profit off the toil of others.' That's what he told me after the first time they came poking around our campsite." At this point, my impulse was to run over to the cell and try to strangle them both through the bars.

"Relax, and be quiet, Ollie," the marshal barked at me. "Tuba followed the tracks back to wagon tracks at the side of the canyon. There, he found the spot where the shoes had been removed."

"It wasn't us, Marshal. That boy don't know nothing about us!"

"Shut up, Brown!" the Marshal yelled with eardrum-busting force.

He must hate them just as I do, I thought on hearing his outburst.

"Everyone knows you two have been trying to swindle prospectors out of their profits. Well, you went too far this time," the marshal continued, with a noticeable effort at controlling his vocal level. "Ollie, when I spotted 'lode claim' markings nearby to your campsite, I took a trip down to Blackhawk and got their names from the claim filing," the marshal informed me. I found them partying at the saloon in Center City on my way back. They were bragging on how they made this big hit of a quartz outgrowth. I still didn't have enough proof to say for sure that they killed your Pa, until you marked the map for me," the marshal explained, while removing my drawing from his vest pocket. While walking over to the cell, he unfolded it, showing it to the scoundrels inside. "You see where he drew the large, flat-topped rock? That's the spot where Swenson planned to be digging, while Ollie was out hunting that day—the exact spot where you two murdering polecats made your big find! You'll both swing for this!" the marshal bellowed out, apparently losing control of his anger again.

"We heard the old man cheering and jumping about with that stone in his hand, and Brown told me to get our horses unshod," Jeffers blurted out as he turned toward Brown and took a step back away from him.

"You filthy, lying bastard," Brown shouted. He chased Jeffers backward and reached out to grab him. Jeffers fell over the bench behind him, with Brown lunging down on top of him. Taking hold of Jeffers's head, he began smashing it into the cell wall.

The marshal quickly grabbed the keys, unlocked the cell door, and swung it open. Jumping in ahead of him, I grasped Brown around his throat as the Marshal jumped in behind me. In my outraged state, I actually expected the marshal to join me—that, together, we would strangle the life out of these worthless murderers. So I was somewhat shocked when the marshal pushed me to the side, causing me to fall against the cell bars. He wrapped his arm around Brown's neck, and cocked his head to the side as if he were trying to snap his neck. Brown reached back and grabbed the marshals forearm, but in but a few seconds, he dropped lifelessly to the floor. Quickly rolling him onto his stomach, the marshal was able to cuff Brown's hands behind his back.

"Help me get this one over to the doc's," the marshal said as he lifted Jeffers by pulling his arm up across his own shoulders.

Jeffers was mumbling inaudibly about the murder, in a half-conscious state as blood flowed freely from the back of his head on down his neck, turning the back of his shirt a bright red.

"So, it wasn't Injuns at all," I said to the marshal as we lumbered over to the doc's office with the half-conscious Jeffers strung between us.

"No, it wasn't," he replied. "Those two must have been planning something like this for a while to be carrying Comanche arrows about with them. No telling if they had faked any other attacks before this one. They'll hang for this one though; that's certain."

"I've got to tell Captain West. I don't have to join the military now," I said, realizing my motive for doing so had suddenly been undone.

"That's not going to be easy," the marshal replied.

"But I was only joining to avenge my family," I continued. "Who knows, maybe Kurt's death wasn't the Injun's fault either," I said.

"That just may be," the marshal replied. "But that isn't going to mean a hill of beans to West."

After we rolled Jeffers onto the doc's table, the marshal cuffed him and left a revolver on a desk near the door on our way out. "Don't hesitate to use this, Doc," the marshal said. "You'd be doing us all a big favor."

When we stepped out of the office, the marshal told me that we had one more item of business to take care of. He had brought a form back from Blackhawk with him, expecting to have ownership of the claim officially transferred to my name. He directed me back to his office to fill it out.

"It'll be my claim?" I asked, not having considered that facet of the situation up till then.

"Sure, you don't get to keep what you claim jump, do you?" the marshal asked. "It was your father's find. And you, being the only heir, have right to it by inheritance. The problem is I don't think you'll be in a position to work it, with your military obligation confronting you. And working it is a condition of owning it. If you think it would suit you, I'll talk to Russell for you. I can have him look at the assay and give you an offer for the claim."

"Can I talk to the captain first," I asked, "to see if he'll release me?"

"Sure, Ollie. We can't do anything until we get the claim transfer anyway."

"Thanks, Marshal," I said. After completing the form, I headed to the saloon, thinking a cold beer might help me regain a perspective on the new twist my life had taken and what was in store for my future. If the marshal was right, that was out of my hands. Perhaps I was destined to be a soldier. There seemed to be little else I could pursue. Apparently, Pa's dream had come true. Judging by what the assayer had said about Pa's flowstone, I might get a lot of money by selling the claim—assuming, of course, that my claim was the source of Pa's stone. But seeing how we had excavated near to all of the surrounding countryside, that seemed likely. If this were the case, what would I do with the wealth—having no one to share it with? I'd have that beer, go and see Captain West, and then decide.

"Hello, Captain," I said as I walked up to the recruiting table, behind which the Captain was seated. "If you don't mind, I've decided to withdraw my enlistment application."

"Too late for that; your application has been accepted," he replied.

"But, Captain, you have to understand, it wasn't Injuns that killed my Pa at all. It was done by a couple of ruthless desperados trying to jump his claim. And I never was too sure that Kurt didn't instigate his own demise at Julesburg. That would be the likelihood, considering his nature, and seeing how no other riders have been set upon."

"Hold on now, trainee," the captain said while rising to his feet. With his hands on his hips, he glared at me from under the wide brim of his hat. That's what you are, you know—until you prove yourself to be good enough to wear the stripe of a private. What makes you think you have anything to decide? You're done deciding while you're in the army. From now on, you'll follow the orders of your officers—which I am one of—and I am ordering you to be out here, ready to march, at six hundred hours, sharp! And understand this, trainee: You have joined the Army of the United States of America during a time of war," the captain continued, his face flushed red at that point, with blood apparently boiling beneath the skin. "If you do not show up, as ordered, ready for duty, I will consider it desertion and have you shot on sight!"

How had I so insulted the captain to incite him to such a state of rage? I wondered, while feeling somewhat fearful that he might resort to violence against me at any second. "I just thought ..."

"You didn't think!" the captain yelled, interrupting me to continue with his indoctrination. "If you did, you'd be thanking me for the opportunity to serve your country in its time of need and, perhaps, to make an honorable and capable man out of that boy's body. Now, I don't want to see you in front of me again, until we are ready to form up at six hundred hours. Have you got that, trainee?"

"Okay, Captain," I replied.

'That's not how you address an officer, trainee. From now on, you will refer to me as sir, and your reply to the affirmative is yes. Now, put them together," he commanded through clenched teeth.

I stood there looking at him for a moment and then, realizing the reply he was looking for, responded, "Yes, sir."

"Then move out!" he commanded, sending me scurrying off without any idea of where I was scurrying too.

The captain was not the same man I had talked to just a few days prior, I thought. Was this because he was now in a position to have power over me? I remembered the marshal's warning—not to abuse a position of power. Obviously, the captain had never learned that principal, I decided.

Actually, it was me who had a lot to learn.

After the indoctrination by Captain West, I felt a strong need for friendly conversation. So, I headed to the post office—hoping there'd be a letter from Jenny waiting. I had the letter open before I got back out of the door. And, I plopped right down on the front stoop and started reading."

Dear Ollie,

I'm sorry to hear about Kurt. It's so terrible it's hard to believe it to be true. I know how close you two were and hope that this won't discourage you with life.

Things haven't been going good for me, either. Would you believe I actually was thrown in jail for three days? My parents had to come down to get me out. We had two slaves hiding in a barn, out behind the farmer's house where I'm boarding, and the slave hunters came with bloodhounds tracking them down. The slave boys took off running across the field, but the dogs ran them down and took hold of them. It was terrible. They took us to jail and wouldn't have let us go if we hadn't given them Henrietta's name. She had been a slave once herself and has been going back and forth rescuing others for years. I hope they don't catch up with her. I was really scared that they wouldn't let me continue in college. It's very hard work, but I'm determined to finish.

Ollie, I don't know where my mind was when I thought of giving you up for John English. He's not the kind of person I want to spend my life with. In fact, I don't expect to ever find another person with a heart like yours. That's why I want you to come back home. I'll even quit college if it's the only way to get you back. I'm here, if you still want me.

Love Jenny

Don't that beat all, I thought. I had to read each line over and over. She'd even quit college for me. How had I ever doubted in my Jenny. Then the reality hit me. I couldn't run to her. I was in the army! I had Jenny back. I had a claim on a gold strike, and I couldn't go to either. What could I do about this? I wondered. There was no dealing with Captain West. Perhaps the war would end quickly, as Simon and Earl had said—once the Union found out that the Rebels were ready to fight to the death in order to maintain their sovereignty.

A month back, the Union had been defeated at Bull Run and had run back up north to safety. But Union ships were still trying to blockade Southern ports. Once the Confederacy was able to build enough ships to run the Union ships out of their harbors, I suspected, the North would abandon their efforts and depart. Then the new recruits, such as I, would no longer be needed.

On the other hand, I had heard much boasting by the Yanks, in the tavern, how they would soon revenge their loss at Bull Run. This made me wonder if the war might last for months or perhaps even a year. No, not a year I decided. Not once both sides realized that Americans were actually killing each other—and, for what, only to decide if states could function independently as many had already done? This, they would surely realize, was not a reason worth killing each other over. In any case, I would not be involved in the war, I reasoned. And if the Indians behaved themselves again, when they saw the military return, it would be likely that the only shooting I would have to do would be in practice.

All in all, it seemed that there was no course of action for me to take, but to let the situation work itself out. The only thing I needed to do, I decided, was to write an answer to Jenny's wonderful letter and let her know, with no uncertainty, how she did then and always had owned my heart.

I went on to explain to her why I couldn't come racing back, as I would have liked to do. I didn't mention my gold claim. There was one thing I wanted to be sure of; if Jenny was going to wait for my return, I wanted to know that it was for me and not for what I might have. I told her about Pa's murder but not that it was a claim jump.

"As always, you will be in my dreams. Love, Ollie," I concluded.

Writing that letter was easier than mailing it. If I threw it away and rushed to her in Saint Joe, I'd be returning to her as a deserter of the military—not much of a start for a life together. Perhaps we could run south and find sanctuary in the Confederacy. But if we did that, the Rebels might find out that I was avoiding the military and force me into their own army. Also, there was the gold to consider. For my part, it would be easy to give it up, if it was keeping me from Jenny. But knowing how much finding it had meant to Pa, abandoning it would cause all my reflections, on our life prospecting together to be plagued by guilt. In addition, might there not have been a good reason for Pa's belief that wealth was necessary for happiness? Although, it would be easy for me to turn my back on the gold, might the gold not be necessary for providing Jenny with what she would want from life?

After having completed the deliberation, I dropped the letter off at the post office and resolved myself to confronting the situation at hand—my military commitment.

The government paid me fifty dollars for Jingles. I could have received one hundred and fifty dollars apiece for Spirit and Flash, if I had not elected to designate them as "personal property." As my property, they were to remain with me in a cavalry company of the 1st Infantry Regiment of the Colorado Volunteers. The horses had to be determined "fit" for this duty. Many of the volunteers had this same desire, but their mounts were turned down by the inspectors. Most of those rejected were bought by the army and assigned to "miscellaneous service." There were thirty-eight volunteers that turned out for the morning formation. Eight of us were with mounts. Jingles was with the other animals that had been sold to the military at the livery coral, including various farm livestock. We stood about jawing for a bit, about our travels and such, before Captain West demanded our silence.

"Men, you are all in the military now. But don't call yourselves soldiers. As of now, you will be referred to as trainees. With a little bit of luck, and a lot of hard work, you will all become real soldiers before you are needed in battle. That being said, I want to thank you all for recognizing your country's need and offering your services in that cause."

"We'll be heading out to Camp Weld this morning and arriving there in two days. For those of you who don't know, it's just this side of Denver. So we'll be setting a good pace in the doing. Before setting out, we'll chow down here beside the road. We're going to be eating, not jawing. In ten minutes, you will be back out here, formed up. So grab yourself some grub and let's get to it.

The food was hot and good—scrambled eggs, bacon, potatoes, good coffee. And to my surprise, they let us have extra scoops of potatoes in the chow line. Setting upon the stoops and rails along the side of the road, we immediately got to making introductions and storytelling, until Captain West's voice boomed out, "Five more minutes!"

Most of us—having hardly touched our food at that point and not wanting to leave it behind—quickly exchanged our conversation for mastication. We were quite right in doing so too, for some men had to discard a large part of their meal when the captain ordered us back out on the road.

"You men with mounts will be driving the herd. If you feel that you can't handle that, give your mount to someone who can ... Swenson!" It was unexpected, hearing my name stated, as we had all, up to that point, been referred to autonomously. "You have two mounts, I see. Can you ride them both at once?" the captain asked.

"Yes, for some spell, sir," I answered, recalling one of my show tricks and not immediately realizing the cause for the Captain's question.

"Is that so?" the Captain responded, with an air of agitation. "Give one of them to that man next to you," the Captain ordered. Saddened by my comprehension of the captain's command, I reluctantly handed Flash's reins to the man to whom he was referring.

After a bit of organization, we started down the valley, joining more volunteers from Central and Mountain City. Farther down, we were joined by a group from Blackhawk, recruited from there and from a mining town south of there by one Captain Cook. With each stop our herd also increased in size. As well as horses, we had a variety of farm animals. Those animals that couldn't be herded were loaded on wagons for transport. We arrived at Camp Weld with over seven hundred men. The following day, a group organized as the Denver Home Guard, joined our ranks, adding another three hundred or so.

And with them came a fright—our commanding officer, a boisterous monster of a man, announced to us as Major Chivington. I was later to learn that the major was previously a Methodist preacher from Denver. This was something of a relief to learn—since, I thought, surely a minister could not make too coldhearted of a commander. His ministry must have been quite unique, though. For it was said that, although his congregation was large, his attendance was small—that due to the fact that it was possible for many of his parishioners to hear his boldly delivered sermons from the comfort of their homes. Although, I was sure that that was an exaggeration, it was apropos as a description of his extraordinarily loud voice. It was also said that he had refused an offer to serve as the unit's chaplain, demanding instead the position of an infantry commander.

"Good morning, my fellow Coloradoans," the major boomed above the din of the thousand plus men assembled before him on the following morning's formation.

"Yes, if you haven't heard, I'm a Coloradoan myself. It's good to be something, isn't it? I'm also an American—just as I suspect each and every one of you are. It's been nearly a year since February 28. That was a proud day for each of us—being granted our own territory. And I, like you, do not intend to let that territory be threatened by anyone—the Injuns or the Rebels! I'm proud, again today, to see the response of my fellow Coloradoans to the call of their territory and country. And you can rest assured that I will stand beside you in that defense.

"I know it's the Injun raids that are at the top of concern for many of you standing before me today. But, as I stand here, I am telling you that that is not our biggest battle. You probably think that the Texan takeover of Fort Filmore in New Mexico doesn't pose a threat to us up here. But that is far from the truth. Although their numbers are small now, many units are being formed throughout Texas. In short course, they will be making major assaults up the Rio Grande. If they are successful in defeating our forces in New Mexico, there will be nothing between them and our doorstep. If we don't act immediately in curtailing their plans, they could be marching into Denver before the year's end! The Injuns we can always deal with. But if the Rebels get control of this territory, it might be for keeps!

"I'm sure you all know that some of our neighbors are sympathetic toward the secessionists and will gladly give them support if they are successful in reaching these parts. So also are there a large number of sympathizers on the West Coast. That will be the next conquest on their agenda. With the wealth of our mines in their control and our West Coast ports added to their trading ability, the Confederacy will take on a new look in the world's eye. Arms and support would grow readily available to them from overseas. And the Confederates could become the dominant power on this continent! I, for one, do not want to see Denver City changed into Dixieland! I don't want a few wealthy landowners using an army of slaves to confiscate the wealth of these mountains or to continue with their plan of using camels to grow cotton across our plains!"

The major's violent arm swinging as he made his statements indicated the anger that these notions instilled in him. "The government has asked us to immediately attach some of our recruits to the Regulars, in the south of our territory—to support them against the Indian uprisings. They will also support in the event that the Texan assault should occur before our major defensive force is prepared to engage them. In response, since my Home Guard is already outfitted and has had an introduction to training, we have decided to move them out immediately. We have assurance from the federal government that formal training will be given to them at their new duty station. Since you men of the guard have only a short-term enlistment, I'm sure you will be glad to have this opportunity to make an important contribution to our cause during your service.

"The remainder of you will be required to train long and hard, so as to learn the art of field combat, as quickly as possible, before deployment against the advance of the Texans. I will push you men—push you to perform as superior soldiers against those arrogant Southern aggressors. Now, listen well to this, men. This is the last time I will explain any of my actions to you. From here out, you will receive and obey orders. And, hopefully, we will be successful in representing ourselves as a formidable army against the Confederate assault."

Only a short-term enlistment! I thought. Why hadn't I gone to Denver and joined the guard? The volunteers who had claimed we would be in combat with the Rebels were right! I had no desire to fight the Texans. In fact, my good friends had volunteered to join the Confederates in Texas. What if I had to shoot it out with them? Could the army actually expect me to risk death trying to curtail the Southerners? For that matter, could the Confederacy expect their troops to be willing to die in order to bring slavery to the western border? This whole thing was crazy. But how could I change it?

"Now, before we get to work outfitting and organizing you men, my commanding officer, Colonel John Slough, has some words for you."

Slough was an average size man with, I was to find out, less than an average temperament. "Greetings, gentlemen," the colonel began. "I'm going to tell you all, up front, that we have a tough row to hoe. And I'm going to be the one that ensures the job gets done." He would also have had a loud speaking voice if it was not that he was speaking through tightness in his jaw and lips. He gave me the impression that he thought the enemy was standing in the field in front of him.

"Your training will be long and hard. You can work with us and learn to be soldiers or be shot dead in a field by a Rebel. Any soldier who becomes an obstacle to the success of this training, will be dealt with quickly and harshly. Obey your orders. Do what you are told, and we will get along just fine. Let us all resolve ourselves to the success of this endeavor, and I'm sure we will represent ourselves proudly in battle.

Remain in place now, and your officers will direct you through the outfitting."

"When we gonna get after them Rebels, Colonel?" the words came from a scruffy fellow in the second rank, who looked a bit too old for soldiering.

"Correct that trainee," the colonel, who was walking off, snapped back at Major Chivington, who had already started moving toward the offender.

"You don't speak until you are told to speak. And, when you speak to an officer you address him properly!" the major barked, assuring that everyone would hear his reprimand. "Do you understand that, trainee?"

"Yes, sir," the offender's reply came, muffled by the wall of a man in front of him.

"I didn't hear that!" the major shouted down at the scrawny figure that his own was totally dwarfing.

ACCEPTING THE MILITARY CAUSE

So, my future was defined that morning, on that field. Learn to be a soldier. Go fight the Rebels. And don't ask any questions about it. At least, it did appear that I would be on horseback, if I were to go into combat. My company was the only cavalry company in the regiment. It was to be commanded by Captain Charles Thompson. The captain was a large-framed man but seemed to be more subdued in mannerisms than his superiors. He was a local landowner-rancher and obviously a capable horseman. He rode a sinewy, black stallion that he called Sootie.

"You have all expressed desire to be cavalrymen. Unfortunately, not all of you will qualify. A cavalry soldier has to be a unit with his mount. If either you or your horse cannot meet the army's performance requirements, you will be off to the infantry. Therefore, my suggestion is to give it your best shot if you want to remain in this unit," the captain announced, after having been introduced to us.

"Looks like I made it," Smitty called to me, coming into the general-purpose army tent that was, at that time, serving to house my half of the company. Smitty's bunk was next to mine. "The captain says that the testing is over," he continued.

Our company had originally consisted of over eighty trainees. But our number had, at that point, been reduced to forty-eight, by the elimination of horses and riders that failed to meet the requirements. The testing had started with the horse's ability to tolerate gunfire, which eliminated a dozen or so horses and one rider. "Of course, I know it was Flash that got me through it," Smitty admitted, dropping his gear on his cot and beginning to work at his bootlaces.

"You sit the saddle as well as any," I responded, already enjoying the comfort of my cot.

"Maybe so, but I'll never be able to 'stand' a saddle," Smitty said with a broad smile crossing his face.

"I know. I really pulled a boner that time," I replied.

Smitty was referring to my antics during a test I was in with Spirit earlier in the day. The test was simply to mount quickly, ride across a field at a gallop, round a pole, return, and dismount. I guess I was feeling a bit cocky and couldn't resist the opportunity to show our company a bit of trick riding. An earlier rider had done a running mount, and it seemed to have been received positively by the captain. So I did the same. But in addition, when I had passed the pole, I slid off the side of Spirit. Then, "Back!" I commanded, when he was some feet to my front. Spirit knew to turn to the side I had dismounted from and return at a gallop. Grabbing the saddle horn as he passed, I swung back on, did a standing ride for a bit on the return, and then slid off behind him and commanded Spirit to "Halt!" at the finish. My ride went well and was rewarded with the claps and hoots that I was accustomed to receiving at shows.

"I had every intention of sending you to an infantry company, when it came to me that your being a trickster might come in handy some day," the captain explained after riding up on his mount after my performance. "If we ever find our company hopelessly surrounded and outnumbered by the Confederates, we might need someone to try and get through to command with a message requesting support. Since there might be no way a normal rider could penetrate their lines, we'd need a trickster. Wouldn't we? Then I'd be glad to have you along." After hesitating for a bit to allow me time to reflect on his statement, the captain concluded, "In the future, it might pay you well to try and perform as a regular member of our unit." Then, pulling Sootie's head to the side, he quickly rode off.

"Yeah, I heard the captain chewing you out," Smitty said. "It was quite an impressive ride though. Was your brother as good on Flash?"

"Kurt wasn't much into tricks. He liked racing," I replied. "Do you think the captain was serious about what he said to me?"

"Some, I suspect," Smitty answered, before falling backward onto his gear, obviously as tired as I was from our long day of activities.

"The officers sure seem certain that we will be fighting the Rebels soon," I said. But it doesn't seem to me that the Union would want another repeat of Bull Run anytime soon," I declared, fishing for an opinion.

"We just took another beating in West Virginee," John Paxton, who was bunking on my left side, joined in. John was sitting on the edge of his cot, cleaning off his boots. His use of "we" instead of saying "the Union" as I had made me realize that I was not yet considering myself to be a part of the Northern force. "The Rebels sneak-attacked them while they slept. But we got them back, the same way, some days later—even a good bit better—at two of their North Carolina forts," he reported.

"Where did you hear that?" I asked, desperate to uncover his information as rumor. For, if it were fact, the implications would be disastrous. The possibility that the Union, upon recognizing the determination of the Confederacy, would find a means of defusing the situation, rather than engaging in a full scale war, would now be less than remote.

"I heard the major reading a report to the colonel," John explained.

John was of the serious and reliable type. I had already observed that during our test periods. He acted older than his age would dictate, as was common given the lives of hardship these times had brought to so many.

"What will we do—kill each other till one side runs out of men?" I asked.

"Or one side recognizes their situation to be hopeless," John replied.

"Everyone knows the Rebels would have no chance of winning a long war," Smitty added. "They don't have enough men, arms, manufacturing facilities, or support from other countries for supplies," he explained, echoing my opinion. Smitty's hairless face, fair complexion, and neat appearance gave him a boyish countenance. But in contrast was his large, straight, muscular frame. And also in contrast was the decisiveness he displayed on matters of importance, as he did then.

"The major said that that could all change if the Confederates win the West," I remarked.

"My parents died getting our ranch started out here. Nobody's going to take that land off of me." Though softly spoken, the deliberate slowness and exactness of the pronunciation of John's words left no doubt as to his conviction.

"What about you, Smitty? You came up here from the Texas Bayou. I don't understand your enlisting with the Union," I said.

"To stop slavery," Smitty quickly replied.

"I don't like it either, but I guess I'm not as righteous as you are. I sure wouldn't put my life on the line trying to defeat it," I stated.

"You would—if you had a sweetheart and a son that were trapped in it," Smitty explained.

"How'd you get into that fix?" I asked.

"Working on a ranch and meeting up with the loveliest girl I had ever seen. The rancher thinks her boy is his. But I could see that he was mine right off," Smitty explained.

"Wow, that's a hell of a situation," I admitted.

"Yeah, from a hellish practice," Smitty added. "We had a parson that spoke out regular against it. He turned up floating in the swamp one Monday morning. We have to put an end to their wickedness right now."

So Smitty too was deeply committed to "the cause." Like John, I had lost my family by starting a new life in the West—with, in my case, only a mining claim to show for it. Would I share their conviction if the Rebels were to attack us? All I knew was that I didn't want it to happen.

"Swenson, the major wants to see you in the command center, ASAP!"

"Yes sir!" I replied. The captain had appeared in the doorway, made the announcement, and disappeared as quickly. On his appearance, a shout of attention had come from the front of our tent, and he'd returned our salute upon departing.

"Damn, it looks as if I might be going to the infantry after all. Bad enough having to go into battle, without having to walk into it," I stated, somewhat seriously as I reached for my boots.

Hearing a roar of laughter coming from inside the command tent as I approached was surprising to me. It stopped short upon my entrance.

While saluting the major, I announced, "Trainee Olof Swenson, reporting as ordered, sir!"

"At ease, trainee," the major replied, tilting his head back to return my salute directly from his seated position at the table. "The marshal has some business to discuss with you," the major said as he rose and started to depart to his quarters. When the marshal is done with you, return to your tent. You'll have to show me that fancy riding that I heard about one day," he commented on his way out.

The captain must have told him about it, I thought. But hadn't he also told him about the reprimand I'd received?

"I have an offer for you," the marshal announced. "Russell had an assay done on your claim. And he showed me how it compared to others he had purchased. Only one of the others was better. He's sympathetic toward the losses you have suffered, appreciates your volunteering in the military, and doesn't intend to give you less than a fair offer for your claim. How does ten thousand dollars sound?" The marshal tried to say this under his breath, but his excitement broke through a bit.

"My jaw probably dropped open, as I stood there in something of a shocked state. "Great!" I answered, after an indefinite length of time.

"Sit down. I have the release forms here. All you have to do is sign them, and the money will go into an account at the bank for you."

"I'd like to ask you one question first, Marshal. If the Confederates take over Colorado Territory, will I lose the money?"

"Not entirely," the marshal replied. "Ten thousand would help you start up quite a few campfires," he said with a chuckle. "The South has created Confederate currency. That's the only money they recognize. Therefore, yes, if they took possession of this territory, US currency would be useless here. But in that case, they'd take ownership of all of our property too—including, for sure, gold mine claims. Thus, you wouldn't be any better off if you still held ownership to the claim. The best thing you can do is to help make sure that that situation doesn't come about. That's why we've got you boys up here training."

"Yes, sir. I think I'm starting to get the idea," I said, while taking the form from the marshal's hand. "Where do I sign?"

"Right on this line," he said anxiously.

Although I suspected that Russell had made it well worth the marshal's trouble to ascertain my acceptance of their offer, that was quite fine with me. The offer had far exceeded my expectations. I was, in fact, quite wealthy. Could I possibly use the wealth to buy my way out of my military commitment? I wondered. There was no way I could present such an offer to any of my commanders. It would, most likely, infuriate them and farther reduce their acceptance of me as a soldier.

If only this damned war would end. I had my Jenny back. And I had a fortune with which we could start a life together. I felt a need to write her and tell her of my desires. I would still avoid mentioning the money. I would, however, express my confidence to her in my ability to create a happy life for us, if we could again be together.

The vision of our reunion occurring in the near future or possibly ever became quite blurred on a mid-February morning. The wind lashed snow against my face, as it did those of my comrades, while our regiment stood at attention, and Colonel Slough described both his and our situation.

"Good morning, gentlemen and 'murderers.'" The colonel's normal salutation had been shockingly modified. He stood on a platform at the head of the field. Between his hands he held a twelve-pound Howitzer shell. "Do we have Confederate sympathizers in our midst? Or are there some among you that are so lacking in brain power as to not recognize that the reason I have been pushing you to the limit is so that you will have a possibility of surviving the upcoming battles that you will most certainly have to endure—whether or not I am alive to complete your training? The fuse went out as this rolled into my quarters. If you are a patriot, you will help me identify the perpetrator of this treason."

Though I sympathized with the colonel's plight, his choice of the words *most certainly* and *endure* when it came to battles trumped all my other concerns. He wasn't exaggerating about pushing us. And my belief that being a horse soldier would make soldiering easier had been quite amiss. It had, in fact, made the training all the more demanding. When our training began, Captain Thompson, our training officer, had said that the European horse soldiers were trained for over two years. Since the trainees in our company had been selected for their horsemanship, we didn't need much time to master the handling of our animals. But, there were still many combat tactics that required repeated practicing. In addition, we had to train on all the procedures of the infantry.

"A horse makes a damned good target," Captain Thompson had explained. "If he goes down, guess what—you are automatically, and immediately, reclassified as an infantry soldier. So you had better be ready to handle that job too."

The consequence of this enlightening was that we didn't finish our training till usually hours after the main body of the brigade had finisher theirs. The captain took us through most of the infantry drills as a company, rather than with the brigade, which did save much time. The brigade had to go over simple maneuvers like falling into formation repeatedly. This simply required lining up at your assigned position in file, while maintaining an arm's length distance from the man in front of you and while touching elbows with those at your side. The main body had to go over this for days. It became quite frustrating for them, standing in position as the entire regiment was inspected, corrected, and then reconfigured and reinspected, all while their feet were freezing in place on the ice-covered turf.

Since we used short-barreled carbine breechloaders, while the infantry used musket rifles, we did our own firing practice. We were expected to deliver five rounds a minute from horseback, which was difficult, even for me. Though, at the sake of being considered a braggart, I admittedly thought of myself as the best in our company at the task.

Yet a night sweat often came over me as I envisioned myself trying to get a cap in position on the nipple during the heat of a battle. We also carried a horse pistol as a backup, which we also practiced loading and firing from horseback. It would have been nice to have one of the Colt revolvers that many of the Eastern units, as well as the Rebels, had been issued. But like our pay, those were "forthcoming." If I had been issued one, I thought, I would be inclined to use it after the first volley from our rifles. Since we were not allowed to issue that first volley until we were within two hundred meters of the enemy, it would be but a few seconds on horseback before we would be within the useful range of the Colt. The Austrian rifles that the infantry were issued had a little better range and accuracy. This inspired the infantrymen to brag regularly about their ability to drop Texans with them—as if it were something they were actually anxious to do. All I wanted to do was to have the war end so I could get on with my life. But since our training was entirely geared toward our upcoming battle with the Texans, this eventuality was beginning to appear as an inevitable one.

This training that we received through February was directed toward large-scale, open-field confrontation. We repeatedly drilled as an entire regiment, responding to the calls of our buglers. Our first attempts at this were so bad that they would have brought laughter from onlookers. But instead, they brought outbursts of condemnation from our officers. Between not knowing what the bugle call was instructing us to do and not knowing the right way to accomplish the task, we often found ourselves intermingled in a mass of confusion. Eventually, we had become somewhat proficient at the flanking and turning maneuvers, firing from rows and columns, rallying into various formations, and reassembling as a battalion—that as a result of performing those procedures repeatedly. On realizing that we were developing this proficiency, our officers marched us out into a valley and had us practice the same procedures in a more confined area.

"That hurts even more without the gear," I said to Smitty as he lay flat on his back atop a boulder.

"Yeah, this is one time I'm glad to have toted it along," he replied weakly, his lungs having been somewhat deflated by the impact of his fall.

A right flank command had us climbing over the snow-covered boulders while trying to manage our weapons. This task was increased in difficulty by the fact that our movements were hampered by our heavy winter coats and the forty pounds of gear that was strapped over them.

"Sounds like experience talking," Smitty remarked as he quickly arose.

"Yeah, I'm reminded of times back at the Atlantic shore, fishing off the jetties and falling on the slippery rocks," I revealed.

"In the warm summer sun too, I bet," Smitty suggested in jest.

"No, actually the blustering may have been even more striking, laden with sea salt as it was. But, the joy was in the endeavor," I explained.

"What greater endeavor then the protection of your homeland?" Smitty asked, his wit concealing his motivation as always.

Get Jenny and take her back to New York with me, I thought as a bugle call that I didn't immediately recognize sounded.

"Too the colors," I heard Captain West shout out. Looking to the valley, we saw the flags had been positioned at its head, allowing for a full regiment assembly. Next, there came a call that I recognized as "on the double quick."

"Excellent, men." Major Chivington's boisterous announcement could be heard clean across the valley as we completed the assembly.

I had noticed that the carriage of Colonel Slough had crossed our flank, and pulled up, off to the side of the Major's position. As the colonel stepped out of the carriage, he seemed to lose his footing in the snow, sliding down, half in and half out of the carriage. His aid quickly grabbed his arm, keeping him from completing a journey to the ground. When the aid attempted to help right him, the colonel's feet did a bit of a dance beneath him. He clung on, suspended between the carriage and his aid. Something about a slight bobbing of his head gave us the impression that it was not just the snow beneath the colonel's feet that was causing his instability.

"Shit-faced again," came a comment from a trainee to my rear, the voice of which I recognized as belonging to Jake Popp. Luckily, it was only loud enough to be heard by those of us close to Jake.

Realizing the futility of his effort, the colonel decided to return to the safe confines of his carriage and dispatch his aid to summon the major. After a short conversation with the colonel, the major returned to the flag post and climbed up upon the boulders, between which the flag had been fixed. With his legs spread across the boulders, his massive figure appeared to be battling the flag for dominance. His head stood a bit above the flag in the configuration.

"Congratulations, soldiers! That's right. You are no longer trainees. As of now, you have all been promoted to the rank of private first class in the United States Army," the major announced.

This aroused much clapping and cheering, of which I partook, though somewhat reserved in the doing.

"Now, we are going to head south. It seems there are some Texans down there that need killing!" the major boomed out.

Quite a fantastic pronouncement from a clergyman, I noted. The cheers this decree produced were deafening.

Wondering what reaction this absurdity was producing from Smitty, I took a quick glance in his direction. Though not showing the ignorant joyousness that I saw all about me, he joined in. But his cheer was a reflection of determination, as though he were already heading into the midst of an enemy assault. I cheered to, though through remorse.

"The Texans have charged up the Rio Grande and attacked Fort Craig," the major announced. "We have got to get down there quickly to assist the troops at Fort Union, as most of the troops from that fort have already been deployed to their south. If the Rebels are successful in reaching Albuquerque and Santa Fe, they will capture enough supplies to allow them to continue right on up to our own homesteads. Do you intend to let that happen?"

"No, sir!" the response was again passionate, and I joined in, reluctantly.

"After double-quick back to camp, make ready for departure at first light. You will pack nothing that isn't military issue. Anything found in tote that isn't, will only add to our kindling pile. I'm sure you all understand the importance of getting down there as quickly as possible. Therefore, I have confidence in your cooperation."

Before the major had completed this statement, the colonel's aid had appeared in front of him. The major bent down to listen to the aid and then straightened up again, loudly emoting, "Correction, be ready to move out tonight—directly after chow!" The major had started this sentence in something of a reluctant tone, but his voice gained in strength and volume with every word.

"That colonel has no heart," Smitty commented. "He could at least have given us a chance to get letters off."

Typical—that would be what would bother Smitty. Never mind that we had already spent the day, since sunup, drilling. Now what—march all night? The reality was even worse than I'd expected.

A DISCHARGING OF MUTINY

We formed up after chow preparing to move out. Captain West had us march our mounts down to the supply tent, where they were strapped with bags of rations. "I know you would all feel bad about riding, while the rest of the regiment was on foot," the captain postulated. He probably was right about that I decided, after a bit of contemplating. But it was still some disturbing to lose the one bit of luck I had had so far in this military exploit—the ability to ride my way through it. The trip would be some easier on Spirit and Flash though, as well as the rest of our mounts, since they were only loaded with about half the amount of weight that they would have been by carrying their normal charge.

"That Slough has gotta go," I heard Jake state as soon as the colonel was out of earshot. I expect he intends to march us clean down to Texas on the double-quick, without even letting us catch some winks." His voice came muffled from under his winter hood. We all had them drawn up tight against the mountain wind that came as cold and steady as was natural for Colorado in this, the last week of February. At least the sky was clear, with the moon and stars lighting the way to whatever destiny was awaiting us.

"Lean into your march," I said, not really concerned that my words would reach the ears of anyone—more likely, to reinforce the mind frame Pa had taught me while crossing the plains. "Attack the challenge and make it welcome," I heard myself say.

"Texas is more than four hundred miles away," I heard a voice from beside me reply.

"But it can't get no farther," I responded, more quietly. "Our bodies never give out; only our minds do. Keep pushing, and Texas will keep getting closer."

"He probably expects to get a star for pushing us, while he's back there in his carriage nursing a bottle of gin," Jake spoke out again.

"It ain't the march that bothers me—it's the arriving," I said to no one in particular, but somewhat relieved to have aired this sentiment.

"Ain't you anxious to get into battle with them Rebs?" Jake asked.

"Far as I've heard, those Texans are raised with a gun in there hand. They're practiced hunters and experienced soldiers, known to be fearless in battle. I really wouldn't want to be set upon by the prospect of having to ride straight into their shotguns and Colt revolvers," I admitted.

"Comes up—we'll do it," I heard John Paxton, from behind me, profess somewhat sternly. "We agreed. This job's got to be done, and we'll do it together. That was the lot we drew. So be it."

"That be a fact, John—just, it ain't something I pleasure in anticipating," I replied, hoping that my confession had not been received as an expression of cowardice—for, I had not heard one utterance of fear from anyone else. Perhaps all of my comrades had found this, the same simple truth that John had aired but that I was missing. There could be no taking off and running back to Jenny. Whatever awaited us in Texas would be the fate that I would have to accept. My honor depended upon it! I'd think no more upon any other resolution. Thanking John inwardly, I leaned back into the march.

"Welcome the challenge," I heard John state in return of my encouragement.

About halfway to Texas, we were to meet up with three more companies that had been sent south a month earlier. My hope was that they would greet us with news that the Texans had given up their campaign in defeat. This was a hope I decided against vocalizing and one that was soon to dissolve.

After two days more of marching south with these additional companies, a dispatch from Governor Weld arrived. The news it brought dashed the last of my hope that the situation to the south would no longer require our participation. The troops from Fort Craig, including our own Home Guard, which had been sent south in January to help guard the fort, had suffered a defeat at Valverde. The Texans were, it continued, continuing up the Rio Grande toward Santa Fe. After making this announcement, the major concluded, "The imperative nature of this situation requires us to increase our marching pace."

"Can he be serious?" Jake asked, dipping a hardtack in his coffee in order to soften it enough for chewing. "We're going on nothing but four hours sleep, this stuff, and jerky," he said, lifting the somewhat softened square of solidified flour from his cup. "It ain't enough to keep a man going on, even in good weather."

"He says we're going to be covering forty miles a day. That should put us down to the New Mexico border in a few days. It should be a darn site warmer down there," I predicted, remembering some of the stories I had heard around the mining camps about the heat in them parts.

"Not till we cross the Sierras," Smitty replied. "Those mountains are just as bad if not worse than the Rockies this time of year."

This affair was turning into a real trial of endurance. Luckily, I had Jenny and my ten thousand dollars to reflect upon, less I'd have not one pleasantry of thought. Where were the others finding their strength? I wondered.

When the bugler sounded "attention," we had to chug down our coffee, putting an end to any further contemplation of our situation and forcing us to return to the distraction of physical effort. Perhaps Smitty would be wrong about the weather, I thought.

After joining up with the three forward companies, we started up the Raton Mountain Pass in nothing less than a blizzard. Several inches of snow had already fallen, making it difficult to maintain a foothold, and the brutal wind against our faces seemed to be trying to force us back down the mountainside. Several men, who had succumbed to the cough, had to be left behind to fend for themselves. We left them huddled around a campfire, beneath the shelter of a rocky alcove, on their promise to rejoin us after gaining strength and on the hope that the latter was actually a possibility. The sorrow their misfortune instilled in me waned away that day as we trudged up the pass, fighting for footing, with the cold gusting wind ripping at our faces. Leaving them three behind had, indeed been unavoidable, I decided.

If the weather and trudging were not, in themselves, enough to contend with, in addition, I had the misfortune of overhearing a muffled conversation between Jake, who was to my side, and Hardin, who was to my rear.

"We'll wait for him behind the brush beside his tent. When he comes out to relieve himself of his alcoholic piss, a good blow or two from the butts of our rifles should be plenty enough to deliver him to the land of the worthless," Hardin said. "We'll leave him bleeding on a pillar of rock so those that find him will note that he had obviously struck his head upon slipping," he continued. "We can swish away our footprints with a switch of brush, and our part in the accident will be brushed away in the like."

"It will be a deserved fate too, 'tis sure," Jake added. "The man would push us to death before a bullet's ever fired, to prove to Washington that he ain't slow—though Slough he be of the mind that is. There'll be no crying at his passing, it's sure," he continued. "And the command passing to the competency of the major will be as welcome to the regiment as it is to him. I doubt anyone will be interested in finding any wrongdoing either," he surmised.

"So be it then," Hardin affirmed.

Damn, they are planning to kill the colonel, I thought. But I also thought that it wasn't my place to interfere. Indeed, it did seem insane for a drunken sot to be in control of our fate—but murder? Was there no other way to rectify the situation?

The wind blowing against the ice on my face pulled painfully at the short hairs, hampering my digestion of the situation. It was near nightfall before we rounded the summit of the pass and came in sight of the way station that marked the Colorado-New Mexico border in the valley below. The valley was walled in by a snow-covered mesa on each side. The vertical walls were as white as the trees above and the tree-covered slopes below due to their limestone composition. The plateaus dropped off in the distance, forming a perfect vee at the exit of the pass. The rise at the end of the pass was noticeably marked by three mudded wagon trails. The one we were on came from Colorado, to the north. A trail broke off of it, going eastward to Leavenworth and Saint Louie. The other broke to the west toward California. Together, the trails formed an arrow at their convergence, pointing the way out through the vee in the southern end of the plateaus. The large open area in the center of the valley, to the front of the way station, made for a convenient camping area. We drew our supply wagons into a circle at its center, to form the corral we employed to contain and protect our animals. The Indians were notorious for sneaking into a night camp to stampede off a herd. And Comanche and Apache were said to be all about in these parts.

After we had removed their packs, Smitty and I checked Spirit and Flash for chafing from the straps. They looked surprisingly well, compared to most of the mounts. We would grease their sides for protection before re-strapping the bags on departure. For a spell, they were free to graze on the grass shoots that had risen since the last wagon train had put in at the station.

Smitty had cleared away an area next to mine and was trying to wedge a tent peg between the frozen rocks that were the makeup of the valley floor.

"Did you hear Popp and Hardin planning their deed?" I asked Smitty, while stretching my pup tent to the last peg I had driven with my trenching tool.

"I heard Hardin say something about alcoholic piss, so I suspected they were complaining about the colonel again," Smitty replied with a chuckle.

"They're aiming to lay for him in the bushes tonight."

"They may be doing us all a favor, if they do," Smitty suggested.

"Maybe so, but it wouldn't be smart of them, nonetheless. "A man can't live with himself after wronging another that badly," I said, the same way I had heard Pa speak those words on several occasions.

"Doubt it'd be the first time for either of them to do a man in," Smitty replied, having moved on to do battle with the next peg.

"Still, I'd like to think that we have the Lord on our side, if we're about to go into battle with the Rebs. The deed they're planning isn't likely to put us in His favor." Putting this thought into words was a bit of a revelation to me, in that I hadn't previously thought through why their plan disturbed me so.

"It's no doing of ours," Smitty snapped back with a bit of agitation detectable in his tone.

"All the same, it doesn't feel right," I replied, unrolling my bedroll into my tent and then dropping in upon it.

"Listen," Smitty said as his head appeared in the tent opening above me. "Leave it alone. We got enough to worry about fighting the Rebs. We don't want to have to watch our backs too."

"Do I look like I'm planning to get involved?" I asked him. "I'm just planning on getting as much shut-eye as they'll let me."

"Yeah, and you ain't alone. They'll probably have us back on the trail by sunup," Smitty said as he ducked back out of the tent opening.

Sleep came to me instantaneously. But in what would have seemed a matter of seconds, were it not for the amount of snow that had drifted up beside me and had found its way under the collar of my topcoat, I was awakened. The unfastened flap on my tent had blown open and was being held open by a foot-high drift of snow. Reaching out to grab the flap, my glance took me to the stationhouse. The colonel's coach had pulled up beside it. To the rear of the house, in the twilight, I could see a figure lumbering to make its way to the outhouse. The staggering bulk was unmistakably that of the colonel. I watched him slowly make his way down and into the outhouse. My stomach sickened slightly as two hunched figures, with rifles in tote, appeared from behind the brush, scurried over to the outhouse, and stooped down beside it.

They were actually going to do it! I felt like yelling out a warning to the colonel but didn't, knowing that Smitty was right. If they knew that I had warned the colonel, I'd be even higher on their hate list than he was. I could run down, on the pretense of wanting to use the john myself. But that wouldn't fly, because none of us, other than the officers, had use for a john, since leaving the fort, considering it a luxury that served to slow our advance.. Besides, they'd probably pull me aside and expect me to cooperate with their deadly contrivance. I could only turn my back on the wintery murder scene about to take place behind the stationhouse.

The figures beside it appeared only as motionless, dark mounds, as the wind-driven snow attempted to blur out the entire scene—except there was a motion occurring in the background. A buckboard had come through the pass and had taken the eastward fork at the arrow tip. The moonlight flickering off of its rounded, rear cover presented a sight I was familiar with from the medic's station at Fort Weld. No sooner had the buckboard turned full broadside to me than it disappeared behind a bluff. Grabbing my rifle from the tent, I quickly loaded it with a ball.

This had nothing to do with the scene unfolding behind the stationhouse, I told myself in reassurance. Yet, I noticed, as it happened, that my muzzle was pointed about directly above the figures at the outhouse, where the concussion from its firing would be the loudest in projection.

On its resounding, the dark mounds moved quickly out to the rear of the scene. As I ran toward the captain's tent, I glimpsed the colonel's heavy figure waddling toward the stationhouse, while simultaneously trying to pull up his trousers. Captain Thompson had jumped out of his tent, which was some distance from and above my own, and was run-sliding toward me.

"What the hell do you think you're doing—robbing these men of the little sleep they are afforded?" he shouted.

"It's an ambulance, Captain!" I shouted out. "I saw an ambulance come from the south and take the trail east."

"Well, quit wasting time. News from the south could change all our plans. Get your mount saddled and head them off, before there's too much distance between us. Don't kill your mount doing it though," the captain said to my back as I stepped through the high snow cover toward the coral, in a joyous state—relieved that my action had apparently been acceptable to him.

"Won't need a saddle, Sir," I replied back to the captain. "There won't be any problems."

"Don't know why you had to wake us all, instead of just heading out after them," the captain yelled after me.

"Sir, I feared the major might shoot me clean off my horse if he thought I had decided to just ride out of here," I yelled back.

Distance would save me from any further conversation on the subject. And the captain would surely understand this reasoning—seeing how the major had, on more than one occasion, threatened to shoot any deserters.

To shorten the distance to the ambulance, I contemplated leaving the trail and cutting across the valley but decided against it. With darkness all but set in, and with the snow covering prairie dog holes and the like all about, I feared having Spirit chance an injury. I was determined not to let Spirit suffer an injury as a result of my unnecessary provocations.

In a few minutes, we were riding beside the ambulance. "Sir, I'm Private Swenson, with the 1st Colorado Volunteers—sent by Captain Thompson to ascertain any information you can afford us on the campaign to the south."

"Can't stop for you, Private," the corporal holding the reins of the buckboard replied. "I've got to get the captain to Leavenworth for treatment. I'll tell you this though: Sibly's taken Albuquerque and Santa Fe and has given them a thorough sacking. We passed a wagon train a ways back that was heading to Fort Union with supplies. The Rebs had ambushed it and were in the process of confiscating everything as we passed. I do have to give them credit, though, for having the decency to grant us safe passage. If you boys can get to Fort Union before Sibly, I'm sure you'll get a welcome from Colonel Paul. Right now, the eight hundred men in our regiment are far outnumbered by the Rebs."

"I'm sure our command will see the need to respond at once to their aid. May I tell them whom it was I have spoken to, sir?" I asked.

"Gladly. I'm Corporal Prestly B. Waite, under Colonel Paul's medical command."

"Thank you, sir, and farewell," I replied, happy to be able to ease my gait on Spirit at last.

"Farewell, lad," the corporal called back as the medic wagon continued to jostle down the trail.

"No more need to hurry, boy," I said as I hopped down off Spirit and raised a handful of oats from my sachet to his mouth. "I'm sure there'll be plenty of hurrying in store for us when we get back with this news," I told him.

How I had become involved with this correspondence, I wasn't sure. But, it was likely to have grave consequences, for which, I suspected, I bore the responsibility—responsibility I would have to see through.

The camp was dead quiet on our return—not a sound except that of the wind howling through the tents and a canvas or two flapping at its passing. Slowly, I walked Spirit passed the sleeping sentry on the lead wagon and into the corral. Before going to see the captain, I tended to Spirit's needs, to ensure nothing would prevent me from doing so in the aftermath of my pronouncement. The worst that could come of this episode, which I had produced, would be that the exertion from it might have weakened Spirit and his ability to affect the effort that would be demanded from him in the campaign ahead. But the sharpness of his movements and the affectionate nudges he bestowed upon me lightened my concern in this matter. Our lone journey seemed to have pleased him. Perhaps it had acted as an assurance to him that we were still an entity, rather than two separate parts of an army.

The captain was startled on hearing my report. "Come with me," he immediately ordered. I had to all but run to keep up with his long, quick strides up to the command post.

"Private!" Captain Thompson barked at the colonel's aid, who sat beside the command tent entrance on a case of hardtack. The aid's head hung in front of his chest, his cheek pressed against the side of the musket that he held wedged between his thighs.

"Sir," the aid replied, quickly jumping to attention on recognition of the captain's appearance.

"Awaken the major immediately," the captain commanded.

The private had not fully stepped into the poorly lighted abode before the unmistakable rasp of Major Chivington's harsh voice proclaimed, "Step in, Captain."

The captain took hold of my arm as he stepped into the large tent— the intention of his expecting me to follow being, therefore, clearly suggested. "This is Private Swenson," the captain announced. "He was the cause of the undesirable weapon discharge earlier this evening."

Through the pale flicker of light that the flare of the kerosene heater was producing, I could see the major's countenance immediately harden.

His reply came in a low growl. "If you brought this man in here for a disciplinary action—" The strength of the major's voice grew with each word he spoke.

And defensively, the captain replied in interruption, before the pending explosion manifested, "No, not at all, sir. Though the private's action was somewhat impulsive, it was motivated by patriotic exuberance."

"Let's have the story, Captain," the major demanded, his voice only a bit gruffer now than its norm. As I stood silently at attention I delighted in the warmth of the tent and contemplated the consequences that would arise, were I to tell the rest of the events that had evolved in that wintry sunset behind the stationhouse.

"It happened that the private saw an ambulance racing through the pass from the south and taking the eastward fork up ahead. Not wanting to let it get out of range, he acted with all means available to get immediate permission to pursue this possible source of information on the situation to the south—which he was successful in ascertaining."

"It seems strange that a private would have the insight to recognize the importance of a situation report. Have you any previous military experience?"

This would be the first time that I would be directly addressing the major. There was majesty about his personage that seemed almost godly. I knew, instinctively, that to deceive him would be out of the question. "No, I have not. It's just that I have been aching to know the situation in New Mexico, insofar as our success and my own fate is at stake in the forthcoming affair."

"From your answer, I'm not sure if it's your insight or fear that's extreme. But since your report is of such importance to me, I will excuse your motivation, whatever had been its inducement, in appreciation of your service and ask you to proceed forthright."

"Yes, sir."

Before I completed the telling of Corporal Waite's information, the canvas, concealing another area to the rear of the tent, opened. The dumpy figure of Colonel Slough appeared in flannel underclothing—his unkempt appearance not in the least bit a depiction of authority. Yet when my report had ended, his absolute command became upfront.

In the rear portion of the tent, from which the colonel had emerged, I could see a second heater flickering from the foot of a cot. Beside the cot, a small keg served as a table, upon which there sat a bottle and a glass. Had I saved this man's life? I wondered.

"John," the colonel began, addressing Major Chivington "we've got to move them right out." The slur in the colonel's voice was unmistakable.

"That'll be all, Captain," the major said, dismissing Captain Thompson. "Good work, son," he added to me, his sincerity appearing obvious to me through his hard eye contact, though I now believe this to be the norm for all his conversations.

"We'll have to give them a couple hours to recoup," we heard the major clearly state from outside the command tent.

The conversation inside continued as the captain and I walked away. Its conclusion would soon become woeful knowledge to all in our regiment.

No sooner had I fallen exhausted upon my bedding, it seemed, then I heard the bugler sound "assembly." This was quite unacceptable to me. The rest of the men had had at least a couple hours of sleep time, while I'd had next to none.

"Let's go!" Smitty hollered in at me.

"Okay," I replied. *If I drop, I drop*, I thought. That'd be it. *Then, I'll be able to get some rest.*

"What in the hell was the shooting about?" Smitty asked as I emerged from my tent.

"I saw an ambulance come up the pass and had to get the cap up quick, to get his permission to run it down."

"I'd never go that far," Smitty replied. "I'd have just run down to his tent, if I had a notion to go chasing it."

"Well, between us, there was something else that prompted the shot," I confessed as we hustled down the hillside toward the assemblage. "It seemed there was an ambush about to take place behind the stationhouse."

"Ollie. You ass! I thought I convinced you to stay out of that matter."

"It just sort of happened," I explained.

"I hope them two don't put two and two together," Smitty concluded, before we got in earshot of our company.

"At ease, men! But listen up!" The major paused after giving these commands to assure quiet would prevail across our ranks. "I want to give my sincere thanks to each of you for the effort you have given us these past days. Our drive to this point has been remarkable, particularly against this weather. However, news has reached us from the south that the Texans have already sacked Albuquerque and Santa Fe. They have helped themselves to whatever they had a liking of, raped the women, and burned the towns."

I thought, for a second, that the major had intercepted another messenger but, on second thought, didn't give much credence to that possibility. It was more likely, I suspected, that the major had added to the message as a means of festering increased hostility in us toward the Texans. Yet I was later to learn that his fabrication was close to the actuality of the events as they had occurred—except that, the burning had actually been done by our troops, before they pulled out of the towns, in an effort to rob the Rebs of their bounty. However, the Texans managed to save some supplies from the fires.

"We also know that, just today, they attacked a supply wagon that was on its way to our troops in Fort Union. What does all this mean? Well, Albuquerque and Santa Fe are now confederate territory, and New Mexico itself will fall with Fort Union. And fall it will! The Texans have our troops far outnumbered and have all the supplies they just captured. But there's one factor they're not aware of—one that's going to spoil their onslaught. The Pike's Peakers are going to show up! We are the only thing between them, Colorado, and perhaps the entire West. Right now, they are riding high on victory. And that's just what's going to make it all the easier for us to drop them on their asses! They'll be in shock when they find themselves confronted by a force of real fighting men, rather than by a group of half-hearted local militia, as they have been in the past. So that is the situation we have arrived to in New Mexico. We've come to do a job. And do it we shall. It has become of the utmost importance that we get down to Fort Union as soon as possible. If we beat the Texans, we can save our troops, adding them to our own numbers before the battle with the Texans comes about. To do this, we are going to have to make much better time."

A groan could be heard throughout the formation at this outrageous announcement. The major had the outright gall to make this statement to totally exhausted troops, who had been called back into formation after but a little over two hours sleep, in what was nothing less than a winter blizzard.

"This won't be as hard as it sounds," the major continued. It's going to be downhill from here on out. And we're going to do it without packs weighing us down." A bit of a muffled cheer could be heard at this statement. "We'll only take what we need to reach the fort. We're going to leave a company of men here as a corporal guard for our supplies. Anyone feeling he is too weak or ill to keep up can fall out now. And form up at the medic's tent. Examinations by the medics will determine who is to remain. It has been a proud journey that you have all been a part of to this very spot. And I would suggest to you that a lifetime of pride will be the reward of this campaign. Don't trade that for the embarrassment of having tried to shuck your duty—especially since the medics will sort you out just the same. If, however, you are unable to hold your own in this venture, your efforts will be nonetheless honorable for stepping out now. And you should do so."

The major looked out over the formation as some thirty or more men broke ranks and made their way toward the medics' tent. The demeanor of those who decided to fall out, for the most part, reflected their ailing—except one or two—namely, Popp and Hardin. It was a relief for me to see the two elect to remain. The Texans were, in themselves, enough of a threat to contemplate.

"Your blankets, weapons, and canteens—that's all the gear you'll be toting from here on out. Turn the rest in to the quartermaster and then fall back out for coffee and smoke. We will be forming back up at twenty-three hundred hours and moving out on the double-quick. Fall out, men!" the major concluded.

As we broke formation and started heading toward our campsites, I noticed Paxton hacking and coughing, just as he had been for several days ongoing. *Wouldn't I have tried for the guard duty if I were in his place?* I asked myself. Embarrassingly, I decided that I would have. Paxton was still with us and still with the cough as we moved out. Unfortunately, so were Popp and Hardin. Apparently, the medics had not believed them to be unhealthy enough to necessitate remaining behind.

The wind had actually increased in intensity after we left the pass and started down into New Mexico, making it hard to determine if the horizontal snow falling was coming from the sky or blowing off the rocky terrain that surrounded us. Although we were on the double-quick, the march seemed close to effortless without the packs that had previously become a normal part of our body weight. Though it was much easier to cover ground, I did not feel any joy in hastening to a battlefield. My anticipation was even farther eroded by Popp's words as he passed on my flank.

"This is all of your doing, Swenson," he said, engaging me with a glaring eye—to which I had no response available.

It was sunup before we stopped for a break. By then, neither Popp, nor the Texans, gave me much cause for worry. The drudge of the march had eclipsed all other concerns at that point. The duration of the blizzard was unprecedented in my memory. It seemed to me that the Lord must have been trying to keep us from reaching the fort. Could it be that I was on the wrong side of the conflict? I wondered.

The conversation around our hardtack shindig ranged from patriotic to mutinous. But it was mostly fixed on punishing the Texans sufficiently for the torture we had been enduring.

24

BATTLE PLANS AND EXPECTATIONS

Thirty-six hours after leaving the pass, we had arrived at the gates of Fort Union. We had covered a distance of ninety-two miles, while stopping only once for a few hours rest. My body had proven to be more of an indestructible mechanism than even I had contemplated—seeing how it was operating entirely on coffee, water, hardtack, and bouillon. Before we had come in sight of the fort, my brain had become just as numb as my body. Rather than having rational, conscious thought, I seemed to be in something of a sleepwalking stupor. Spirit's stride had also become labored, even though his load was reduced to half of what he had carried across Colorado. I seriously doubted that he could go on more than a few more miles without rest.

Passing through the gates of Fort Union, I was brought back to reality. The major had, to our surprise, packed our drums and pipes on some of the burrows and brought them out to accompany our colors on arrival. The entire company of the fort whistled and cheered upon our entry. And not a man among us, I'm sure, felt any guilt over enjoying the pride our accomplishment instilled in us, since we all knew that the trial we had undergone was nothing less than an ordeal.

"Where the hell did you come from?" I heard one member of the fort's company call out.

"God's country," was the response. And it was one that we all had in mind.

"Who be you then, angels?" another of the company questioned.

239

"Just one step lower—Pike's Peakers," Captain Thompson responded, for all of us.

Once settled in, we slept long and hard. While we slept, Slough negotiated. The commander of the fort, one Colonel Gabriel Paul, was under orders to sit tight and await the arrival of General Canby's forces. Adding Canby's regiment would create a force superior to Sibley's Confederate regiment. Paul, having been a West Point graduate and highly acclaimed Mexican War hero, outclassed Slough in experience. Slough, however, though of the same rank as Paul, outweighed him in seniority and, under high protest from Paul, used this technicality to take full command of the fort's body.

"The order still stands!" Colonel Paul insisted.

"All standing orders are not passed on with command," Slough contested. "Our orders are generated as a result of a situation report, presented by the field command. Since it was not I who presented the report, which generated the orders, the orders do not therefore apply to my command."

"And how would your situation report have varied enough to impact headquarters toward accepting your ambitious plan of attacking, with little more than an equal number of troops as has the enemy—while, on the other hand, we could simply sit in the safety of the fort awaiting a large reinforcement from Canby that would assure us of an easy victory."

"I understand that Sibly simply bypassed Canby at Fort Bliss, in order to move on and capture Albuquerque and Santa Fe. Why wouldn't he do the same thing here and then move right on up to Denver? As I understand it, he is already well stocked with your supplies."

"Well he surely wouldn't cut himself off from Texas, with this large of a force to his rear," Paul contended.

"And why wouldn't he? Denver has a large contingency of Southern sympathizers, as do the California and Oregon territories. If the Confederates promise business concessions, like a stake in the mines and railroad, to be divided among the populus in these territories, they could very easily swing the entire west over to their cause, leaving us as an isolated fragment in the new, huge western Confederacy. No, Colonel. The Texans have to be confronted and stopped here, in New Mexico.

And we aren't going to do it by sitting in this cluster of adobe huts you call a fort. If the Rebels set up a cannon battery on the mesa to the west, they can use the big guns to level these huts and leave our diminished forces in the open for a slaughtering," Colonel Slough contended.

"While they set up on the mesa, we could always pull back to beyond the creek, a mile to the east, and defeat them as they try to ford its water," Colonel Paul contested.

"Retreat in their wake? Colonel, you are a war veteran. Surely you know how the sight of the enemy forced into flight offers the greatest inspiration an army can obtain. They will run us down and mow us down as the creek hampers our retreat. That's not a picture I want to see materialize. In the least, they will have control of the fort and can leave it manned by a small force as they continue their siege. My men have pushed themselves to get here—over four hundred miles in thirteen days—across snow-whipped plains and mountain ranges. They did it to help you defeat the Texans, not cower in front of them! I am enforcing my seniority and usurping your command. You are to order your company to make ready for an immediate attack on the enemy," Colonel Slough forcefully demanded.

"Colonel, you will take full responsibility for this action. I will see to that. If you think I have any reservations in reporting thusly, you are badly mistaken. It is the safety of the men that should be of greatest concern here," Colonel Paul concluded, displaying sternness in his countenance.

"You have my orders." Colonel Slough's response was harsh and dismissive.

On March 22, Colonel Slough marched us out of Fort Union, along with most of the Fort's garrison troops. Colonel Slough's carriage, as usual, followed to our rear. We were to march down the Santa Fe Trail and attack the Texans in the New Mexico territory's capitol city of Santa Fe. With the best part of the forts troops added to or own, we now had over thirteen hundred men. This number included members of the Colorado Volunteers 2nd Regiment, Company B. They were the ones who had marched to New Mexico in February and had partaken in the battle at Valverde Ford. They were under the command of a Captain Dodd. It was from two members of this company that I got my first insight into the actualities of combat.

After disengaging from the battle at Valverde, Canby had returned to Fort Craig, and was sent an ultimatum from the Confederate commander, Colonel Sibly—"surrender or die." When Canby refused to surrender, Sibly simply marched his forces north, intent on capturing supplies from the cities there, rather than attacking the fort as he had threatened. Canby sent his New Mexico Volunteers to harass Sibly's rear guard and slow his advance. New Mexico's Governor Connelly had joined the volunteers in hope of reaching Santa Fe before the Confederates, so as to be able to prepare his government for departure. Two of Dodd's Coloradoan troops were sent as personal aids and guards to assure the governor's safety. During a hardtack-soaking break, we listened to these two troops recanting their tale—in a bragging fashion to which they apparently had a legitimate right.

"During the assault at Valverde, we were sent far to the right and had to wade, waist-deep, across the ice-covered creek. The Texans were taking cover in a grove of trees at the end of the ford," a member of Dodd's Coloradoans named Rick recanted. "We were all yelling mad by the time we got across the creek. The icy water made it feel as if our ankles and nuts were being squashed in a vise," he went on. "All we knew was that we had to drive them Texans out before we could set about wringing the ice water out of our trousers. So we charged right into the thicket, bayonets to the front, and chased them back across a field, where they found cover in a ditch. But that was the ones that were still standing."

"We'd have jumped right in after them too," another of Dodd's troops, named Will, added, "except our captain had us form back up for another charge, to help the men in the middle of our line hold off an assault. But no sooner had we formed up than we saw a charge coming right at us. It was the damnedest sight we're ever apt to see too. Ain't it so, Rick?" Will asked, passing the conversation back to his companion, so he could enjoy listening to the telling.

"It sure enough was. A forty-man cavalry company of lancers was charging toward us in columns of four, carrying nine-foot poles topped by a bayonet and waving red flag. They let out a chilling yell when they got close. In our two-rank formation, the captain had us wait until they were about a tree length to our front before we let a volley fly. When our kneeling rank, including Will and me, opened up, there was a pileup of horses, poles, and Rebs. After our second rank had fired, their forces were completely reduced to a pile of twisted bodies. Some of the lances had come down to the front of their column, and as they plunged into the ground, their bearers were lifted right out of their saddles and tossed about in the melee. Soon, the red flags they had flown blended into the blood covering the ground. After we got off our second volley, there were but three men that I saw scampering back toward the creek," Rick proudly emoted.

"I wonder why they were using lances," I said. "Maybe they don't have enough guns for all their troops."

"No way," Rick quickly replied. "There isn't a Texan alive that hasn't got several weapons. Most are toting more than two. They probably thought they could scare us into cowering. Don't think they knew they'd be fighting Coloradoans. If it had been a bunch of Mexican volunteers they were attacking, the Rebs would have had them hightailing it, for sure," Will suggested.

"Not Carson's Mexicans," Rick added, apparently correcting Will's assertion.

"No, not them Mexicans," Will agreed.

"If Carson had taken the left, instead of following us to the right when we moved to help Duncan, we might not have lost McRae's guns," he continued.

"The Rebs captured your gun?" I asked in surprise.

"Yes, a six-gun battery," Will confirmed, somewhat sheepishly. "Then they turned them down on us! We had the Texans scurrying off into the hills on the right, before their big guns started opening up on the left end of our assault. They put our guys on the run, so we moved to help them. But some seven to eight hundred Rebs were right on their ass, along with their big guns, cutting them down in the water. They probably would have kept on them till they dropped them to a man if Colonel Canby hadn't sent out a white flag and asked for a mercy truce, to allow both sides to collect their dead and wounded."

"Sounds like the Confederates came out ahead then," I suggested.

"Well, they got the guns," Rick offered. "We both lost a couple hundred men. But the big advantage to the Rebs was that they got past the fort and got to raid the stores at Albuquerque."

"They also left Canby stuck between them and the Confederate troops in El Paso," Will added.

"I don't suspect they would have been much of a threat to us if Canby could have managed to hold them to the south of the fort. Would they?" I asked.

"Sure wouldn't," Will replied. "They'd have probably had to hightail it back to Texas and might have had a problem with that. Supplies mean victory out here—like Lynde found out."

"Lynde?" I asked.

"Oh, that's right. You fellows haven't heard anything about the Texan victories down here, have you?" Will asked.

"No, not much," Smitty and I both conceded.

"When the Confederate Colonel Baylor moved north from El Paso to threaten Fort Filmore, Major Lynde decided to abandon the fort and retreat to Fort Stanton—this, even though his forces were half-again larger than Baylor's," Will began, further informing us of the recent events. "What Lynde failed to consider was how much water his men would need to cross a hundred and forty miles of desert. And it's been said some of his men, not so cleverly, filled their canteens with whiskey that they had previously been ordered to burn. When Baylor's men caught up with him, they found Lynde's troops crawling on all fours and begging for water. Baylor not only got the Fort but was also supplied with a new herd of cattle—allowing him to further his advance," Will explained.

"They probably were some of the same cattle Paddy Graydon went after at Fort Craig," Rick added, continuing this extraordinary report.

"That's a story you'd be sure to get a kick out of hearing. When Baylor sent Major Sibly farther up the Rio Grande to attack Fort Craig," he went on with the story, "he had his men camp out on a mesa across the river from the fort. After having his cattle led to the river for watering, the Confederate herd was left to graze freely at the foot of the mesa. That night, Paddy, being the clever ex-dragoon fighter that he was, lashed boxes of twenty-four-pound Howitzer shells to the backs of two mules. With the help of some fellow scouts, he led them across the river and toward the Rebel cattle herd. They lit the fuses and whacked the mules on the tail end, sending them prancing straight for the herd. Problem was, when Paddy and his boys turned and started running back toward the river, those mules sensed trouble coming and did a quick turnaround. Before the group got back to the river, mule parts were flying all about them. Upon returning, they found the troops at the fort had been rudely awakened by the blast. But, it seemed, Paddy was too embarrassed to detail the cause of the explosions. Still, although Paddy's exploits failed to damage the Confederate cattle herd, it may have contributed, indirectly, to a success for our side.

"After Paddy's shenanigans—the Texan guards must have been soundly asleep—their mules, about a hundred fifty of them, were enticed by the smell from the river to saunter down to its bank. Espying them, our guards herded the mules across the water and right into the fort without being detected. In the morning, while Paddy took credit for the entire affair, the Texans were busy torching some of their own wagons— seeing how they were now some shy of mule teams. This was probably what spurred them into leaving the fort and heading north. They know an army can lose one battle and go on to other victories. But without supplies, it's time to head home."

"If that's the case, why won't the Texans just pass us by and take Fort Union with the small garrison we left guarding it?" Paxton asked.

"No way to get by. They probably would if they could," Rick explained. "But there's no way through these mountains except through Glorietta Pass—straight up in front of us. The pass is narrow with near vertical walls, and the terrain above is too jagged and sharp to travel over."

"It seems as though God has cut us a roadway," Smitty said.

"Us or the Texans," I added, perplexed by the entirety of what I had just learned and of what was forthcoming.

The 2nd Regiment veterans had begun telling us about another skirmish they had had with the Texans on the way up to Albuquerque when we were called to formation. Their tales had set me to wondering. Since their regiment had been sent in advance, with only a small amount of training, and yet they had been subjected to such bitter combat, what would our command be expecting from us? I wasn't anxious to find out.

Colonel Slough marched us out fifty miles to Bernal Springs. Since there was still sunlight remaining, he sent Chivington with us Pike's Peakers on ahead as skirmishers. In selecting us to be sent ahead, I suspected Slough was glad to be rid of the hostility toward him that he knew existed in our company. And I knew exactly how he felt. Jake Popp seemed more threatening to me than the Texans did at that point—probably due to the frequent glares and spiteful comments he would throw my way.

At nightfall, we made camp at a Polish emigrant rancher's spread. The major sent scouts high into the rocks at the side of the trail to watch for Texans that might be coming through the trail ahead of us. To our delight, our troops managed to capture four Confederate scouts and return them to our camp. Upon questioning these young men, we learned that they were trappers from Mississippi, who saw the Confederate Army as a chance to gain recognition of their tracking and marksmanship ability.

"How are you at escaping?" the major asked the Rebels pointedly. "You see, we have no stockade facility available for you at the moment. And since I can't spare any men to accompany you to the rear, it seems to me that the only thing left to do is let you try to escape and then shoot you dead on your way out!" The major's voice had reached its normal, earth-shaking intensity by the end of this sentence.

The four youths sat in front of him with mouths agape—too shocked to comment.

"That is, unless your loyalty to the Confederacy can be disproved, by a report on your company's size, location, and armament. In that case,

I could accept an oath of honor on your part to remain uninvolved in this war henceforth. And, in so stating, you would be allowed to return to your native state and remain alive."

Of course, it was easy to predict what decision these boys would come to. The major took their long guns before sending them off to the north. I suspected that they might not live up to their oath to remain uninvolved in the war. But whether or not they did was insignificant to the major—since, they truly would have been too much of a burden to maintain as prisoners. In any case, the information they supplied us with was invaluable to our mission.

The major stated that they would not return to their company, on fear that they might be forced to admit their disclosures to us. The question was, was their information to us truthful? If it was, Sibly, in Santa Fe, had sent out a party of skirmishers behind them. They were about equal in number to our four hundred men. But, they had the advantage of having in their possession two of the six-pound Howitzers from McCrae's captured battery. This party, they informed us, was one to two days south of us, making its way up the Santa Fe Trail—that is to say, heading straight toward us!

In the morning, we set out, cautiously, making our way up the tree-covered western slope to the mouth of the pass. It was good to have Popp's squad to my front as we ascended—good to have him in view, that is. In the event of an engagement with the Rebs, which seemed inevitable at that point, I would attempt to keep him to my front. Having him to my front relaxed my fear. Also, the situation at that time was too intense to allow for the fear of combat, which I had previously anticipated having to deal with. My senses were heightened in a way that only an instinct for survival can induce. And the dominant effect this produced was alertness. How favorable fate had been to those four Mississippi Rebs, I thought. They were actually committed, by honor, to get out of this war. It was not likely enough to happen that I should store any hope in being saved from the forthcoming combat by a situation like theirs. I had to concentrate on protecting my life by the only means I had available—that being by defeating my enemies.

As our advanced scouts rounded the summit and viewed the descending trail that led to the floor of the pass proper, they spotted several columns of smoke arising from a thicket of trees at the side of the trail. Further observation revealed that a group of thirty-two of the Texan forward skirmishers had taken refuge for the approaching night in the thicket. These skirmishers were referred to by the Confederates as brigands. Although, they didn't wear a confederate uniform, and were in fact, an unkempt bunch, the scouts knew to expect them at the forefront of the the rebel advances. They were actually a group of criminals and ruffians that used the war as an excuse to plunder the countryside. And for that reason, they always demanded to be to the front of a troop movement. This trail offered them nothing in the way of plunder. And since combat confrontation was not actually part of their motivation, they apparently felt no need to further their advance after sunset.

On hearing this report on the presence of the brigands, the major sent half of our men down a ravine at the side of the trail, where they were out of sight. Remaining on the opposite side of the summit, the only task we in the cavalry were assigned was to keep our mounts subdued during the action. At the base of the hillside, our men crawled slowly and silently upward, while spreading out around the brigands. They had gotten within a hundred feet of them before a Reb noticed a movement of the brush. The Confederate strode out, pistol in hand, and stood directly over one of our troops, one Bud Wilson. "On your feet, Yankee. You're captured!" he commanded matter-of-factly as he pointed his gun down at Bud.

"Not so," Bud replied, loud enough to be heard by all of our party, which at that time had the brigands completely surrounded. It's you that has been captured!" Bud pronounced as he rose.

At his statement, our two hundred men stepped out from behind the rocks and bushes, their guns fixed on the brigands. From their three campsites, the brigands jumped up and started toward their rifle stands. One round was fired into the air, followed by a bluster that dwarfed the rifle retort.

"I wouldn't do that!" The major's majestic voice rang out like a reproaching at one of his Sunday sermons.

The brigands froze in their tracks and were taken, to the man, without incident.

The major used similar tactics to extract a report from them as he had used on the Mississippians, except, instead of releasing them, he had them bound head to foot. He left four men with them as a guard before we moved on.

"These are not the kind of men you can commit to a pact of honor," he said. "We will hold them here until we return with the rest of the Texan invaders. We know where they are now!" the major announced. "They're right in front of us—walled in by Apache Canyon. What say we corral the rest of these Texans!"

The major's excitement was contagious. My cavalry unit had come down from the summit to join the rest of our company. And I too felt exalted as a cheer, "Hurray for the Pike's Peakers," rang out.

Not one thought by anyone, I suspect, was given to the six-pound Howitzers the Confederates were toting—unless it was by the major himself.

25

RECOGNIZING THE ENEMY

"Men, the battle is at hand. Leave everything but your weapons with the guard. No buffalo robes, overcoats, or canteens. We are going to rain down on them before they make it out of that canyon. And we'll be fighting loose and wild!"

The major's words had us worked into frenzy as we anticipated a plummeting of the Texans. But as we hastily moved down into the walled roadway, aptly designated as Glorietta Pass, my ardor toward the swiftly approaching confrontation waned considerably. I was once again keeping Popp in the proliferation of my vision.

With our encumbrances now reduced to nothing more than our weapons, our pace was increased to a notch or two below one that would have had our troops running. We were running to capture our prize—the Texan army. Perhaps it was a result of the exhaustion of our monthlong campaign that I was finding myself in a state of utter confusion. Could it really be a sensible and even joyous thing to be running toward an enemy army? Yet, so far, we had captured thirty-six Texans without sustaining a single injury. Could it be that they were also reluctant to have their bodies dashed by enemy fire? Perhaps they would simply lay down their weapons on sight of our exuberance.

Or so it would have seemed until we rounded a bend in the road that opened to Apache Canyon proper and pulled up abruptly on the command of, "Take cover!"

About six hundred feet to our front, a mounted company of soldiers had pulled up. The banner they were sporting was an unmistakable one—the Lone Star flag. Next of notice were the two six-pound Howitzer guns. They were being unlimbered in front of columns of infantry. It was a force nearly equal to ours in manpower yet far superior in firepower, giving consideration to the two, ominously pointed cannons. We quickly scurried our mounts into the pines that lined the left side of the canyon.

Their cavalry had apparently done the same—allowing their infantry to exchange pops of muzzle fire with our own. These pops were indicative of the launching of a small ball of lead through the air—a ball that could rip through semisolid matter, like human flesh and bone, or could flatten out on impact against the solid rocks lining the canyon walls. As nondescriptive as these little pops were to the destructive power of their counterpart, so too did not even the loud booming of the cannons totally warn of the devastating capability of their hellish projectile. The two cannons fired about simultaneously. The first ball came straight up the middle of the roadway. And since our infantry had fallen to the prone, it soared over them. Fortunately, the fuse was of sufficient length to carry it past our company before exploding, harmlessly, against the hillside at the bend of the road. The swoosh it made in passing did, however, cause a good deal of damage to our fighting spirit.

During our journey to Pike's Peak, my brother Kurt and I, on occasion, had practiced throwing bolos. Just as the swish of the bolos or that of a bullwhip lashing through the air gives a discernible indication of their power, so too did the loud swoosh that the cannonball produced in its passing project an unmistakable warning as to its prodigiousness.

The second ball was more effectual by far. It slammed into the pines to my front, sending everything from splinters to log-size chunks flying in all directions before exploding and adding hunks of metal shrapnel to the projectile spray. Wailful cries of pain indicated that more than one of our men had suffered the effects of the second cannon boom.

Once into the pines, with a large number of trees protecting my front, I felt somewhat sheltered from the cannonballs for the moment. Then, while assessing my safety, a bit of panic stirred me with the realization that I had lost sight of Popp and Hardin as we'd scattered into the trees. Quickly, I checked to my rear and just caught a fleeting glimpse of several mounts rounding the bend that led back out of the canyon. Popp, Hardin, and another rider appeared to be deserting! *What a break*, I thought. The only enemy I had left to worry about was to my front.

"Pike's Peakers, take to the hillside! Leave your mounts. Get above them guns and get them silenced. West, send some of your men to the right flank to get above them. Do it now!" Major Chivington was giving the commands from his mount—the only mounted soldier on the canyon floor at the time and by far the biggest target. *He must be fearless*, I thought.

"You heard the major! All squads in company A—leave your horses here. Get across the canyon and work your way above them guns," Captain Thompson ordered. "Move out now!"

I quickly wrapped Spirit's reins around a tree trunk and joined my company in a low crawl back toward the road. Before we had crawled fifty meters, a cannonball exploded directly to our front, freezing us in place.

Then immediately, we were brought back to reality by the major's booming orders. "Go now, before they can get off another round. Get across now!"

Ceding to the insight of the major's command, we jumped to our feet and sprinted for the shelter of the rocks on the other side of the canyon, accompanied by the whiz and smack of musket balls. Winded but unscathed, we were recovering our strength in what shelter we could find, on the opposite side of the canyon from the rest of our company, when another ball burst to our front.

Without hesitation, we jumped to our feet again, applying the major's wisdom and quickly scurried from boulder to boulder or rock or tree or whatever presented itself as cover.

Cameron Catny knelt behind a boulder to my front. As I sprung to his side, I grabbed hold of his shirt and gave it a tug. "Cameron," I called, intending to get him back to moving up with us. But he dropped over, offering no resistance to the fall. The other side of his face was missing. It had been replaced with a slab of raw meat. Realizing, after a second, that the cannonball must have burst near that spot, I grabbed him by the shoulder and began to drag him back while yelling for a medic.

"It's too late for that," Paxton said from behind me. "He never even bled."

"Hush!" I shouted on first hearing his words—still somewhat shocked by my discovery.

"He's gone. He must have been killed immediately by the blast. Let's go, mate—got to stop them guns is what. Let's get on!"

Feeling somewhat foolish, I gazed down at Cameron. *Blazes*, I thought. He had remained totally sustained, kneeling behind the boulder before I'd released the inert mass—a mass that shortly prior had housed a human spirit. My tug had allowed the empty mass to drop, insignificantly, back to its affinity with the earth.

Once above the enemy's position, I sprawled behind a rock, and took aim on the Rebel gunners below. Several bodies had fallen behind the big guns and were being dragged away by fellow Confederates. Having drawn a bead on one of them, I was about to fire when it occurred to me that he was grasping his comrade by the armpits, just as I had done Cameron. Would it be right to shoot a man who was engaged in the rescue of a fallen companion? Just as I decided it was not, I saw the soldier drop atop his comrade's body. A recollection flashed in my mind. Had I fired unknowingly, as I had on the Indian buck I had killed back in Colorado?

No. My flint was still primed. One of the pops that were filling the air had been his demise. Our troops on the opposite hillside apparently had the guns silenced before we had gotten into position and were now moving down closer to the Rebels in the roadway, who were frantically engulfed in limbering the guns for a withdrawal.

"We got them now, Ollie!" I heard Smitty's voice from beside me joyfully announce as he jumped to my side. "Let's get after them!"

The Texans were running for the first time since invading New Mexico. They hadn't been expecting the battle they found themselves in. Our troops at Fort Union, they knew, had become accustomed to defeat at their hands. And the New Mexican Volunteers, many under short enlistments that had already expired, had neither the motive nor the desire for a full-scale life-or-death confrontation. Indeed, the Texans were not aware of or prepared for the Coloradoans. Some of our company, who had gotten within earshot of the Texans, heard one Texan inquire of his companion, "What are they, men or devils?"

"Neither, Pike's Peakers," our man responded to the Texan's dismay, before sending forth a leaded greeting.

As for my part in this, my first combat experience, I seemed to have been functioning as a spectator. Before I had made my way back down to the roadside, I heard our bugler sound, "Cavalry, charge."

How? I wondered.

They knew we'd been sent up the hillside without mounts. *I haven't gotten even one shot off at the enemy*, I thought.

Jumping behind a rock again, I looked for a Texan to take my revenge out on—for the ordeal they had imposed on me. Their guns had already moved out, and their rear guard was back stepping as it held our troops, in the roadway, at bay. As I again took a bead on one of their numbers, I realized they were in total retreat.

Did it make any sense to kill a man who was retreating? Perhaps they wouldn't stop until they were back in Texas. Whether wishful thinking or irrational logic was in control of my reasoning, I'm not sure. But instinctively I moved my aim to the source of this foolery. I sent my ball flying at the waving Lone Star, which was moving up with their columns, and felt a tinge of joy on seeing a speck of light appear through their tapestry. "Bull's-eye," I announced, in self-congratulation.

"Give it up, Olof!" I heard Smitty shout. "We've got to get back pronto."

Balls were flying in both directions along the roadway, so we had to stick to the hillside as we scurried and stumbled back to the pine grove. Quickly crossing the road and mounting, Smitty and I were among the first in our company back to the roadway on horseback.

"Make sure those guns are loaded," Captain Thompson called out as our columns were forming up—mine wasn't.

Then there was silence. After a few final pops, the firing had ceased. The enemy had moved out of sight, around a curve in the road to our front. The captain was lining our troops up in columns on each side of the road, when Major Chivington came galloping up.

"Where's the charge?" the major shouted at Captain Thompson.

"Sir, the enemy was out of sight before my men could get formed back up."

"Your orders were to charge! That means to charge! I don't give a damn if the enemy is in sight or not! When I order a charge, by God, you will charge! We had them on the run—now we will have to do it again. If you don't lead your men in charge at its next command, I will have you shot for treason!" the major shouted threateningly at our captain. "Keep your men mounted and ready to move out!" he ordered in conclusion.

"Make ready to move out!" The captain made his way up to the front of our unit, repeating the major's order.

After we had advanced about a mile and a half up the roadway, the major sent two scouts ahead to monitor the enemy's movement.

Seeing the scouts quickly returning was not a promising sign. The enemy was now, we were told, about a half mile to our front, around the next bend in that old wagon road. *Here we go again*, I thought, *running into another death fight.*

Everything had worked out in my favor so far. I hadn't been killed or even had to kill. But how far could we be pushed before we became, to the man, involved? With Chivington in command, it seemed there'd be no other possible conclusion.

The major ordered that we hold up and await the bugle call to charge. We were to remain mounted with our bayonets fixed, while the major led the ground troops charging around the curve and into the enemy fire.

They were no longer in our sight at the first firing of the Howitzers, causing our troops to once again hit the dirt and scurry for cover. This time, the Rebels were determined to prevent what had been their demise in our previous engagement, by sending their troops into the rocks, partly up the hillside, on both sides of the roadway.

"They're Texans," the major announced to our men. "They think they've climbed up the hill, but they're use to wearing those pointed boots. Show them how to climb, Pike's Peakers! Get above them again, and we'll drive them back down—and into the ground! Get above them Pike's Peakers!"

Riled into frenzy, our men charged up into the rocks once more, yelling as they went like a party of charging Injuns. It was later said that the Rebels truly thought of them as devils—flying from rock to rock, without the need of touching a foot to either and undaunted by the musket balls striking around them.

Back at the head of our infantry line, the major pranced among our troops in the roadway and to its side who were firing at the Rebels from what little cover they could find, against the onslaught from the enemy fire. The major, with one gun in each hand and another under his arm, road among our men and rallied them to their feet.

"God damn it, men, I'll charge them on my own if need be! They're Texans. Let's go get them! Join me in the charge!"

The men rose to their feet behind the major's stallion, forming columns again on each side of the road. The Howitzers were directed toward the approaching columns, and a ball was fired from each into our advancing forces, leaving a path of dismantled forms through their ranks. Some in the path of each ball cried out in agony at the wake of its blast.

Most of the cries came from those who had suffered the least physical injury. The more severely injured were no longer capable of an utterance or were too shocked to contemplate the need.

One individual who omitted a shout caused by the sting of what he assumed to be shrapnel smacking into his face and side found, upon inspection, that he had actually been smacked by flesh and bone fragments from a soldier at his side—the latter having had the misfortune of losing the larger part of his chest in a ball's passing.

The inanimate state of those immediately transformed into lifelessness was easily acceptable. But the severely wounded living were difficult to ignore. Later, one volunteer, who had been a settler on the Kansas plains, described to me how the rhythmic surges of blood from the shoulder of a comrade whose arm had disappeared, reminded him of the discharge of spring water from the artesian well around which he had centered his homestead. And, in tears, he added how that water was the lifeblood of the earth. To stop this precious loss, he had torn off his shirt and tied off the gaping wound as best he could.

From our position, around the bend from this traumatic development, we were spared involvement. Yet by the sound of the blasts and nearness of the enemy fire, we surmised that many casualties were being sustained by our companions.

Above all the dastardly sounds of combat, I heard the bellowing command of our major to, "Sound cavalry charge!"

Before the bugler had completed airing the refrain, we were rounding the bend in the trail at full gallop.

"Don't give them time to limber the guns," Captain Thompson commanded as we started the charge.

The importance of this order was absolute to us all, as we raced headlong into the enemy fire. After passing though the columns of our infantry, with about half the distance to the enemy guns remaining, there was a bridge in the road that the Rebels had destroyed after crossing. The remaining twenty-five-foot wide arroyo threatened to bar our way. And it most likely would have undone our charge had it not been a requirement of the captain that our mounts possess jumping ability. That being so, with hardly a break in our stride, we forded the breach and continued with bayonets stretched out before us. Yelling furiously, we charged behind the essence of might, our Major Chivington's invulnerable form.

My plan was to fire my musket at a frontline Reb and then plunge my bayonet into another. Following that, if there was still a need for such, I suspected my instincts and the butt of my musket would support my efforts.

As it turned out, things did not unfold to this agenda. Two of our mounts dropped in front of me as we neared the Rebs, forcing those of us behind them to pull up sharply. Circumventing the fallen carcasses around their left side, I saw the captain's mount drawn up facing me. He indicated that I and several others including Smitty were to take a left fork in the road, leading to a cabin homesite.

"Secure that structure!" the captain ordered, pointing at the domicile.

Veering in the direction of the cabin, we continued our full-paced gallop.

On first glance, I noticed several musket flashes in the cabin windows. Had I been saved by this turn of events, or was my situation now even more precarious? The enemy on the roadway was, at least, out in the open. Men behind a fortification had the capability of defeating a large number of attackers, and we were but six. Examining the situation, I had to wonder what exactly it was that we were in the process of doing. We certainly would not fare well in continuing this charge, I thought. As soon as we were in target range of the cabin, we would most likely be blown off our mounts.

Collecting my senses, I decided to veer Spirit off to the side of the trail and indicated for the others to follow.

Smitty shook his head no, while pointing at the cabin.

"It would be suicide—" I started to say.

"No sweat," Smitty said, interrupting me. "Look!" He nodded toward the cabin to draw my attention to the weapons being tossed out of the front door. This was followed by four Rebels, their hands raised above their heads, exiting from the door.

At this sight we returned to full stride, overjoyed by the aspect of taking our own prisoners. This was quite a shocking development. With the reputation the Texans had of being fearless fighters, who would have expected that they would abandon their fortification, where they had the ability to defeat a large number of troops, and surrender forthright? Certainly, to me it was nothing short of a miracle. What would these Texans be like? I wondered. As we rode toward our forlorn enemy, my old friends Earl and Simon came to mind—their stature holding a resemblance to a pair in this group.

"Ollie!" I was shocked by the call and by the realization that it was more than just a resemblance they bore. Jumping down from Spirit in front of my old friends, I stretched out my hand in greeting.

"Keep those hands in the air!" I heard Paxton yell from behind me. "You know these cutthroats, Swenson?" he asked, in a confused tone.

"Yeah, I do," I replied, turning toward Paxton so that he could detect my sincerity. "Spent many days, we did, panning together back at Mountain City. This is Simon, and his brother here is Earl. Texans or not, I'll stand for them any day."

"That doesn't change anything," Paxton declared. "They're the enemy. And we can't let them keep us from getting the job done."

"I say shoot them and let's get back to the battle," Wilson, added angrily.

"Now wait a minute," Smitty said, quickly jumping into the conversation, while swinging Flash around to confront the antagonist. "We haven't completed our orders yet. We're supposed to secure the cabin. If we abandon it, the Rebs might move back in. I say we collect the weapons and then torch the place."

"Good. You and Swenson do that then … and march them back, too, if you want. It wouldn't take all of us for the doing of that," Wilson said.

"Let's get on with it then," I said in agreement, happy to be able to separate the Daltons from Wilson's hostility. "Tell the captain we'll be bringing back the prisoners," I added as our companions headed back toward the battle.

"And make sure you do!" Paxton called back to me before our four companions broke their mounts into a gallop, back toward our company.

"You men start walking back to the cabin," Smitty commanded of our prisoners. "Keep them to our front, Ollie," he said to me under his breath, after holding me back a second by grabbing my upper arm and allowing the prisoners to establish the safety margin of a slight lead. "I'll go up and collect their weapons," he added before running up ahead of us.

"How is it that you didn't stand us off from the cabin?" I asked the prisoners in general.

Simon responded, "When your boys in the hills pushed us down to this cabin, we decided to give it up if you Yanks took control of the road. We sure weren't going to try and hold off the whole Union Army. Besides, it wouldn't be long before you'd decide to torch the place and shoot us down as we came out the door. What would you do, Ollie, if you were us?"

"Same as you, I suspect …except, till now, it seemed that I was the only one in this war that had any concern about staying alive. Guess I suspected you boys would be with those of the martyr mind frame."

"Might have been, if we were fighting to protect Texas like we joined up to do," Earl said, joining in the conversation. "It wasn't our idea to try and usurp the entire Western territory. We got no choice but to cater to the whims of our old, drunken colonel, who cowards off at every battle."

"Sounds familiar," I replied while restraining a chuckle.

"Sure ain't something we want to die trying to do," Simon said in concurrence.

"It wasn't so bad driving off the Mexicans and the tender bellies they sent from up north, but we weren't expecting you boys to show up down here," a third member in the party of prisoners contributed.

"We're only down here to keep you all from coming up there. If we could call the whole thing off, I'd be a damned sight happier," I admitted.

Strange, I thought. This was the first time in a long time I'd felt safe in expressing my true feelings about this war. And it was with a group of Confederates.

"Bring them down here," Smitty yelled out to me. He had collected their weapons and was stowing them with ties to our saddle straps. "Grab some dry brush and pile it against the walls," he continued. "We got to get back before the captain thinks we're ducking the fight."

There could still be heard constant musket fire, but I noticed that the Howitzers hadn't fired for some time, which was definitely a good sign.

MORE TROOPS, LESS HOPE

The cabin was full ablaze when we got back to the main road. Captain Thompson was back on the far side of the arroyo with a large group of what looked to be Confederate troops and several members of our company. A lot of musket fire could still be heard coming from farther down the canyon. Apparently, we had driven the Rebels back down the trail in the direction they had come from, that being west.

"I see you've brought us more of these Rebel bastards to deal with," the captain said in greeting us. "Let them climb across the gully, and then you boys can jump it. That's the safest way for your horses. Did you leave any dead ones at the cabin?"

"No, sir. These are all that we encountered," I replied.

"Well, good work bringing them back alive. I know it's hard to keep from shooting them where they stand."

"Actually, it wasn't, sir. You see, those two are Simon and Earl Dalton," I said, pointing at the brothers who, together with the two other prisoners, were sliding down into the gully. "We spent two winters together working a cradle and got to be good friends, sir."

"Well, they are prisoners now—just like the rest. You remember that. They aren't going to side with you against those Rebels back there," the captain said, pointing down the road toward the still raging battle sounds.

"Actually, it seems they haven't got much interest in their army's campaign anymore, from what they've told me, sir." I hoped explaining this to the captain might help the Daltons get a release, if our commanders were to contemplate one.

"You just treat them the same as the rest. Do you understand me, Corporal?" the captain ordered sternly.

"Yes, sir," I replied.

Smitty and I started a short gallop toward the arroyo, while our prisoners were straining to pull themselves up the steep embankment on the far side, hampered by poor footing on the loose rocky slope.

Upon landing on the captain's side, I addressed him again. "You called me corporal, sir," I said, questioning if it had been an error on his part.

"All privates of the regiment have been granted corporal rank," the captain explained. "You are combat soldiers now ... Once them prisoners are properly tied off," he continued, nodding toward the seventy or so prisoners to his rear, who several of our troops were guarding while others lashed their arms behind their backs, "you are to help march them to the hostelry that we passed back down the road. If any more are taken, we will march them back with us once the battle is won."

With that, the captain turned and, with a grunt, spurred his mount into a gallop. Having jumped the gully he called back to us over his shoulder, "Now I can return to the battlefront."

As he continued galloping down the road, I wondered, was it bravery or stupidity? Everyone seemed to be anxious to become part of the carnage. Perhaps openly displaying their desire for combat raised their self-image a notch. But was that worth dying for? I felt relieved and remarkably fortunate to be, for the moment at least, out of the combat. Nonetheless, a pang of guilt coursed through my being at the thought of the death of my companions occurring just a bit down the trail.

"I feel like riding after him," Smitty said, indicating he was dealing with the same torment that I was.

"You don't have to be a hero, Smitty," I said. "Once this war ends, nobody is going to care about your part in it. Hey, I guess we'll be getting more pay now that we're corporals," I added, delegating to worthlessness our former topic. "If they ever really do give us a paycheck, that is. And that probably won't be until this war's over."

"At least, we'll have a nest egg coming once we get out," Smitty replied, indicating his interest in having a future. "Let's go join your buddies!" Smitty yelled to our four Texan prisoners. "We've got quite a herd to manage here, haven't we?" he asked of me.

"Yeah, we'll have to keep our wits about us and our eyes on them," I replied, acknowledging that our assignment was, in itself, somewhat perilous and demanding.

But as it turned out, we got the prisoners back to the hostelry without incident, other than a constant barrage of insults from our captives.

The hostelry was a small cluster of buildings known as Pigeon's Ranch. It was so named because the Frenchman who owned it did a peculiar dance that resembled the common contortions of a pigeon.

The engagement in the pass broke off when dusk set in, and the Rebels decided to withdraw. The colonel marched our bedraggled unit back to join us. Again my guilt set in—guilt at the sight of men and horses toting the dead and wounded, guilt for being alive.

"We run them off." Paxton was the first to speak to me. "Those notorious Texan marauders were running for their lives from the charge of the Pike's Peakers. We beat them soundly," he concluded. Yet, though glorious in their victory, our company of newly indoctrinated combat troops found that sullenness prevailed over them in the accompaniment of their fallen comrades.

"Take time to chow down and tend the animals, but don't get comfortable. The major hasn't given us any new orders, but we might hit the Rebels again before the night is over." It was Captain Thompson maintaining our readiness. He then moved on through our company, repeating a version of the same to the fatigued ensemble.

"That's disappointing," I said to Smitty, who was gathering the makings of a fire pit. "I was hoping that the Rebs would keep on running, clean out of the territory." Though jokingly spoken, I was admitting my desire for the end of the battle.

"What's this," Smitty said, pointing up the wagon trail at a Confederate in tote of a long stick, to the top of which was affixed a square of somewhat blood-splattered, white material.

The major walked out to meet him. Quiet came over our company—except for groans and occasional yells of pain from the wounded, who were under the care of our medics. I remember wondering why they didn't use an ax, in the hands of a capable axman, to do the removal of tattered appendages with one swift blow, rather than subjecting the patient to the torture of multiple passes of a saw blade through their flesh and the unacceptable reality of having the saw teeth chew through their bones. It was said that the wound must be clean—where an axe would do too much crushing to allow for proper healing. But it was also known by all that an amputee's chances of surviving would require nothing less than a miracle in any case. The likelihood was that infection was near certain to end the patient's life before a few months of dejection had passed by. Yet later, in a conversation I had had with one Bob Pitt on this matter, I recall his telling me that he had no feeling at all of the saw's passing through his thigh. He had only yelled out, he recalled, in obligation to his departing appendage.

"Sir," the Confederate officer bearing the white flag addressed our commander, "Major Pyron of the Confederate Army respectfully requests that we both restrain from further hostilities until 8:00 a.m., as a means by which to collect our dead and tend to our wounded. If that be agreeable with you, sir, I will so inform our major."

"You can tell your major that he need not fear us until 8:00 a.m.," Major Chivington replied, the inference in his phrasing being that Major Pyron would need to fear us at the stated hour.

There it was. Eight o'clock, and it would all start again. In my current state of exhaustion, I realized that, as soon as my eyes closed, I'd be awakened by a formation call, and we'd be on our way to another battle. *I mustn't dwell on this*, I thought. It had to be done. Yet I knew that the odds of my survival were decreasing with each assault.

That thought was broken as the captain announced, "You've got twenty minutes before you move out," just as our fire had gotten started below our pot of java. "This company is going to move the prisoners back to Kozlowski's Ranch, immediately. There isn't enough water here to sustain us. The rest of the company will join us as soon as the medics have completed treating the wounded," the captain concluded before moving on.

"That's a hell of a thing," Paxton declared. "We'll be giving up our chow time because these prisoners take so damn long to move."

"We couldn't expect them to double-time it with their legs tied," I replied. Though equally frustrated as he by the order, I saw no reason to attribute the blame to the prisoners, rather than to the total absurdity of warfare.

"Don't see why we can't just drag them along behind our horses," Paxton added spitefully.

"It doesn't seem fair that they should be able to get out of the battle so easily," I added, realizing that I had sounded sympathetic to our prisoners with my previous response.

"You could ask the captain to let you stay to the rear with the wounded, to guard the Rebs, if you're afraid of fighting," Paxton said to me, apparently upset by my lack of disdain for our enemy.

"Don't worry. Ollie might not like it, but he'll be up front in the charge," Smitty said in my defense.

"I'll do what needs to be done," I said, calmed somewhat by Smitty's intervention from the fit of anger Paxton's comment had provoked in me.

"I can't wait to get another crack at killing those Rebs," Paxton said, his gaze fixed on the flame beneath the coffeepot. The flickering of the fire reflected over his face in the cold, semidarkness of the winter evening.

After ten minutes, our twenty-minute break was over. We prepared to march our captives back to Kozlowski's ranch.

Whack! A whip cracked above the heads of the prisoners at the rear of their group. "Move it, you varmints. Move it!" Paxton shouted, obviously trying to agitate them.

"We'll see who's prisoner when Colonel Scurry gets here," a prisoner retorted.

"Maybe you'll scurry a bit faster when we throw him in there with you," I added. I was glad to hear this bring a laugh from Paxton, since I wanted him to know that I was on the same side as was he.

We made it to Kozwolski's a short while before the rest of our company and had a chance to chew on some dried beef and bacon before falling in for the night.

Colonel Scurry—the prisoner expected him to be his rescuer, I recollected. His past successes had been mentioned by the troops from Dodd's company. This was a name that I suspected would become more meaningful to me before long. And so it was.

Just before sunup, one of our scouts came galloping into the ranch with news of a large group of Confederates riding into the west end of the canyon. "A force of near to a thousand men," he estimated.

It appeared that, when the Confederates had sent their messenger to ask us for a cease-fire, they had also sent one back to their main force, requesting that they come to their aid at once.

"That would be Scurry," Major Chivington replied to the scout. "The question is, was that his entire force that you saw?"

"Can't say for sure," the scout replied. "They had just entered the canyon when we got there. There may have been others ahead of them."

"Captain Thompson, get two riders out straightaway with a message to Colonel Slough to move up the regiment at once. Tell him that I don't like being outnumbered three to one," the major ordered.

"Yes, sir," the captain replied. "And should we put the rest of our company in defensive positions, lest they attack soon, sir?"

"No, we don't. That would only invite a charge. They don't know that we're aware of their increase in forces. They will be expecting us to attack. We must foster that impression on them by preparing for an assault. Hopefully, they will sit in wait on us."

The major's plan worked. We spent the day acting like we were preparing to attack. We never did, and the Rebels never came. At 11:00 p.m. of that evening, much to our delight, our main force was spotted approaching the canyon. That entire day had been spent in relative leisure. Yet it was one of the most difficult days of our campaign—having to deal with the stress of expecting an attack by an overwhelming force at any minute.

Fortunately, the Rebels had misjudged our intentions, and that allowed us the time needed for Colonel Slough to march the main body of troops to our aid. Seeing a thousand of our men, with cannons in tote, entering the valley gave quite a lift to my expectations for the future. It seemed that fate was protecting me once again. *Perhaps, with this much fighting power, we can drive the Texans off without sustaining many casualties*, I thought.

Unfortunately, the colonel was developing a plan not at all favorable to my renewed optimism. His plan was, in fact, even somewhat alarming to the unshakeable Major Chivington. Shortly after our regiment had settled in with us at Kozwolski's, Captain Thompson's voice came to me from oblivion and caused me to abandon the comforting warmth that I had developed in my blanket.

"We're going to see the colonel," the Captain said to me directly. "But first, he wants us to fetch those two prisoners that you're friendly with."

Simon and Earl were startled at our appearance, I noticed—it being somewhat after the midnight hour. But relieved they were also, after being freed from the corral post to which they had been tied in a manner that forced them to sleep in a sitting position with their arms tied behind their backs.

"Did you talk them into setting us free, Ollie?" Earl asked.

"That just might be so," the captain answered in my stead.

Earl didn't reply. Something of a pleasured expression tried to emerge on his face. However, cautious skepticism curtailed his enthusiasm. "Good," he replied, somewhat placidly.

"You go in with him. I'll wait out here with this one," the captain said, allowing Simon and I to enter the command tent, while he kept Earl out of earshot of the pending conversation.

In the dimly lit interior of the tent, I could recognize Major Chivington and Colonel Slough at once.

"Corporal Swenson, what's the name of this prisoner?" the colonel asked me.

"Simon Dalton, sir," I replied, somewhat shocked to discover that the colonel actually knew my name. Obviously, Captain Thompson must have prearranged the details of this meeting.

"Mr. Dalton, your brother is outside with Captain Thompson."

"I know my brother is out there," Simon replied.

"Did you notice the two mules tied to the sapling alongside the tent?"

"Yes, sir, I did," Simon replied. The pitch of his voice had risen slightly with the hope that this conversation was leading toward his release.

"I am going to put a proposition straight forth to you and your brother. Corporal Swenson has indicated to us that you and your brother have lost the desire to continue in your Colonel Scurry's campaign. Is that a fact?"

"That's been so, long since passed," Simon replied. "Don't neither of us cotton to the idea of dying just to aid them brigands in looting the countryside. We'd have taken down your Fort Union weeks ago if we hadn't had to wait for them to get their fill of ransacking Albuquerque and Santa Fe," Simon explained.

"This is my offer then. I have two simple questions to put to you and your brother. If I get the same answer from both of you, you will set right out of here on them mules. But you will have to give me your word that you won't take up arms against the Union hereafter."

"No, I couldn't promise that. If the Feds send troops into my beloved Texas, my cause would be back to where it was when I enlisted. And Earl would feel the same—I'm sure. We'd die before allowing it, and I can't say any different."

"I'm glad you didn't. Or I would have taken you for a liar right here and now. And, that would have been the end of our conversation. The truth is, we have no plan to invade Texas—now, or ever. The territory is too vast. And Texas holds no strategic geographic significance to our effort. In other words, I can accept your word, if it be on the terms that you will not fight for the Confederacy, outside of an attack on the state of Texas."

"You can have my word as a Texan on that," Simon replied.

The colonel's statement caused me to wonder if he was actually that informed on the Federal war plans. Perhaps, it was a totally hollow statement, designed only to extoll needed information from Simon. Or perhaps, and I hoped it not be so, he had no intention of living up to his end of the arrangement.

"How many men are under Colonel Scurry's command?" was the colonel's first question.

"Was some over a thousand, less them of us you killed or captured. Right about that number—a thousand—I'd suspect," Simon answered.

"And cannons?" the colonel asked, apparently finding excitement in the first answer he was given—seeing how we were now over fourteen hundred men strong.

"The four six-pounders we captured at Valverde," Simon replied. "But I think that one of them was probably destroyed in the battle. For I heard that one of our artillerymen, fearing you were about to recapture it, threw himself upon it and ignited its ammunition. In so doing, he blew it and his self apart.

"Swenson, take him out to the captain and bring in the other one," Colonel Slough ordered. "There is to be no conversation between you and your brother out there, or the deal is off. Is that understood?"

"That's understood." Simon replied.

I led him out of the tent.

"The Colonel made the same offer and asked the same questions of Earl. In return, he received the same information—about a thousand troops and four cannons. The only variation was in Earl's response to the proposition of not rejoining the Confederate campaign.

"The weather's about to break," Earl stated in response to the question. "We've got a whole season ahead for panning. Simon and I have been talking about heading back up to the diggings. It's probably wide open up there, now that gold fever's broke. And with half the men caught up in this war that's not apt to blow over before next winter sets in, there's sure to be plenty of vacated claims. If the war doesn't end by next winter, we'll just have to spend our time keeping the ladies in those snowshoe places happy."

Wow, did that hurt! I was contemplating asking the colonel for a third mule about then, but the major spoke up at that point, for the first time since our arrival.

"I'll take him out to his brother," the major said. "They had both better understand that those mules keep heading north from these parts. I'll have my sentries shoot them dead if they try to head back down this canyon." The major spoke to us, but his words were for the Daltons, and his sincerity was as clear as a sermon. The major grasped Earl's arm and led him out, as if he were carrying a broomstick.

"What did you think of their replies?" the colonel asked me after they had gone out.

"Same as you, I suspect, sir. They have about a thousand men and the three Howitzers."

"You know them men well, do you, Corporal?"

"Yes, sir. I do."

"And do you think that their answers were honest?"

"Absolutely," I answered immediately, not having given any thought to the possibility that they might have somehow fabricated their answers. As I thought of it, I quickly dismissed the possibility. If there was anything the Daltons would be incapable of, it would be the perpetuation of a deceitful performance.

"We can't do it!" the major, who had suddenly reentered, stated impetuously to the colonel, truncating our conversation.

"We can. And we will," the colonel responded, his calm and quiet response being the only effective arguing technique possible against the major's vocal fortitude.

"Once they realize that they are trapped, they will turn on us with three men against each one of ours, and charge right through our line," the major replied, obviously exerting a strong effort to curtail the loudness of his heartfelt response.

"They will have to keep us under engagement, or they will have our guns and bayonets tearing them down from behind," the Colonel offered in contradiction.

"Exactly, and making them all the more desperate to crash through my line." This statement by the major was actually made through clenched teeth—that being the only means he had to lock in his anger.

"They will have nine hundred of our men and twelve, twelve-pound Howitzers to one side of them—on the other side, your Pike's Peakers.

Isn't that like being trapped between a rock and a hard place?" the colonel questioned. The way the Colonel had intoned *Pike's Peakers* seemed to reflect a bit of sarcasm. Perhaps the major had been doing too much bragging or had taken too much credit for the successes we had had so far. Could the colonel be acting spitefully, in retaliation, with our lives serving as a tool of punishment? It was such that this conversation indicated to me.

"You will be sacrificing my men. And if the battle turns back your way, your reduced number might not be enough to repel the attack. Still, if you insist on splitting our forces, the larger number should be with me—seeing how your twelve cannons will more than balance out our strengths," the major contended.

"No. We need to protect the supply wagons at all cost. We need to maintain the superior troop power, as well as the cannons, up front in order to assure impenetrability to the wagons. Nothing results in total defeat, in these parts, as assuredly as having your supplies compromised," the colonel argued.

"Then keep our forces unified in their defense. Fourteen hundred men and twelve cannons would be an impenetrable force against an assault by one thousand," the major contended.

"You will take your four hundred men up atop that cliff. And when the battle ensues, you will charge down behind them to attack them from the rear," the colonel stated conclusively, raising his voice a notch for the first time in this conversation.

With that, the major turned and strode out, quickly and silently.

"You are under direct orders, not to speak a word of anything you've heard here tonight, to anyone. Do you understand that, Corporal?" the colonel asked of me, in what was clearly a direct order.

"Yes, sir. I understand, sir," I replied with sincerity.

27

DIVINE INTERVENTION

Formation call awakened me after but an hour or two of shut-eye. Together with a group of Mexican volunteers, who were along mainly as guides, our 1st Colorado Volunteer Regiment, under the command of Major Chivington, was ordered to the attack mode. We were to ascend the canyon wall and proceed to a vantage point above the main body of our forces that would still be in the canyon below. In the midnight's darkness, those of us in the cavalry readied our mounts.

The sun had not yet arisen as we had a short chow down while watching our regiment preparing for battle down below us. After walking back out of the canyon, we had ascended the rocky ridge that led to the top of the canyon. Under the order of silence, I resisted the temptation to talk to Smitty about the assignment we were about to undertake. Perhaps his words would help me accept the disaster I knew awaited us. A thousand Rebels would be charging directly into our midst, fighting desperately for their lives, against our force of what was now 490 men, counting the Mexican volunteers.

When the Confederate Army arrived, we would be moving down the canyon to their rear. It was reassuring to know that it would be too steep, at that point, to descend to the floor on horseback. So Spirit and the other horses would have to remain above in safety. Would Spirit end up as a Confederate or Union mount? I wondered. Feeling a need to ponder the forthcoming battle in privacy, with my coffee cup in hand, I walked some passed the boulders behind our campsite, where it would be possible to view the approaching sunrise. As I stared at the subtle glow of sunlight, not yet an actual illumination, I sipped my java and tried to imagine what Smitty's response would have been if he had heard all that I had.

There in the dimly lit horizon, a figure took shape, off a short distance to my right. It appeared to be a man seated beside a donkey. Rising, I walked toward the figure, which I feared must be one of the Daltons. The possibility that they had disobeyed the major and returned was dreadful. He would certainly have them shot if they were discovered. Nearing the silhouette, I discerned a robe and waistband about a man's body—the unmistakable garb of a Spanish monk.

"What are you doing here?" I asked.

"Olla, I'm Padre Cordona," the man responded softly. "I have come here and am here in the Lord's service—as I do, as is my life. I am hoping that my service may be used to aid the adobe tribes that live here and who have suffered long and hard under the hands of both my people, the Apache and Comanche Indians and also under those that you have engaged in battle—the Texas Army. The only support that these tribes have received in their history has come from the government that has sent you. By being here—perhaps by praying or simply by talking to you, I may in some way affect the will of the Lord and, in so doing, may help to stop the slaughter and tyranny that these tribes continue to endure. I'm sorry. I'm not being polite. What of you, my son? How is it that you have felt the need to so approach me?"

"I fear death, Father. I don't understand why our loving Father in Heaven allows men to take each other's lives," I said, allowing the whole of my suppressed underlying thoughts to be stated.

"Don't forget, my son, He knows what awaits us in His kingdom. Perhaps, if we were as informed as He, we would not have the determination needed to stay alive through even the slightest of life's difficulties. The Lord's concern is only that mankind continues to flourish. In His love, He has supplied us with all of our needs. As our needs have grown, so has His bounty. Be sure to realize that at the basis of every miracle of nature, and every implementation of science, there lays the imprint of His hand alone. In recognizing this fatherly attention toward mankind, His lack of protection for the individual can only reflect death's insignificance. Our task is only to stay attuned to the fact that, as individuals, we are always guided by His hand toward the implementation of His providence. Now, you tell me, my son, what then has brought you to this fearful state?" the padre asked, after pausing for a moment to allow me to reflect on his explanation. This padre had probably seen a lifetime of deaths among the pueblos between plagues and enemy attacks, with his faith only being strengthened by it all, I presumed.

"A battle awaits us in the morning that is likely to mean the death of most of those you see up here before you," I explained.

"And what will this gain?" the Padre asked of me. ""Will your sacrifice lead to a victory for your army?"

"That can't be determined beforehand," I replied. "It will be a major battle. That is all I am sure of."

"But, if you win the battle, will the Texans be totally defeated?"

"Nothing assures the total defeat of an army," I said, "lest it's the loss of every man or all of their supplies," I said, recalling the words of the colonel.

"Then, why not attack their supply wagons, rather than attacking them? Wouldn't that be an easier victory?"

"That probably would make sense," I replied, "If we could locate and get to the supplies."

"I sat above them earlier today and gazed down upon them, just as I'm gazing upon your army now."

"Tell me what you saw, Padre," I said, interested in the possibility this conversation was alluding to.

"There were perhaps eighty wagons, weighted with goods, and a bit farther back five hundred or so horses and mules."

"Could our army transverse the terrain to this place?" I asked, somewhat excitedly.

"In a few hours, I'd expect. But there's a sheer drop of several hundred feet down to Johnson's ranch, where they are setting."

"Would you lead us to this place" I asked anxiously.

"Perhaps that is why I live," he responded in the same monotone as all he had spoken.

"Please wait at this spot," I implored the padre. He agreed, and I hastened back to find Captain Thompson. Jogging back past the boulders, and across our campsite, fate stepped in to help me in this endeavor.

Staring, hands on hips, at the glint of sunlight appearing on the horizon was the massive figure of the major. "Sir," I said as I approached my superior at a non-threatening walking pace.

"What is it, Corporal?" the major replied in an unthreatening tone.

"Forgive me for approaching you directly, sir, but I have knowledge of a matter that I believe to be of the utmost importance."

"Aren't you the troop that awakened us with gunfire to report the news of the ambulance in the pass? And the one who captured his old companions at the cabin?" he asked.

"Yes, sir. I am," I said, fearing that I may have overstepped my better judgment in approaching the major.

"You are the bearer of the information I am seeking then—no doubt. Let me hear this knowledge that you have acquired in my hour of desperation."

After telling the major about my conversation with the padre, his attitude changed to one of extreme seriousness.

"Stay right here, Corporal," the major commanded, before running off toward the command tent. Soon he returned with Colonel Chavez, the commander of the Mexican company in our detachment, as well as with one of the colonel's lieutenants, Lieutenant Morales.

"Take us to the padre you spoke of at once," Major Chivington ordered of me.

Leading the way back to the ridge of rocks where I had left the padre, fear that he might not be there waiting was overcoming me. So it was with great relief that I viewed the image before us as we neared of the Padre sitting beside his pack mule.

The padre rose as the colonel and lieutenant approached and then prostrated before him. Laying a hand upon each of their heads, the padre began to converse with them in Spanish. After rising, the colonel led the conversation, with the lieutenant occasionally joining in as the padre responded to their questions. At the conclusion, the colonel explained to the major the facts that he had ascertained.

"Father Cordoba does know the location of their supply wagons, but there is a sheer two hundred-foot drop at that point to the canyon floor. He feels he can lead us there, along the canyon, in perhaps three and a half hours. Lieutenant Morales has never followed the canyon over that exact stretch, but he knows the terrain to be extremely rough. Yet Father Cordoba assures me that it can be done. Morales says that, from here, there is a trail to a village southwest, and from there the terrain would be quite flat and manageable to the western stretch of the canyon. The priest agrees with that but says it would take more than twice as long by that route," Colonel Chavez explained.

"If he could make it over these plateaus with that old mule, I'm sure we could do the same," the major stated. "But we wouldn't want to start out too early. If we attack before the battle starts back here, the Rebels might hear our gunfire and race back, not giving us time to finish destroying their stores. Then, too, they might spot us moving along the ridge and recognize what we are about. It's likely that they have scouts spotting along the ridge at this minute. We will take the lieutenant's route but invite the priest along to lead us to the cliff face," the major said to the colonel.

The manner in which the major made this decision alone, though outranked by the Mexican colonel, was surprising to me. I attributed it to the fact that this was an American army campaign but was not certain that the major's aggressive nature was not in influence.

"What is your name, Corporal?" the major asked me.

"Swenson, sir. Corporal Olof Swenson."

"You are to find Captain Thompson. Tell him that these are my orders. Have him take some troops and extra mounts down to the supply wagon. Get all the spare ropes, straps, and anything else that we can tie together to scale a wall and get back here straightaway. If you are questioned down below, you are not to mention our plans to anyone other than the captain. Just tell them that I am requisitioning these items to get us down the canyon wall, as it might be quite a drop. Make haste, Corporal Swenson!" the major concluded.

When I got to the command tent, I found Captain Thompson seated on a cot, writing what I suspected to be a letter to his family. I had planned to do the same, to let Jenny know that we would be engaging a far superior force in battle and how the thought of returning to her would motivate me toward survival. Also, I intended to let her know that, if that were not to be, I would die with a heart full of love for her. Now that the battle plans had been changed, we would have a much better chance of survival, I thought. Instead of being outnumbered three to one by our enemy, we would probably outnumber the force they had left behind to protect their supply wagons. Yet, if they should anticipate or gain knowledge of our planned attack on their supplies from their scouts, we might have an unpleasant surprise awaiting us. At that point, I had a horrifying thought of being shot at while hanging from the side of a two hundred-foot cliff. Whatever was in store for us, I certainly had been involved in fashioning the upcoming events and possibly in determining my personal survival—or perhaps the opposite.

"Sir," I addressed the captain.

"What is it, Swenson?" he replied. Relating the events of the morning to him, I started with my having discovered the padre. There was an air of pride in my recanting, I'm sure—as I felt that I had made a significant contribution to our campaign. For that reason, I expected something like a congratulations from the captain. And it came as something of a surprise when his response came strongly in disapproval.

"Still trying to stand on your horse, are you, Swenson?"

His remark shocked me so that I could not think through a response.

"Do you feel you are too special to follow the normal chain of command? In the future, you will never directly address any of my superior officers, unless approached by them. Is that understood?"

"Yes, sir. I was on my way here—" I started to explain how I had crossed paths with the major.

But the captain, having no interest in hearing my response, interrupted it. "Go get the rest of your squad and a few extra mounts. Then carry out the major's order. We are going to need thousands of feet of rope, so get every bit you can find. Then go to the maintenance wagon and requisition all of the lubrication oil. Do it, fast!"

"Yes, sir," I replied.

"Thousands of feet," I remembered the captain saying as I stared at the pile in front of us. We had rolls of rope and thick leather strapping, which we carried for harnesses and to tie down supplies on the wagons. But would this actually be thousands of feet?

"Get every bit," the captain had also said, emphatically. There was still a lot of rope holding the bonnets to our wagons, but it would take some time to remove, and the captain had said, "Do it fast!" Not wanting to get into any more trouble with the captain, I decided not to take the decision on as mine alone. Talking it over with the other seven members of our squad, we attempted to calculate how long it would take to try to get our near to five hundred troops down and up a two hundred-foot rope. This led us to conclude that extra ropes would be a large factor in saving time at the wall and we should attain as much rope as possible.

"Time it takes removing the ropes from the wagons, will be multiplied in time saved at the cliff," were the last words spoken. They came from Smitty.

It took us a little over an hour to pull all the bonnet ties free and wrap the bonnets over each wagon's content to protect it from the dust and sun rays that had taken hold of the day.

Apparently, we had made the right decision, for the captain was pleased when he saw our four packhorses loaded down with the precious cargo.

It was after eight in the morning before we started heading west. Our regiment was preparing to move out down below us. One of Morales's troops led us safely to the village and, from there, to the west end of the canyon. Nearing the canyon we could hear the almost rhythmic, booming of the cannons resounding off the canyon walls. Though not loud at their distance, the implication of their thunder was shocking. The battle was fully underway, somewhere along the canyon's length. The major had us pull up some three hundred feet from the canyon wall.

It was strange to hear him try to speak softly, but he did. "Our lives depend upon maintaining absolute silence. You can cough or sneeze all you want. But don't make a damned sound doing it, or you will be signaling your own death. When you get to the bottom, look for cover in the rocks. But don't knock any loose while doing it. If your arm gets stuck in a crevice in the wall and snaps off at the shoulder, you will keep your pain to yourself, if not I'll shoot you myself.

"Men," the major continued, "the total success of this operation depends upon our getting down this wall unnoticed. I will hold each of you responsible in seeing that we do. Before you climb over the edge, make sure that your rope is secure on the saddle. Use your hands and feet to keep off the wall, but don't let me hear you kicking or smacking it. Before you start down, sling your weapon across you shoulder and don't have anything on you person that might be knocked off and fall. When your feet reach the ground, push up on the knot above your head and the sling will release from around your chest. Then signal the top to pull the rope back up. I can't stress enough how important getting down this wall is. I'm depending on your good sense and effort to pull this off. Our lives depend upon it. Don't let me down, men." The major seemed out of character in asking, rather than demanding, but I thought this made his words all the more potentiated.

Everyone seemed to be in a state of alert concentration as we watched the saddles being stretched across the ledge, as close as possible to the cliff's edge. There were eight saddles, each with one stirrup tied to a stirrup of the neighboring saddle. The captain said that the saddles would act as pulleys by allowing the ropes to slide over their seats. Back at the village, he had us cut down a tall, straight spruce and stripped off its branches. Along the way, he had us notch it at nine evenly spaced places. The notches were spaced by using a saddle with the stirrups outstretched. The captain had selected the length of the cliff we would use for our descent by its possessing cracked rock, to which we could wedge and tie this spruce pole directly behind the outstretch saddles. The right spot was actually quite easy to find on this craggy, rock plateau.

The pole lay a few feet behind the saddles, and we fastened a length of rope from each notch in the pole to a saddle stirrup. Along the way from the village, we had also fashioned eight long lengths of rope by tying together all the lengths of rope and strapping we had brought along with us. The captain had us tie one end of each of these lengths of rope to one of eight strong, two-foot lengths of branch that had been cut from the spruce. Each rope was tied to both ends of a branch in a triangular configuration. These branches were to serve as seats for us while we were being lowered down the cliff.

As the saddles were being lashed together, the captain asked if there was anyone among us who felt he couldn't handle facing the height of the drop. I recognized that, by responding, I would be removing myself from the danger of the ensuing battle, but I didn't let myself dwell on that thought. Six men responded. Together with these six, the captain then selected thirty-four of the biggest and strongest men from our ranks. He informed this group that they would be the pullers. Five from this group were assigned to each rope. He then asked the Mexican colonel for sixteen capable men, short of stature, to tend the saddles. Two of these men were assigned each saddle to aid in our decent. They helped us get into the lowering configuration—seated on the branch with the slip noose tight around our chest. They also applied oil to the saddle to keep down the rope friction.

As we descended, they signaled the pullers to stop lowering us if they saw that we were in trouble. This happened frequently as the ropes tended to put us into a spin, leading to hard contact with the wall. When we reached the bottom, and freed ourselves from the noose, these Mexicans signaled the pullers to walk back away from the wall, dragging the rope back up as they did so. We continued this process till, in a little over an hour, over four hundred of us were lying behind the rock boulders at the bottom of the cliff, waiting for an order to charge.

When it came, it was given silently, and we commenced our assault in silence.

28

THE COMPROMISE

As we passed the wagons that circled their camp tents, not a single Reb came into sight. But when the first of our men entered a tent, several Rebels drew pistols and yelled out warnings. The silence was broken by their shouts and by the shots that silenced them. A group of ten or so Rebels took off on horses, with another six running after them on foot. The major kept us from shooting at them. "They pose no threat to us," he said. "By the time they reach their regiment, we will be out of here."

When three of us jumped into one tent, we found the Rebels were still engaged in drinking and card playing. They either failed to recognize the alarm or were too engaged in their activity to care. Since their rifles had been left standing by the fire pit outside, they offered no resistance, just profanity, to having been captured. Five Rebel medics were treating wounded in their medical tent. The major left them to continue their work. In the end, we had a group of seventeen restrained prisoners.

To these, the captain posed one simple question: "Did your commander actually leave but this handful of men to protect your entire wagon train of supplies?"

"It turned out that way." It was an older man who had spoken up. He was dressed too formally to be a soldier.

"And who might you be?" the major asked.

"The name's Whitcum, Giles Whitcum. I'm the Regimental Reverend, as well as Colonel Scurry's personal secretary and drink mixer. Before the fireworks started up the canyon, there were also a hundred and fifty German mercenaries in our company. But, like Odysseus's men when lured to the Scopuli Islands by the song of the Sirens, they found the music of the cannon fire irresistible to their maniac intellects."

"So they rode off—up the canyon?" the major asked.

"Ten minutes after the firing started," Giles replied.

"Danke schoen," the major replied. Then turning to us, he commanded, "Torch the wagons. And, Captain Thompson, send a group of men west, up the canyon, to bayonet their animal herd."

The padre had mentioned that there were about five hundred horses and mules in a grotto about a half mile west of the ranch, I recalled. Hearing the major's remark, I quickly moved out of the group of men surrounding the prisoners and over to a campsite where men were preparing torches from tent posts and oil-soaked linen. Torching wagons seemed much more acceptable to me than bayoneting livestock.

The wagons went up effortlessly and actually provided, for some perverse reason, a somewhat enjoyable activity. Making my way through the smoke of the flaming wagons, I could still hear the popping of the big guns. But these pops were dwarfed by the exploding ammunition from the first wagons we had torched. This entire episode had become exhilarating to me. The Confederates were still engaged up the canyon. And it would take hours for them to reach us, even if they had the notion to disengage from the battle and return immediately. We were in the process of destroying their entire means of waging a campaign. And we were, in effect, winning the conflict for the Union, without sustaining any casualties in our effort. Best of all, I had played a major part in bringing the whole strategy about. Indeed, I had circumvented the threat of combat and still completed my obligation. However, my inadequacy as a soldier was about to be exposed at that very moment.

"Swenson." It was the voice of Captain Thompson. "Over there." The captain was pointing to a small group of cottonwood that was being illuminated by the flames of nearby burning wagons. In the midst of the trees, three Confederate mounts had been tied. They were in the process of pulling viciously at their restraints in an attempt to gain freedom.

"Run those horses through," the captain ordered of me.

What can I do? I thought in panic.

"No need for that, sir," I replied in desperation. "If I turn them loose, they're sure to run long and far from these fires."

"You have your orders, Corporal. Now run your bayonet through them animals, and let's get on with our work!"

The one mistake I had made had come back to foil my attempt at soldiering. Unintentionally alienating the captain had negated all my other successes. "I'm sorry, sir. I can't," I replied remorsefully, knowing the consequences this refusal could produce.

"Kill those horses!" the captain ordered of two troops that were running past us. They did so without hesitation, and in an instant the horses lay beneath the trees kicking in futility.

The captain was gone before the deed was done, but I realized that I had not heard the last of the incident.

It had taken less than an hour to destroy all of the Confederate Army's supplies, kill all of their livestock, and start our first eight men back up the wall. Pulling us up didn't take much longer than dropping us down had taken. One man on each side of the saddle had to keep a foot against it, to keep the saddle from being pushed back. And there was some difficulty in pulling us over the ledge once we had reached the top. But by six thirty that morning, we were all, including seventeen prisoners, back up the wall. We noticed that the cannon fire had stopped again, as it had done on two occasions earlier, suggesting that one side or the other had made a concession of territory. The major's concern had become to get back to the regiment and help in the battle. There was no longer a threat of failing in our mission as a result of being discovered by the Confederates. So, we followed the priest's shorter route along the canyon wall on our return. There were no more cannon retorts heard all the way back.

Apparently, we had passed the enemy in the canyon below as they headed back to Pigeon's Ranch without notice by either party. The battle had ended at after six that evening. Our troops had pulled all the way back from Pigeon's Ranch to Kozlowski's. The Confederates had caused our withdrawal by flanking and threatening to capture our guns on two occasions. Colonel Slough was surprised by the Confederates asking for a truce after our withdrawal, when they seemed to have gained the upper hand by being in command of the field of battle from above. He was not aware that Colonel Scurry's request had been provoked by a report, which he'd received from the troops that we had run off of Johnson's Ranch, notifying him of the destruction of their stores. Knowing that the Germans had deserted the protection of the supplies in order to join in the battle caused Major Scurry's main concern to shift from the battle to salvaging whatever he could of his supplies. That attempt proved futile, however, since we had been thorough in the destruction of all of the Confederate supplies and animals.

It was about nine at night when we got back to Kozlowski's. On hearing the news of the enemies debauching, Slough decided to abandon the canyon and head back to Fort Union immediately. He knew that the rebels had already totally stripped Albuquerque and Santa Fe of supplies on their way north and that the only supplies remaining in the territory capable of sustaining an army were at Fort Union, which he had left poorly guarded. If Scurry had managed to fight his way through our position at Kozlowski's in the battle, he could have taken the fort and our supplies easily—winning the battle in total. As it was, Scurry was forced to retrace his steps through Santa Fe, where he found only meager rations remaining. This was the start of a disastrous, death-strewn retreat by the Rebel Army, back to Texas.

The battle, for our immediate future, was over. I had survived but felt no joy over that. Our side, like that of the Confederates, had had a hundred or so men killed and twice that number seriously wounded. Reflecting on my fallen companions, there would be no salvation from guilt, shy of joining them. If I had been the bravest and best fighting man in our unit, survival, in itself, would still be disgraceful. The only honorable end for a combat soldier is falling before the enemy's bullets, I decided. Perhaps, in the next campaign I wouldn't be as lucky, or should I say as unlucky, as I had in this one, I thought. But I was to find out that it wouldn't be either of these two.

The morning of our return to camp, I was delighted to find that I had received a letter from Jenny, though I really had hoped to have several waiting. It had been written three weeks earlier. The "word she was hearing" was that the war would probably continue for years. She couldn't possibly go on waiting for me that long, not knowing if I'd ever return at all. That's the only reason she decided to "start dating" one of her colleagues, it read. This should have been devastating news to me. But it was not. The years of dreaming of Jenny had turned into, just that—a dream. And as much as we want dreams to materialize, we really know that they are just dreams. She had become unreal to me in this estranging environment. I had taken the letter well. But what did shock me was the news I received that evening when summoned to talk to Major Slough.

"Corporal Swenson, I have received a letter from Captain Thompson informing me that you failed to fulfill your duty in battle by refusing to obey a direct order. Is that true?" the major asked.

"Yes, sir. I suspect it is. But, you see, he wanted me to slaughter three sturdy mounts. And, well, sir, I love horses."

"He *wanted* you to slaughter them? Corporal, he *ordered* you to slaughter them. You do not decide whether or not to follow an order!"

"But, sir, it wouldn't be right—no more than it would be if they were men he was asking me to slaughter."

"And what do you think your job is?" the major asked, obviously irritated by my responses. "Your job *is* to kill—men, horses, or any other damned thing you are ordered to kill!"

"But, Major," I responded, a noticeable squeal in my voice, "we kill men that are trying to kill us. That's not like slaughtering."

"Let me ask you this, Corporal. What if we had prisoners that we were incapable of transporting, and they had information that, if we set them free, might be reported and possibly abet our demise? There are times when slaughtering, as you call it, can be unavoidable." The major ended this analogy by staring me hard in the eyes. "The course of action our codebook dictates in a case such as this is discharge without honor," the major stated, his voice returning to a normal conversation level.

My legs had succumbed to weakness at the citing of the ruling, but the thought of discharge sent a glint of hope coursing through my being.

"However, the contribution you have made to our campaign, through good judgment and initiative has been immeasurable. For that reason, I believe, although you are not cut out for infantry, you have the makings of a good officer. Therefore, I am ready to refer you for officer training, in a noncombat capacity."

"Thank you, sir," I responded, somewhat panicked by this unexpected offering. "But I really have no desire for a military career at this time." I considered telling him how I had enlisted through misguided reasoning but decided that that would be as ineffective as it had been with Captain West, back in Denver. "You see, I have dreams that I want to pursue as soon as this war allows me," I continued. "And—"

The major cut me off just as I needed him to. "You want to get out of the army?" the major asked. "Do you realize that you are giving up an opportunity to serve your country and bring honor to your name and your life?"

"Sir," I said, "begging your pardon, but the only thing I want from life is to return to the girl I love and start a family with her." This was indeed what I wanted, although I already knew it was no longer awaiting me.

"Corporal, I feel personally in your debt, for the information you provided during this campaign. And, I repay my debts ... Therefore, I will muster you out, honorably, with the Home Guard. Their commitment has expired, and they will receive papers the day after tomorrow. But understand this; I expect you to recognize that these conditions are unconventional. And as such, I require you to maintain them confidential—that is, between you and me alone. Do you understand, Corporal?"

"I do, sir. And I thank you wholeheartedly, sir," I replied, overjoyed by the major's charitable offer. "But I entered two horses with my enlistment, and leaving them behind would be difficult ..."

"They were listed to accompany you in service, and since your service will discontinue, they will remain as your personal property on discharge.

"I am sure you are an honorable man, so I will accept your word on this, and prepare the papers," the major concluded.

What I had given my word on, I wasn't sure. But, I was sure that he had said I would be getting out. And that was exhilarating.

Thinking over our conversation, I realized that the major had insisted I maintain silence about my discharge. But I couldn't simply disappear without an explanation to Smitty. To keep my promise to the major, I decided to solicit Smitty's promise of confidentiality on the matter, before revealing the details.

Smitty's final analysis of the arrangement was, "He wants all the credit. He doesn't want you around because he doesn't want to admit it was you who thought of hitting their supply train."

"Actually it was the padre who thought of it," I replied in correction.

"But, you suggested it to the major. If you'd have gone to the captain, he'd want the credit. Believe me, your name won't show up on the battle report, anywhere."

"That's fine with me," I said. "I hope he makes general."

The colonel resigned shortly thereafter, over the distress he received from higher-ups, brought about by his decision to move against the Rebs, which was contrary to standing orders. It was determined that his doing so had resulted in Fort Union and our supplies being left in jeopardy. Additionally, the troop hostility toward him had surfaced again during the battle. It was said that the colonel was in fear for his own safety while in the regiment.

The major, on the other hand, was promoted to colonel, as a result of his display of leadership, bravery, and ingenuity.

Three days later, on April 1, 1862, I was heading north with most of the Denver City Home Guard—all of us then having civilian status. This unit had fought at Valverde, as well as at Glorietta Pass, under a mere six-month enlistment. Some of their numbers had been killed or incapable of travel, some reenlisted, and the rest were my companions heading north.

Whether I would accompany them all the way back to Denver or take the eastern trail when we exited the canyon, I had not decided. Perhaps it would still be possible to get Jenny back. But did I really want her? Not that I harbored any anger toward her for abandoning me. The situation, after all, made that understandable. A young, beautiful woman, ready to start a family life shouldn't be put in a position where she had to spend years alone. Yet, if I were to win her back, there would always be a question in my mind as to whether or not she really wanted to be with me. Even justifiable broken promises leave lasting scars, I thought. Also, there would be hostility in Saint Joe, toward men of my age who were trying to keep from getting killed in the war. This situation would require my providing a mandatory explanation of my situation to every person I met. This didn't seem to be worthy criteria to use in determining my future, but it was reality. Denver would be hospitable to the returning guard, and I could use my association with them to avoid the embarrassment of having to admit that I was incapable of slaughtering. There was still some winter left for snowshoeing. And if nothing else came up through the summer, I might get back into the diggings, in order to keep myself occupied. It would be interesting to see what Russell was doing at Pa's claim, I thought.

With ten thousand dollars in the bank and no responsibility other than tending to Spirit and Flash, I suspected that I should have felt exhilarated about my future. But as days passed, and stories were told around our campfires of each man's future aspirations, I found mine to be, basically nonexistent. My future had always been centered on Jenny. Now, I had found myself at a loss for inspiration.

When we cleared the Raton Pass, fourteen members of our party took the eastern trail. Probably all were heading back to the towns they had hailed from before the call of the gold. About halfway back to Denver, a storm started setting in. Dark clouds had dropped from the mountaintops, and the wind was coming in forceful gusts. When a gust sent a spray of cold water against my face, it gave me a pleasant sensation, as an event occasionally does when it produces a mental association. This association was from a time in my past, when the earth's bounty was, in itself, inspiring to me. The pleasant sensation was easy to extract from my memory. It was from the spray of the sea, as Kurt, Pa, and I spent our days fishing the sea wall back east. The pleasure of contentment with life that I had felt then was unexplainable. Perhaps it had come from knowing I had all that I needed between the love of my family and the sea's unending gift of sustenance. However, the thought of returning to New York Harbor was a fleeting one. Besides the difficulty of the trip, the hostility the war had evoked there, in conjunction with the chaos the labor parties were experiencing, eliminated returning there as a desirable alternative.

Shortly after the rain had started falling, I noticed two figures taking a left fork of the trail. "Where are you heading? I asked as I trotted up beside them.

"To the home of the angels," one responded.

"The Pacific," the other added.

"Mind a little company?" I asked.

"Takes a lot of hard riding, 'cross Injun country, through canyons as high as these mountains, and over desert that takes two weeks to cross. We'll travel mostly at day through Apache country …grub up and camp at station houses. Probably take near to two months to reach the Pueblo of Los Angeles. That's if the Apache don't have other plans for us. Think you can handle it?" one of the deviants asked.

"I'm Olof Swenson. I'd surely be glad to tag along and see the last stretch of land this country has to offer."

"Ned and Will Pratt. Glad to make your acquaintance, Ollie. I've just one thing to ask of you, son. That pack animal of yours isn't toting much. Can we hang a sack or two on him, to lighten up our mounts?"

"Sure, but that's no pack animal. That's Spirit, second fastest horse in the West. This is Flash. He's the fastest." I said, opening the door for some storytelling.

We pulled up and strapped two of their bags to Spirit, as I was riding Flash at the time. Not wanting either horse to feel unimportant, I divided my riding time between them.

We had gotten our back pay on mustering out at Fort Union. If I made my way up the coast when we reached the ocean, I could have the bank wire my savings out to me, since the telegraph had recently been put through to San Francisco. As I glanced down the trail, the Home Guard was continuing north along the Rockies. Their number would virtually assure their safety in travel. My spontaneous decision to head west was again putting my life in jeopardy, I thought. But what did that matter? If we were killed by the Apache or not, no one would ever know. So what would be the harm? The important thing was life had again taking an exciting turn. What in life could be better than not knowing what lay ahead? Given a new land and a new life to explore, I felt truly gifted.

"Joining family in Los Angeles, are you?" I asked.

"No, just resting up there a bit," Ned responded. "And, reacquainting ourselves to the pleasures of society. After that, we'll be heading up to Stockton."

"They're building a new prison there. Our uncle Jim has been assigned as the warden. He's signing us on as guards, soon as it's occupied. Near to fifteen dollars a day, guaranteed," Will explained.

"Little more than half our day's pay will buy us each six acres of flat valley farmland," Ned added.

"Now that the Mexican grants are but used up, the Government has gone to open sale at $1.25 an acre. And, that's flat tillable farm land," Will clarified.

"Sounds like you've got things in order, for sure," I replied, as I recollected a field of wild flowers, which I had been quite taken by outside of Saint Joe. "Keep in mine, the cost and availability of supplies needs to be considered when you're planning on setting up a spread," I suggested, hoping for an incite as to the feasibility of their plan.

"Nothing to think about," Ned replied, in a bit of a huff, perhaps taking aback a bit by my inference of a flaw existing in their means of attaining the realization of a long-planned dream. "Dry goods are pouring into San Francisco, more than New York harbor- Coming from all over the world," he boisterously stated.

"And Stockton is close by?" I asked, using my ignorance to offset my previous audacity.

"But a day's ride out," Ned replied, assuredly.

"Plenty of long-shore work right in Los Angeles or up the coast, if your of the mind," Will offered, in the case that I was in lack of hopeful expectations. Such of course, would be needed to persevere through the demands of the challenging journey awaiting us.

"No, but your talk of the land sale has peaked my interest," I replied, and acknowledged simultaneously.

"Looking to set up a homestead, are you?" Ned asked.

"I would have been, but I lost plans for that several days back, when I lost my reason for wanting it."

"Dumped you did she?" Ned asked, in a display of his insight of the obvious.

"It seems she's found a need to take up dating," I replied.

"The fickleness of women. It comes as a result of their motherly instinct to seek out security. Like water seeking the lowest level, they gravitate to the best offer," Will stated, displaying a pre-consideration of womanly motivations.

"I'd like some land to run ponies on," I realized as I stated. "Perhaps, with a race track. I'd raise and train Injun ponies for their speed." That would be something, I thought.

"Add a rodeo, and I'll sign on," Ned offered, joining in my imagining.

A horse ranch, with stables and a track- what a wonderful dream that would have been if I still had Kurt and Pa to share it with. But alone, it would only develop as an empty undertaking- What would Jenny think of it? She always had a love for her horses, even as far as to enjoying their tending. Perhaps, I was wrong in not revealing to her that I now had the means of providing for our life together. Will's incite, as to the importance women bestow on security, did ring of the truth. And, as Pa would say, "Having hope for the fruition of a dream, provides our daily sustenance." If I provided hope for our future together, might she once again vision me as her future?

June 19, 1862

Los Angeles, California

Dear Jenny,

I can not deny that reading of your decision to start dating had left me deeply distraught. But, your reasons for doing so were understandable and as one would expect.

I'm happy to say, that my commitment to the military has been fulfilled, and I was honorably mustered out. If your wondering as to the addressing of this letter, it comes as the result of a fateful turn of events. Before leaving the service, I was notified of my receipt of a substantial inheritance. It seems that after my pa died, he was awarded a large sum for a claim he had offered to a mining company. The money from the claim sale has now come to me. This lent itself perfectly to a plan I had developed after conversing with two California bound comrades. Listen to this Jenn:

As you know, California has a wonderful, sunny and mild climate. The Government is now offering level growing lands, at remarkably low costs. I'm presently heading for a town called Stockton, outside of San Francisco. The plan I have is to purchase about a thousand acres of grazing land, which I intend to set up as a horse ranch. It'll have stables, corals and a training track. Jenny, if you would have an inclination towards joining me there, it will also have a cottage, barn and gardens. *I actually have the money to make this happen*!

I wouldn't ask you to give up your schooling. The Stockton area is in a development boon. The future is sure to bring the area a large demand for educators. So, you could easily find work teaching if you still desire doing that. In any case, it will certainly take a good amount of time for me to act on these intentions. I won't mention your dating, that way you may believe that I don't find it significant. Jenn, I too have had other associations since we've been apart, but it is you that I have loved through all of them.

Before deciding, consider the hardship that will await you, of spending near to a month of days on a stage. I can afford to ticket the two front benches in a Butterfield Coach. These face each other, and would allow you to spread out and nap with some comfort. But, nights are cold. The ride is dusty and sometimes sickening. Layovers at a way station are possible, but may mean many days of waiting for another coach that can accommodate you. The benefit of enduring these days of hardship would be: An opportunity to view the beauty of the wide open American west; and, finding the arms of a would-be husband, waiting to embrace you at the journey's end.

I know this letter will sound somewhat imaginary to you, but know that it is my undaunted intent. Whatever you decide Jenny, know that I WILL LOVE YOU FOREVER, OLOF.

"Sounds good to me," a somewhat teary-eyed Will responded.

"I'd hold off 'til after seeing San Francisco's working ladies if I were you", Ned suggested with a smirk. "Mexicans, Injuns, Negros, China dolls, you can take your pick- even Germans and French!. The gold rush brought them in from all over the world."

"Yea, and for only a month's worth of wages," Will sarcastically added.

"No thanks, there are none could compare to my Jenny," I replied. "One look at her, and you will be knocked into jealous agreement."

"I sure do hope that does come about," Ned responded with sincerity.

"Well, there's one thing I know sure: If it's meant to be, it will be," I concluded.

THE END

Printed in the United States
By Bookmasters